M000267882

SUNRIDER

The SunRider Saga: Book One

SUNRIDER
BOOK ONE IN THE SUNRIDER SAGA
By Rafael Hohmann

This is a work of fiction. Names, characters, places, and incidents are either the product of the author's imagination or are used fictitiously, and any resemblances to actual persons, living or dead, business establishments, events or locales is entirely coincidental.

All rights reserved.

COPYRIGHT © 2017 RAFAEL HOHMANN

ISBN: *978-0-692-92817-2*

This book or its images may not be reproduced in whole or part, by mimeograph or any other means, without permission. Making or distributing electronic copies of this book or images constitutes copyright infringement and could subject the infringer to criminal and civil liability.

For more information:
http://rafaelhohmann.com

DEDICATION

For Jess and Dave: Jess, without many months of support and encouragement, this story never would have come this far. Dave, our long hours of debate and discussion have made Lenova wider, scarier, and more exciting.

Table of Contents

SUNRIDER

The SunRider Saga: Book One

RAFAEL HOHMANN

prologue:

from the sky

—I have seen men become Gods, and I have seen Gods become dust—

The Priests and Priestesses walked in parallel lines, shoulder to shoulder, chanting songs of suffering. Thousands of black robes flapped like dying crows, hanging to shoulders, beaks swallowing heads. Moans and whispered chants swam in the wind, swallowed by the ashen land. The cracked earth was a dead beast, and the long line of hooded forms was the last of the maggots patrolling on bones. They were a collective, a sacred tribe, the last living history of what once was a great people, eons ago. They were… a cult. Glints came from beneath their robes—quick flashes of yellow. In devotion to the ways of sacrifice many had replaced organic limbs for ones made of gold. They hobbled and limped across the Kingdom of Rot, flesh matched by metal.

Mal'Bal strolled at the front of the parade, his hairless head pulsing with purple veins. He was the only one who didn't wear a robe. He chose to expose his glorious body for all to see. In his devotion to pain and the hate he felt for life, Mal'Bal had ritualized and swapped each limb and organ with gold all the way to his neck. One could no longer call him human; he was something else entirely. The Golden Agony. The Necromancer of Rot. Mal'Bal the Lich-Lord.

In his yellow hand he held a charted map marked with crisscrossing lines representing the common trails where the enchanted dead roamed. He tossed the parchment without thought or aim toward a nearby follower. The man scrambled to catch the paper before it blew away, knowing punishment would be severe if it slipped off, twirling in the gray air. Mal'Bal was confident that they would return home before their smell drew in a corpse-swarm too large to handle.

The voices of the cult meshed and separated, becoming one, then splitting into a cacophony of noise. Harsh prayers of pain and death brought euphoria, brought ecstasy. They were lovers of self-immolation. There was predictability to their energy. When excitement built-up to crescendos of shuddering limbs and rolling eyes, there was always one or two who would stop and flay themselves. This was tradition: a part of their yearly mecca around the land. They would leave their home, the young adults with eager pale-pink skin—a glinting baby purity—following the elders who tread the steps of their ancestors. When they returned, the smooth bodies of the young would be split and broken, marked by metal. It was an elevation of status, an opportune enlightenment into a state of higher being. There was nothing more glorious. The cries grew louder and as if on cue, a form shouted and broke formation, hood falling back and revealing a shadow-haired woman. She unsheathed a scythe, the common weapon of the cult. "Oh Great One, from weakness to mastery of the flesh, behold my sacrifice!"

The woman slammed the blade behind her right kneecap, with eyes like daggers focused on Mal'Bal's expression. She shrieked, and blood splattered the dim rocks. Mal'Bal raised an eyebrow, cruel pleasure flickering across his features. The woman, face scrunched in suffering, bared her teeth. Sitting on her rear, she plunged the scythe behind the other kneecap. She moaned and shuddered as Mal'Bal closed his eyes, savoring the woman's pain like a sponge soaking up water. He let the moment linger.

"Bless her." he hissed, his voice a smooth poison escaping a fissure.

Three robed men came forward, eager to please, putting golden ingots into chalices shaped like knee joints. As they did so, Mal'Bal chanted in rhythm, low in pitch. He spoke faster, voice growing harsher and angrier, demanding submission over the elements. The golden ingots shook in place, ready for a final command. Mal'Bal waved a metal hand.

"*Gasta.*"

The ingots melted, forming liquid yellow puddles. Green Apex gems—stones holding dark energy—were placed within the gold as more words were spoken to solidify the material. Hooded forms brought the hemorrhaging woman her new knees, laying her back and cleaning her wounds. They worked quickly. The smell of blood would attract the dead from hundreds of kilometers. When the cult members had done their part, they gazed to Mal'Bal in waiting, most with blank worshipful faces. Yet hidden in the crowds some cowered, others scowled with defiance—but never openly. Not all wanted the man as their leader.

The Lich-Lord whispered the final words to the ritual. Blood flow was sealed, gold melded to flesh, and the woman slumped back, her pain subsiding. The magical energy that left Mal'Bal was insubstantial, yet he took a break, staring into the night sky. The sky was cold and silent, unresponsive to Mal'Bal's conscience. The smattering of stars almost seemed as if nature had botched its attempt at covering the emptiness beyond their world. The lights were an ineffective veil, unsuccessfully masking that they were alone in existence. Many in the cult were content—complacent even—with the lack of *more*. But for some reason Mal'Bal couldn't accept the silence. His lot was temporal, and it made him angry. If he couldn't have more, no one could. He wanted to yell at his people, to command that they look up into the void, and understand. If only the dim glow from those small dots would grant them a sign, perhaps acknowledge him as correct… As if hearing his thoughts, an answer came. It was in the form of falling white lines trailing red tails. His followers paused, observing Mal'Bal's stiffened back.

Falling stars were a new sight to Mal'Bal, one who'd seen events most mortals couldn't imagine. One headed toward him: a blinking white light shining brighter and brighter. It whistled as it tore through the stiff air. His cult yelled in exclamation, *finally,* finally looking up. At the last minute, Mal'Bal stepped away.

The star—no, the small object no larger than a boot—smashed in front of him, throwing the crowd back. Upon touching the ground, it let out a pearly ring, like the loudest of church bells. Then—there was silence but for the crackling of melted rock.

Mal'Bal, his golden body too heavy to be toppled, stood alone while cult members struggled to their feet. His wild eyes found the object smoldering by the light of red-hot earth. Many other stars fell from the sky, crisscrossing the distant horizon, no other landing anywhere near his lands. Approaching the crater caused by the event, Mal'Bal studied the piece of armor that lay at its center: a bracer. It glowed white in the night, metal popping as it cooled. It exuded the promise of power and confirmed all he had believed in. Mal'Bal's face split into a horrifying grin.

cave-diver

1

—For thus the King of the Gods, Abealon was blind to his younger brother's scheming. The rebellious dark God Miza-Tirith worked in secret from the shadows of unformed space, where his workshop was born in the heart of a dead star. And so, experimenting with forbidden forms of creation, Miza-Tirith's boredom grew into a belief that the Avengelions should not abide by rules or limitations. And when his older brother Abealon slept, Miza-Tirith would whisper into his ear, working his mind over to the idea that they should loosen the laws of creation. —
-Domolov, the Three-Fingered Cleric's Historic Book of Speculative Deity Theology, page 12,803

Two male bodies struggled in the ghastly heat of the desert, churning up a curtain of terra-cotta tinted dust and sacrificing the little water they had in their bodies. A film of salt coated their foreheads, sweat evaporating as quickly as it was formed. They slid down a knoll—apart from the crags to their backs, it was one of the only slopes as far as the eye could see. The ground was an unforgiving enemy to both forms, uncaring to the subject of the fight or the lifeforms involved in it. It clawed at their bodies and drank of their energy, soaking up whatever it could take—and it could take it all. In this land, dreams and aspirations were as brittle and as quick to die as the plants that grew upon the bleak surface.

A stone smashed into Finn SunRider's cheek, drawing blood. The flat-faced teenager who'd hit him gave a quick laugh. The older boy's pockmarked features and brutish cement-block head filled Finn with infuriation. It wasn't Finn's fault that the boy looked like the back-end of a Vat-Pig, but having the guts to call him ugly—especially since the miner was twice Finn's build—had been the *least* smart choice Finn had made all day. He lay on the ground with hot sand and rocks beneath his fingers: part of a familiar consistency. It was a texture he'd known all his life—forlorn and boring. Grit clung to his nails and wind siphoned moisture from his pores, leaving a stale taste on his lips.

"You're stuck here like the rest of us, talc-licker." the bigger boy spewed. Talc was weakest of minerals, softer than dirt. Finn hated the name.

Finn forced a large bloody grin, even though deep down he wanted to bare his teeth in rage. He wished he could muster the spit to hawk at the miner, but instead he chuckled. "What? Does the outside world scare you?"

Finn jumped up and swung his right fist, using a chunk of diorite as a weapon. It smacked across his enemy's ear, ripping cartilage, and the older teen staggered backwards, fighting to keep his balance. The fresh wound—already drying—only enraged the older boy. Before new wounds could be inflicted, two elder miners stepped between them. The burly men grabbed both teenagers by the nape of their necks, holding them apart. Finn blew a kiss to the other boy and the large boy howled, trying to break free from his captor.

"Let me cave 'is face in, let me!"

Finn was dragged away from the middle of the gravel trail running between a sad toolshed half-buried in discarded stone and an abandoned ventilation shaft still open to the hollow depths directly below their feet. The man holding him let go, pulling at his sticky shirt collar hugging his wide chest. "By the Vat-Worm's dung, what's going on?" he barked. "Finn? Gunther? Either of you want to explain yourselves?"

The older boy, Gunther, snarled. "Talc-licker wants to see the big wide world." The boy shook himself free and pointed at Finn with a grubby calloused finger. "He's an ungrateful cave-diver. Make him work our shift Maggs. Let him break rocks for a while."

Maggs, the sun-wrinkled man that'd pulled Finn back, reprimanded the spry teen with a stern gaze. Finn turned away, chewing on the corner of his dirty cheek. It tasted like dirt. Everything tasted like dirt.

"Again Finn? Talking of leaving? You know you can't, you don't have the funds."

Finn kicked at the ground, scattering gravel. How could he convey his longing for freedom? His desperation for a life beyond drudgery and monotony, a meaninglessness filled only by work that would never benefit him? He couldn't speak the words out-loud. What he felt couldn't be expressed in sentences, but only wishes fragmented by his lack of knowledge of the world. He didn't know what smells skipped off the surface of a lake, but he would like to. Or if he'd enjoy holding snow in his hands, but he wanted to give it a try. What he would give to experience the liberty to go where he pleased and do what he wanted to do. "Of course I don't have the funds." he hissed to Maggs. "We'll never be given the funds. The supervisors are nothing but slave-drivers."

Maggs rolled his eyes. "Get back to your shift. Be grateful you don't get kicked out into the Slaglands." The elder miner picked up his dropped pickax and called over his shoulder as he turned. "And afterwards go to the practitioner for salve. Your face is cut." The men dispersed, taking Gunther with them. They walked with hunched, bent backs, feet following the same path they had for years. They were forms defeated by the heat. It had stolen both their moisture and hope. Shuffling downhill, they entered a drab granite barracks, hunger driving them forward. Shift-change.

Finn threw his diorite chunk against the half-buried tool shed. Dust billowed from the impact. He was surrounded by an ocean of dirt and rock—a desert landscape of jagged stone cliffs, forming an inescapable border to one side, and plains of desolation everywhere else. The smell of iron lingered in Finn's nostrils. The colors yellow and orange saturated the landscape, the sky, and the people, sinking through skin and swirling within their dreams at night. It drove a man mad for a change in hue.

The desolate *Crust,* with three mining outposts distanced along its crags, was a name given by the miners to describe the torrid environment they endured in. Its official name was unknown, and perhaps only House Crumm knew the answer. With their pointedly proud emblems of a ball and chain attached to a broken sword—a mocking sigil to those enslaved by the house—House Crumm took on the role as the overseers of the desert. With their lack of care to the old laws of Lenova, it was they who condoned slave trade and forced man-labor within miserable camps. It was they who were willing to beat a young boy to death for refusing to work. Yet for all its hot misery and although overshadowed by the corrupt House, the Crust was livable—unlike the Slaglands. Poising at the edge of their camp like a black sleeping lizard covered in cracked scales lined with lava, the Slag swallowed most the desert. There was life in the Crust— tough life—but it was there. The Slag…it was a blot of sterile heat. Legend told that the Slaglands was once an ocean of lava, created by titanic forces long ago. It had pushed and stretched, shaping the Crust into a crescent-moon dotted with cliffs and crags that resembled stone toes and tables pointing to the sky. The natural terrain formed an opportunistic area for those who wished to mine jewels from the depths. It was a death sentence for many, but an opportunity for businessmen.

Finn had seen wealth; diamonds, rubies, and even the elusive sapphire. He'd *touched* the wealth. But none of it belonged to him. No, he collected precious ores and gems for far-away nobles. Crumm would trade with any that were willing to sully their bags with blood treasure. It was always a temptation for the miners to pocket what they found, but to steal a stone was to be outcast into the black Slag. This had been Finn's life for as long as he could remember. He was orphaned at birth like so many unfortunate children of Lenova, with no recollection of his parents. Perhaps they were dead. Perhaps they were uncaring and had tossed him to the slavers as a baby. He didn't know, and he never would. As a child, he always cared for an answer to his past, but time and the desert had beat the desire for conclusion right out of him. To Finn, the past was long gone and to be forgotten. The orange heat of the Crust was his oldest memory, and that was all it would ever be. He'd picked up his first pickax at the age of two.

Finn trudged up the knoll, passed the half-buried closet, and overlooked the outpost. Forms bustled below him: men and boys with rough-hewn shirts made gray by work. Their clothes stuck to their bodies and sweat glistened like jewels on their skin. A hundred meters away Finn could see a black line marking the edge of the Slag. Massive heatwaves danced over the horizon. The temperature emanating from the Western landscape was immense.

He kicked over a tiny knot of sage brush. It exploded into dust. Behind it was a *Mole-Hole*—a cave-diver entrance into the mines beneath his feet. The passage was drilled straight into the ground, like a thin entrance into the hollow space within a vase. He crouched at its edge and balanced in place. To fall through the Mole-Hole would be certain death— a hundred-meter plummet down the central mineshaft to a hard bottom. The wide mineshaft itself was all underground, with sole entrance coming from the collection of holes cut across its ceiling. He adjusted his mining shoes. Made of Sponge-Marble, they protected him from jagged stone and prevented his feet from burning in the desert heat. Reaching through the hole along its edges, he found what he was looking for: a thick dusty rope held by a clamp. He unlatched the end of the rope and pulled it up, hearing a pulley system creak in place. For the millionth time, Finn imagined the ground giving in, sending him into the dark abyss. He was sure Gunther would throw a party for the whole outpost if Finn died, yet it sounded a better fate than to wake up another day in the Crust.

He took the metal clamp attached to the rope and connected it to his belt, tugging to make sure it was fastened. Finn rappelled through the hole and let go, free-falling into shadow. The sounds of desert wind were replaced with the hum of the depths. His stomach lurched, then settled as the rope can e to a stop. The ingenious pulley system contained safety devices that slowed his descent if he fell too fast. With his free hand, he grabbed at the goggles dangling around his neck as he swung within the sunbeam streaming into the dark. Like sibling pipes standing in rows, lines of light filtered from the Mole-Holes above, cutting into the sunless chamber. Fitting the goggles over his eyes, the dark expanse took on a bright orange definition. The goggles were made of a crystal that allowed the user to see in dark spaces such as the mine. Without them, miners and cave-divers would walk into walls, getting lost all throughout the Crust.

The noise of a thousand pickaxes clinked, sending sparks flashing into the dark as metal met stone. Commanding shouts rang out in bored tones as miners switched shifts, carted material, and wished for better lives. Like a large beehive, rows of groaning scaffolding and precarious wooden ledges ran to the bottom of the shaft, forming horizontal ridges that grew smaller and smaller, creating a cone shape. Platforms carting men and supplies were pulled up and down between the superstructure, their movement giving life to the construction. Spaced in patterned intervals along the layers were hundreds of oval caves and offshoots, worn smooth by decades of miners. Men bustled over them, appearing and disappearing like ants. A boy was reprimanded for dropping a shovel and another sang of sleep, before he too was reprimanded.

Flicking a metal switch on his belt, Finn free-fell once more. When he gained sufficient speed, the rope again slowed him to a stop, causing the switch on his belt to revert back the other way. Turning the switch, he dropped further. The pattern continued until he was at the bottom of the mine. Finn unlatched the rope and adjusted his rough-hewn, stained shirt. Around him stood eight other boys all between the ages of seven to fifteen. They also wore goggles and their faces were dirty with cave dust. They greeted Finn with nods.

Apart from basic commands, they hardly spoke to each other. There was no friendship between any of them: they couldn't afford it. Cave-diving, unlike quarrying the walls of the mine, was a job where death was not only expected, but occurred frequently. The boys were tasked with finding natural crevices and cracks in the stone. They would squeeze their bodies into them, following the sharp tunnels in search of mineral veins. They went where no human had ever gone before, into the cold hard dark. They bent and shoved through erratic turns and holes so small, mice would have turned the other way. Sometimes one would get stuck, or there would be a cave-in. Many mummified bodies haunted the mines of the Crust.

Finn, sixteen-years-old, was the oldest and most experienced of the cave-divers. Having survived two cave-ins, and one time a rock trapping his leg for three days before he was rescued, he'd grown into an expert. He'd been told by many a miner to stop dreaming of traveling Lenova, he had plenty of exploring to do underground. Because of those words—and not only his enslavement—Finn despised his job. But as shift lead, it was his responsibility to stay motivated and organize the other boys, telling them where and where not to go.

"Digger, Tunnel Six. Lindo, Tunnel Two. Goblin and Mudd, with me to Tunnel Fourteen."

He commanded with his mind only half-aware, shouting over the noise of grinding rock and chiseling. Instead, his thoughts wandered to what lay beyond the Crust. Beyond the Slaglands. He imagined places of water and of green vegetation. Well, he tried to. He'd seen pictures of cities painted in mud by wrinkled miners, stared with longing at strange artifacts worn by passing merchants, and grew jealous of the gleam in the eyes of those who'd once been free. He'd heard their stories and starved for a life he'd never experienced. The desire ran deep into him, nestling into his core.

Before the boys left down their respective tunnels, Finn reached into a small pouch at his belt and handed them a blue pebble each. They were Aquamarine Tears: small magical stones that when sucked, brought moisture to a miner's mouth and kept them hydrated for a few hours. The stones were only one of many types of enchanted rock found in the Crust, and one of the few that miners and cave-divers could use for themselves. Materials such as the Ghost Topaz, which could multiply a man's senses, were for nobles and those rich enough to afford it.

He led Goblin and Mudd to Tunnel Fourteen. The two had arrived only the day before and Finn chose to keep the new boys with him to supervise over them. The three were to explore a cave which had formed by temperature change. The opening was temporary, and when the Summer season waned, the rocks would once more shift and hide its passage. The fluctuation of the ground was an infrequent event, but when it happened, the mine supervisors were eager to send boys to their death over the potential for more wealth. The two younger cave-divers didn't ask Finn about his bruised face, marks of his fight with Gunther. In return, Finn didn't ask about them, or where they'd come from.

Following a narrow but tall crevice in the shape of a doorway, they came to a chamber housing dozens of cave offshoots. Finn scraped his shoulder, but accustomed to the scratching of the rocks, his body didn't register the injury. Puddles lined the ground and a distant drip echoed and bounced between the walls. Mudd pointed to an opening near the floor and to the far left. It could have been a mere slit cut from where floor met wall. With his goggles, Finn made out a chalk-drawn arrow, indicating the unexplored section. He rubbed the skin on his arms to stay warm. In the deep it was easy to have all your heat stolen from you.

Mudd took lead and one by one, they crouched and wiggled through the tight space. Finn sucked in his chest and squirmed his body, using techniques learned through years of practice to move forward quickly, even though he was the largest cave-diver. He bent at the waist around a curve, hissing in discomfort and thinking about what trees looked like.

The tunnel opened into another cavern. The chamber was full of tan crystals embedded into the walls and ceiling. They looked like glass hands glued upside-down, reaching for the boys. Finn pulled out a small parchment and marked the discovery with a coal pencil. They trudged onward, annotating and exploring tunnels, finding dead-ends and veins of various types. Coming across a small oval passage only knee-high, Mudd pushed forward. Although brand new, he was confident. Had the boy had done something similar before being enlisted by the Crust? The tunnel they followed was long—longer than Finn was used to—and halfway through, the boys took a break, the ceiling and floor pushing against their bodies. It was easy to panic: they were swallowed by the earth, compressed by the looming weight touching their neck hairs. It was hard to breathe without choking on the dead dust spores that kicked up when disturbed. They were deep, sliding through a forsaken intestine of stone. Cave-divers had gone mad with hysteria in the depths, hugged tight by solid matter thicker than existence itself. Yet there was no room for claustrophobia in the Crust. Those who lost their nerves—died.

Feeling his lungs throb with lack of air, Finn wiggled a pinned arm into his pouch, contorting his limb to pull free a stone fragment. Like the Aquamarine Tears, this was another material the miners *could* use: Miner's Pumice. The cream-colored sponge chip was light and fragile in Finn's hand. He cracked it open in front of his face and fresh air broke free from the fragments. He sucked in a breath, his companions doing the same. Breaking Miner's Pumice in a confined space was dangerous. If one smashed a large enough chunk, the pressure released could set off a cave-in. For want of air, one could die, crushed beneath rubble. The boys began to crawl again.

As minutes passed, Goblin grew tired and slowed, causing Finn to match the younger cave-diver's pace. Mudd pulled ahead and disappeared. Finn swore under his breath. He knew better than to crawl alone in an unexplored tunnel. But Mudd, being inexperienced, overconfident, and untrained—didn't. Once Goblin had caught his breath, causing Finn to use another piece of Miner's Pumice, they continued after Mudd. Finn crawled for what seemed like an eternity, each minute adding to his worry. Where was Mudd? What if the tunnel ended? They'd have to crawl backward for kilometers.

Finn spat out a dry Aquamarine Tear and stuffed another into his mouth. He sucked and small rivulets of liquid ran down his dusty throat. The movement was an echo of his entire life. Mechanical; copied and repetitive. How many more tunnels would he crawl through as the years went by? Thousands? Millions? Not even finding rare gems could change the monotony. He figured tedium would kill him before the Crust did. Ahead, Goblin vanished with a thud, his body sliding free into the next chamber. Finn dragged himself forward, elbows scooping at the small space, fingers splayed. The rocks leaned down, wanting to pin his head to his chest, push his thighs together, flatten his feet. But then it let go, opening up and spilling Finn out of the tunnel. He lifted himself and stretched his legs and arms, arching his sore back in the new room. Turning in place and looking for Goblin, a strange mix of sounds met his ears: quiet panicked breath and wet splats, as if someone was jumping in a puddle. With his goggles on, he searched the dark room, hued orange by the lenses.

There. Goblin's form faced away from Finn and slowly backed to him. The boy's body trembled and without notice, pushed closer. "What's wrong?" Finn asked, perplexed. The wet sound echoed again, and Finn looked about, searching for water.

Something moved in the dark. Finn froze in place, feeling his limbs grow cold. A strong musky smell hit his nose, the smell of mold and wet rocks. What he thought was the chamber contracted and stretched open, as if shrinking in the middle, then expanding. It was like watching a magic room change size. The walls, floor, and ceiling seemed to peel backward, splitting free and wiggling. They glistened; wet, round, and fleshy.

Finn was horrified. The cavity they'd nearly stepped into was no chamber at all, but the mouth of a limbless and tube-shaped form, wiggling like a living pipe. It was the mouth of a vat-worm, contracting and expanding, yet not attacking. It was still, as if unaware of their presence. Finn's body shook with tremors and his nostrils flared. He was unable to blink, and his eyes wobbled. The hundred-meter-long insects were deep-dwelling monsters of the Crust, feeding upon rocks, gems, and whatever unfortunate life-forms that came across them. Talked of in whispers by the miners late at night, they were the source of nightmares by many in the mining community. If it weren't for the massive chewed-out tunnels they left in their wake, many would believe the vat-worms to not exist.

Each vat-worm's outer skin was encrusted with its favorite flavor of gem: some made of sharp crystals, others of flaming coal, and some—in the case of this vat-worm—made of Orpiment, a dark yellow rock full of arsenic and sulfur.

Finn spotted something small resting along the edge of the sleeping vat-worm's mouth. A body. Finn nearly shouted in terror. Mudd's corpse leaned against the lethal rock shell, sagged and sunken. The dead boy's eyes were milked over, and his skin looked scaled. Having gone ahead of his companions, Mudd must have come across the vat-worm first, not even realizing what he'd walked into. *He'd unknowingly gone to his toxic death.*

The vat-worm closed its mouth once more, then opened it, exposing row-upon-row of sharp trowel-shaped teeth glistening black and gray—perfect for cutting through the toughest of minerals. Fetid breath misted the chamber and Finn's goggles fogged over. He gasped and stifled a cough as the snort heated the room. For all he knew, the atmosphere had suddenly grown toxic. It became quiet. Finn swallowed, copying Goblin and backing as well.

Without warning, the vat-worm awoke. The entire chamber exploded into movement: contracting, sliding, and twisting. There was a hollow groan from deep within the yellow beast's throat. The enormous mouth slammed open and shut, tasting the air a hairsbreadth away, teeth bending out and shaking; hungry. Unfortunately, it seemed Finn's meaningless existence was about to end—just not in the way he wanted.

worm chase

2

—Thus awakened! Thus awakened! Glorious King Nelmir has found the prime well of magic! Now our sleep-veil dissipates! Praise to our race! Hear and heed the secret whisper of our King! Come in, come in to the coven, we the Enlightened Few! Let us unite science with the archaic arts! —

-Faded ancient description found in the depths of the city of Pania, estimated to be over 200,000 years old.

Finn howled, spinning in place and scrabbling for the tunnel. The vat-worm barrel-rolled in place, shattering rocks and shaking the confined space. Its immense body pulsated, and grating sounds crackled from its toxic shell. It snapped out like a predatory bird, trying to suck Finn and Goblin into its tooth-lined gullet. Its mouth was so big, it had a hard time getting to them. Instead, its gut moved forward, followed by its body, dragged in a rippling movement. It wedged itself closer. Chewing through rock and stone, its teeth overextending to dig at the sides of the walls, it widened the chamber.

Finn, goggles slipping away from his eyes, shoved at Goblin, who'd thrown himself headfirst into the compressed narrow tunnel they'd come from. The boy grunted with strain, wiggling forward. Despairing, Finn knew no matter how fast they moved through the tunnel, the vat-worm would catch up, crunching through everything and swallowing them whole. Their bodies would be crushed between millions of tons of dirt, rock, and ore, shredded by the beast's bite. The only way to survive would be to either kill the beast—a feat no human could possibly do—or outpace it.

Backed against the chamber wall and watching Goblin's feet disappear, Finn held his arms over his head in protection as stones crumbled about him in the vat-worm's glutinous fury. The creature shoved itself forward again, trying to pin Finn against the chamber, or at least graze him with its Orpiment hide. Finn curled up, making himself as small as possible, his body trembling in horror. The beast let out a monstrous moan and its teeth gnashed in waving patterns, as if begging for Finn to jump inside. Deep within its moist terrible mouth Finn could see the last bits of Mudd sliding into oblivion. Bile rose to his throat and his bladder quivered.

Goblin was out of sight, finally giving Finn the room to escape. The vat-worm smashed against the chamber wall again, coming so close, that an Orpiment shard jutting from its lower belly nearly poked Finn's eye. As it reared back, contracting against itself in the confined space, Finn got a brilliant idea—a suicidal idea.

Before the beast could strike again, demolishing and eating another section of the wall to make room for itself, Finn reached into the pouch hanging from his belt. Years of experience working with rocks allowed his fingertips to recognize the chunks of unbroken Miner's Pumice—four pieces of hearty size. As soon as his fist closed around them, drawing the material out of the pouch, he dove into the small tunnel. The enclosed space ripped at his sides, tearing lines into his shoulders, back, and arms. Finn didn't care, nor was he cautious with his movements. He shoved himself forward, meter at a time, grunting with panicked strain. Behind him, he could hear the frustrated bellows of the creature, the stone walls around Finn shuddering as the beast chewed a path forward. Finn knew as soon as the vat-worm had enough wiggle room, it would plow ahead at full speed and there would be nothing Finn, Goblin, or all the miners in Lenova could do to stop it.

Thought of the creature's immense size urged him on. Finn had only seen the beast's head—the vat-worm was a giant. It had to have been Finn's terrible luck that he'd crawled right into its lair, waking it from its nap.

As soon as Finn put a few meters between himself and the chamber, he dropped the Miner's Pumice, and as carefully as he could without breaking the pieces, crawled over them. Using small bits of the material was dangerous enough, only called for when there was no air to breathe, but to use *four large chunks* all at once—it was a guaranteed cave-in. Finn was counting on the vat-worm to chew its way forward and he hoped if the beast moved in a straight line to them, the pumice would be crushed between its teeth and cause a concussive explosion. Would that be enough to stop it, or even throw it off their tracks? Finn doubted it, but all he could do was crawl for his life. He applied all his expertise into moving, body shuddering in time with the walls as the vat-worm tore the chamber apart behind him.

Going as fast as his skills allowed, Finn caught up to Goblin, who was panting in uncontrolled fear. The younger boy was making a critical mistake. It was a lesson drilled into them since day one, a lesson that'd taken Finn his whole life to master. *In a deadly situation, control your breathing. If you don't, the Crust will have you.* Finn had found himself stuck many times, panic and claustrophobia sinking in as he tried to break free, deep within the bowels of the earth. Air ran out in the abysmal mines and cave systems. Chastised by the cave-divers of the time, now all adult miners or dead, they'd reprimanded Finn for not controlling his breathing. Years later, it had become second nature, Finn's lungs working separately from his terrified mind. Goblin though, brand new, had yet to learn the technique. Being ahead, the boy was sucking up the limited oxygen far quicker than Finn would like.

The cave system behind them gave a gut-wrenching shudder. The vat-worm had made enough room for itself. It was on its way, at a speed seemingly greater than a running stallion, its unbreakable rows of teeth moving as a blur, its body swallowing and projecting everything it broke. Already going as fast as his body would allow, Finn gritted his teeth, expecting to be smashed flat as the tunnel caved in, carved by the monster. His face pushed into Goblin's feet and he was forced to slow down. He wrestled with the mania trying to rise out of him. He nearly screamed for the younger cave-diver to move faster but knew to stay quiet. The boy was at his edge and it would be the end of them both if he froze in terror. Finn squeezed his eyes shut, feeling the tremor behind him grow stronger and stronger. The vat-worm was coming.

There was a rock-cracking *pop!* The tunnel filled with pressure and both Finn and Goblin were forced forward, shot like wads of wet paper blown through a pipe-straw. Their shirts were torn to ribbons and their chests and backs were ripped by the rough stone. A massive amount of fresh air rushed around them, whistling through the narrow gaps their bodies formed. The oxygen expanded Finn's lungs to a painful size. So as to not choke, he coughed out the Aquamarine Tear still in his mouth. The crunch of stone and rock doubled as the tunnel behind them collapsed. A pained haunting groan reverberated around them. The vat-worm had bitten the Miner's Pumice.

He didn't let the moment go to waste. Instead, he shoved at Goblin, who lay in the tunnel, dazed. The boy twitched, then darted forward, crawling without caution. Finn followed, ears listening to the commotion behind him. The beast sounded more distant now, bellowing and sliding about as it tried to find where its prey had gone. The chances of it crunching its way toward them were still high, so Finn continued to move, not letting up.

The farther they crawled, the more distant the noises of destruction became. After a while, Finn knew the vat-worm had either changed its course, going the wrong way, or had given up the chase. Goblin came to the same conclusion, slowing his pace. The two boys stopped, laying on their bleeding bellies and shivering in relief.

"You did it. You're okay." Finn croaked, patting the younger boy's leg.

The tunnel grew uncomfortably hot and Finn flicked Goblin's Sponge-Marble sandals, indicating they should keep moving. They readied their bodies and once again wiggled forward.

Sweat poured from Finn's face and he reached back with a pinned arm, maneuvering to get at his pouch. He had a score of Aquamarine Tears left, but no Miner's Pumice to give them fresh air. He popped one of the light blue stones into his mouth and sucked, then passed another to Goblin. The magical pebbles raised their energy and they maneuvered forward, crawling for what seemed an eternity.

Ahead of him, Goblin disappeared. Finn heard the boy slide free, his body echoing as it hit the floor of a larger chamber. Finn did the same, pulling himself out like a creature birthed from the dark. He stood, wavering, and with blood rushing to his head. He adjusted his goggles, regaining his orange-tinted vision, and grinned at Goblin. They'd made it.

Finn came forward and patted the new cave-diver, forgetting the restraint he was supposed to maintain. "I can't believe that happened on your first dive! And we're still breathing!"

Finn was impressed with the amateur. Most on their first day panicked going down the main mineshaft, much less the tunnels. When Finn had first started, it'd taken him four dives before he'd worked up the courage to crawl through a chamber the size of his body.

Finn stopped himself from praising the boy. Cave-divers couldn't have friends. As the vat-worm had proved: death was all too near in the Crust. Losing someone was a lot easier if you didn't know them. Like when Mudd had died. There was a brief moment of sadness, then acceptance.

Goblin, not knowing friendships were taboo, grinned back, his innocent dirtied face looking relieved. Finn bit his lip and turned away without a word. Instead he took lead, heading back to the mineshaft. He knew the action must have hurt Goblin's feelings, but he clamped on his hesitation and squeezed it to non-existence. *No friendships.*

The returning trek was quiet but for their footsteps. Caves and tunnels passed around them and Finn's experience took them in the right direction without getting lost. When they stepped out into the bottom of the central mineshaft, they were greeted by the other cave-divers, who'd already returned, holding their etched parchments full of notes on their explorations. Finn knew they noticed Mudd's absence and their torn clothes, but none spoke out. Just another death.

The cave-divers each handed Finn their parchments and fastened their belts to the hanging ropes attached to the pulleys far above. Finn watched as Goblin struggled with tying himself up. The boy looked to Finn, eyes asking for help. Finn worked his jaw and forced his gaze away. Goblin eventually figured it out and had himself strapped in. Finn attached his belt to the last rope and called to the mineshaft roof, voice swimming up the chamber. "Cave-divers ready!"

The ropes tightened, and the boys were lifted off their feet, pulled high above the working miners and their mine carts lugging precious materials though the network of tunnels. As they neared their individual Mole-Holes, Finn could see a miner working a lever in a nearby tunnel. The man controlled the pulleys via intricate gears and weights, allowing the cave-diver to return to the surface. The ropes came to a stop and Finn grabbed the edge of his Mole-Hole by a worn hand-hold, pulling himself out. Light blinded him, and he yanked off his goggles and detached his belt. As his vision cleared, he watched Goblin struggle to pull himself out. He finally succeeded and staggered in the harsh light.

Finn noticed that the boy's dark skin color was like an umber stone—a unique exotic color. Finn liked it, contrasting it to his pale skin earned from so many years underground. With enough time, perhaps Goblin would be as pale as him.

He approached the boy—*formally*—and got his attention. "We need to report Mudd's death and the vat-worm to one of the supervisors. And we need replacement shirts as well, we're drawing attention. Come on." The boy nodded, detaching his rope and following Finn.

"Hey look!" a voice called out, "Talc's got himself a pet grub!"

Gunther, sneering at him from a crowd of miners, approached the mine holes for his shift of rock-chipping. The men around the bully chuckled as they attached their belts to the mole-hole ropes. Gunther pointed to Goblin with his chin. "Hey newbie, I'd watch his back if I were you. Finn's got his head in the clouds. If he dies, you'd be all alone!"

Goblin furrowed his brow, looking back and forth between Finn and the miner.

"I'm talking to you, newbie!" Gunther growled.

Goblin, as silent as the moment Finn met him, didn't reply.

Gunther dismissed them with a wave of his hand, attaching his rope and dropping through a hole. Finn shook his head in disgust and walked toward a sand-colored complex. It resembled a box-shaped fortress, with thick pillars supporting balconies and wide stairs leading to various entrances. It was nestled against the massive sandstone crags sitting upon the edge of the Slaglands.

Approaching the large yellow structure, the two boys wove between miners and cave-divers leaving and entering the building to make their reports. Some took the time to rest against the cracked pillars lining the entrance before hurrying off, hoping to not get caught. A group of men who were known for sneaking gems into their supervisor's pockets gambled in the shade of an archway, rolling dice and betting work shifts. If regular miners like Finn were ever caught doing relaxing, they'd lose all privileges—including breakfast and lunch. Finn would never kiss up to a super, the thought alone making his fists clench.

Finn explained to Goblin that the outpost headquarters was a hub of operation where House Crumm kept organization over the mine. Finn knew of two other structures like it, both to the South across the spine of the Crust. Orphans, those running from the law, or men who couldn't pay off debts all ended up in the mines, working under the careful eye of the operations office. Finn and Goblin were nothing more than property, *investments*.

Goblin stared at the dusty high-walled building in amazement. Far above, curtains blew out from oval windows and the smell of cooking meat wove down, teasing hunger.

"Don't get your hopes up. You'll be living in a limestone hut like the rest of us." Finn told. "Don't get caught staring or someone might think you're planning on stealing something."

They walked below a large arching doorway, cool shadow hitting their faces, protecting them from the desert heat. Finn's feet stopped treading on sand and instead tapped across ceramic paving. He pointed out to Goblin the various earthen-toned halls, stairs, and landings. "Those offices are for finances. These rooms are for incoming merchants buying stones in bulk. They'll have negotiations with a supervisor to determine prices." Goblin took everything in without a word.

Finn led Goblin past a group of orphan sellers who eyed them coldly. Women with bruised faces and eyes cast down served drinks to hooded men. Three men from another House looked around sneakily before swiping a silver urn into a sack. Finn guessed House Abhurdean based on the symbol of two hand-palms, one above the other, adorning their travel cloaks. So even the Noble Houses outside of the Crust were willing to stoop to petty thievery and accepting to slavery. Finn wondered as to how far the corruption spread. To all nine houses perhaps? To the King's throne room? Not staring at the scenes around him for too long lest he got sick to his stomach, Finn climbed a set of stairs to a second-floor terrace. Turning a corner, they entered a small domed room smelling of incense. Inside, a lean man wearing a turban sat behind a desk counting on a mechanical abacus. Finn watched little magnetized beads slide back and forth within the metal contraption, assisting the supervisor with his duties. Thick purple carpeting, designs painted on the ceiling, and dark wood furniture decorated the room and boasted of a pampered lifestyle. The man stopped his work and beckoned them forward. On his turban was an embroidered rectangular badge, signifying his blood relation to House Crumm. Basing on the size of the man's office, Finn guessed him perhaps a distant nephew to the Noble Lord, nothing more.

"Special report, I assume?" the supervisor mumbled, a distasteful sour look to his face. It seemed he didn't appreciate having a small office nor having cave-divers barge into his space. "It doesn't take two people to turn in parchments."

Finn handed over the mapped areas drawn by his young crew.

"Yes sir, we have a report."

"Well, spill it."

"Tunnel fourteen—it's marked on my record—was destroyed on purpose. There was an Orpiment vat-worm. We were lucky and escaped with our lives, but we lost Mudd."

The supervisor didn't blink an eye. He grabbed a piece of paper and took notes. "I see." he drawled. "Anything else?"

"No sir."

"Good. Get back, end your day, and stop at the practitioner for poultice. I don't want to hear word that your cuts spread an infection in the mine." The man reached into a bin beneath his desk and gave Finn two copper vouchers which could be traded for new shirts.

Finn thanked the super, leading Goblin out of the room. There was no appreciation. No *are you alright*? Finn was used to it; the supervisors weren't his parents. They were unforgiving bosses who only cared for money and productivity. Finn could tell Goblin struggled with the uncaring detachment by the way he shot the man a frown. Leading the young cave-diver out of the building before they both got into trouble, Finn walked them back to the limestone field where huts, barracks, and medical tents awaited.

Finn had them both looked over by a practitioner, who cleaned and dressed their wounds. In a round stone building used both as a supply hut and a payment office, Finn gave his vouchers to a man with a crooked nose. In return, they were both handed gray shirts, the garments already looking pre-worn. Finn hated the building. Once a week he would make his rounds to the place, receive payment for his work, and immediately give it to a collector, owing every coin. The supervisors made sure rent for his hut and cost of his food and water equaled how much he made. Thus, he was indebted for life, stuck in the Crust until he withered or died in an accident. Finn knew that in the days to come, as Goblin learned his place in the outpost, the younger cave-diver would grow to hate the building as well.

He had them stop for food and water at an open shack with a sagging roof. The man behind the counter marked their names on a ledger and Finn knew his debt had increased by a few coins. He left Goblin there, munching on a piece of cactus-bread, forcing himself to not say goodbye to the boy. Why was it so hard to not be friendly? He'd never had problems distancing himself from others before.

Although his hut was in the far West limestone field near the Slaglands, he didn't complain. Being close to the border where it was hottest meant he had more privacy: less bored miners to kick-in one of his hut's walls, laughing as he scrambled out before being buried alive by limestone. It meant he could sleep at night without having to hear the snores, crying, and flatulence of a thousand men.

He approached his small modest hut, a white bumpy-walled dome made of poorly-shaped blocks. He ducked inside, pushing the curtain he used as a door back into place to hide the unforgiving sun. Laying on his straw mat, he gazed at his dark ceiling. There was nothing else to look at; no furniture, no decorations—only a failed half-finished attempt to etch an imaginary forest on his wall. No light filtered through; he had no windows. He was used to the dark; he was a cave-diver after all; always would be a cave-diver, hollow and without hope. He closed his eyes, trying not to think of Mudd, the vat-worm, Goblin, or the fact he'd never leave the Crust.

a quiet friend

3

—*Circa 5,599 E.E. (Economic Era-The 17ᵗʰ Era): King Tipidus the First takes three-hundred men up North to unmapped lands as part of a "holy quest" to bring knowledge of past historic events into light, hoping to shed truth on what has led to the extinction of ancient races whose existence is only recorded on the scrolls of Lyria's Grand Library. He does not return and his young eight-year-old son, Tipidus the Second takes the throne. Men search for the old High King for years but only three ever return, none of which sane enough to explain what has occurred to them, others, or their King. —*

The following morning, Finn awoke to the sound of deep clay horns bellowing a heavy tune. It was early, and the hot sun was still to peak over the crags. Finn dressed and stepped outside. Other miners, ready for the day's work, yawned and looked to the barracks. Following their gaze, Finn made out shadowed forms stepping out of wagons and walking in lines to stand in front of a waiting supervisor. New workers.

By their build, they were all male, meaning the women must have already been separated and taken to the Hub to become maids and servants. The Crust had ensnared more victims: fugitives, vagabonds, criminals, and debtors. Men and women with history. Yet Finn didn't fear them. They may have gotten away with crime wherever they'd come from, but in the Crust, if you got caught doing something you weren't supposed to, there was only one punishment: banishment into the Slaglands. No one was stupid enough to risk that.

"Welcome to the edge of the world!" one of the miners shouted with a laugh. "You can't get any farther West than this! Hope you're ready to die under a rock!"

Some of the miners snickered and Finn let out a smile. He'd seen this scene play out a thousand times. Some of the forms—difficult to define in the low light—shifted in discomfort, yet others stood straighter. Those were the ones that had come willingly. They were the ones with nothing left to lose or crazy enough to think the mines would provide safety.

Finn looked forward to when new workers arrived. They always brought in word of the outside world. They described strange and magical locations, odd cultures, and fascinating people. Heart beating faster, Finn went to breakfast wishing for his two work-shifts to pass quickly. Hearing new stories was a treat. It was his only sweet taste of freedom.

He spotted Goblin leaving his hut, a spot near the center of the limestone field. The boy looked exhausted, as if he hadn't slept all night. Finn grimaced; Goblin had chosen the worst location to make residence. The miners lived miserable lives and many cried and wailed in their sleep. Goblin, with his hut in the middle of the field, would have to accustom to the sound. It was something that would take a long time.

With the consistent amount of death in the mines, homes were often freed-up. Most surviving miners were ones who'd been raised by the Crust. It was rare for adult recruits to last long. They didn't move through the system like the orphan boys did, gaining experience from an early age. Unused to the dangerous labor, the new miners would get themselves killed. In contrast, the orphans would be trained in the Hub by veteran miners until they turned seven and could be promoted to cave-divers.

Although they were coached thoroughly, seven-year-olds sometimes died on their first dive. It was no wonder trainers often committed suicide. They interacted with the young boys for years, finding fragile solace and joy. Out of all the jobs in the Crust, being a trainer was the task no one wanted. Finn's instructor—an elderly veteran by the name of Glob Sumtick—had died years ago. The man had suffered a heart attack in his hut. Whether the cause had been sadness or old age, Finn didn't know. The only memory he retained of the white-bearded man was one of him laughing as Finn crawled through a wooden tunnel made to represent a lava tube. He'd been practicing for his first dive and didn't know why the trainer hooted. Finn shook the nostalgia away. It wouldn't do him any good to focus on the past.

After a breakfast of stringy meat, brought in with the batch of recruits, Finn hiked to his Mole-Hole, skirting around a sour-looking Gunther who seemed to have gotten about as much sleep as Goblin. Using his belt and the pulley system, Finn was lowered to the bottom of the mineshaft. He gave his cave-divers their assigned locations, finding by accident he'd left Goblin in his group once more. Hoping the boy wouldn't grow even more attached, Finn tried his best to ignore him, instead focusing on the other two cave-divers tagging along.

They mapped out a large chamber shaped like a basin. The room could have housed ten-thousand people. Using their orange-tinted goggles they found traces of titanium veins painted along the walls. He was disappointed to not come across anything unique in the awe-inducing space—a change in pace could have made his day pass faster. Although the mines were old, new types of magical stones and colored crystals were discovered every year. The most prized material on the market were SolarStones, which were shaped like thick white staves with rounded ends. The superstitious rumored them to imbue positive magnetic energy, and anytime SolarStones were brought out of the mines, merchants lined up to place their offers.

Following the titanium vein, Finn marked his parchment, and then showed Goblin how to note minerals on his paper. The boy listened to his every word and tailed his every step. When the shift ended, Finn left the caves to take his break. At the bottom of the central mineshaft he passed Gunther. The bully scowled at him as was his usual routine. Finn was grateful another fight hadn't broken out between them like the day before. He regretted ever having mentioned his desires to see the outside world out loud. Finn had no idea why the words had prompted the volatile miner into harassing him.

Above ground, while eating oat paste in the shadow of a boulder, he watched as the new adult recruits were fitted for their Sponge-Marble sandals. In the daylight, he could now make out their features. Many looked like farmers and scared refuges. Finn frowned. It didn't seem like there were any pick-pockets or pirates, they always had the best stories to tell. Even though one had a chance of walking away with their pockets mysteriously empty, Finn found listening to thieves' tales worth it.

He returned to the mines for his second shift, awaiting dusk when he could go to the barracks and overhear news from the world beyond. The work passed slow—Finn had to hold his patience in check as he was again dogged by Goblin. The boy was his shadow everywhere he went. When the day was finally over, Finn nearly climbed his pulley-rope hand-over-hand to get outside. By the time he found the new recruits in the eating area sitting at a large wooden table, many other miners had already crowded around. Finn jogged to the men, his ears perked, trying to catch their every word.

"Oh sure," one of the recruits barked, "times have changed. The land's shadowed, I tell you. Rumors and whispers are spreading about."

Maggs—the large miner that'd stopped Finn and Gunther's fight—stepped forward with arms crossed. "Rumors you say?"

The recruit nodded, a man of solid build and a strong tan. "Indeed! I was fishing off the shores of Lake Everston—had to catch my dinner you see—when from the dirt trail comes a half-crazed lone traveler. I could tell this was a man who'd once seen wealth in his life: some young buck with torn clothing and a rat-like complexion. All he had left to his name was a ring on his finger. He staggered to me with a wild look and warned me in these words: *Beware fisher, men are awakening with demonic powers. Cities are burning. Strange magic's running rampant!*"

Maggs coughed out, halting the tale. "Demonic powers! Sounds to me the young con was trying to swindle you out of a meal!"

The recruit frowned and shrugged his shoulders. "I'm telling you like it was! You're the ones who asked me to share news of outside!"

The other miners shushed Maggs and urged the man to continue. The recruit shook his head. "I brushed the crazed traveler aside and stole his ring. Apart from that, the world's the same: the rich tax the poor, them noble fools run all the trade in Kazma, the king cares nothing for his people, and decent ale's hard to come by."

The miners laughed, walking away to their respective huts. Finn rushed forward, and in an act of thoughtlessness, grabbed the man's arm. "Wait!" he spoke in a rush. "Is there any more? What of far-off lands? Wars? Voyages?"

The tanned man shook him off, sighing and standing away from the table. "Look kid, I just got here. Having to run from the debt-collectors is one thing, but life in the mines will be difficult. I need my sleep."

The man brushed past Finn before he could protest, abandoning him with a bitter sense of disappointment. The crowds dispersed, and Finn was left alone with Goblin, who'd been at the edge of the pavilion. Irritated, Finn waved a hand at the boy. "Go to your home and leave me be."

Finn stomped back to the edge of the limestone field and looked to the Slaglands. Hot wind dragged pebbles across the black glass rock toward his home. His frustration grew into desperation. He'd never escape and see the world.

It was the first time in Finn's life someone was showing him genuine attention. Goblin followed Finn from the barracks to the mine, holding himself in check, as if worried that if he stepped too close, Finn would snap out. It made Finn hate himself for how he'd acted the night before. Someone finally looked at him with the attitude of friendship—with worth—yet he couldn't bring himself to return the act. Goblin had been through an adventure with him. They'd survived danger together. How could Finn brush that off? A hundred logical reasons for why he shouldn't interact with the boy ran through Finn mind. But acting on impulse, he caved-in with a sigh, concluding he didn't care anymore: he wanted a friend. He *needed* a friend.

Finn looked over his shoulder. Goblin slowed his pace and in turn, Finn slackened his own stride, allowing the boy to catch up. Goblin tilted his head, perplexed, and Finn let out a genuine smile. "Hey Goblin. Hot day isn't it?"

The boy stared at him with wide eyes, mouth turning from surprise to a pleasant beam. He nodded, wiping his brow.

"You don't talk much, do you? *Can* you talk?"

Goblin shook his head, frowning in disappointment. He pointed to his throat.

"Your throat-strings?" Finn guessed, "They don't work?" Goblin dipped his chin. Finn cringed, unable to imagine having such an awful impairment.

Goblin pointed to Finn and frowned. "What?" Finn asked as Goblin pointed again.

Goblin rolled his eyes and poked the bruise on Finn's face. Finn winced and felt the injury. "Oh yeah, that's from the vat-pig that teased us the day before, Gunther. Watch out for him." Goblin's hands mentioned for Finn to go on. Finn sighed. "I made the mistake of speaking out loud. I said I wanted to leave the Crust. Wanted to see the world."

Goblin pointed to himself and Finn, making a funny motion with two fingers. It looked to Finn like a man walking. He scrambled his brains to understand what the boy was trying to communicate.

"You and I leave?" Finn snorted, struggling for words. "Ever felt as if you were meant for a different life than the one you were given?" He immediately shook his head. There was no point in wishful thinking. It wasn't Gunther's fists that had beaten the hope out of Finn. It was time. "We're getting distracted. Today will be a change from routine—we won't be doing any cave-diving."

Goblin gave him a questioning look.

"Last night, miners cut free a large supply of SolarStones. It'll be the cave-divers' job to sort and categorize them by size when the cart's hauled up."

Goblin rubbed two fingers together, the universal symbol for money.

"Yeah, they're pricey. Worth a lot more than we'll ever make. Oh, and don't think they *pay* you here. What you make only covers the cost of living and food. We're slaves. Look, they're drawing the cart up now."

The dark-skinned boy followed Finn's gaze toward a large square Mole-Hole. A metal cart full of white round rods was being raised by a wooden crane. Cave-divers slid a thick metal plate below the cart, covering the Mole-Hole. The cart was then lowered back down. Boys came forward with various bins marked in increments. Finn grabbed one of the bins and Goblin followed. Finn showed him what they were to do. "We'll sort out the small SolarStones. Ones fit only for jewelry."

A supervisor yelled at them to get started. As they worked, Finn made rude comments about Gunther under his breath, humoring Goblin. Like a wave of water washing out of him, Finn spoke of his wish to escape, to be free. And once he started, he couldn't stop. It felt good—*great*–to have a release. He talked of trees and monsters, cities and magical locations he'd only heard of. Goblin listened and nodded, smiling and doing what he could to communicate back. Had Finn made a friend? If so, Goblin was Finn's first. Exhilaration coursed through him.

Finn sorted alongside Goblin until their bin was full and the burning sun hung straight above them. Each grabbing one end of the container, the boys wobbled their way over to a waiting cart, dropping the heavy bin into the vehicle. The two were patted by hired security paid to oversee that the cargo made it to where it was supposed to go. Finn was shoved around and had his shirt torn off. He didn't fight back but held his tongue, accepting the abuse. Having found no stolen stones on them, the boys were pushed back to sort a pile of amethysts. Finn picked his shirt from the dirt and put it back on, patting himself down.

At the end of the day, after separating and organizing a dozen different caravan shipments, they stood straight, wincing as their backs popped. They made their way over to the barracks for whatever pathetic dinner they'd be given. On the way there, a voice shouted out, drawing their attention. They turned, facing Gunther, who passed by with the look of one who'd come upon a large sum of money.

"Talc and the new grub, side-by-side like two lovers! Hey Finn, you going to let him move into your hut?"

Finn growled under his breath, wishing for nothing more than to shove Gunther into a Mole-Hole and watch him plummet to the bottom of the mineshaft.

"How long you two gonna stay friends Talc? You think he'll die tomorrow or next week? He's not a veteran and he's not a mine-orphan. I bet he gets stuck in a cave and suffocates in three-days-time!"

"Eat dirt, Gunther." Finn growled, leading Goblin away from the laughing miner. Goblin gave Finn a look of worry and Finn shook his head.

"Don't listen to him. You won't die in the mines. I promise."

Inside his hut, Finn was about to remove his shirt when he heard footsteps outside. He moved the curtain covering his door and found Goblin, standing with his head hung low. He held his fist out and Finn could tell there was something there.

"For me?" Finn asked.

Goblin opened his fist and pushed his hand forward. Finn took the proffered item and examined it. To his surprise, he found a small SolarStone interwoven with twine, forming a wristband. The knots holding the precious stone were intricate and beautifully designed. Beside it was a note written in thin scratch. *For saving my life. Perhaps you can buy your freedom with it someday.*

Goblin!" he exclaimed in surprise. "You stole this for me?"

Goblin made the motion of Finn hiding the object. Finn tossed the present onto his sleeping-pad before anyone could see it. He didn't worry though; he *was* at the edge of the limestone field after all.

"How'd you sneak it away from the cart?" he stuttered.

Goblin pointed to his mouth, a proud grin on his face. He stuck his hand out. Perplexed, Finn took it. Goblin shook it firmly. Making a shushing motion with his finger, he turned and left without a sound. Finn stood in the fading evening light, watching the boy go. In his mind, a thousand thoughts rolled over each other like a falling rockslide. He was overwhelmed. Could there be a weak fluttering wingbeat of hope in his chest? He possessed a treasure, albeit stolen. Yet he could care less whether it was illegal or not. House Crumm had stolen his life. It was only justice that he took something back. And of Goblin! The decision he'd made to befriend the boy was already changing his life. He owned something of value! No, he owned *two* things of value: a SolarStone and a friend.

RAFAEL HOHMANN

nozgull the earthbreaker

4

—*Circa 1,744 E.E. (Economic Era-The 17th Era): The soothsayer, Yvonne the Talon-Walker, rises to power through subterfuge, controlling seven of the nine Lenovan Houses. The War of the Soothsayer begins and the capital of Lyria is razed. Many ancient artifacts and documents are destroyed. King Gabrin wins back power over the Houses after promising the House Lords each two cities of their choice to control and govern as long as each house swears permanent allegiance to the King. The political maneuver is dubbed "The Separation of control". Yvonne the Talon-Walker is forced to swallow mortar and is tossed over the side of the floating islands to fall four kilometers to her death in the SeaLake below.*

—

SUNRIDER

When Finn awoke to the sound of morning horns, his mind hand went straight to his wrist, grabbing Goblin's gift. He gave a soft chuckle, wondering when and how he could use the valuable treasure to buy his freedom. Who could he sell it to without getting caught? A greedy merchant willing to smuggle him out of the Crust? And would it pay for both his and Goblin's escape? After what the boy had done for him, he couldn't leave his friend behind. Standing and rubbing his face to clean the grit from his eyes, Finn hid the treasure and left for breakfast and morning shift, contemplating the small sliver of hope he'd been given.

He walked with a quick pace, thinking of how the day's monotonous work would be improved with a friend. Finn made it to the barracks, and being handed a piece of cactus-bread, chewed slowly, waiting for Goblin to arrive. The boy was running late. He doubted Goblin had gotten used to the sounds of the miners at night. He might have slept in, exhausted from uneasy rest.

Before Finn could make up his mind on whether to go to the boy's hut and check on him, another horn sounded. The noise was quick and commanding. Finn recognized it: an emergency meeting. Following the other miners, Finn jogged to the outpost Hub nestled against the crags. The horns went off again and the miners increased their pace, not wanting to get into trouble.

Finn frowned. Public meetings, even emergency ones, were rare; they interrupted with the work-flow. The last gathering had taken place the year before when a large section of mine had collapsed and supervisors instructed them on how to proceed. Two miners had taken advantage of the situation and ran away. The supervisors noticed but let them go. Where could they have run off to but their death? Without a week's supply of water, there was no escaping the Crust. In the two-hundred years the mines had been operational, no one had ever escaped alive. Skeletons dotted the edge of the desert where miners had fallen to their deaths trying to scale the crags. Other skeletons littered the single road leading out of the outpost. The one place free of mummified remains was the Slaglands. With nothing beyond but black desert, no man—sane or not—dared travel there. Wondering whether any of the new miners would attempt escape, Finn reached the Hub.

A well-dressed supervisor stepped forward, ready to address the crowd. It took a moment for Finn to recognize the form. With elaborate robes cut almost to look like the wings of a butterfly and a turban wrapped with golden ribbon, the House Lord cleared his throat. Finn had heard rumor that the man—Ublah-Kan—was a eunuch and a procurer of spice. The miners went quiet. "We've lost communication with the other two mine outposts within the Crust. As well, we have had no new merchants come up the Southern road. We have reason to believe these areas have been raided and pillaged. We have sent out some of the Hub guards, but they have not returned."

The men went into uproar, everyone shouting and exclaiming their worry. The House Lord raised a hand, and all went as silent. The man's eyes were sunken into his skull, as if having spent years trying to escape the harsh light of the sun.

"We'll continue operations as normal. We can't treat this as a danger yet. Don't fear, those that have invested their wealth in our products won't allow us to come to harm! We'll be alright. That is all."

Maggs stepped forward. "That's all? This meeting can't be over! We need protection! What if it's a large band of marauders?" Gunther and other miners shouted their agreement.

A guard stepped forward and swung a wooden staff across Maggs' head. The blow was hard enough to break the stick, yet Maggs, being a miner as tough as they come, only fell to one knee with a strained grunt. Gunther tended to Maggs while giving the supervisors a look of rage. Finn knew even Gunther wasn't thick enough to fight back. Many of the supervisors carried gems with magical properties granting them subtle, yet terrifying power such as the Whistling Stone which when aimed at a man, could make his bones vibrate. If pointed at a target for long enough, every bone in the body would obtain stress fractures and begin to crumble. Finn had never seen it done before, but had heard from older miners such as Maggs, that it was a terrible scene to witness.

The House Lord didn't blink. "Don't you risk your lives every day? Have you not grown accustomed to the dangers of the mines? You cower like children. Do each of you suddenly find yourselves in the need of comfort and a loving embrace?"

Maggs licked his lips and wobbled back upright as the other miners shuffled their feet. The House Lord continued, sneering. "Get back to work. We've already wasted enough time. All will be well. Serve the mines and the mines will serve you. It's the standard we live by."

The miners shuffled off, many raising fists in anger as the supervisors turned their backs. One could nearly taste the fear and resentment in the air, a bitter flavor carried by the sand-laden wind. Had the other mines had been attacked. And if so, by whom? A guild of thieves? Finn couldn't imagine anything short of an army fighting a thousand strong miners.

As the week passed, no merchants arrived, leaving the outpost quiet. Stress and worry built up, boiling under the edge of everyone's skin. Many more guards were sent out to investigate the other outposts, but of all that left, none returned. The remaining Hub guards stayed near to the supervisors, numbering barely a score. If only the miners could be given weapons of their own to defend themselves... but Finn knew the House Lord Ublah-

Kan would never take the risk. Through keeping them busy, unarmed, and focused on chipping rock, he could control them. Yet anxiety strengthened, blanketing the camp and even showing through the supervisors' calm facades. They were harsher, jittery, and spent most of their time indoors. House Crumm and their elite were on the verge of barricading themselves in the Hub. The days passed, and gems piled up in the mine, unsold.

It was upon Finn's second shift's end when a meeting horn called out, one for only the leaders of the mine. Finn, hanging by his rope from the central shaft, had to wait as he was raised to the surface before able to learn what was transpiring. As he pulled himself out of the Mole-Hole and detached his belt from the pulley rope, he gazed to the distance. All the miners and cave-divers around him were frozen. When Finn saw what they stared at, he froze as well.

It was a peculiar sight. A glimmering cloud—like mirrors in the sky—hovered on the edge of the Southern horizon. Goblin, having climbed out of his own Mole-Hole, pointed to the distant shape.

"I see it, but don't understand it." Finn told the boy. "It's never rained in the Crust."

They walked to the shade of the food barracks. Were the supervisors meeting to figure out how a cloud had come upon them? If it were to rain, water could get into the mine. There were many volatile minerals inside that would turn deadly when mixed with liquids. Finn ate his supper in silence side-by-side with his friend, watching the distant shape. It wasn't growing smaller and it wasn't moving sideways, meaning it would either dissipate—or come toward them.

That night as Finn readied for bed, he wore Goblin's present. His dreams were a mix of riches, dirt, and rainstorms. Awaking to the morning horn, he stepped out of his hut ready to go and wake Goblin. Still unused to the schedule, the boy had slept-in more than once before, already getting into trouble. Finn heard a shout and spun in place, remembering the storm cloud. Looking to the center of the outpost—as were the other miners who left their huts—they bore witness to an inexplicable sight.

Strolling into the camp with an air of confidence walked a goateed man in a metal suit. The man's suit, only partially covering his form, wrapped around his brow, hands, and stomach. A deep rich brown glowed from the abstract designs inlaid on the armor. In one hand, he dragged a large travel bag. It looked empty and was coated in dust. With the other hand, he tossed to the ground an empty water-skin.

But the strange partial suit was not what Finn focused on. Instead, he stared in amazement at what was *above* the man. It was a cloud: the massive cloud they'd seen in the distance. Finn opened and closed his mouth, body wobbling at the view. It was no ordinary cloud. It glinted with a million hues of color and sparkles. It took Finn a moment to recognize its composition:

The cloud was made of enormous gems, crystals, and precious stones—floating in the air.

No one made a noise or moved. The man walked past the limestone field and came to stop between them, the mine, and the Hub. The massive cloud followed him, making the softest of tinkling sounds. Squinting his eyes, Finn and the other miners stepped closer—like hypnotized cattle—moving between the huts in a daze. Astonished, Finn walked into colored shade. Looking up, he could see greater detail in the low-hanging cloud, resting what could only have been fifty meters above him. A massive pearl the size of five horses floated above his body, slowly spinning and reflecting light. Red, pink, yellow, and green tint swam across his pale cave-diver skin. How could a pearl have made its way to the Crust? Were they not found only near large bodies of water? How far had this man travelled? The other miners looked about with childlike wonder to their faces. Nearby, Gunther wobbled, mouth open and face turned upwards.

The strangely-clad man stretched out his hands. His combed-back curly hair reminded Finn of an animal's mane.

"Men of the land." he called to the miners; his voice loud, clear, and confident, his lips cracked from travel. He acted powerful, but his features were of a common man. "I thank you. I thank you all for your work and your sacrifice."

Finn could see a band of supervisors leave the Hub, knit together in a tight group and led by Ublah-Kan. They moved forward in shock and fear. The reduced and remaining guards surrounded them protectively, iron spears at the ready and swords drawn. The stranger gave them a nod.

Ublah-Kan stepped forward, turban wobbling, pock-marked skin gaunt. His mouth tried forming words. "What—how... Is this magic?"

The suited visitor smiled, showing straight yellow teeth. "It's much more than what you can comprehend, mine-owner."

The supervisor stuttered, hands wringing together. He looked to the cloud and to the man so quickly, Finn worried he was having a seizure. It couldn't be real. What they were witnessing wasn't possible.

"Oh great mage, what do you require of us?" Ublah-Kan asked, falling to one knee. He raised his arms outward. "To show such might and force! To command the very gems! What's the purpose to this grand show?"

Most miners followed the House Lord's example and knelt as well. A few others, in great fear, stayed frozen while many in House Crumm held onto defensive magic gems, gripped tightly in their hands as if warding off evil. Finn stood still, distracted by the pearl above him. A question hounded him. Where had all these riches come from? Were these... from the other mines? The partially-suited man, watching miners stoop to his power, smiled even wider.

"What do I require? I require everything. I want it all."

Ublah-Kan was unable to reply. He cocked his head to the side, sunken eyes full of questioning. The magical man continued. "I am Nozgull the EarthBreaker. Now-appointed Commander of the Crust, Lord of all Lenova. I am a Star-Child and I *will* be the richest man in all the land."

Finn turned his gaze away from the cloud to study the visitor. Something was wrong. The way the man stood, poised like a predator; Finn felt something in his gut—the feeling that arose before a tunnel collapse.

"A Star-Child?" Ublah-Kan asked. "I'm unfamiliar with the term. Are you of a magician's guild? Or perhaps of another Noble House?"

The strange man laughed, his voice echoing across the crags. He raised his right arm, indicating a metal piece of forearm armor meshed with the metal suit covering his hand. *A bracer.*

"This. This fell from the sky to land at my feet! I was chosen by the heavens themselves! Chosen to be more than mere drudgery! Chosen to rise above mortal coils! Chosen to abide by a different set of rules than those of Lenova! *My* rules. By the power granted to me by fate, I forge my future!"

There was silence across the land as the simple miners and their confused supervisors tried to understand what was being said.

"Great one, what is your command?" Ublah-Kan asked, trembling beneath the visitor's might. The suited figure, center of attention, relaxed his shoulders. He took in a deep breath and Finn heard it from all the way at the edge of the crowd.

"I declare unto you your law: all that comes from the land is mine."

Ublah-Kan froze and looked toward the Hub. "You mean the stones? The gems? My lord, those—those aren't yours!" The House Lord blundered over the words, terror cracking his voice.

The armored man nodded as if in resignation. "Why do I continue playing with you?"

"My lord?"

"You're not my subjects. You're not even worth the dirt beneath your feet. You already bore me."

Ublah-Kan made the move to stand, his hands still wringing together. The armored man stepped forward.

"If you won't give me what I want, then die."

Without warning, a gem the size of Finn's hut shot down at the speed of lightning. It smashed on top of Ublah-Kan, burying itself a meter into the ground. The man was snuffed, like a miner stepping on a dry bug husk.

The miners stared at the semi-translucent object, then to the shifting cloud, and back to where the House Lord was no more. Sprinkles of blood coated the faces of the front-row miners. Finn couldn't think, his mind had frozen. Before anyone could move or say another word, jagged crystals flew like spears, impaling the rest of the supervisors and their escort of guards. Members of House Crumm bled into the sand, their lifeless eyes open far too wide. And thus, the slavers died on the very grounds were rested the bones of their slaves.

Finn fell backward onto his rear, air hissing through his throat. All around him, boys and men screamed in terror. Precious stones, rocks, crystals, gems, ores, and other riches of the earth pelted like rain, striking miners dead as they ran away. One collapsed from a blow to the head. Twelve were smashed flat by the very pearl that'd hung above Finn.

Finn, shaking in awed fear, tripped backward and scooted across the limestone field. He was unable to look away from the partially-armored man. The *Star-Child*, as he'd called himself, waved his arms as if conducting silent music, controlling the stone cloud. With a flicker, thirty men were crushed, smeared as paste across the ground. Immediately the terrain soaked up their blood. A hard look came over Nozgull's features as he lifted both hands above his head. With a scream of exertion, he brought his arms forward. The *entire cloud* exploded down. Finn yanked himself to his feet, running for his life as all around him $_{me=n}$ and huts were obliterated. He was shouting, but over the sound of destruction, he couldn't hear himself.

Turning to look over his shoulder, dodging falling stones worth the same as a small city, he spotted the man making a claw motion with his fingers. The man's lips moved, as if beckoning something. His eyes... his eyes were *euphoric.*

To Finn's far right, the ground exploded, throwing screaming miners in all directions. Their bodies spun like dancing leaves, cracking against stones, and bending in odd angles. From the dust and dirt, a massive form moved and wiggled with violent rage. It shook itself free, unable to comprehend a world of light and space. It was a coal-coated vat-worm.

Unlike the Orpiment worm Finn had encountered some time ago, this worm smoked and sizzled, thick dark fumes billowing out of its circular mouth and from the cracks in its shiny black hide. Teeth wiggled in patterned waves, tasting the air, feeling the vibration of running feet.

It gave a hideous groan and barreled forward, its maw gaping wider than seemed possible. Both boys and men were swallowed whole, snatched into the black, putrid inferno of its mouth. They bubbled and melted faster than they were chewed. The worm carved a path across the outpost, killing, crushing, and destroying. Those who dodged to the side were rolled over by its fuming body, ripped to bits between the worm's weight and the ground.

Finn fought his lungs, trying to stay calm like he'd been trained—*impossible, it was an impossible task*—and watched as the suit-wearing man focused all his attention on the vat-worm, as if he was controlling it. The worm was wiggling, Finn observed, fighting its own movements. It didn't like the surface world, it wanted to return to the dark, but the armored man was commanding its coal skin. The worm spun in place, cutting back to catch the men behind it. None of them escaped.

Nozgull released his hold on the vat-worm and the creature thrashed in place, becoming a self-twisting rope, scaring the land and crushing many before diving headfirst into the ground. Earth billowed up into a pillar as the beast let out one final bellow, its fat open tail projecting chewed dirt and human remains. It disappeared, running away from the madness.

Nozgull turned to the Hub, where many had fled for protection. With another strained scream, he swept his hands to the side and the entire building rumbled and vibrated. Cracks ran down the walls and pillars, and stones slid sideways. The foundations grated and snapped. Like a deflating bag, the Hub caved-in on itself, collapsing into debris and dust. The tops of the crags above seemed to fold down like hands cupping over bugs, burying alive those trying to climb the cliffside to escape.

Nozgull, suit glowing as he panted, turned and stomped between the huts; collapsing those hiding within their homes and entombing them with flicks of his hands. By some miracle, Finn was still alive, having stayed near the edge of the attack. Turning in place, he wove between the small limestone shelters to escape the man and his line of vision. Those seen were killed.

The ground jumped, throwing Finn in the air. A sound rang through him unlike he'd ever heard before. It was the noise of Lenova tearing apart, the sky collapsing, the world breaking. The mineshaft exploded, its roof launching into oblivion, evaporating the Mole-Holes and exposing its insides. Dirt shot a thousand meters up and rained across the outpost. Dust billowed in rolling waves. The land dipped as cave systems below their feet shut closed. Gems, ores, and crystals flew out of the open shaft like upside-down rain, joining the cloud above. Nozgull was shrieking—screaming about wealth and power—his phrases jumbled like a lunatic, spit flying from between his lips. Stone slabs fell like walls laid by an invisible god's hand, picking off escaping miners. The barrage came at insane speed, like comets turned arrows, leaving behind the smell of iron and salt.

Gunther came out of the dust, a crystal wedged through his neck. He made eye contact with Finn, opened his mouth, and collapsed. *Like meat—he'd fallen over like meat.* As if in a dream, Finn staggered past him, arms out like a crazy man, doing all he could to not drop to his knees and curl up. He made it to his home and dove inside, having no idea what to do or where to go. Beyond his hut, screams and explosions rang out. The ground shook, and men died. Out of instinct, he grabbed his cave-diver belt, containing the stones he used in exploring. He wrapped it around his waist with trembling fingers. As he did so, a thought struck him: Goblin! Where was Goblin?

He jumped back through his door and was met with silence. There was no more yelling, no more running, no more movement. Blood and dust hung heavy in the hot air, hiding the landscape in a yellow curtain. Finn shuffled forward, his eyes grabbing at shapes, hardly able to see in front of him. What he thought was a rock was a body and a body, a rock. Finn didn't know whether to make himself small or run back-and-forth. He could get hit at any second and he wouldn't even see the incoming projectile. He froze in place, hearing a grunt in front of him. With terror controlling of his body, he stood still as a statue, waiting for the dust to dissipate.

It settled around two shapes, forming human outlines. Goblin and Nozgull! Squirming in silence, the young cave-diver was being dragged out from behind a rock by the armored Star-Child. The man wasn't killing the boy: he was binding him. Nozgull looked exhausted. He was gasping and his lips were white, yet he still had the strength to subdue Goblin.

Noticing Finn, he grinned.

"Last one? I commend you on surviving! Unfortunately for you, I only need one servant to tend to me and my wealth! This one's lucky I have an open spot! My last servant found himself out of my favor. I made him eat his own weight in opals. Literally."

Cold fear clawed at Finn's heart. The man took a tired step forward to attack and Finn threw himself to the side, smashing his shoulder against a limestone hut. The force broke the wall and Finn fell in a heap, barely missing the wave of crystals magically thrown by the Star-Child. Untangling himself from a bedsheet, Finn jumped again. The movement saved him a second time as the hut behind him imploded like a door slamming shut, nearly crushing him to the size of a loaf of bread.

Finn ran for his life, arms over his head, objects whizzing all around him. More huts collapsed, and stones flew at his heels. Finn didn't know if he imagined it or not, but there was less aggression to the attack. Nozgull had no energy left. Either way, Finn was still in mortal danger. A glancing blow to his calf sent him to the ground but he popped back up, fear hiding the pain.

With no plan, no thought, and with nowhere to go, Finn sprinted in the only direction available to him: the Slaglands. He could see where limestone became black glossy rock. He aimed for the line, determined to live long enough to cross it. A shard of stone cut his arm and he cried out but pushed himself faster.

"Run miner, run! Leave your friend to me. I shall care for him!" Nozgull laughed out. "Run from death, *to* death! Let it be so. Let the Slaglands eat you!"

With tears running down his face, with terror clutching his heart, and with the terrible thought he was leaving Goblin behind to that *monster*; Finn crossed into the Slaglands. He ran without pause, the fading laughter of the Star-Child chasing after him. Eventually he collapsed, falling against the blazing hot rock, his conscience leaving.

RAFAEL HOHMANN

lines crossed

5

—*Circa 4,200 E.E. (Economic Era-The 17th Era): Mount Khun erupts, spewing ash across most of the eastern desert. Rivers of gold and lava spill down the mountain for five years. Seizing control of the mountain, House Crookshanks gathers the wealth and builds massive forges to process the materials. Paying off their debts and bribing the King with gold, they are given a boon—which ten years later they use in the form of healers and medicine when their forge workers develop a volatile contagious illness dubbed the Stone Apoplexy. —*

There was a line and Wahala crossed it. A border, a contrast; corroded death to verdant life. Next to her, the cult leader Mal'Bal inhaled the fresh air of Lenova, exhaling the stale mist of the Kingdom of Rot. His golden body glinted in the sunlight as he left dead land and stepped onto grass. Wahala was certain that the man couldn't feel the vegetative texture with his golden feet nor could care less for what the sloping fields provided. Each heavy step he took made the landscape shudder. His yellow naked body created furrows in the soft ground.

Wahala and the cult had left the only land they'd ever known and entered a place of calm and tranquility. The color, the vibrancy, and the warmth more than offended: it brought them outrage. *"False! It was a false state of being,"* they hissed. *"Only pain and putrefaction measure reality!"* Their barren lands of death and lifeless terrain: *that* was symbol of existence. Life was calculated by how it decayed.

By Mal'Bal's stance, Wahala knew he was confident in his mission. He had found a purpose far greater than just surviving. If life was only a path to death, he would assist the cycle. He would kill all species, races, and people. Through it, he would end the process of creation. There would be no cycle, for there would be no life to start it. Glorious non-existence would be all that remained.

A bee fluttered past the cult leader and he roared, swinging at the insolent beast. It dodged his hand and he swiped again, determined to crush it into goo between his fingers. Beside him, Wahala watched, her eyes narrow slits as she stared at the leader. Her new golden knees creaked as she shuffled her feet. The bracer had changed the Lord-Lich. The rituals and yearly sacrifices done to the million-dead walking the Kingdom of Rot were no more. Abandoning the Cult's sacred lands and temple, Mal'Bal had cajoled his people to come to the forbidden lands of light, an alien landscape the cult had never seen.

Wahala scowled. *She* could feel the grass under her boots—she didn't like it. Where was the sharp stone? The ragged cracks in the ground making a man's feet blister and bleed with each step, marking a red trail across the land? She wanted to return home. Many others did as well. But the bracer, Mal'Bal's gift from the dark between the stars, had opened the man's mind to a new opportunity: evolution, destruction, a change from tradition.

Wahala looked at her legs, examining her joints and how they gleamed. They were her only modification, her only sacrifice. Rage enflamed her. The entire cult had been dragged into folly. They reveled in death and the lack of an afterlife. They worshiped the *process* of decay. Mal'Bal would take that away. He would take even *them* away when the time came. They were marching with their chins up, right into the maw of omnicide. To think, her first sacrifice had been done in the name of Mal'Bal when she could have instead done the mutilation in remembrance of her ancestors.

The leader of the cult caught the buzzing insect and snuffed its life. He turned and beckoned Wahala to stand at his side. Obediently, she complied, hiding the way she looked upon him when his back was turned. Mal'Bal pointed to the lands of the North. The horizon was green and pure grass.

"There, Wahala my handmaiden, my righteous. Beyond we'll find the path to the end. Beyond are many who will be ours to purify."

Wahala bobbed, not foolish enough to reply. Mal'Bal's mood could shift in a heartbeat. She'd seen him rub shoulders with a man, to only a few seconds later disembowel him. She locked onto his eyes: a mistake. His hypnotic stare was wild, his pupils only pinpricks. It was as if Mal'Bal was attempting to force his mad thoughts into Wahala.

"We'll end all life as I have ended the life of this creature." He held out his hand where remnants of the bug fluttered to the ground.

"Yes, Golden Agony." Wahala stated with a bow.

Mal'Bal pushed past her to face his large gathering of gold cult members, their entire people. Thousands of mutilated men and women looked to him, many with praise. But now, Wahala observed, there were many with faces like stone—those unhappy with Mal'Bal's decision to leave their lands, disgusted by Mal'Bal's *delusion*.

"Born from a golden womb, was I." Mal'Bal spoke, voice like the rumbling of thunder. The veins on his face and scalp pulsed with the dark energies of the Apex gems infused into his body. "You know of my mother, the previous Queen Priestess. Fatherless was I. Her insides were given to her, already prepared to bear fruit. Given by the dead lands themselves! By my birth was she torn in two! From blood, bone, and gold was I born. You knew then as you know now, I was to lead our people!"

Many cult members raised their arms, screaming into the sky. Some fell to the ground, rolling and wailing. So entranced were some by the man, they immediately pulled out scythes and flayed themselves. In disgust and outrage, Wahala watched as they ritualized in the Land of Light. Her body trembled. Spread throughout the crowd, many others had the same angry reaction. But caught up in his own words, Mal'Bal didn't notice.

"We'll spread ourselves beyond the borders that have confined us! We'll cover the entire world in blood and darkness! Depravity will wash as a flood through homes and cities, eradicating life!" Mal'Bal leaned forward as if about to whisper a secret. The men and women went quiet, eyes wide with anticipation.

"I have seen our future." Mal'Bal whispered out. The cult was as silent as the stars. "By this device I was granted a vision!" The man lifted his hand. A metal bracer gleamed in the sunlight. "Through my inheritance, was my mind focused! I saw what we were to do!"

The cult, even Wahala, perked their ears, curiosity staying their voices.

"I'll bring movement to which is inanimate! I'll reverse the order of existence! All organic life will die and be replaced by a purer creation! I'll become a God to a nation of anti-life! You... will be my heralds!"

The cult stayed silent, trying to imagine how the man could

accomplish such a feat. They *knew* he had the power of necromancy on his side, but how was one to create anti-life?

A voice spoke out from the crowd. "But we are alive! Will you kill us as well? Have we fallen so far from our traditions?"

The crowd turned, trying to find the speaker. Mal'Bal's breathing grew shallow, his face one of a predator sniffing blood.

People parted, revealing a wrinkled elder leaning on a cane made of carved bone from her dead husband's spine. "This is folly I say! Heresy! Anti-life belongs to the dead roaming our home!" She coughed, stomping with a clawed golden foot. Others around her nodded.

Mal'Bal slid past Wahala like smoke, smelling of sour rot and rage, and approached the old woman, his hulking form overshadowing her. "It's a new age." he spoke, muttering under his breath as if talking to himself. "There are new rules to abide by. Tradition won't let us become more. All we do is stagnate and die!"

The elder stepped back, pursing her lips defiantly. "Death is what we worship! We embrace it! A Queen Priestess would never allow this!"

Mal'Bal loomed over her, hands twitching like large vices. His back and his jaw stuck out. "Born from a Queen was I!" he hissed. "I am more than a Queen ever could be! I am the mandate of the earth itself!"

Many in the cult cheered, few dared hiss. Mal'Bal's arm blurred out, catching the elder's neck. "If you embrace death so much, then I grant you exaltation!"

There was a snap as he broke the woman's neck. There were cries of outrage among the crowd. Wahala staggered back, shocked. Mal'Bal ignored the sounds.

"Those who oppose the cult, hold us back! Will you listen to her, or the earth itself? I am the earth!" He shook his bracer-adorned arm. "I was verified by the heavens! I am the will of our people! Of the world!"

There was silence. Many were nodding, eyes like blank sheep, worshipful. Wahala's stomach churned. What was happening? Her entire world, all she'd believed in, was turning upside-down.

Mal'Bal motioned for an Apex gem to be brought to him. A teenage girl carried one forward, grabbing it from a supply cart. Mal'Bal lifted the green stone into the air.

"Behold the power granted to me by the skies! For death!" he screamed.

Suddenly, his bracer came to life. It contorted and spread, metal growing and covering his arm. The cult members jumped away from him, scared and cowering. Was this some form of new spell the man had learned?

Metal encased the golden body, forming a suit that covered Mal'Bal's chest, legs, and other arm. When it was over, not one bit of Mal'Bal could be seen. The entire man was enclosed in dark metal armor, a metal frill growing from the back of his skull-shaped helm. Intricate, curved designs ran along the arm braces, shin guards, chest piece, and head covering. They glowed golden.

In his hand, the Apex gem glowed as well. It thrummed to the same beat as Mal'Bal's heavy breathing. He waved his hand, pointing to a covered cart. Dumbfounded cult members pulled the cloth off, exposing boulders of various sizes. Mal'Bal stomped forward and his suited arm shot out, jamming the Apex gem into the pile. All was still. Wahala licked her lips. Then the pile of stones moved, grating and cracking, rolling off the cart. Cult members dove to the sides, screaming and falling back.

Wahala watched in awe as the boulders piled one over another, forming the basic shape of a ten-meter man. It wobbled and straightened out, animate. By the power of the bracer, Mal'Bal had constructed a crude—living—stone idol that towered above the crowd. An evil feeling came over the area. The form shuffled and Wahala gasped.

Something was happening to Mal'Bal. She turned and watched as his suit collapsed, hiding within itself and returning to the bracer. His head, the only flesh left to him, was covered in sweat. Although the bracer was once more normal, the stone golem stayed upright. *Still alive.*

"I have transcended to Godhood." Mal'Bal whispered. "I bring existence to new creation. Life to which was not meant to have life, formed from any material. I am a limitless… God."

He spread his arms and looked to the sky. "We will end this world and bring about a new age."

Mal'Bal walked to his golem; his creation. Around him, cult members fell to their knees in worship. Wahala stepped back; disgust, terror, and betrayal hammering against her chest.

"It's time to change our ways." the leader spoke. "We're no longer a cult of stagnancy. We're harbingers, bringers of the end."

He beckoned Wahala over. Startled, she approached him.

"My butterfly." he purred. "I'll need you to learn words in the ancient tongue. If many are to ritualize in our campaign, you'll be the one to join gold to limb. I cannot waste energy and time on such trivial matters. I shall make you my…acolyte."

Wahala was astounded. She didn't know whether to be insulted at the mention that ritualization was trivial or feel the rush of power at the responsibility given to her. *Necromancy!* Mal'Bal had made only himself privy to the art, hiding the knowledge from all others.

"Come," he spoke, "I'll teach you some words. Our people are cutting themselves now."

Mal'Bal stopped and put a hand to the belly of the stone man. He touched it in loving wonder and looked to the horizon where lay the lands of humanity. His eyes, as wild as ever, vibrated with a promise to bring death to all.

"Anti-life." he whispered.

fate wrought

6

—*Erstwhile in a day gone by, oft stalwart men die: not by blight, sword, nor rod, but by Aluxim, the Baron-God. A warning: be wary of a pillar of light, to hither transport you to endless night. Venerate Aluxim, shall the weary chant, venerate, venerate! Yet I shall reply, armor-donned God will I not obey, for the sake of my freedom, I can't. —*
-Old forgotten song, tuneless, believed to have come from the 14th Era, roughly 20,000 years prior to modern age (E.E.)

Agurgling scream full of pain and terror disturbed the dead sky. Finn pulled away from black rock, shocked by the noise that'd come from his throat. He was a baby, violently born into a hot, unforgiving world. Everything he'd ever known: gone.

His skin, like one large swollen welt, refused to stretch. Invisible fingers were pinching the sides of his brain, rolling the meat between knobbed digits. The headache in his temples flooded his senses and he staggered about, dodging steam as if the ground was spitting at him. Heat waves the size of mountains rippled the landscape, distorting reality. Air thick as mud and hot as a furnace forced its way down his throat. He fell, tearing the skin on one knee. He let out a moan. His mind—his mind couldn't take what he'd seen. How could one man have caused so much death?

An image of Gunther flashed through Finn's mind, already dead yet still stumbling about. He dry-heaved, tasting sour bile. Hot, it was way too hot. Half-running, half-falling, Finn entered the shade of a stone spire shooting to the heavens like an enormous tooth. There was no change in temperature. Everywhere he looked, he couldn't see signs of life, not even cacti, birds, or bugs. The only movement came from steam, trickles of lava pouring from rock.

Finn's mind huddled into the corners of its own depths. Nozgull the EarthBreaker: how had the man obtained such power? What Nozgull had demonstrated—it changed everything. The scales of Lenova were tipped. Magic and armies, artillery and navies, they were nothing to a man who could create clouds from gems. Memory of the Star-Child shimmered before Finn like the heat waves vibrating the landscape. Nozgull held his arm up, showing a piece of armor—a bracer—his yellow teeth glinting in the heat. His eyes mocked Finn.

"This. This fell from the sky to land at my feet. I was chosen by the heavens themselves!"

There was something about that bracer. Nozgull had shown it off, like a knight brandishing a beautiful sword. Was that what had given the man such power? If the article had fallen from the sky, what could have manufactured the event? Why send it to Nozgull, a man full of greed? *A murderer.*

SUNRIDER

Rage engulfed Finn for all the miners who'd died. They'd struggled so much, fought so hard, just to stay alive. Then with the wave of a hand, Nozgull swept it all away. He'd even taken Goblin. Finn howled into the air, his voice weak. Why had Finn made friends with the boy? He'd taken the risk, promised himself he'd watch the younger cave-diver knowing full-well Goblin could die in the mines. Yet fate was too strong a thing to change. Danger had found them in the end.

Helplessness boiled within his veins, forcing his muscles to clench and his burned skin to throb in agony. What could he do? He spun in place. There was nothing but black rock stacked and poised, ready to cut him to ribbons. Spines pointed to the sky in accusation, bristling in curved rows like petrified liquid explosions. The Slaglands, he was lost in the Slaglands. Panic squeezed his chest and his stomach muscles clenched. The Slaglands meant death. He was going to die, the meat on his bones slow-roasted, peeling back to reveal bone cracking under heat. He could already smell it; the cooking flesh sliding off him. He wanted to giggle, the edge of madness tempting him into an easy slide down into the dark.

But his cave-diver training fought back, assessing the situation. Think Finn, what do you have? Finn patted himself, grabbing his cave-diver belt. His fingers ran over the satchel hanging from his right side. He tore it open. Inside, were various stones Finn had stored for the day's work, a job he'd never do. Eight Aquamarine Tears waited within, staring back at him. Water!

In frantic greed, he stuffed one of the stones into his mouth and sucked as hard as he could. A small cold trickle hit his throat and he cried out in relief. Standing in the shade of the large stone spire he closed his eyes, drawing on the stone with relish. It wasn't a lot. No, it wasn't nearly enough. But it would do for a while.

He opened his eyes and continued to riffle through the bag: four lumps of Miner's Pumice, an empty parchment, and a coal pencil. He searched his clothes to see if there was anything else. His eyes were drawn to the small wristband on his arm, Goblin's gift to him. It would have one day paid for his freedom. The SolarStone shone in the sun, its white surface flawless. It caused something to stir within Finn, an emotion that'd only previously come to him with his desire to see Lenova: determination.

Goblin was still alive—had to be. Nozgull was keeping him a slave. But Finn couldn't save him, he was lost in the Slaglands. Adding to the problem, there was something wrong with the terrain, as if the air was heavy-laden with a curse. The sun wasn't changing position. It hung perfectly at the center of the sky, giving no indication of his bearings. In the time Finn had been underneath the stone spire, the rock's shadow hadn't wavered even a fraction of a hairs-width. He scratched a line at the edge of the shadow with a stone shard, then watches it obsessively. What seemed like an hour passed and his body grew heavier and heavier in the heat. The shadow did not shrink or grow. The Slaglands, it seemed, was timeless.

With no indication of a way out and without the help of the sky, Finn spun in place, knowing his next decision would determine whether he'd die or not. Looking one direction, Finn could see more black spires like the one he stood under. He was unsure of whether it was the correct path, but he knew the rocks would provide shade. He clenched his jaw, closed his belt satchel, and took a step into the blistering sunlight.

Finn trudged the land as an endless wanderer. Vats of smoldering lava bubbled out from natural terraces, layered like stacked black tubs. Thick sludge rose to the surface, spilling to the steps below, then was swallowed by jagged cervices. The lava waterfalls hissed, greeting Finn as he hobbled past, sucking on his Aquamarine Tear. *Welcome stranger. We've never seen your kind before.*

Over a sea of waved hillocks and unnatural cliffs Finn walked. For all its danger and lethality, the Slaglands was a wonder. How had it been created? A massive volcano? No, one volcano couldn't span such a distance and change the landscape so drastically.

As he hiked beside a sheer wall of rock with his shirt over his head, Finn took a break, marveling at the sight. The wall, possibly eighty-meters tall, looked like a large frozen wave in mid-movement. Finn put a blistered hand on the burning-hot facade. It was perfectly smooth. He imagined a castle standing on the spot. The wall could have been the remains of a cathedral the size of a city. He spotted the faint outline of a form burned into the surface. Was it a beast with tentacles coming from its head or perhaps a woman with splayed hair? Finn tore his gaze away, spitting out his second Aquamarine Tear. Not wanting to tarry long, he continued. A macabre, haunting feeling trailed after him.

Finn passed open lava tubes resembling the shed skin of snakes abandoned on the ground. They were large enough for armies to march through. He traversed spires and stones that were melded back, as if once liquid. Even though his Sponge-Marble sandals were designed for walking in hot places and protecting his soles, they weren't strong enough for the continuous stomping through volcanic rock. Chips and nicks were appearing, and Finn knew if even one of the two sandals broke, he would no longer be able to continue and would die in the Slaglands.

Anxiety mounted in him as he spat out another dried Aquamarine Tear. The pebble, once blue, was now gray and could have passed off for any other common stone. There were only four left. He knew he'd gone the wrong way, but it was too late. If he changed direction, he would potentially go in circles.

Finn walked on, body sagging with exhaustion and the weight of the sun's heat. Whether he was heading deeper into the slag or toward its edge, he didn't know. He rested in the shade of a rock, using his shirt as an ineffective barrier to help stifle the heat of the ground. Meters away a wide stream of lava ran by, hypnotizing him to sleep.

The heat bent and broke through Finn's scalp, piercing his skull and cooking his head. He was being roasted alive. With eyes squinted half-shut, he nearly staggered into a vent, sure the hole—resembling a well—led to some deep magma-filled chasm. Finn pulled out his seventh Aquamarine Tear. They weren't doing him any good. They didn't have enough water. Not enough... How many days? Two? Three? Perhaps still only one? There was no way to tell time. He was going to die.

Finn caught himself whispering, apologizing to Goblin. Turning to ask the boy why he wasn't responding, Finn saw he was alone. He neared a steep hill and to his weakened state, it looked like a mountain. His body shook, trying to cry without moisture. He sucked at his last Aquamarine Tear, tongue swollen enough to protrude between his cracked bleeding lips. The stone was empty; had been for a long time. There was no way he could return the way he'd come. He focused on the hill in front of him. Like a dying animal determined to go on a little longer, Finn fell to his hands and knees and crawled up. The skin touching black rock burned, but Finn no longer felt it.

With conscience fading in and out, Finn made it to the top. His eyesight cleared, and he witnessed the full scope of what he'd climbed. The hill was no sole mass, but a ring curving to his right and left: a full circle. Turning in place, he could see for kilometers in every direction across the Slaglands. The entire landscape curved as massive concentric rings, or frozen ripples in water. The tall stone waves and spires, like castle walls and towers, all leaned away from the area Finn stood on. The rivers of lava, the rocks—everything—looked as if made and pushed away from this spot. And at the other side of the hill—no, the lip of the crater—he spotted a shape.

His mind had to have been playing tricks on him, for in the middle of the basin was a man, arms outstretched in greeting. In a movement Finn knew looked ridiculous—it couldn't have been a man down there—he raised a hand and waved. The form didn't respond. A stone, it was a stone.

His knees wobbling, Finn staggered to the epicenter, the heart of the Slaglands. His tongue tried to move and form words, but only quivered. He wanted to speak, to laugh out. Of all the directions he could have gone, he'd chosen the worst way. Coming closer to the mysterious mound, he made out more detail. The center pushed up, like a stack of boulders forming a platform, and there was something on top of it.

He slid the last few feet and fell forward, body protesting that it had nothing left to give; no energy, no water, and no hope. He had to see the center though, the core of the Slaglands. He forced himself to his feet and walked to the mound. When he was close enough, his cracked mouth dropped, and he wheezed out in shock. If he could have, he would've shouted. *It was a man!* Well, the rough form of one, as if chiseled from volcanic rock, or fossilized.

To Finn, it looked to be kneeling, hands outstretched to the heavens, close without touching, as if pleading with the skies or pointing to them. Where the face would have been, a crack ran down the center. A tiny rivulet of lava poured out, down across the chest. The scene was...*holy*. Finn couldn't comprehend it.

Silence abounded around him; even the hot wind died down. He climbed the pile and stood near the form. It was the size of a man. Could it have been human? If so... what had it been doing here, in the center of a crater?

A glint caught Finn's eye and he studied the stone man's arm. Leaning in—careful to not touch the thin line of lava—he examined what he saw. Partially covered by volcanic rock and meshed with the figure was a... Finn fell off the stack of boulders, landing on his back. He tried speaking.

"N—no! It can't be!" he rasped out.

There on the man's wrist was a bracer. Not just any bracer, but a thick, wide, metal one like Nozgull's. The bracer of power. The bracer of a Star-Child.

Shaking his head, Finn pushed himself up, his mind roiling and pulsing with heat exhaustion. His heart hammered in irregular pulse. A bracer in the middle of the Slaglands, resting on the statue of a man. Could the man have been a Star-Child? Could the man have caused an explosion big enough to create the Slaglands? If Nozgull's ability to move gems came from his bracer, then had the bracer on the statue held power to terraform the landscape? Finn couldn't fathom the force necessary to achieve such a feat.

But the Slaglands had been around for forever. Stoneworkers in the Crust with the skill to detect age in rock told that the Slaglands had been created many centuries back. If it were true...had Star-Children existed long ago? Finn held his head between his burned hands. Too much, it was all too much to process. Nozgull once more shimmered before Finn, repeating the same words as he had back at the miner's camp.

"I was chosen by the heavens themselves!"

Finn revisited Gunther's death. Remembered the bully punching him for saying he wanted to leave the mines and see the world. Remembered his desire to be something more. Goblin had supported that dream.

"By the power granted to me by fate, I forge my future!"

Finn narrowed his eyes, his focus on the bracer. His heart beat faster, the lava pouring from the stone man's face glowed with welcome, and the air thrummed with potential. With a mental apology, Finn leaned against the stone arm, putting all his frail weight on it. The arm shattered, launching fragments of rock and droplets of lava. Finn howled as a drop hit his face with a sizzle and bounced to the side. He fell, still on top of the severed arm, and rolled off the mound. The rest of the stone man cracked and fell apart like brittle ash, scattering around him.

Finn rolled to his side, wheezing and choking on his depleted Aquamarine Tear. He spat it out and sat up. He'd crushed the arm into powder. The bracer waited in the dust, shining as if from a jeweler's store. Durable—maybe unbreakable?

Finn picked up the dark smoky-gray object, awed. It was long, as if it would fit from the wrist to a fingers-length away from elbow. It was also heavy and solid all around—it didn't clasp over the forearm like an archer's bracer but slid from over the hand. Overlapping pointed plates went along its back as if scaled armor on a beast. Strange runes indented the metal—inexplicable symbols. Finn found a word carved on its edge.

Akuun

He recognized the letters but not the language. Having only basic training in reading and writing, Finn could scribble out *granite deposit, diamond mine, emeralds are rare*—rudimentary sentences in standard Lenovan. This was not Lenovan. Was it a name? He didn't know.

Holding the bracer, he was faced with the decision on whether or not to *put it on*. Nozgull said he'd been chosen—that his bracer had landed in front of him. Finn had obviously not been chosen—but he had found one. Did that make him a Star-Child?

Goblin's terrified face returned to his mind. He had run away in panic, leaving his friend. He hadn't protected Goblin. His hand squeezed the device to a point where it shook. Finn's entire life had been written for him; forced upon him. In his hand, he could change it all; he could be the master of his own fate.

With a deft movement, Finn slid the bracer on his left wrist, opposite to Goblin's wristband on his right arm. The bracer gleamed in the sun. Without warning, his entire body stiffened, and an electric shock coursed through him. Something was within him, burning him from the inside-out. His veins were full of lava.

Finn let out a scream, falling to the ground and convulsing. Visions of stars, black space, and faces shot past his eyes. He saw the Crust from on-high and a writhing black mass in the depths of a far-away abyss. He watched vat-worms tunneling and a friendly man with a curved sword laughing. He saw waves of lava swallowing an army. He glimpsed a dark obelisk and lands of gray where shambling bodies walked aimlessly for eternity. He saw another man—full of rage and made of gold—scream at him. A mountain in the shape of a spider crawled across an ocean of grass.

The visions came as a blur, pushing through his conscience at incomprehensible speed, memory of them flaring and fading. A word came to mind, repeated over and over until he lost conscience, falling to the ground: *yours, yours, yours.*

There was a pulse as the bracer tightened and grafted to him. Finn's body ceased its movements. The wind picked back up and nearby, the remnants of a fossilized man blew away.

my devotion

7

—Circa 4,622 E.E. (Economic Era-The 17th Era): Scientists from the House of Phure find sediment evidence along the beaches of the SeaLake confirming that near one-million years ago, Lenova was temporarily swallowed by oceanic waves, terraforming the landscape. Faint magic still clings to the ancient sediment, too frail to be tampered with. The slightest human touch dissipates evidence. Through it, a few radical scientists make the claim that Lenova and the world of Sirramar is many millions of years old and used to once house far more potent wild magic. —

Wahala watched the Lenovan village of Castor burn. Screams rang out into the sky as an oblivious sunset turned the land orange to match the color of the flames. Creatures such as the villagers had never seen before wandered the streets, tearing flesh from skin and ravaging the land.

Looming rock golems, their backs and chests huge and thick, their heads hunched low and forward, crushed the simple homes with merciless blows from their fists. Oak-tree wicker men with roots wrapped around glowing hearts, faceless heads, and moss beards, collected bodies. Hooded humans with limbs made from gold plundered private belongings. But of all the monsters roaming about, killing the villagers that ran and gathering the rest into town square, the worst was Wahala's master, the changer of cult tradition, one who spat upon everything Wahala had dedicated herself to: *Mal'Bal!*

With his bracer activated, forming a magical suit around his body, the leader tore a child from the arms of her father and tossed the youngling to the golems. Chanting and prayers of sacrifice were shouted in the act. Although some had argued for using them as slaves, Mal'Bal had temporarily decided that the children and elderly were of no current physical use to the cult: they were to be disposed of. Their moment of passing was to be relished. It was the piercing of the veil between life and the beyond. Sacrifice brought a brief glimpse into the blank yonder: endless nothing. It was why cult revered pain over all other feelings: the stab of agony was the strongest of tastes, the only echo to be taken into the void.

Wahala half-watched from the shade of a fountain, chewing on an apple and reading a necromancy book she'd been assigned to study. Her master approached Castor's town square, where the remaining villagers awaited their fate. Some wept uncontrollably while others stared off to the distance, lost to reality. Yet a few glared at the cult leader with defiance. One such man, straw hair parted in two, forced himself to his feet. He jabbed his bound hands toward Mal'Bal, showing no fear. They were the hands of a mill-worker. "Foul demon! You'll suffer at the mercy of Almus for what you've done!"

Wahala clicked her tongue and shook her head. The villager was a scrawny fool. His brash tongue would be his end. He was brave—Wahala admitted—brave to a point of stupidity. She fingered the next page of her book, repeating ancient words under her breath to memorize them.

Somehow controlling the heavenly bracer—catalyst to the cult's fate—Mal'Bal mentally commanded his helm to retract. The frilled skull-like piece sank back, split apart, and slid away to his neck. The villagers shouted at the sight of the cult leader's true features.

The mill worker's eyes went wide. "What are you?" he whispered out.

Mal'Bal ignored the question. Instead, he drew close to the man. "Almus." he growled out. "Your God is false. Only his name exists."

The man shuddered, disturbed by everything Mal'Bal was. Wahala could tell it pleased the cult leader. The Lich-Lord motioned for cult members to hold the man in place. Around them, villagers begged to be spared and released. "What do you devote to your God? Time? Money? Flesh?" Mal'Bal's voice was a dangerous sweet tone.

"My life." the mill worker stuttered. "I devote my life to Almus, master of on-high."

Mal'Bal purred, coming even closer. "Devotion. I *adore* devotion." He reached out a hand and a cult member brought forth a small locked chest. The man eyed the chest nervously.

"My followers are devoted. I'm devoted. Have you seen our proof? Wahala, come forth!"

Wahala's heart lurched. What did Mal'Bal want with her? She dropped her apple and book and stepped forward, face like stone. She spoke no words. Mal'Bal pointed to her knees. "Her devotion to me and me alone."

Wahala held her scowl in check. Her knees had been sacrificed to an ideal. Standards Mal'Bal had never followed.

SUNRIDER

The mill worker was sweating—cracking. Wahala could see the fear creeping in. "Will you show me your devotion?" the Lich-Lord whispered. The villagers went silent. So did the cult members, and— maybe in everyone's imagination—even the roaring fire of the burning buildings.

"My devotion?" the man stuttered.

"Yell out the name of your God." Mal'Bal commanded. "Call out to him in worship. Let's see if he answers." The mill worker opened and closed his mouth in silence. "CALL OUT TO HIM!" Mal'Bal roared, spit flying out of his mouth all over the man's face.

"Almus, Master of on-high! Bring forth thy light and exuberance!" The man stood rigid and with teared-up eyes heavenward. Around him, villagers shook in terror. Mal'Bal stared at the sky, fists clenched. "Come on…" he growled. "Come on."

Wahala frowned. To whom was Mal'Bal talking to? It was as if he wanted to see the villager's words come true. Had his obsession with death and the lack of anything beyond sank that deep into his core?

"Just prove it! Just mark me wrong." Mal'Bal half-chuckled. His eyes were wobbling and his eyelids shaking. Wahala's frown sank lower. Just how insane was her master?

"Almus…" the villager groaned out, pleading.

"It isn't, it isn't…" Mal'Bal repeated under his breath, his voice almost holding a touch of tortured agony. Then he suddenly snapped back, wiping sweat from his forehead and looking down to his victim. Mal'Bal's cheeks were flushed. He looked to the cult member at his right, still holding the locked chest, and motioned for it to be opened. The cult member brought out a key.

"Almus, the Father of the seven God-Kings, allow my pastures to flourish and my children to sing praise to thee…"

The chest opened. A golden ingot and a chalice came to light.

Mal'Bal picked up the two items, one in each hand. Clenching them in his fists, he turned back to the man.

"Almus, the deliverer of peace..."

"FOR DEATH!" Mal'Bal screamed, his voice far louder than the villager's. The mill worker stuttered and continued. "...release the bonds of suffering from these hands..."

"FOR DEATH!" Mal'Bal screamed again, overwhelming the man's voice. The man was shaking, panic quivering in his eyes.

"...so I may labor in thy presence and forevermore..."

"FOR DEATH!" Mal'Bal bellowed in the man's face. The villager staggered back and stopped his prayer. The cult members tightened their grips on him. All eyes were on Mal'Bal, fearful and worshipful alike. Wahala's skin tingled.

"You see," Mal'Bal whispered with a shrug, his voice as quiet as a mouse's footsteps. "there's nothing out there. You feel it, don't you? You hesitate, your words fumbling in fear. My devotion's greater than yours. Let me share it with you. Hold him still!"

Mal'Bal kicked the man's legs and the mill worker fell to his knees. Mal'Bal began to chant in rhythm, his voice rising and falling, growing in volume. Fresh tears came to the villagers' eyes and they wailed out. Urine trickled down the mill worker's legs and Wahala stepped back in disgust. Nearby, the stone and wooden golems held their ground, still as statues.

Mal'Bal put the golden ingot into the chalice and lifted it above his head. "Gasta." The ingot melted into liquid. There were no fumes, no indication of heat. The process had been pure magic. All awaited with bated breath.

"My devotion." Mal'Bal said, one hand shooting out and grasping the man's jaw. He pried the mill worker's mouth open with two large fingers. The man flailed but was held in place. "I give it to you." Mal'Bal poured the liquid down the man's throat, shoving his face against the man's.

"FOR DEATH!"

Mal'Bal stepped back from the floundering mill worker. Cult members released their grips on him. The villager choked and bubbled, thick wet noises coming from his spastic form as he fell over. The man's eyes rolled back, his limbs dancing about.

Mal'Bal pointed to a cult member. "Take three others and bring me more gold." He looked to the dying man. "And I'll need Apex gems. I have an experiment to perform." Mal'Bal grinned, teeth bared like a wolf. Wahala frowned, wondering what the leader was up to.

"Lich-Lord." one cult member called out, his ragged black clothes flapped in the hot wind billowing from the burning village. "What of the others?"

Mal'Bal faced the remaining survivors of Castor. "Give them knives. If any feel like living, let them ritualize claim their God as false, and prove themselves as members of our fold. The rest—those defying, fearful, or the ones who can't bear to join us—throw them to the flames." The villagers of Castor shrieked. Wahala knew the sound was music to Mal'Bal's ears. Her master turned to her. "Wahala, you've practiced for long enough. By now you should know the words to the rituals." She nodded and Mal'Bal purred, "Good. Then then prepare limb casts and liquefy gold for those who cut themselves."

Mal'Bal disappeared into the depths of the village and Wahala walked back to the fountain to retrieve her discarded apple and book.

A quiet cult member approached her. He was tall, rugged, and sported the hint of a beard. He was like a strange, beautiful animal appearing from nowhere; handsome if Wahala allowed her emotions to think for themselves, but she didn't.

"Queen Priestess." he whispered to her.

Her eyes widened. For him to call her by the title was sacrilege. Mal'Bal had disbanded the high order of Queen, the long-held traditional role of leader: thus, not allowing anyone to usurp him. After Mal'Bal's mother died giving birth to him, the twenty-year process to choose a new Queen had been halted in its eighteenth year, when Mal'Bal had all the possible successors killed.

"Don't be offended, my lady." the man whispered. "I understand it's not your rightful title—yet."

She held her breath, preparing to push the man away. If Mal'Bal overheard someone calling her Queen, *she* might get gold poured down her throat.

"You may deceive many," he chuckled, voice like velvet. "but for those of us who court deviousness, your face is easily read."

The words made Wahala's heart jump. "What do you mean?"

"Mal'Bal has overstepped. He's changed the ways of the cult." The man stared at the ground spat in disgust, an act contrary to his looks. "Even now, many of our own *ritualize* in his name. You should know—the Lich Lord has forced you into being his gold caster."

Wahala wasn't alone in her feelings. She grabbed the man's chin and lifted his face so he stared into her eyes. He was tall. "What's your name?"

"Salastine, Queen Priestess."

Something stirred within Wahala. A wind of change. "I'm not a Queen Priestess." she hissed.

The man pointed to a far-off decrepit farmhouse. Wahala could see a small gathering of cult members waiting at its doors. They watched her with observing eyes. There was a sneaky quality to them, as if they were a group of lounging snakes.

"Mal'Bal shall run out of gold sooner than we think in his mad campaign."

SUNRIDER

Wahala could hear the screams of the villagers who'd chosen to replace limbs with gold. She'd have to go and perform the necromantic magic to graft gold onto them soon or they would bleed out. She could also smell the cooking flesh of those who refused. Salastine spoke the truth, Mal'Bal had been using all their supplies. Salastine put his soft lips against Wahala's ear, making her shiver. No man had ever approached Wahala this way. Was he trying to play her emotions or was he genuine?

"He'll need to send some of us back to our homeland for more gold. He holds you close—he's made you his acolyte; his little helper. If you play to his trust and are chosen to go..."

"You can endow me as your Queen at our temple." Wahala finished. Their eyes burned into each other and refused to look away.

"The right hand of Mal'Bal shall become his successor." Salastine affirmed. "The proper leader of our cult has always been a woman. Possibly you—with the exception you don't break the ancient rules of the cult as the Golden Agony has done."

Wahala stepped back from the handsome cult member. There *was* a wind of change blowing around her.

Salastine faded back into the crowd, his words lingering in her ear. "You'll be surprised at how many want to rebel."

inheritance

8

—And three were called forth, the booming voice of Abealon full of joy and energy: Come hither Jamiir, come hither Lovattimarsh, come hither Ballion! For by the work of your hands—more beautiful and far greater than the other Gods—have by this your victory been granted. Hark and listen all existence, for three winners have been selected. Let it be noted in the books of time that the competition stands at a close. Let us enter a time of rest and witness the reward, let the three first mortal races flourish to their full capabilities! Thus we shall call this the first measured Era, the second Era after the time of the Gods, the Era of First Birth! —
-Domolov, the Three-Fingered Cleric's Historic Book of Speculative Deity Theology, page 34,007; sub-section 9

Finn opened his eyes. The Slaglands were no longer hot. It took a moment to reorient, but when he did, he jumped to his feet, spinning in place. He brought his left arm up and stared at his wrist. The metal bracer rested there, bound like it was part of him. He tried pulling it off, but it wouldn't budge, as if it was woven into his skin.

"What is this?" he shouted in frustration.

He remembered putting it on, falling to the ground, and seeing visions. Visions of... already the memory of what he'd seen faded. He could only recall small fragments. A golden man screaming and... lava. Or fire. He couldn't remember. Finn shook his head. A Star-Child bracer on his wrist. Did it make him like Nozgull? Did it make him powerful? Would he be able to control gems and stones?

Finn pointed to the center of the crater. He focused and waved his hand to the side, imagining black stone breaking free and flying about. Nothing happened. The stone didn't move. With a growl, Finn tried with both hands.

"Move!" he shouted.

"Obey me, stone!"

"Fly!"

There was no response from the inanimate object. Was the bracer too old and the magic worn away? Or had Nozgull lied about the origin of his power? But if so, why had Finn come across a bracer just like Nozgull's at the epicenter of the Slaglands? *Epicenter...* Maybe this bracer had another ability? Maybe... it caused detonations?

Finn imagined a small explosion happening in the distance. He tried waving his arms. He stomped his feet in an angry dance and screamed out every foul curse he could think of, knowing it was no use; the bracer wasn't going to work for him. He wasn't going to achieve the power Nozgull had shown back at the mining outpost. If Nozgull could see him now, he'd be on the ground rolling in laughter. *And Goblin*—Finn had made a promise to protect the boy yet had turned and ran for his life. Now he was in the middle of the Slaglands, about to die from thirst and heat and...

Finn wasn't thirsty. Neither was he hot.

The realization made him freeze and blink. How could that be? With sudden shock, Finn jumped. Was he dead? He slapped himself and yelped. No, he wasn't dead. So how was he not experiencing the effects of the Slaglands? It was as if he was spellbound or using a magical gem or...*the bracer.* He lifted his arm again and stared at the object in open wonder. Could the device have made him immune to heat and in turn made him resistant to the base need of drinking?

Finn paced around the epicenter, careful to not step in the trickle of lava pouring from where the stone man once stood. No, he could feel the distant need for water. He would have to drink... eventually, but he felt he could go days more without a drop. The bracer hadn't made him impervious to thirst, it had enhanced how long he could go without water. Enhanced it a lot.

But what about heat? Stopping and examining himself, he found another surprise. All the spots on his skin where he'd been burned by contact with the sun-soaked rocks were healed. He also had no sunburn. In fact, his once-pale cave-diver skin was now a hue darker, a little tanner. It was as if he stood at the bottom of a mineshaft; shaded and cool, yet nothing but bright, harsh light hit him. Was he now immune to high temperatures?

Finn's eyes turned to the lava trickle. His mind mulled over the idea and he tried to talk sense into himself. Yet he couldn't shake the feeling—the curiosity to try. Finn walked over to where the small stream of lava came from the rock. Originally having poured from a crack in the man's face, it now flowed from the base stones where the figure had rested. Finn put his hand above the trickle, trying to sense the temperature rising from the glowing liquid. His hand felt nothing but cool air. He brought it lower, hovering it above the flow. Still no temperature change.

What if he did touch the lava? What if it burned, sticking to his skin and peeling away his flesh? How would he get the liquid off himself then? But the bracer...the potential power... Finn swallowed hard. He wouldn't know unless he tried. Using his non-dominant hand, he lowered a trembling finger until it touched the red rivulet. Finn clenched his teeth and closed his eyes, heart pounding and expecting to feel unimaginable pain.

But he didn't feel anything at all.

His eyes popped open, bugging out of his head. He didn't feel anything at all. There was sensation of thick slow-moving liquid, but there was no heat. He put his hand flat against the ground and watched in amazement as lava flowed over his fingers. Not even the hairs on the back of his hand burned. He turned his palm and let the lava collect into a puddle. He rubbed it against his other hand and thick heavy globs fell to the ground with a sizzle. Finn let out a laugh. Unbelievable!

He brought the lava close to his face and examined the red glowing liquid. He could see flecks of melting rock, reds, yellows, and oranges; all intermixed into the substance. On an impulse, Finn did something crazy. *He stuck his tongue out and poked the lava.* There was nothing but a tingle. Finn laughed again. He flung the lava in an arc across the sky, spreading his arms as it rained around him.

With a hiss that made him jump, lava hit his clothing and the material burst into flames. Finn yelped and danced, batting at his shoulders. The fire didn't hurt, but instinctively frightened him. Once he'd put out the flames, he groaned, staring at the many charred holes in his shirt and pants. Examining the rest of his outfit, Finn took off his Sponge-Marble sandals. The pair were destroyed by his long trek and the ground was somehow cool to his soles.

The stone man—a figure petrified by ash and lava long ago—must have been able to harness the bracer to its full extent. Did that mean one day he would do the same, turning entire landscapes into slag? And for that matter, why had the wearer been petrified? Had the man not been granted the same power as he? Had the man not been immune? Or did each wearer gain unique abilities? There was so much Finn didn't know.

Looking about, Finn assessed his situation. Although immune to heat, he was not immune to hunger. His stomach ached from lack of nutrients and his hands quivered with weakness. He'd been accustomed to malnutrition at the outpost, eating small unsatisfying meals, but he'd never experienced this much hunger. He had to get out of the Slaglands—and he had to save Goblin. There was no time to waste. He walked away, content in knowing he wouldn't see the place again. For all it had done to him— bringing him to the brink of death—it had also changed his life. He trudged up the crater wall, leaving behind the quiet rocks.

The journey was long yet made much shorter by Finn's new immunity to heat. It could have taken him hours, or days. His legs moved in monotony, his mind degrading into a state of stasis. Over hills and past jagged pillars, even taking his clothing off and holding it over his head as he waded through a shallow lava river. He napped occasionally, the strange landscape haunting his sleep and making his rest unstable. He walked barefoot and because of wearing Sponge-Marble sandals all his life, his thick callouses kept him going. At least the typified black rock was glass smooth.

He knew he neared the edge of the terrain when he looked to the sky and noticed it was darker—the sun was setting—time had returned to him at last. Finn grinned, spotting an orange and green horizon. *Green.* Finn shivered. He had all Lenova to explore. Yet he narrowed his eyes and boxed his excitement. He had a duty to Goblin. No matter how hard, he would first save his friend.

Finn hiked the last kilometers out of the Slaglands. Black rock transitioned to dirt, spotted by weak desert shrub and gravel. Soon, it turned to yellow weeds buzzing with crickets, and eventually to grass. When he came across the bright vegetation, he fell to his knees. His hands pressed onto the green. It was prickly. Finn couldn't help but chuckle in wonder. He spotted desert crags and cliffs far to his right a long way away. Straight ahead and to his left were sloping verdant hills leading into trees. Finn tried to orient himself. He'd escaped West into the Slaglands and at some point, miscalculated his direction coming back. He was in a new land; a place he'd never heard of before.

Finn caught himself staring at the trees in amazement and wondering what it would be like to climb one. Giving in, he ran forward, spending the last of his dwindled energy to reach a branch. He pulled himself up and grabbed another. The tree was large, and the bark was a dark color—nearing deep blue. Fat leaves sprawled out and heavy cones pulled down, giving off a tangy smell that made Finn's nose run. He climbed as high as he could and stared across the horizon. The trees spanned a forest running to the far East. He could see distant snow-capped mountains, hills, cliffs, and even rivers.

He descended, plucking one of the tree cones along the way, and sat on the ground. He pulled at the brown stems, revealing small nuts cocooned within. He took a gamble and popped one in his mouth, biting down. It was bitter at first, but after a couple of chews, gave off a creamy flavor. Feeling no strange effect, he ate the rest of the nuts within the cone and climbed back up, plucking more. When he finished, belly full and tired of the taste, a large pile of disemboweled shells littered around him. It didn't take him long to fall asleep, a small breeze kept his body covered in goosebumps the whole while.

The following morning, Finn set out into the forest with no idea on where to go and his belt satchel stocked with more tree nuts. Yet although lost, Finn was far from panicked. This was his first time in the heart of nature. He remembered his half-finished attempt to etch a fake forest into the walls of his hut. He'd never imagined it to be so…explosive and disorderly. In his etch, tree trunks were duplicates of one another, standing in even rows, but this forest far from obeyed any rules. Trees interwove and tangled, forming walls and ceilings of bark and plant-life. Birds sat in rows, watching him from above with cautious chirps and cocked heads. Lines of ants wove on the ground, agitated by his presence. The smell of crisp vegetation was euphoric. Finn spent more time stopping and observing than he did moving.

At one point, as he aimlessly wandered beneath the tree canopy, he thought he saw the faint glimmer of a shining cloud far ahead. Running forward, he lost track of the oddity, wondering if it was Nozgull. He spent the rest of the day lost in the forest, following game trails and climbing trees. The sky was blue and only white clouds greeted him. If Nozgull was out and about, he was activating and deactivating his power, making himself hard to track.

Finn found a natural spring bubbling from the base of a small hillock and gulped the cold water until he couldn't stomach it anymore. With his newfound powers, he drank only four gulps, finding his thirst easily sated. He finished off his tree nuts, unsatisfied and wishing he had meat. Wandering until sunset, he found no trace of civilization. When the depth of night hit, Finn laid himself against the base of a tree, and settled uncomfortably. Stirring, he gave up finding a fitting position and climbed the branches above, seeing if he'd have better luck off the ground.

As he climbed, something caught his eye and he squinted. Deeper into the forest where the trees grew taller and thicker, a faint glow flickered between leaves and branches. A campfire. Finn marked the location in his mind and climbed down, his stomach rumbling in hunger.

He pushed into the forest, weaving between tree trunks and tripping over roots as the last of the sunlight fled the incoming presence of darkness. In the distance, three low *caws* came from the mouth of some strange beast. Averting from the direction, Finn continued toward the light. The moon was high in the sky by the time Finn neared the reflection of dancing flames. When he was close, he heard a voice call out, but not to him, to another individual. The voice was familiar, and Finn's heart raced.

"Get more soup boiling! I'm still hungry! If the meal isn't ready soon, you'll find yourself with diamonds through both eyes! Then you'll have some value."

There was a sound of someone being shoved and landing heavily. Finn peeked around a tree trunk and his suspicions were confirmed. Lounging in the center of a nice-sized clearing was Nozgull. His cloud of gems hung without pattern like lazy fog above his head, but below the tops of the trees. It was no wonder Finn hadn't seen the cloud from a distance.

Another form moved, picking itself up and wiping leaves from his front. Finn suppressed a gasp. It was Goblin. He was alive!

The Sound of Closing Tombs

9

—Circa 5,204 E.E. (Economic Era-The 17th Era): Lilith the glorious, the most beautiful woman in Caronas, marries six-hundred men. Three days later the many husbands find out Lilith is in fact a homeless ninety-year-old woman with incredible shapeshifting abilities. Stealing all their collective wealth, Lilith disappears into the night. Soon after, she dies of a weak heart, having spent all the money gambling against House Pallock.

—

Finn fell back into the shadow of the trees, heart fluttering like a dying animal. His arms—his arms were trembling. He crawled under a bush and gasped, dust clogging his throat. He fought the urge to cough. Fear had overwhelmed him.

Nozgull was more dangerous than any person, animal, or event

Finn had heard of. He was a force of nature, like a sandstorm. No one could stop such a power; only get out of its way. Visions of miners, ghosts hiding in the dark between the trees, opened and closed their mouths, hollow eyes staring, warning him to run—run far away. Ublah-Kan's turban flying through the air, blood spraying out in an arc…

Finn's fingers clawed, his body mutinous, his emotions out of control. He could smell iron in the air. His eyes scanned for each movement: the wobble of a leaf, the firelight waving against the trees, a beetle near his elbow. Nozgull laughed at something and Finn nearly lost it, his body spasming. The overbearing fear of making a sound was the only thing freezing him, halting his trembling.

What was this? This uncontrolled terror? It was strong, too strong. His loyalty to Goblin, his promise to keep the boy safe—was an egg, tittering on an edge. How could he do it? Run away again? Yet if he stayed, how could he stop Nozgull? Something glinted on his wrist—not the bracer on his left wrist, but the small SolarStone interwoven into a fiber wristband on his right.

Goblin had no one else. It was either Finn or death. If there was any hope of Goblin being saved, Finn had to get control of himself. How could he ever achieve his goal of exploring Lenova by starting it with an act of cowardice? But the miners…slabs of stone and shards of crystal moving down like omnipotent hands crushing bugs… His whole life, all he'd known—gone. All except Goblin, the last remnant of what had once been. Finn's body clenched and unclenched, fear scratching furrows into his bones. But he had too… He had to try.

Finn crawled out of the bush and peered around a tree, studying the clearing. He spotted Nozgull, lounging on his side as Goblin handed him a steaming bowl of soup. The Star-Child wore his strange partial armor, covering his brow, hands, and stomach. Finn sniffed the air. Wild onion and something sweet and nameless danced in his nose. He wanted to curse Goblin for having cooked something that smelled so delicious. His stomach contracted painfully.

Nozgull took the bowl and sipped slowly, eyes half-closed. He stopped and motioned for Goblin to sit with his back against a tree at the edge of the clearing, opposite from where Finn hid. Nozgull stood and Finn jumped back, falling to his rear. He stifled a hiss, angry with his own terror, and moved forward to spy once more. Nozgull approached Goblin, removing a length of rope from a satchel. He tied the boy against a tree, binding his arms so he couldn't escape. The Star-Child returned to his soup, laying on a thin mat near the fire.

Nozgull purred. "Keep cooking me grub like this and I'll keep you around until the end of the week, miner. Too bad that friend of yours ran off to his death in the Slaglands. I might've spared him and had the two of you fight to the death for my amusement." Finn shuddered.

The fire grew lower and Nozgull drained the last of his soup. He moved to the pot hanging over the flames and poured himself more. Finn dropped back behind the brush and worked his jaw. Something tickled him and again, he jumped, mind returning to when the supervisors had been crushed. He slapped at a bug on his arm, unable to see the critter.

With the sun gone and the moon moving behind thick clouds, the only light came from Nozgull's dwindling campfire. It was getting as dark as holding one's eyes shut. Finn remembered a piece of equipment hanging about his neck. His mining goggles. He'd grabbed them right before the attack on the mine. Having been in the Slaglands where it never grew dark, he hadn't given a second thought about them.

He fit them over his eyes and the landscape took on a clear orange hue. Finn peered from around his hiding spot. The light from the fire blinded his sight and he yanked his goggles off.

Goblin's head had drooped to his chest. He must have been exhausted. Finn cursed Nozgull under his breath. As if in response to Finn,

Nozgull stirred from his resting position. Finn ducked, petrified. Nothing happened. Peering around his tree, Finn watched as Nozgull yawned and stretched, smacking his lips. The Star-Child pointed to the sky at his cloud of massive gems. Finn's heart froze, his eyes widened. Like an animal at its last moments, he was mesmerized into stillness by incoming death. Was Nozgull about to send a crystal shard through Finn? Did he know where Finn was the whole time?

Nozgull waved his arms and the cloud spread out, lowering. He controlled the gems to form a ring around the clearing, evenly distributing large and small gems across the grass and dirt, swathing the landscape in wealth. Once the gems all rested on the ground, Nozgull went off into the bushes to relieve himself. When he returned, his armor was gone.

Finn frowned. Had the man dropped off the pieces among the trees? It made no sense. Nozgull went back to his mat and sipped once more at his bowl before tossing the rest of the contents to the side. With a sigh, the Star-Child lay on his back, arms behind his head.

Why had Nozgull lowered his cloud? The answer came right away: Nozgull was tired. He couldn't control his power in his sleep and had to release the stones. It was no wonder he'd spread his vast wealth around the camp: if anyone were to try to sneak up and assassinate him, they would have an entire field full of stones to tip-toe over. It was Nozgull's security measure; meaning Nozgull was vulnerable in his sleep. Finn dared a smile. Could it be his chance? If he snuck around the clearing after the fire went out and while Nozgull slept, Finn could free Goblin and run away in the middle of the night. He even had his goggles to assist him.

He was again assailed by visions of the mining outpost, halting his excitement. Finn studied the man, waiting with impatience. Nozgull had common features, curly hair, and plain clothes—nothing resembling a threat. Again, Finn wondered where the man's strange armor had gone. He remembered the beautifully carved lines in the black metal and the rich brown glow coming from the designs. A magic suit. Finn's eyebrows went up. What if that was why Finn couldn't access the power of the bracer? What if there was a suit to go with it? There had been no armor on the fossilized man. Without a magic suit, would Finn only have fire immunity? He licked his lips and shook his head, trying to dislodge the thought.

The fire shrunk lower, synonymous with Nozgull's eyelids. Finn had to fight his own exhaustion. His body, harshly beaten by days of trekking, was sore and begged for sleep. Only a while ago he'd been trying to find a comfortable position under a tree.

It took time, but Nozgull's form relaxed and Finn heard the man begin to snore. The fire died to glowing coals and the forest took on a cloak of deep darkness. Finn stood, careful to not make any noise, and put on his goggles. He was rewarded with orange vision. He stopped, thinking on what if Nozgull awoke. What if he added more wood to the fire, once more brightening the clearing? He shook his head, the cobwebs of doubt not releasing their hold. He walked around the edge of the camp, trying to reach Goblin without entering the open gem-strewn ground. As he moved, he calculated each step to not snap twigs or crunch over leaves. It took him longer than he liked to approach Goblin's tree, and in the end, he was forced to make his way over a few gems to reach the sleeping boy. Throughout that time, Nozgull slept on without being disturbed.

Thanking the stars above, Finn wiped the sweat from his face and crouched behind Goblin. He wrapped his hands over the sleeping boy's mouth, pressing tight. Goblin startled awake, grunting out and shaking.

"Shhhh!" Finn hissed into Goblin's ear, his body tensed and with eyes on Nozgull. "Goblin, don't make any noise! It's me!"

Goblin froze. Nozgull snorted and rolled to his side, facing them. Finn winced but the Star-Child's eyes stayed closed. Goblin turned his head. He couldn't see Finn but recognized the voice. His eyes, wide as the moon, looked about in the dark. Finn pulled off his goggles and put them on the younger boy. Although Finn could no longer see, he was certain Goblin was staring in open fascination at him and the clearing, covered in precious stones.

"Never thought I'd have to tell *you* to be quiet." Finn whispered before taking back his goggles and putting them on. Goblin was grinning, relief overcoming his features. Tears dotted the boy's face. Finn knew Goblin had questions.

"Yeah, I survived the Slag my friend, and a tale it is! But first we must get you out of here. Don't make any noise."

Finn went behind Goblin's tree and found the knot Nozgull had tied. He glanced at the sleeping man, pausing to check his status. Nozgull stirred, as if in unrest. Finn needed to hurry. He grabbed the knot and worked it, moving as quickly as he could. The man had done a good job, too good of a job. In fact, Finn couldn't undo the knot. With rising frustration gnawing at his chest, Finn went back around to face Goblin.

"Goblin, the knot's too tight. I can't get it loose." Goblin froze, then pointed his chin out around them.

"What do you mean?" Finn whispered as quietly as possible, terrified his voice would wake the Star-Child. "The land? I don't know what you're getting at." Goblin again pointed out around them, gesturing at the ground. Finn tried to guess the boy's meaning. "The ground? The Earth? What's on the ground? The gems? Oh, use a sharp gem to cut the ropes!"

Goblin nodded with a smile. Both boys were sweating at this point, ears poised for Nozgull's movements. Finn looked about him, able to see what Goblin couldn't. He spotted a sharp piece of sapphire, dagger-like and long. It rested a few meters in Nozgull's direction. He would have to venture out into the open—exposed. Finn bit his cheek. There had to be another way, but the only knife he saw was sheathed on Nozgull's waist. Finn's hesitation was wasting precious time.

As carefully as possible, Finn moved forward, tip-toeing and rolling his feet to control his step. He skirted the massive pearl that'd once hung above him back at the Crust. It permeated the air with the sweet smell of rot, both hair and bone fragments matting one side. Up close, he could see many of the gems held dried blood, or more. Finn gagged at a crushed limb too disfigured to be identified, impaled by a long, glistening, purple rod. Nozgull had killed many, the gore being all that was left of those Finn once knew. Each gem was a grave marker; a somber, morbid symbol of Nozgull's evil. But just as there were stained gems, there were also clean crisp jewels, an uncountable wealth tempting death. Finn looked away from the red stains in disgust, both anger and horror fighting for dominance within him.

Moving forward, something cut Finn's foot and he froze, hearing the noise of two stones grinding against each other. He nearly yelped as he wobbled in place, gritting his teeth in pain. Lifting his foot, it took him a moment to spot what he'd stepped on. Two orange garnets, nearly invisible because of the goggles' hue, rested together. The noise had caused Nozgull to stop snoring and Finn stared at the man's form in terror. Nozgull rolled the other way, muttering under his breath about the price of rubies and how rich he was. Finn swallowed hard, wanting to vomit, and continued toward the sapphire shard with even more care. He reached the sharp gem, grasped it firmly, and returned without stepping on anything.

Goblin, looking about ready to jump out of his own skin, thrashed when Finn crouched in front of him. Finn reassured the younger boy it was him and went behind the tree to cut the boy's bonds. He knew there would be a problem the second he began to slice downward. The noise of sawing the rope with the sapphire was loud—like a bear scratching at a cloth. Finn glanced to the Star-Child, cutting as fast as possible. He had to move fast, or the noise would wake the man.

He was halfway through when he checked around Goblin's tree

once more. Nozgull, sitting upright, was looking about in confusion, awakened. In horror, Finn went stone-still. Would death be immediate? A flash of crushing pain so swift it was barely registered? The man was feeling around for sticks to put into the fire-pit. His hands fumbled in the dark without results and he frowned.

"Who's there? Miner, is that you making noise?"

Heart to his throat, Finn shook in place. He was terrified of Nozgull. Everything about him: his simplistic clothes doing nothing to warn of his danger, his greedy attitude, and his power. The man could snuff Finn's life in an instant.

Panicked, Finn went back to work. As he resumed cutting the rope, the scratching noise rang out again. Nozgull stood, spinning in place, eyes wide and unable to see. "Who's there?" the man shouted. Nozgull raised his bracer-wearing arm and Finn froze.

His mouth dropped open as Nozgull's bracer came to life, sliding and expanding. It separated into multiple sections, gliding along the Star-Child's body. A piece stretched and grew thin, wrapping around the man's brow like a crown. Two others formed around Nozgull's hands, shaping into black-metal gloves with sharpened fingertips. One piece grew large and hugged the man's stomach. The magic suit came from the bracer. The intricate designs glowed a soft rich brown, casting enough light to illuminate the man, but nothing else. Still unable to see Finn or Goblin, Nozgull flailed in the dark, a haughty, even prouder demeanor coming over him.

"You'll not be pleased at knowing whom you've disturbed!" the man shouted. "I'm not the simpleton you thought I was! Step forward night-prowler and face this Star-Child!"

Nozgull lifted his arms and the gems throughout the encampment shot into the sky, spinning and forming a cloud. Finn, using the noise to his advantage, jumped back to his work, cutting at Goblin's ropes for dear life.

In his hand, the sapphire trembled, wanting to fly upwards.

"I can hear you!" Nozgull screeched, waving an arm and launching a pillar of formed silver into the brush, far to Finn's right. The metal tore through trees and branches, snapping them like they were brittle twigs. The misjudged attack caused both Finn and Goblin to jump. Goblin gasped, and Finn clamped a hand over the boy's mouth. Finn's blood was cold, as if it no longer pumped.

Nozgull twisted his head in their direction. "Aha!" he shouted, throwing a wave of stones, gems, and crystals all about them. The pieces missed the two boys by a hairsbreadth and ravaged the forest landscape. They froze as Nozgull cocked his head to the side, listening for movements. He was trying to determine their exact location. Finn grabbed a nearby rock with a trembling hand. He tossed the piece over the Star-Child, making a commotion on the opposite side of the clearing. The man yelled and spun in place, throwing the massive pearl. It barreled through the forest, crushing everything in its path. With Nozgull distracted for a brief moment, Finn went back to the ropes, cutting the last of the bonds. With a snap than made Nozgull spin around, Finn threw the rope to the side and helped Goblin to his feet.

"Trickster! I've located you now!" Nozgull yelled. The man raised his arms above his head, lifting all his precious materials.

"Run Goblin!" Finn yelped, diving to the side as stones and crystals smashed all around him. The shard he'd used as a blade broke free from his hand and flew up, cutting his palm. In horror, Finn remembered Goblin couldn't see without goggles.

He rolled across the grass and sprang to his feet, searching for his friend. Goblin, arms out to feel in the dark, ran toward the Star-Child. The boy moved in an uneven line and Nozgull, hearing the incoming steps, swept out a hand. A raw chunk of red ore flew at the boy, striking Goblin across the shoulder. He fell to the grass with a heavy gasp and didn't get back up. Sensing he'd hit someone, Nozgull raised all his stones back into the air, condensing his cloud into a thick pile. Visions of the outpost spinning through him in a loop, Finn did the only thing he could.

"Knuck! You vat-pig!"

The words left Finn's mouth before he could take them back. With a roar, Nozgull swept his clawed hands and the entire cloud of gems launched in Finn's direction. Running for dear life, Finn dove behind a massive oak tree with a trunk as wide as a wagon. Stones and gems pelted the forest, though none of them strong enough to break through the oak. There was a solid *thunk* as a chunk rebounded off the center of the fat tree. Nozgull gave a grunt of pain and Finn risked peering around the trunk to see what'd happened.

Nozgull, staggering in place, held a bleeding ear. Finn could guess what'd happened: one of the stones had ricochet back toward the Star-Child, grazing his face. Finn's terror was roiling, changing into anger, making him feel drunk. "You're a curse upon Lenova! A blight!" He spat. "Star-Child demon!"

Nozgull staggered and yelled, sweeping an arm without focus. Stones bashed and smashed around the place, but none came close to Finn.

"How do you know me? How do you know of the Star-Children? Who are you?" Nozgull called out.

Finn pressed against the oak, sweat stinging his eyes. "You know who I am, oh EarthBreaker! Your mistake was to let me live! I too am a Star-Child!" The words left Finn giddy but there was a lump in his throat and his entire body shook.

There was no sound from Nozgull. He was no longer stumbling across the clearing. He'd frozen in place. "The boy from the mine outpost? The one that ran into the Slaglands? How'd you survive? How—how do you see me in the dark?"

Finn's anger was no longer roiling now but hammering at his core.

His instincts told him to move. An idea was forming in his mind, perhaps his only option. Finn stepped from around the tree, reaching into his belt and fingering the large, unbroken piece of Miner's Pumice inside.

"Nozgull," he growled, "you can't own the world. Your gems are stained with filth."

Nozgull roared, spinning in place. Blood flowed from the side of his head and matted the man's curly hair. A wave of stones shot in every direction. The massive pearl rolled past Finn, close enough he could've reached out and touched it. Nozgull was blinking rapidly, his eyes adjusting to the dark. He was squinting at Finn, as if beginning to make out his form. Goblin, lying out in the open, was stirring.

"Lies!" Nozgull screeched. "I own this world! Me! I was chosen! I saw the terror in your eyes! The fear as I *slaughtered* all those you knew! You're a mere miner, a dead man walking!"

Rage saturated Finn's bones. Even though he'd desperately wanted to leave the Crust his whole life, the miners hadn't deserved their fate. He looked at his bracer, not feeling any change in the artifact. It wouldn't aid him.

"I *am* a Star-Child." Finn hissed out between clenched teeth. He walked out into the open, treading quietly. He had no idea the impact of the words he spoke—the terms were foreign to him, yet he played along. Nozgull rubbed his eyes and squinted harder. Finn continued talking. "I know how it was to don the bracer. Did you see visions as well? Visions you can no longer remember?"

Even through Finn's orange-tinted goggles, he could distinguish the paleness of Nozgull's face. The man quivered, the first time Finn had seen weakness in the monster.

"How do you know of the visions?" Nozgull spoke in a low voice. "Did you see it? The black? Falling skies and the sound... the sound of closing tombs?"

SUNRIDER

Finn frowned. Although he could hardly remember any of what he'd seen, he knew the visions hadn't shown him what Nozgull spoke of. The Star-Child looked pained.

"The sound follows me... Tell me miner, DOES IT FOLLOW YOU AS WELL?" The man screamed the words, throwing gems at Finn, eyes adjusted to the dark. Finn dropped to the ground, dodging a crystal that nearly impaled his face. Nozgull screamed in lunacy, blood coating the side of his head.

"You won't take my wealth! My power! I was chosen! I am a God!" Nozgull shrieked into the dark, an animal howling at the moon, and formed his cloud again, collecting all his materials. The massive pearl, along with many other large precious stones, flew above Nozgull. They joined into a large sphere. Nozgull, raising his hands above him, pointed his clawed fingers at the mass, wheezing with strain. Spittle flecked his lips. "I can see you, miner!" He giggled, looking directly at Finn. Nearby, Goblin tried lifting himself up—the boy was dazed but uninjured. Finn had only one option left. Miner's Pumice had saved his and Goblin's lives before, perhaps it would do so again. He aimed the porous chunk at Nozgull's head and threw it.

"*My* wealth! *My* power! *My*—"

Finn's aim was true and Nozgull was struck on his wound. The pumice burst, releasing a powerful concussive blast of air. The oxygen hit the campfire and it roared to life, illuminating the clearing. Finn howled, lowering his goggles, half-blinded. Nozgull was tossed backward, arms waving like loose cloth. Rubbing at his eyes, Finn ran to Goblin, reaching the boy's side and lifting him to his feet.

Nozgull fell into the fire and let out a screech of agony. Embers erupted into the air and the Star-Child's clothing caught into flames. The pain must have been terrible. Distracted, Nozgull lost control of his power. Above the clearing, the massive cloud of gems fell apart, raining straight down.

Finn yanked at Goblin, screaming at him to move. His legs dug into soft earth and he pulled them to the forest edge. Half-dragging his dazed friend, Finn yelled and ran. Valuable rocks of every type hit the ground; crashing, smashing, bursting, and crushing. Huge crystals slammed into the dirt, burying themselves meters down. Ores dropped and bounced. Gold chunks and rubies the size of doors showered the land, all causing a noise equal to an exploding volcano. In the middle of it all, Nozgull's scream cut to silence as the massive pearl landed right on him, followed by many more gems. Everything went dark as the fire was snuffed out.

Finn threw Goblin forward using all his strength. The boy launched between two tree trunks and disappeared into the vegetation. Finn dove after him as behind them, the entire cloud of wealth landed, obliterating the clearing with the sound of closing tombs.

Finn's face and chest smashed into a root sticking out from the ground. One of the lenses on his goggles shattered. He rolled into a tree, wrapping around it, and lost all breath. The forest shook. As suddenly as it happened, it finished, leaving only the clatter of rolling gems. Finn held himself, poised for anything, but nothing happened. There were no zooming projectiles. Nothing at all.

He raised his head, and with shaking fingers, put his half-destroyed goggles back on. He could feel a gash on his face. Hot blood ran across his cheek. He stood, wobbling in place, and shook his head. Looking about with his one working lens, he was unable to spot Goblin. Fearing the worst, Finn pushed through the bushes.

"Goblin! Where are you?"

A form moved in the dark. Finn watched as it crawled out of a hollow at the bottom of a large tree. It was Goblin—scared, but alright. Finn released his breath and ran to the boy. Goblin jumped in place, raising closed fists and ready to fight.

"It's me, Goblin!" Finn shouted with a nervous laugh. "We made it! We're alive!"

The mute cave-diver dropped his jaw in awe and danced in the dark. It was comedic and strange; something Finn hadn't seen before. Suddenly, the boy froze. He made a questioning gesture with his shoulders and pointed to his own wrist. Finn knew what he meant.

"I don't know what happened to Nozgull." Finn replied. "Stay here, I'll go see."

Goblin shook his head in a no, but Finn's curiosity drove him to walk back into the clearing. What he saw made him freeze in place. Where once was a campfire was now a hill of gems. Scattered all around were hundreds more precious stones. As for the Star-Child, there was no sign. Finn had his suspicions deep beneath the mound, Nozgull's crushed body lay, a fitting end for the EarthBreaker.

Finn didn't know how to react. A slight wind passed through him and he put his hands to his knees. The miners of the Crust had received their justice, the man that'd killed them was no more. Finn backed away from the clearing, remembering Nozgull's words:

How do you know of the visions? Did you see it? The black? Falling skies and the sound... the sound of closing tombs?

Nozgull's visions had shown him his future. The bracer had shown him what would come. *The sound of closing tombs.* A word came into Finn's mind: fate. He tried to not throw-up.

He left the clearing, but not before stopping and filling his miner's satchel full of small, clean gems. He stayed away from those crusted with gore. He packed his bag to the brim: diamonds, rubies, sapphires, and emeralds. He then returned to Goblin's side. The boy stood in the dark, his lack of vision not allowing him to do anything but wait for Finn's guidance.

"Come on, let's get out of here and find a place to rest. I don't want to stay here. Nozgull is no more."

The younger cave-diver nodded—pensive. What went through Goblin's mind? What horrors had the boy suffered while enslaved to the Star-Child?

The two friends walked off between the trees, guided by Finn's half-broken goggles. Finn's thoughts turned elsewhere. Was he officially a Star-Child? He'd admitted as much to Nozgull. He felt at the bracer on his wrist, wondering if one day it would obey him. He remembered the suit; morphing and contorting to Nozgull's body. Where had the bracers come from and what were they? Above, real clouds broke, black and made of vapor, illuminating the forest in moonlight.

the toad and the ferret

10

—Circa 3,444 E.E. (Economic Era-The 17th Era): Pirate forces led by Malark Oakchest establish a base on the island of Lastiss. The Opal Dominion unites and forms the Black-Dog Navy: a group of rag-tag sailors loyal to justice and peace. The Black-Dog Navy is overwhelmed by the pirate forces and instead of accepting defeat, await for their boats to be boarded. When all the pirates do so, the navy members burn their vessels down, taking all the pirates and themselves into the depths of the waves. —

Finn pushed through a bush that didn't want to let go of his belt. Swearing and yanking himself forward, he stumbled onto a dirt path. He grumbled, pulling a thorn from his bare foot. Goblin—following behind him—seemed to have no trouble with the bush at all. They found themselves on a wide road, the first sign of civilization they'd seen since leaving Nozgull's camp nine days before.

Although leaf beddings and sore legs were easy topics to complain about, the freedom to go where they pleased kept them in high spirits. Goblin had fed them wild mushroom and leek soups, foraged with skill Finn didn't know his companion had. Finn in turn had entertained them by recounting the story of his travel in the Slaglands. Goblin consistently studied Finn's bracer in curiosity and with silent gestures, speculated on its ability. It took a couple of days for Finn to accustom to Goblin's hand signals, but after learning the meaning to many of the symbols Goblin used, he was soon able to have conversations with very few pauses.

"You figure we'll run into other people soon?" Finn asked his friend. Goblin shrugged and patted his stomach. Finn huffed and turned away. "I *know* you're hungry! That's been your only response all day long!"

Goblin patted his stomach again and pushed forward down the path. Finn shook his head and followed, his own stomach rumbling. As they walked, Goblin made a strange movement which Finn didn't understand. The boy rubbed at his throat and made a pushing motion, as if trying to spit or force something out of his mouth. The actions were so comical, Finn howled with laughter. Goblin stared at him with annoyance.

"I can't help it!" Finn grinned. "It looked like you were crawling behind a vat-worm with your mouth open!" Goblin's eyebrows furrowed in confusion and Finn sighed. "You know, vat-worms poop while they eat. Crawling behind one with your mouth open—that's what you looked like!"

Having to explain the comparison dulled the joke and Goblin still didn't seem to understand. Finn waved a hand, chuckling to himself. "It's no matter. What in Lenova are you trying to tell me?"

Goblin made the same gesture again, but also brought his arms out and shook them while closing his eyes. Finn howled with laughter yet again. "That one was even better! It looked like you crawled behind the vat-worm, puckered up, and kissed its rear! The hand thing—that was great! Were you weighing its dung?"

Goblin punched his shoulder, clearly not as amused as Finn. He made the motion of talking and pointed to a passing bird flying above.

"*Singing?* You must be kidding! All that lunacy you did—meant *singing?* I guess you want to be deaf as well as mute." Goblin wound up to hit Finn again and Finn jumped out of the way, bringing his hands out. "Alright, alright! You honestly want me to sing?"

Goblin waved an arm as if to indicate there was nothing better to do while they walked.

"I don't know many songs, only those I heard from elder miners. They always had a happy melody or some sad warble about a beautiful woman. I doubt I could pull that off."

Goblin indicated he should try anyways. Finn huffed. He'd never sung before—only hummed a few tunes under his breath while in the mines. The idea of singing made him feel stupid. But it was only Goblin, and the boy couldn't even complain. He stared at the wide-spaced swathe of birch trees they were passing to the left. A bug buzzed near his ear and the warm sun shone on his neck. Cool air brought a hop to his step and the idea of freedom was still fresh on his mind. Finn smiled. "There was this weird miner at the outpost. He'd always sing these happy little tunes while he worked and a few of us thought he wasn't right in the head. He was transferred to another outpost, so I don't know what happened to him. I recall one tune he always sang."

Goblin motioned for Finn to continue. Finn cleared his throat. "It went something like this:"

> "*A Toad went a-hoppin' from his home one morn'*
> "*You come back home!" said his wife with a scorn.*

RAFAEL HOHMANN

Toad took three hops and landed on shore
replying, "Don't worry, I'll be home at four!"

Ol' Toad sight-saw the dark forest nearby,
using his long tongue to catch a fat fly.
When suddenly Ferret appeared from a bush,
spittin' and hissin' and givin' Toad a big push.

"You got in my way!" said Ferret to Toad.
Toad then replied, "You were in my road!"
The two pulled out swords to joust to the death,
but both being fat, had run out of breath!

Both being fools, not wanting to die,
Proposed 'nother option—on the fly.
"I challenge thee Ferret, to a great eat!
Whomever loses, must admit defeat!"

"Owl can judge and declare the winner,
Rabbit can cook and prepare us the dinner!"
Ferret agreed and set out the plates,
while wildlife gathered to watch the fools' fates.

The large spread was grand, the meal divine,
each dish was superb; each bite was sublime!
They swallowed some soup, Toad gobbled a cake,
They drank some wine, Ferret chewed on a steak.

Faster and faster the two did eat,
until Rabbit cooked so fast, off flew her feet!

SUNRIDER

Owl's eyes burst from trying to follow,
the two foolish blurs, continuing to swallow!

Plates shattered, cups spilled, food went a'flying,
'til both drew quite near to choking and dying.
All that remained was one morsel of cheese,
which ferret scooped up with quite the unease.

He put the last tidbit right into his mouth,
silence reigned, from the North to the South.
With a pop Ferret burst, all over the place,
his body went flying, hitting Toad on the face.

Food bounced about, glazing Badger in honey,
annihilating Antelope and butchering Bunny.
Smashing a stoat and slaying a snake,
the rest drowned in soup, forming a lake.

All that remained, was poor bloated Toad,
flaying about on the soup-wave he rode.
Half-drowned in food, and gargling foam,
Toad finally made it, all the way home.

Where there waited his wife, angry as hell,
about to ring, a late dinner bell.
She forced Toad to sit and forced Toad to eat,
until he was full—from his head to his feet.

Toad died in his seat,
yes, he was quite dead.

Yet his wife had the audacity, to send him to bed!"

Finn finished the out-of-tune song with a bow. He turned to wait for
Goblin, who'd stopped walking, bent with silent laughter and purple-faced
from merriment. Finn gave a broad grin, remembering the first time he'd
heard the song. He'd almost fallen down the mineshaft.

"What-ho!" a voice called out. "What a melody! Makes you feel
bad for the poor toad, doesn't it?"

Finn turned in place. From behind them, a wooden wagon came
around the bend, pulled by a tired-looking brown horse. Neither Finn nor
Goblin had noticed the incoming sound of the creaking wheels. An older
man with a large straw hat waved to them from the wagon's bench where
he controlled the reins. Finn waved back, feeling a blush come to his
cheeks. The man had overheard his song.

The wagon approached and came to a stop. The man, wrinkly as a
dried fruit and tanned from head to toe, smiled warmly and gave a nod.
"The name's Piscus. Where are you two travelers heading?"

"I'm Finn." Finn replied curtly. "And this is my friend, Goblin. We
don't rightly know where we're heading. Possibly East in search of lodging
and food."

The man's smile broadened. "Then hop in, I'm heading East
myself! You two are in luck—I own an inn. It's in Pittance, a few miles
down the road from here."

Civilization! Finn inhaled. He'd get to see his first town beyond the
Crust. "Thank you!" he told the older man, hopping into the wagon.
Goblin followed with a grateful nod. "Pittance? I've never heard of the
town." Finn remarked.

The man shook his reins and the tired horse pulled them forward.
"Pittance is a small town. Moved there myself a few years ago and built
my establishment. Unfortunately, we don't see many travelers there. No sir,

Pittance is a bit out of the way for most folk. It's a religious place, but simple. The townsfolk near-worship the bordering stream."

"Stream?" Finn asked.

The man looked at them and gave a wink before turning back. "There's a small celebration and storytelling going on tonight—the town holds it once a year—and recount the legend of the nearby stream. You're more than welcome to participate!" Piscus yawned. "So where do you two come from?"

Finn struggled with how to answer. He decided honesty was the best option—he wasn't a very good liar anyways. "We come from the Crust—where the mining outposts are."

Piscus' eyes widened. "The Crust? There's nothing but slavery, death, and rocks in that desert! It's no wonder you set out to see the world!" The man scratched his curved nose. His eyes glanced at Finn's shoeless feet and burned shirt. "Doesn't seem like you've had much luck on the road. You—" His voice faltered, and Finn followed his eyes. The man was staring at Finn's bracer. Piscus' entire demeanor grew wary and his eyes showed...*fear?*

"It's not what you think." Finn fumbled, covering his bracer with one hand.

"It better not be, young traveler." the man spoke in a low voice, slowing his cart to a stop. The horse whinnied. "I hope you aren't here to find amusement in killing me. I'll have you know that I'm a proud and brave man. I will not beg for mercy from tyrants and murderers."

Finn shook his head. This man knew of Star-Children. Maybe even more than Finn did so himself. "I mean you no harm!" he stuttered out.

Piscus licked his lips. "I would think one who sang so freely wouldn't be an evil individual, but it's said the Chosen are cunning predators."

"The Chosen? You mean Star-Children? There's a bunch of them?

I mean—a bunch of us?"

Piscus eyed Finn carefully. There was suspicion there, but also doubt. The man was afraid yet was giving Finn the benefit of the doubt. "You don't know much of the Star-Children?" Piscus asked him. "Were you not granted your bracer from heaven itself?"

Finn paused. Should he reveal what had happened to him in the Slag? He mulled it over before deciding to tell a simplified version. "I found the bracer on the remains of an ancient Star-Child, one who'd been dead for many centuries. I donned it and now can't take off the piece."

Piscus studied him without word and turned to face the road. He tugged his reigns and the cart moved once more. "I believe you, Finn. Damn the Divine Stream, I believe you." He let out a sigh. "You don't look to have an evil bone in your body, you don't. But how you found that bracer on a long-dead Star-Child confounds me. I thought them new to the land."

"So you've met one? Another Star-Child?" Finn asked, leaning forward and hoping Piscus could shed some light on the mystery. The man shook his head. "Not directly, no. Otherwise you wouldn't have come across me, I'd be long dead. No, I only hear tales from passing travelers and those coming from the bigger cities and citadels."

"What do they say?" Finn asked. Goblin leaned in as well, curious as to what they could learn. Piscus scratched his nose once more. "They say stars have fallen from the sky, delivering bracers to souls across Lenova. Regular men and women have transitioned to Godhood, achieving feats beyond explanation; able to destroy entire populations with ease. But a few fight the call to power. There are Star-Children who have used their abilities to do no harm, but instead become protectors."

"Good Star-Children!" Finn exclaimed. He looked at Goblin and Goblin nodded. "If I can find them, maybe they can teach me about this bracer!"

Piscus twitched. "Yes. It seems your kind are splitting into two factions: the wild and the controlled."

Finn paused. *His kind.* Was he no longer classified as human? Piscus continued. "The evil ones ravage the land, claiming cities for their own dominion. Some call themselves masters, while others call themselves Gods or emperors. Lenova is in a troubled state. The king has locked himself in his castle, muttering of bracers and more power. He sends out men to claim one for the throne. Citizens have lost trust in family and friends. There's unease everywhere you go. Entire towns have vanished. A storm brews on the horizon, young travelers." Piscus pointed to Finn's bracer, tree-shadow marking his face. "And I'm afraid you've made yourself part of it."

Finn shook his head, not wanting to accept everything he was hearing. The world he'd wanted to explore, the wonder and magic—it was all being threatened.

"I didn't want to be a Star-Child." he whispered, grabbing his bracer. "I put it on to have the power to protect my friend."

The horse whinnied, and an orange bird flew past, dropping a feather. Piscus caught it and wove it into his straw hat. He gave a sad smile. "Then you're a special case, Finn. One who wants power for righteous reasons, words hard to believe." Piscus faced the road. "I don't know whether all the rumors of Star-Children are true. But if they be so, a word of caution my young friend: you won't face others as kind as me or as oblivious as the people of Pittance. You'll see darkness and pain. You'll see corruption. Ready your heart and remember the words you've spoken. You don't wear the bracer for power, but to protect the ones around you."

Finn didn't reply. Instead, he watched the dark bracer glinting on his wrist. Goblin's wristband seemed simplistic side-by-side with it.

"We arrive at the village of Pittance." Piscus spoke out. "Get ready for your first step beyond the Crust."

machinations

11

—Circa 5,610 E.E. (Economic Era-The 17th Era): Finn SunRider, at the age of ten, saves thirty-two miners from a tunnel collapse by wedging his leg beneath a boulder. It takes three days for miners to uncover the tunnel and save him. Miraculously, his leg heals, and Finn SunRider is reprimanded by House Crumm for wasting resources on his life. He is told he will never pay off the debt. In retaliation, SunRider sneaks into the Hub and burns all documentation of his debts. Unfortunately, he does not burn the duplicate copies of the documents. —

"Lich-Lord. It's time."

Mal'Bal paused his gory work, wiping the blood from his face as he knelt on the ground. The dirt floor within the tent had been churned into maroon mud and clung to the golden man's knees and shins. Bone shards and torn clothing were strewn about, as if thrown without care. Flies clumped in large black piles from walls, their collective weight sagging the canvas. Their buzzing was the ecstatic scream of a million flesh-eating dots.

Mal'Bal studied the cult member that'd approached him, watching to see if the man would grimace. The cult member, sensing a test, remained frozen without emotion. Sweat collected on the man's brow and his eyes flickered to the red mess strewn about the tent. Mal'Bal let the discomfort drag until the man looked ready to flee. When he'd been thoroughly amused, Mal'Bal nodded.

"Indeed, it's time. Assemble our people."

The man left the tent and Mal'Bal returned to his work of splitting skin and snapping bones. The noises were wet and loud in the thick heavy-aired tent. Flies collected and scattered in the movement, drawn to the sickly-sweet smell. In the dim light, most would mistake the place as the entrance to some hellish portal.

A cat-like form moved in lithe calculated movements, emerging from the shadows at the back of the tent. "Wahala," Mal'Bal purred, "do you marvel at my creativity?"

Wahala, unlike the messenger, did cringe at the sight; her face a mix of disgust and annoyance, unafraid of what the leader might think. It made the man smile and chuckle.

"Your project should be...finished at another time, my lord." she stated, holding a hand over her nose. Wahala's eyes roved over the state of the decay-filled tent. She'd seen dismemberment and gore, but nothing of this scale.

Mal'Bal broke another bone, revealing gold beneath white. Blood and marrow coated his fingers. He raised his arms wide, facing the woman. "Do you view me as a toddler playing with his toys, Wahala?"

The words were controlled and happy, but Wahala knew better

than to let her guard down. Mal'Bal was the most dangerous when he seemed the calmest. "I believe you must focus outside, Golden Agony. The campaign's about to continue. The cities of Metés and Vestés..."

Mal'Bal waved a dismissive hand and returned to his work. His knees adjusted in the red filth and he pulled at the gold within the corpse. Splitting an arm in half, he let out a grunt of approval. Inside, as if chaliced by bone, was a golden limb, jointed by an Apex gem.

"This experiment is an inspiration, Wahala. The Queen Priestess who thought of it didn't try it out. In fact, she was too insane to do so. Days after her inauguration, she killed herself. Her untested project brings me much curiosity." Mal'Bal's gaze bore into Wahala. "And you bring me curiosity as well."

Wahala froze. "What do you mean?"

Mal'Bal tore another golden limb free from its organic prison. He examined it in approval and grabbed at the dead man's ribcage. The corpse hardly resembled the mill worker anymore. "You were common." Mal'Bal spoke softly, "Fleeting, like this man. But the closer you came to me, the more I exposed what was beneath the skin." There was an explosive wet sound and a plain golden rod, thick as a stick, came loose. "Metamorphosis, Wahala. You're my dark butterfly, like my puppet born from an organic cocoon. You show far more drive than the rest of our people, especially since we've been here. Something has lit a fire underneath you."

Mal'Bal yanked at the golden rod, standing and putting his weight on the corpse. The noises that ensued made Wahala turn and look away, her body shivering. Mal'Bal sighed, loving every macabre moment. With a final pop, it was over. Blood flowed in every direction, expanding in a puddle, turning mud into swamp; washing the entire floor of the tent in red.

Wahala and the cult leader gazed in wonder at the figure facing them. Wahala took a step back—for standing in front of them was a Golden Puppet the size of a man. with stick-figure limbs and a featureless oval face. The entity was bathed in the blood of birth. Its joints, made of green Apex gems, swirled with the fog of power. There were no dents, carvings, or complexities to the being. It was plain, golden, and terrifying. It didn't move, but stared at Mal'Bal, a sense of perverse love floating between the two.

The cult leader stepped back from his handiwork. "My *child,* Wahala, is as important as the campaign. Whatever I deem entertaining is what becomes priority. Not what you *believe* to be important."

The Golden Puppet lifted an arm. Intricate razor-thin fingers wiggled and danced like tapping daggers, as if the creature was learning to move for the first time. Wahala imagined feelers on a bug. The hand spun in a full circle, not hindered by the limitations of ligaments and tendons. Without feature, the puppet was impossible to predict. It could be happy, curious, or murderous. There was no emotion to gauge; no thought process. If Wahala were to come up behind it, it's head would look the same as if from the other side. What was forward could be backward. Mal'Bal had created a monster to be feared.

"But the cult, Mal'Bal—as a leader, that's your duty."

Wahala snapped her mouth shut. She'd said the words out loud. She hadn't meant to voice the thought.

Mal'Bal spun in place, his face scrunched in rage. "THE CULT GIVES ITSELF TO *ME!* TO ME! THAT'S THE CULT'S DUTY!"

He marched to Wahala, shoving his face up to hers. She could smell his breath—like fetid meat, as if he'd been feasting on the corpse at their feet. Behind him, the Golden Puppet leaned toward them, its head cocked to the side—ready to defend its creator. Wahala's eyes went wide with open fear. Mal'Bal sniffed, as if trying to smell her terror. He then stepped back, calm as ever.

"Why do you advise me, handmaiden? Do you question my leadership?" He spoke the words with the happy perkiness of a child. "Do you imagine your wisdom greater than mine? Were you born from the earth?"

"N—no master!" Wahala stammered, feeling lost by his instability. She assumed a meek posture.

Mal'Bal grabbed one of the puppet's arms and raised it, clicking his tongue with a frown. "No, no, no." he sighed. "Can't have this at all. Better give an edge to these limbs—sharpen them like razors. Then you'll be perfect."

The man turned to leave the tent. "I've raised you to be more than a common cult member because of your mother's old role as head acolyte. Yet you stand in the shadow of example Wahala. You forget, I am what you all strive to be."

With the flick of a tent flap, the leader was gone. The Golden Puppet stared—or seemed to stare—at Wahala for a moment longer, then followed his creator, scampering out on all fours like a spider. The creature's limbs moved in an agitated blur, causing Wahala to shudder. She was left alone in the tent, nearly ankle-deep in gore. Within her, familiar emotions stirred: anger and outrage.

Mal'Bal had delved deep into his own madness and manic journey. Who could say what he wanted? Was it truly the death of all living beings and creatures? If so, then he, more than anyone else, was the greatest threat to the cult. Sacrifice might be in their culture, but not their own genocide.

Wahala could care less if the other races were killed, but her own people? No, Mal'Bal needed to be stopped. *Usurped.* If she had what Mal'Bal had, she would be a great leader. The cult taught there was meaning to destruction: order and enlightenment from self-sacrifice. Had Mal'Bal only wanted to spread the cult's ways—the belief of nothing beyond death—whether by force or invitation, Wahala would have gladly followed him into Lenova. But no, the man had seen fit to destroy all life. Wahala knew if Mal'Bal had his way, he'd decimate all creation, taking the cult with him and leaving a black world of rot where only anti-life walked. Nothing would be born, nothing would decay. There would be no existence left. If *Wahala* could be leader though... the cult would be saved.

She left the tent—a place symbolizing exactly what would become of the rest of the world if Mal'Bal continued. Around her, the cult—far larger due to Mal'Bal's forced recruiting—gathered around the Golden Puppet and his master.

How many of their new members were sincere? How many would turn and stab Wahala's brothers and sisters as soon as they got the chance, avenging Lenova's fallen cities? Wahala made eye contact with Salastine and the handsome man gave her a curt nod, disappearing into the crowd like smoke. As she strolled forward to stand by the cult leader's side, occasional whispers rang close to her ears.

Queen Priestess.

M'lady.

Heiress.

It fueled her to walk with head held higher and eyes burning with desire. The cult belonged to Mal'Bal. But there were some—some that belonged to her. They could *feel* her loyalty to tradition.

With the crowd gathered, many eyes gawked at the golden creature caked in blood. Was it like the golems treading within their camp, without sentience or free-will? Or was this entity different? Mal'Bal smiled to his people, ignoring their questioning stares.

"Do any of you know of the power of my mother?" he asked loudly. The crowds stayed silent. "She led as Queen Priestess, overseeing her acolytes, the cult, and our safety."

Wahala's heart jumped. What was this about? Why was Mal'Bal speaking of the old Queen? Was her desire to rule uncovered? Had

Salastine been exposed? Mal'Bal brought forth an intricately-carved wooden mask. Innumerable amounts of eyes had been cut into the dark brown wood. The mask itself looked to be a large, sideways, lidless eye. The crowd gasped. Wahala was stunned. *It couldn't be...*

"The All-Face." Mal'Bal stated with a triumphant nod. "The mask worn by the Queen Priestess herself to gaze into the future and see all possibilities for our cult. With this artifact, we'll march forth in perfect uniformity! The future will be ours to control for we'll know all paths!"

The crowds stirred. Those recently initiated didn't know of the sacrilege Mal'Bal had done. To remove the mask from the holiest of shrines within the temple, bring it to the Lands of Light, and use it even though he was not appointed as oracle? It was unheard of in the history of the cult. It went against the structure of leadership and power. Bugs crawled under Wahala's skin. All she'd known was being desecrated. It had all changed when he'd donned the bracer from the sky. The people of Lenova whispered of him, some calling him a *Star-Child*. If that was what Mal'Bal had become, if that was what he claimed to be, then he was no cult leader, but a heretic. A crime only fixed by death.

Rage ran like pressured fire from Wahala's head to her feet, then back. *The bracer. Star-Children. Mal'Bal.* She would put an end to this madness. She had to.

Mal'Bal raised a hand and his many golems strolled about the crowds, standing five times the height of a man. The cult leader pointed to the twin cities of Metés and Vestés, which rested less than a kilometer away. Distant ant-like forms scurrying about: bringing forth bastion defenses such as catapults and torsion engines which fired crossbow bolts the size of horses. The machines peeked from over the tops of the parapets. Farmers and villagers ran through the gates into the safety of the large stone cities. The massive roofed bridge which rested one-hundred meters above the ground and across the top of the walls of both cities, serving as a highway for trade, was now full of soldiers readying their weapons. Unlike Castor, Wahala knew this battle would take a heavy toll on the cult. But if they won, the resources and people captured would more than compensate for their losses. In fact, it would increase their strength tenfold.

"We'll lay waste to life!" Mal'Bal screamed, his blood-encrusted golden body gleaming in the sun. Near him, the Golden Puppet fell into a spider-like position, ready to crawl forward in blurring speed.

Two dozen slaves taken from the countryside brought forth an open golden litter where rested a black chair. The massive weight pressed on strained hands holding metal handles, pushing the men into bent tortured forms, their collective groans ringing out. Mal'Bal climbed on the platform and sat, leaning an elbow on one knee. The Golden Puppet, showing incredible strength, put itself beneath the litter and lifted it on its own; leaving the liter-carriers open-mouthed and in shock. Mal'Bal's eyes gleamed in anticipation; his pupils but pinpricks. He pointed to Wahala and she stepped forward.

"Have you been studying the dark techniques?" he asked her.

The cult leader was referring to the necromancy books he'd tasked her to read, teaching her the arcane magics of how to graft golden limbs. She'd become his *sorceress*, his acolyte—yet the title of acolyte had been tainted. No longer was it the ancient traditional role of serving the Queen. No, there was no Queen, only a usurper.

The task, like most of Mal'Bal's tasks, was a test. Wahala knew Mal'Bal's cunning—her given responsibility not only freed up his time and energy so he wouldn't have to perform the ritualisms himself, but they held her in check. The man had given her a taste of status to only better control her. Better *use* her. But why? Because her mother had been an acolyte herself?

Wahala could play the mental game. She would use the role to her advantage.

"Master, the books you've given me have been a great fountain of knowledge. But..." Mal'Bal leaned in closer, waiting. "I fear to better perform the ritualisms quickly and with effect, I'll need more knowledge. Knowledge we've left behind in our temple."

Mal'Bal's face was impossible to read. He gave heavy breaths, nostrils flaring in excitement for the blood-fest to come.

He must wonder the true purpose of the request, Wahala calculated. He's no fool. He knows manipulation like he knows killing. But he's distracted by the battle.

"Allow me to take a small group back to our home where I may gather more books and bring back more gold for your campaign, Lich-Lord. We run low and many wish to ritualize their limbs. In addition, master, the gold could be used as a weapon of bribery against the weak Lenovan people." She was pleased with her excuse. For having made it up on the spot, she'd done well.

Mal'Bal stayed quiet for a moment longer, his eyes narrowing. Wahala's heart beat faster.

"I was expecting your aid in this fight, handmaiden." Mal'Bal hissed. Wahala held back on saying a single word, waiting for the cult leader. "I shall have to perform the ritualisms myself. It'll be a waste of my time and energy. Go, your words ring of truth. Bring me back more gold. Take only three with you."

Wahala gave a deep bow, holding in her excitement. Instead she showed gratitude. "Master! Thank you for this opportunity! I'll—"

Mal'Bal cut her off. "Don't think me a fool, woman." Wahala froze, mouth half-open. "You'll read only what you're allowed to. Don't dare access the volumes which only leaders may read. You are but a cult member." He grinned. "I can taste your greed, Wahala. Remember your place."

Wahala bowed lower, swallowing the anger and disgust rising to her throat. His foolish pride! His arrogance! Who was he to change the structure of the cult?

"I apologize, Lich-Lord. I but thirst to one day become like you. I strive forward in your vision."

Mal'Bal smiled, his eyes like that of a snake. "Don't you all?" He dismissed her.

With a flourish, he pointed toward the twin cities. The cult spun in place, brandishing their scythes and screaming in enthusiasm. Stone and wood golems moved forward to the front; a wall of anti-life obedient to their master's will. Their gem hearts glowed from the power of Mal'Bal's bracer.

The cult leader activated the item and a black suit grew about him, cloaking him in otherworldly-metal and glowing runes. He kept his face free to the air.

"FOR DEATH! " he screamed. The cult howled into the sky as a reply, marching forward and pushing past Wahala, who stayed in her bowed position.

Mal'Bal donned the All-Face mask. His body clenched, and he shrieked into the air, every possible future rushing into his mind in an incomprehensible wave. He fell back into his seat, shivering. His breathing grew wild and he moved as if mad, his body jerking. The artifact would show him how to win the battle, *if* he could control it. Wahala doubted it would cooperate to its fullest effect—he was no Queen Priestess. Yet, Mal'Bal had proven to be more than a mere man...

A small breeze, like the brushing of a cobweb, glanced past Wahala.

"Salastine." Wahala whispered.

"*Queen Priestess.* " a smooth voice answered back. "What word do you have on our grand leader's decision?"

Wahala smiled and stood straight, watching the army march

toward Metés and Vestés. "I'm no Queen Priestess yet. But by our lord's blind command, that will change."

Salastine smiled a perfect smile, his teeth white and straight. He bowed to her, his composure perfect even though Wahala knew the man was full to the brim with energy.

"Gather two of our most loyal." Wahala commanded. "We travel back home to our temple. I'll ritualize and preform the rites. *Then* you may call me Queen."

"Your heart for the darkness." Salastine whispered, prayer-like, disappearing into the marching crowd.

Wahala closed her eyes. *Yes, my heart for the darkness. And for leadership of the cult.*

pittance

12

—Circa 5,602 E.E. (Economic Era-The 17th Era): Goblin of the Whey-Weavers is born, mute with no chance of ever gaining a voice. —

Finn jumped from the grating wagon, patting Piscus' horse in thanks. Goblin followed and the two looked about in wonder. The dirt path had led them to stop in front of two large humanoid statues covered in moss. Finn studied the thick tall stones, trying to make sense of what they were. One resembled a naked woman with the head of a deer and Finn averted his gaze, trying not to stare. The other looked to be a man with a snake's body. Moss covered most of the man's face and Finn couldn't make much of its features.

Beyond the statues rested the village of Pittance. It was a place unlike anything Finn had ever seen before. Dirt paths lined with white stones led to beautiful houses of clay brick and wood. To Finn, the homes looked as if living trees were hugging the edges of the four walls. Upon closer inspection, he saw that the four corners on each house *were* living trees. The people of Pittance had used incredible artistic skill and craftsmanship to build their homes into the surrounding wildlife. They were both architects and gardeners.

Taller trees, with layered branches, formed multi-storied homes. Bushes and ferns pulled themselves up, rising in slopes around the walls. By staring closely, Finn could find the trace of human guidance in the growth. Wild bushes formed paths, a particularly long root had been turned into a bench, and the hole in a tree into a window. Open fields of flowers sprawled between the homes. Soft purple, yellow, and orange blossoms grew in abundance all throughout the peaceful village. It was as if they had built Pittance within a large open grove without ever having disturbed nature.

Finn watched as white-robed children ran and giggled, climbing moss-covered statues dotting the fields. He took in the village as a whole. The entirety of the place was a circle. Surrounding the village, farms and gardens flourished; tended by men and women, side-by-side. Beyond the village, Finn caught a glint of sunlight reflecting off moving waters.

Piscus led them toward the center of Pittance. Finn passed a group of adults sitting cross-legged in a circle; chanting, singing, and beating on drums. Their heads were wreathed in vines and their faces reddened as they sipped wine from hollowed goat horns. They spotted Finn and Goblin and waved with large smiles, treating them as if long-lost friends returning home. A young maiden, her lips soft and pink, beamed at them. Finn couldn't help but smile and wave back, his heart jolting. Women had always been rare in the Crust, only used as servants—never miners. The maiden mesmerized him, and he listened to her strike a song as he followed Piscus forward.

SUNRIDER

Betwixt glade and fern,
thrush brings birth,
the smell of spice is in the air!
In hallowed groves,
the couples dance,
their passion burns and flairs!

Finn's cheeks grew hot and his stomach rolled. The way the drums beat, and the way the woman's voice rose and fell: it brought a strange feeling to him, something he hadn't felt before. He wanted to run back into the circle and dance, grabbing at the maiden's fair hands.

Piscus looked at him and laughed. He yanked Finn's shoulder, guiding him forward. "Careful friend, or you'll be lost in fantasies of wild romances and fairie-lit forests!" Finn shook his head and moved on, feeling haunted for something he didn't understand. To his left, Goblin was pulled away from the singers as well.

They walked underneath an archway made of animal bone and strung with leaves. Deer and elk skulls looked upon them, their antlers curved in twisting knots. They passed stone pavilions where tall poles strung with dozens of colored ribbons hung in the breeze. Carvings of suns and moons in various stages of the eclipse topped the poles, each with smiling faces full of frozen merriment. Finn pointed them out to Piscus and the wrinkled man laughed, tipping his straw hat.

"Maypoles, Finn! For dancing and festivity!"

Finn gave the man a questioning look, overwhelmed by the amount of culture and difference the town provided. Everything was new. Everything was... He sniffed the air, a sweet and tangy aroma hitting his nose. It was the most wonderful scent he'd ever experienced.

"Huckleberries, fresh-picked and pressed for wine." Piscus

commented, noticing Finn's flaring nostrils.

"It's amazing!" Finn stammered.

His heart hammered as he was hit with a thought: he was finally doing it. He was exploring the world!

Piscus pointed to the middle of the village where a stone walkway ran around a grass plain full of propped logs and unlit campfires. Four elder men and women were coming their way, kind smiles on their faces. Like the children, they also wore white robes tightened by twine around limbs. Piscus waved to the approaching group and moved forward in greeting. Finn and Goblin followed.

"Have you accomplished your personal tasks in Caronas, good Piscus?" an elder woman spoke. By the way she carried herself and moved in the middle of the group, Finn assumed she was in charge.

Piscus bowed with respect. "Miriam. My travels were successful. How fairs Pittance?"

Miriam gave a kind smile. Her face was wrinkled with time, yet Finn could tell long ago she'd been a beautiful woman. "Pittance stays the same as ever." she responded. "Who are your guests?"

Piscus introduced both Finn and Goblin. "I met these young men on my journey back. They've been good company so far."

Miriam stared at Finn in question. "Why does this one not wear shoes?"

It took a moment for Finn to answer. He hadn't been yelled, reprimanded, or hit by any of the leaders of the town. He'd never known kindness from his betters before. "Travels have been hard, elder." Finn stuttered. "But I have means to buy myself new clothing."

"Do both of you mean to spend the night with us?" Miriam asked, "Our celebration of Lith-Lamma is tonight. We revel in the warmth of summer and remember our heritage. There will be storytelling, eating, and dancing. We welcome all visitors to participate and enjoy their stay."

Both Finn and Goblin nodded in excitement. To begin their first night in civilization with a celebration was too good of an opportunity to pass. Miriam motioned for Piscus. "See to it they wash and change. I'm sure they've grown tired of travel-dust coating their skin."

Piscus bobbed excused himself, mentioning for Finn and Goblin to follow. He led them toward the stream, where Finn could see a humble two-story inn resting near the banks. The corners of the building were four fat oak trees, their branches a tangled mess.

"Piscus," Finn called, mentioning to the homes around them, "the ends of each house are trees. How is that so?"

Piscus winked at him as he passed by a bush full of sky-blue flowers. He plucked a flower and stuck it in his hat beside the orange feather. "The men of Pittance plant four trees at a young age so they can have a home for their families when they grow older. They pick tree saplings of their choosing and a location. For fifteen years they nurture the trees as they grow large and strong. It's symbolic to the people—it shows their dedication to the land and proves their patience as exceptional husbands and fathers. When they're old enough to start their own families, they build walls and a roof around the trees."

Finn looked at the houses with newfound wonder.

They continued walking and approached the stream. As he walked along the bank, Finn stared at the glinting water running past him. The stream was wide but shallow. He could see near-translucent fish dart past. They swam so fast and hid so well it took Finn a while to realize he wasn't imagining them.

Passing a wild bush full of small purple berries, Piscus stopped and plucked a few for himself. The man motioned for Finn and Goblin to do the same. Finn picked a handful and put one in his mouth. A tart yet sweet taste hit his tongue, filling him with energy. His eyes went wide as he stared at Piscus.

"Those are the huckleberries you've been smelling." the man explained. "They're turned into wines and ales. You'll have a greater taste for them tonight. Goblin, I recommend you stop eating. You'll spoil your appetite."

The younger boy, mouth full, stopped but continued to eyeball the bushes. Piscus laughed, continuing to his inn. Finn glanced back at the stream and froze, his mind confused. He'd sworn the water had been traveling from his left to right, but now it moved the other way. Piscus noticed his hesitation.

"Don't worry Finn, you're not crazy. I see you've played witness to the phenomenon that is the Stream of Fate."

Finn looked about, scratching his head. "But... how can this be?" he asked. "Didn't the water move..."

Piscus nodded, face solemn. "You'll hear the story of the Stream of Fate tonight at the festival."

Finn rubbed at his eyes and stared at the water with greater focus. *Now it was moving left to right again.* On the opposite shore, tall ferns and cattails hid most of the land. Willows hung about, covering many small and strange clearings.

"Should it not be called a river?" Finn asked, "It seems too wide to be a stream."

Piscus shrugged. "The villagers deemed Stream of Fate sounded better than The Indecisive River." Piscus changed topics. "Some have tried boating it, but none have been seen again. The stream has no beginning nor end."

"Why sail it?" Finn asked. Goblin looked equally curious and amazed at the phenomenon.

Piscus tweaked his own nose. "You'll know more tonight."

Although curiosity gnawed at Finn to a point where he felt he would go mad, he followed Piscus into his inn: a warm smoke-smelling place creaking at the slightest breeze. Piscus walked through the front door, leading them into a small bar where two grizzly men sat and drank beer. Worn red carpet covered the floor and there were few tables, yet cozy charm was everywhere. Another straw hat like the one Piscus wore rested on the head of a mounted boar. Names were carved all over the walls and Finn assumed they were of previous visitors that'd come before. A large black log cut in half served as a bar counter and a plump woman came forward from behind it, greeting Piscus whom Finn assumed was her employer. She left to serve the two other guests.

Finn could tell by how the men dressed, they were either distant traders or trappers. They looked at Finn's bracer and turned away quickly without speaking a word. Finn was led upstairs before any introductions could be made.

Piscus showed both Finn and Goblin to a small room with two beds and a view of the stream. Through the circular window, Finn still couldn't tell which way the stream flowed as it seemed to change every time he blinked.

"If you hand me some coins, I can make my way into town to buy you both new clothes." Piscus commented. He gave a wink. "Miriam would burn down my inn if she thought I was mistreating guests."

Finn reached into his satchel where he kept all the gems he'd taken from Nozgull and pulled out a small ruby, handing it to the man. "Will this do?" he asked, ready to offer more.

Piscus' eyes seemed to nearly jump out of his head and he spluttered. "*Do?* If you wish to buy a house, this will do fine! To imagine if I'd been swindling you! Finn, where'd you get this wealth? Surely you didn't steal it?"

"I inherited it. From one who died." Finn replied, thinking quickly.

Piscus glanced to Finn's arm, where the bracer rested. Conflict ran across the older man's face—suspicions of whether Finn had killed someone for the money. Piscus was gentle and kind, not one to judge or do ill. If the Star-Children were as bad as they sounded, Finn couldn't take offense to Piscus' attitude. It was no wonder the innkeeper was still suspicious of him.

The man dipped his head, his straw-hat tipping toward them. "I'll bring you clothing and your change."

"Keep what change is left." Finn stated. Piscus stiffened, looking at him in shock. Finn tried not to blush. "You've showed us a lot of kindness, Piscus. You deserve more."

The man's face flushed as he worked his mouth. The innkeeper looked to be struggling for words. "By grace and grass Finn! I don't know what to say! This will keep my inn running for months!"

"Just say you won't buy me any of those strange white robes the townsfolk wear. Get me something for travel. Leather if you can find it."

"Only the best!" Piscus bowed, leaving the room.

Finn turned to Goblin with a smile. The boy was relaxing on one of the two beds, his face exuberant with pleasure. It was the first time he'd lain on something soft since leaving the mining outpost. Even then, the outpost beds hadn't been the most comfortable in Lenova. In fact, they'd felt like one was sleeping on a cloth-wrapped rock.

"I might've overwhelmed our host." Finn stated before he too jumped into a bed of his own. His muscles melted like hot butter on the soft mattress. Goblin didn't reply, but instead rolled over and immediately fell asleep.

Piscus returned, awakening the two boys. In splendor, he produced an incredible arrangement of garments. He gave Finn and Goblin each a pair of thick leather boots with steel tips, thick green-gray cloaks, leather gauntlets, and fresh pants and shirts so soft, it was like wearing a cloud. Finn's cave-diver belt was replaced with a black one boasting more segments for clipping pouches and weapons. Piscus had even bought the boys straw hats, copies of the one he wore. Goblin put his on and strutted around the room like he owned the world.

As Finn tied his cracked goggles to his new belt, Piscus explained to them that the town merchant had nearly believed the ruby to be fake. It took Piscus time to convince the merchant that the wealth was real.

After donning their new outfits and allowing Piscus to burn their old clothes, Finn and Goblin followed the innkeeper outside. The sun had set and torches—Finn hadn't noticed them before in the daylight—burned in the streets, casting warm light across the town. Finn watched as families of birds flew to the trees forming the homes of Pittance. The animals were bedding for the night, weaving into the structures like building materials returning to their proper places. Did the villagers fall asleep and awaken to the sounds of chirping and birdsong?

Men, women, and children throughout the village made their way toward the central field where fires were being lit. Cooks came forward, setting food on groaning tables that bent under the weight of the feast. There were cheers and saliva flowed from mouths. Never had Finn seen so much food.

There were plates with golden pastries nearly bursting by touch alone, exhibiting flaky crusts and cream-filled centers. Tender meats sizzled, fresh from fires where they'd been smoked. When cut, seasoned juice ran down knives. Mushrooms lathered in butter and an assortment of freshly-picked fruits and vegetables too numerous to count decorated each dish, sometimes as topping and other times surrounding the food as art. Soups of a hundred varieties, ales, wines, beers, and even a cake the size of an adult man were all set on tables. Cheeses freckled with nuts and fruits were cut into and spread on thick slices of hot bread. Children and adults alike dipped their fingers into frothy puddings so thick and sweet they left one lounging in their seat with eyelids half-closed. Honey-covered almonds made their way into everyone's hands and lavender ale into each cup.

Finn found himself surrounded by men with moustaches handing him samples of pies. Plump women fought to give him a taste of their broths and blushed at his compliments. Finn watched Goblin dive headfirst into a plate of tarts. The boy used both hands to stuff one morsel into his mouth after another. A group of men surrounded him, eyes wide in amazement. They started a game to see which dish Goblin would eat of the most. Cooks began to ignore all others and rush to Goblin's side, presenting the boy with their finest dishes. They laughed, giddy with pride as Goblin sighed with contentment at each bite.

Music flowed about them in haunting tones, coming from strange instruments made of spinning strings and hollowed metal tubes. Voices rang out, singing of men chasing beautiful nymphs and of ancient forests where animals wouldn't die. Children ran circles around the adults, chasing each other and throwing candied nuts. Some villagers performed acrobatic feats and others showed incredible athletic skills.

Finn saw eight beautiful maidens dance around a maypole, each holding a colored ribbon tied to the top of the structure. They spun and twirled, mixing color and dance under the growing starlight. No one moved forward to cheer or disrupt them. Instead, onlookers watched from a distance, not wanting to interrupt. It was beautiful in the way it was untouchable—as if no power in all Lenova could stop them. Finn knew the scene would stay in his mind forever.

His hand grabbed, Finn was yanked forward into a crowd of gyrating bodies dancing to the melodies of the night. A girl with light green eyes laughed and spun with him, holding his hands. Her cheeks

crinkled the corners of her face and the moon glinted in her hair as it
flowed about them. Finn felt as if in a dream. One which he wished would
last forever. A warbling song washed over him like a wave, sung by an
unknown voice:

> *In the pale snow-forest, my love.*
> *You'll find me there behind the maple tree.*
> *Smiling and leading you on, through mountain and vale.*
> *Where there be lands of imagination.*

The girl he danced with drew close and disappeared, over and over, teasing
Finn with her beauty. With the trace of lilac in his nose, she spun around
him once more and was gone, leaving Finn in the middle of the crowd, his
heart fluttering.

Nearby Piscus sat at a table, joking and laughing with the elders of
the village. Even the two surly-looking traders from the inn celebrated,
eating and dancing, their faces full of wonder like the children around
them.

Finn found himself herded forward with a large crowd as they
gathered about a roaring fire. He sat beside Goblin on a soft well-worn log.
Around him, others flopped to the grass or curled against a loved one.
Piscus came and joined them, sitting to Finn's other side. More feathers
dotted his straw hat. An elder stepped in front of the flames, becoming a
silhouette. Finn recognized the form as Miriam, the leader of the village.

"Tonight, we remember." Miriam began. "Birth and death, love
and loss. Whom we are and whom we become. Tonight, we tell the legend
of the Stream of Fate."

the stream of fate

13

—Circa 5,613 E.E. (Economic Era-The 17th Era): Kind Tipidus the
Second, heavily drunk and without control attempts suicide by hanging. He
is only saved when the rope unravels, not having been properly tied. —

housands of years before humans walked Lenova, there lived greater
races. The Nature-kin, which embodied the spirits of the plants and
animals about them, changing form at will. The Seraphs, obsessed with the
stars above as if they wanted nothing more than to go there. The Forsaken,
whom had been on this earth since before history was remembered.
Because of their differences, the races wouldn't accept each other. In fact,
they waged war with such ferocity and strength, the very ground moved.

The Nature-kin knew the lands, the Seraphs used cunning
machinery, and the Forsaken manipulated magic. In all the turmoil and

death, something unique happened. The son of a Forsaken and the daughter of a Nature-kin fell in love. Fearing their lives and their people would be lost to the wars ravaging the world, they desperately searched for a way to end the conflict. But sadly, they had no means to control the hatred burning in the hearts of the races.

In a frantic act, the two met late into the night, praying under the stars for omnipotent help. They knelt and explained their world, described the evil running through it. They wanted it to stop, wanted the war to end. If only they could obtain a means to break the conflict.

Suddenly, in wonder, water sprang from beneath them: two springs coming from the couple themselves. A terrifying cold voice whispered out as quietly as the shivering of grass in the breeze: "Only by all-encompassing sacrifice can peace be wrought."

But there was nothing the Forsaken boy nor the Nature-kin girl could offer. Their lives were small and insignificant. They held no treasures. All they had was their love. And so, the voice took that from them.

The water pushed the two apart, forming a stream that fought with itself to exist. Farther and farther they were pushed from each other and their wails of sadness could be heard all across the land. When the stream had finished growing, neither of the lovers could be seen, for they'd disappeared into opposite horizons. Never would any living being find where the two ends of the stream came to rest.

Yet the two still live to this day, fighting the push of the stream by pulling back on it, trying to reach each other. Thus the stream changes its course, in constant chaos.

The three elder races, seeing the sacrifice made by the two lovers, grew even angrier with each other. Upon the banks of the newly-formed stream they fought their last battle. They said to each other: let fate decide whom shall prevail.

RAFAEL HOHMANN

For eight years the battle waged, day and night without pause. Hills were formed by the uncountable bodies of the fight. When the dust settled, only three forms remained: one from each race. For behold, the true sacrifice to end the conflict was genocide—a cleansing of all hatred.

Looking around in sorrow at what had become of the world about them, the three dropped their weapons and wept bitterly. For their time had ended upon this world and they knew there was nothing they could do to change it. So side by side they crossed the stream to the banks beyond, to become deities garnished with the responsibility of watching the world be given to the races that would follow: the varying people of Lenova we know today.

It's said that the first to cross the stream to meet with the deities will be granted one wish of any choice. It is also said that any who successfully boat from one end of the stream to the other; they would unite the two lovers once more and be given the knowledge of all time and all space. But none have ever accomplished such feats, for it would take more than what we can give to succeed at such a quest.

And so, the sacrifice made by the two lovers was fulfilled: peace had come to the land, but at a steep price.

Thus is the story of the Stream of Fate.

a call to water

14

—Circa 32 E.E. (Economic Era-The 17th Era): Dalimenarus the Mace leads 10,000 men to war against Viz of the White Nothing. Their battle awakens the Spider-Queen Xhicuxhizzum and her million children. Humanoids from across Lenova unite to save the land. —

Finn opened his eyes as the story ended. Around him, others stirred as well, muttering and discussing what they'd heard. Goblin looked off to the dark horizon, staring past the flames of the many campfires lit in the central field. He too looked to be contemplating the story.

Piscus nudged Finn and gave him a smile. "What do you think? The people of Pittance live upon the banks of the stream. They near worship it."

Finn mulled over the story. Promises of wishes and knowledge earned echoed in his mind. "Do they believe it to be true?" he asked, "Did those events take place and can one cross the stream to have a wish granted?"

Piscus stood and stretched, the movement causing Goblin to come out of his trance. Around them, many villagers were leaving. It was a clear sign the celebration had ended. Finn could see Miriam and the other elders thanking the crowds like polite hosts. Cooks took away what food remained from the wooden tables. Sleeping children were picked up and carted off to bed.

"They certainly believe it." Piscus answered. "Look at the water and tell me which way it flows. You can't. Makes it pretty easy to assume it to be true."

"Has anyone crossed the water?" Finn asked.

Piscus laughed. "It's as if you fancy attempting it yourself Finn!" Piscus helped Goblin to his feet. "Aye. A long time ago one tried crossing it. The village allows any who wish to do so."

"Well?" Finn egged.

Piscus shrugged his shoulders. "No one knows for sure if the man made it. He tried it late in the night as we slept. We never saw him again. Gone like the many who've tried sailing the stream. There are no bodies that wash ashore. No debris. No sign they've ever been in the water. No one ever could locate the ends of the stream. There truly is some form of magic to it all."

Finn looked to where the stream lay. He couldn't see it in the dark, but he knew it was there. Something rolled inside of him, like a hungry dog searching for food. What if he crossed the stream and wished for knowledge of his bracer? What if he could be given power over it? What if he wished all Star-Children gone?

Piscus nudged him. "Hey boy, don't be getting any crazy ideas. I'm starting to like you."

But Finn didn't respond. His mind was like a fish stuck on a line. The more he tried to tug away at the story, the more it reeled him in. The culture. The history. He'd never experienced anything like it before.

"Come on, back to the inn for the lot of us." Piscus stated. "In my opinion, you've more than paid for an extended stay as long as you'd like. Let's get some rest. It's late."

Piscus walked away and Goblin followed before turning to wait for Finn. The younger boy gave Finn a questioning look that Finn understood. *What's gotten a hold of you?* The hairs on Finn's arms stood straight out. He didn't know.

In bed, Finn couldn't sleep. He tossed and turned, visions of the stream plaguing him. *It's said that the first to cross the stream to meet with the deities will be granted one wish of any choice.* His fingers clenched against his pillow and he furrowed his brow. He could feel the Star-Child bracer on his wrist—like a metal graft on his skin. Part of him.

He threw the blanket off the mattress and lay spread-eagle, staring at the ceiling made blue by moonlight. He could hear Goblin's soft snores from the other side of the small room. The boy hadn't been as perturbed by the story as Finn had. Maybe curious, but not driven into a frenzy.

The bracers. Powers running rampant across Lenova. Finn. The lone figure in the Slaglands. The stream. One wish promised.

Finn stood and walked over to the round window at the end of the room. He peered through the glass and stared down. Below, the edge of the stream ran, flickering reflections of starlight greeting his gaze. He blinked and tried to focus his vision. The water was moving in another direction. He stared as intently as he could until his sight blurred. His eyes slid to the side and when he refocused, the stream moved the other way. He gauged its width. Thirty meters across was his estimate. He remembered that it had looked shallow. How was it possible no one had successfully trudged across the body of water? Any man or woman with balance and strong legs should be able to do it, yet Piscus said none had returned from the journey. There had to be something more to the water—something that drowned a man and pulled him under, without a chance for resurfacing. Or maybe the stream washed the crossers to its ends, a place no one'd ever found. Maybe it was there where all bodies and boats piled up, like a mass graveyard. Finn shuddered.

He walked back to his bed and lay down, trying to relax. His desire to know and see all Lenova was hammering at him again, just as it had in the Crust. Instead of the question, *what lies beyond the crags,* he now was haunted by another: *what lies beyond the stream?*

His eyes closed and he fell into a restless dream. In it, a green-eyed maiden danced about him. Maypole ribbons were tied around her wrists and an elk skull was worn like a crown. She drew him to the banks of the water and Finn watched on, mesmerized. She walked backwards, beckoning him to follow with a finger. Her eyes twinkled and her lips curved at the edges. Her face was beautiful.

Finn tried to warn her, to tell her she'd drown, that the many bodies of ancient dead soldiers would pull her beneath the water. Slowly she waded deeper and deeper, her eyes calling to him. Her mouth didn't move but he could hear her voice, like a silk sheet against his cheek. *Come and see. Come and see what lies beyond. Come and seek your destiny.* Her head submerged. Finn couldn't move. His legs worked in place, not drawing him forward. He couldn't save her.

Not that way, Finn.

He turned around against his will, facing away from the water. *Like this.*

Finn was shaken awake by Goblin, sleep still in his eyes. Finn sat up, nearly knocking heads with the boy. Goblin put his hands to his hips, as if chiding him. Finn rubbed his face and waved an apology.

"Is it morning already?" he mumbled.

Goblin responded by throwing Finn a shirt. The cloth hit Finn across the chest and fell to his lap. Goblin motioned for Finn to dress. He rubbed his belly, indicating he wanted breakfast.

"What is with you?" Finn asked with a laugh, donning his clothes. "Did you not eat enough last night? I swear I saw cooks in tears trying to keep up with you! How are you not full?" Goblin rubbed his belly again and winked.

"Fine." Finn chuckled, making his way to the door. "Let's go see if we can find Piscus, shall we?"

The two went downstairs, finding the bar empty except for the plump barmaid. Upon questioning, she informed them Piscus had left to eat breakfast with the elders. Piscus had instructed her to tell them they were more than welcome to join. Goblin led the way out of the inn and Finn was forced in a half-jog to keep up.

They spotted the gazebo which they'd been instructed to find and made their way to the forms which rested under the shaded white platform. Decorating the grass around the structure were poles topped with animal skulls, staring off into the dawn. Upon seeing Finn and Goblin, Miriam and Piscus nodded a greeting.

"Behold, our guests!" Piscus shouted in cheer. The group was eating a light breakfast of bread and butter. In their cups they held a curious white liquid.

Piscus had them sit on one of the benches beneath the gazebo roof. He served them their meal. When given a full cup of the white liquid, Finn stared at it in hesitation.

"Have you never drunk cow's milk before?" Piscus asked him,

eyebrows knit together.

Finn shook his head. "No. What is it?"

"By grace and grass, Finn!" Piscus shouted, "Have you done anything in your life at all? You seem to be in wonder at everything about you! Perchance this is the first time you've seen the sky as well? Surely you jest?"

Finn again shook his head. Even Goblin looked shocked.

"There wasn't much variety in food and drink where I came from."

"Variety!" Piscus spluttered. "Milk, water, wine. It's not complex! You should return to your home, find whomever raised you, and shove your foot so far up their—"

Miriam put a hand on Piscus' arm, chuckling in mirth. "Just try it, Finn. I'm sure you'll like it."

Piscus rolled his eyes good-naturedly and ceased his rant. Finn drank from the cup and his eyes grew wide. "It's creamy and soft!"

"Well of course it is! It's milk! What did you drink as a child, boy? Mud?" Piscus forced a pitcher onto Finn. "You'll drink this all to compensate for the years you've missed!" Finn nearly dropped the ceramic jug, laughing.

"I didn't take you for such a milk enthusiast Piscus." Miriam chided.

"Milk, milk, milk! It goes with all meals!" Piscus preached. "I drink it for breakfast, lunch, and dinner! I'd have milk tattooed on my arm if I could! That, or your name, Miriam!"

The elder rolled her eyes and threw a chunk of bread at the innkeeper. Piscus dodged and tipped his wide hat. Miriam acted offended, but Finn could see the small smile she tried to hide. Finn was sure Piscus could see it too.

As they ate, Piscus and Goblin debated over food. It was humorous to watch Piscus argue with the mute boy.

"Of course carrots go in stew, Goblin! It's traditional!

"What are you doing with your arms? You wave them about as if you've lost control of your body. Quit that, it confuses me!

"Cabbage? *Cabbage?* You're as insane as Finn! Cabbage works with nothing! Maybe as compost! What in all Lenova are you getting at? Your arms are bouncing around the gazebo! I have no idea what you're trying to tell me."

"Finn," one of the elders called out. Finn turned to the bearded man. "What do you carry there on your wrist?"

Finn jolted and he stared at the bracer.

"He dons the mark of a Star-Child, elder." Piscus answered for him, face calm.

Finn worried at the reaction the elders would have. Would they be as scared as Piscus had been when first meeting him? Would they kick him out of town?

"Ah, merely a noble from far away then? How quaint. 'Tis good to have you, lad." The elder turned and continued his meal.

Confusion welled within Finn. Did they not care he was a Star-Child among their midst? Piscus leaned over and spoke into Finn's ear. "It's alright Finn. They don't care much for events that don't affect their village. Pittance is a peaceful place of self-reliance. Whatever happens beyond the borders is of no concern to them."

Finn looked to the now-solemn-faced innkeeper. "Don't they hear the stories of Star-Children destroying and killing?" he whispered back.

"They do, but they brush it off as mere political battles between lords and nobles. It doesn't concern them."

Finn found the words disturbing. How could the people of Pittance not care about the rest of Lenova? Were they blind to danger? Piscus nudged Finn. "Don't take their judgement harshly, Finn. Look about you. There is but peace and tranquility here. They know nothing of the evils beyond as we who have traveled there do. Let them enjoy their bliss. It's such a rarity."

Piscus spoke truth, yet it was hard for Finn to accept it. The village of Pittance was free from the darkness and death sweeping Lenova. Free from corrupted politicians, swindlers, robbers, and killers. But, if someday the village was to be attacked, how would they defend it? The people had their innocence, but would innocence be their demise?

He wiggled in discomfort, mind preoccupied with the village and with thoughts of Star-Children marching toward them. He overheard Miriam talking with another elder.

"Never will I eat sausage links before bed again, Stephan! The dreams I had, I tell you. Quite disturbing! Poor Miller was being chased by a goat down that ravine near Quo'tul Pass..."

Dreams.

An image of a green-eyed maiden beguiling Finn to water came to mind. Finn shot up from his seat, dropping his cup to the gazebo floor. *The dream. The girl. The stream.* Everyone jumped, staring at him in confusion.

"Finn! What happened?" Miriam asked. "Were you stung by a wasp? They do tend to linger about the place."

Finn shook his head in a no. "I—I'm sorry."

"What goes through your head, Finn?" Piscus asked, eyes narrowed.

Finn licked his lips and stared toward the distant stream. *One wish to those who could cross it.* Something was calling to him. *Destiny.*

"I'm going to cross the stream."

He stated the words with confidence, his voice flat. Throughout the white gazebo, no one spoke. Eyes widened and mouths dropped open. "Finn," Piscus whispered, "don't you remember my words? Not one's ever crossed successfully!"

The dream rushed in repetition from beginning to end through Finn's mind. *Not that way, Finn. Like this.* "They haven't succeeded because they didn't know the secret."

"What are you talking about?" Piscus spluttered. Goblin grabbed at Finn's arm, brow furrowed. Finn didn't reply. Instead, he hopped down the gazebo steps and ran toward the stream.

RAFAEL HOHMANN

beyond the stream

15

—Circa 4,900 E.E. (Economic Era-The 17ᵗʰ Era): House Silverskin and House Glover develop a feud over possession of land. The feud lasts three hundred years, affecting the economy of many cities, who are left without coveted Fibermoss-nets and orange wheat. —

The rushing sound of water grew stronger as Finn drew close to the banks. He ran around a grove of trees and slid down an embankment covered in dew. Ferns and tall grass swept past his face, slapping him as he skidded to the edge of the water. In the distance, he could hear voices calling his name. Finn had a strong feeling he shouldn't answer, but instead stay quiet and cross without being seen. There had been something about the dream that'd spoken to him in a deeper level, as if it had been a secret message. There was a way to accomplish this challenge, a method no one had thought of doing before.

His new boots carved into dark mud and crushed rotting vegetation as he walked to the water's edge. The smell of wet wood hit his nose and a finite mist tickled his skin. Standing upon the banks, he examined the water once more, still unable to determine which way it flowed. On the other side, tall grass and closely-knit willow trees hid the ground. Anything could be there, watching and waiting.

What would happen if he did cross? Nothing? Or perhaps his wish to activate his bracer would be immediately granted? Or would he die? No one had ever come back from crossing the stream and no bodies had ever been found. He fought with himself to make up his mind. What if this was his only opportunity to have a wish granted? He had to stop thinking. The voices in the village were still distant but growing closer. Finn didn't have time to hesitate. He remembered the dream: how the green-eyed girl had turned him around. *Not that way. Like this.* He rotated backward, preparing to walk into the water while facing away from the opposite bank.

The bracer and Goblin's wristband were splashed with water as he took a blind step, putting one foot into the churning waves. Nothing happened. He wasn't swept away. Hands didn't reach out and drown him. The near-translucent fish wove around his boot, curious to his presence. Still looking away, he put his other foot in the water, now standing in the stream. His heart pounded and he swallowed hard. He might never see Goblin again. Might never see all of Lenova, his biggest goal in life. Instead, he might drown.

Finn stepped again, the water rising to his calf. He remembered he couldn't swim—had never been taught to swim. He walked backward and the water moved to his thighs. It was cold... yet warm. Everything about this stream contradicted itself. Its flow, its temperature, and even the way in which one had to cross it. Finn continued to move, the water mounting around him. As it hit his waistline and he walked even deeper, he was buffeted back and forth. The strength of the water grew and he did what he could to not slip on the rocks his feet tread upon. He imagined sliding under the waves and he knew if his head submerged, he wouldn't resurface.

A fish splashed near his face and distracted, Finn slipped, chin dipping into the water. He waved his arms in windmills to maintain his direction. Upon finding his balance, he coughed out the water that'd splashed into his mouth. It was sweet. He continued, shedding the stream as he rose from the opposing banks. As he drew near to shore, tall cattails pushed about him. He was soon only treading ankle-deep in water. In the distance, he could see villagers led by Miriam, Piscus, and Goblin. They walked to the edge of the ravine which he'd slipped from. They were trying to find him.

Weeds pushed about Finn, hiding him as he walked backward until his feet hit dry ground. With his heart pounding, he worked up the courage to spin in place and face the other side. Nothing fatal happened. Surrounded by willows and weeds taller than his head, he tasted the earthy smell of untouched vegetation and was relieved to be alive. Near his foot a fox ran by, stopping to stare at him in curiosity. Perhaps having never seen a human before, it wasn't scared. With a flick of its tail, it was gone.

Weaving between the green, Finn climbed a small rise, pushing through curtains of foliage. Birds cawed out, gossiping over the strange human that'd intruded upon their territory. Butterflies flew past, not taking the time to disturb him.

Finn rested a hand on a mossy trunk and looked about. Nothing had approached him. No magic drew itself about him, changing anything. His bracer was dead weight. He knew no wish had been granted. Had the story been just that? A story? Disappointment washed over him and Finn sighed, sitting on the ground. He felt foolish for having walked backward across the stream. What if the wishing magic had faded over time?

He was on the verge of leaving when he saw the crevice. Near his position, a rock outcrop grew from the ground. From it, Finn could see a dark line running through its center. Above, small carved symbols arched over the entrance. They were faded—sanded by the elements—and he didn't recognize their meaning.

Finn approached the crevice, his body electrified with excitement. It was narrow, barely the width of a child. If he sucked in and squeezed, he knew he'd fit through. Benefit of being a cave-diver: one knew how to maneuver through tight spaces. Wiggling his body and scratching his chest, Finn left the world of light for one he was much more familiar with: a dark place of stone walls and chill air. The crevice opened up, moving downward. Being able to straighten out, Finn used his hands to guide himself in the dark as he scooted his feet forward.

He knew to be careful—one overconfident step and maybe he'd walk over a hole, dropping into the bowels of darkness. He sniffed, catching a whiff of something pungent. It gave him discomfort. He knew of many toxic caves which could poison a man's lungs.

Finn remembered the story told by the elders. After the ancient battle between the three races, only one of each remained. Had they carved the tunnel, a final symbol to a time so primeval none could remember it? It was indeed man-made: as Finn slid his palms across the walls he could feel chisel marks. His fingers rubbed against those indents, also finding curves and patterns. There were pictures and words. If only he had a light to see them...or had thought to bring his miner's goggles. Finn had a feeling many secrets could be learned from the walls.

The tunnel widened even more, becoming large enough that Finn could stretch out his arms to either side and not touch the edges. At first mistaking it for his imagination, Finn thought he saw the flicker of a far-off glow. He continued to walk, treading carefully until his eyes confirmed the light. There was a sharp bend, the walls lit by something beyond. A shushing sound could be heard. He stepped around the corner, stopping to examine a carving of a scaly giant plucking scores of men with one hand and dumping them into his open crooked mouth. The image was foreboding and eerie in the stillness of the cave. The giant's left foot crushed the stone wall of a citadel and with his free hand, he reached for more victims. Around him, small humans ran, were brutally crushed by the collapsing structures, or lay prostrate, worshiping the monster. The violence was detailed and highlighted a darker more primitive time in Lenova, an era of brutality, pain, and terror. It made Finn wonder if the depiction was fiction or a historical event. He moved on.

Around the corner, a rectangular room opened. It took Finn's breath away and he was left gazing in wonder at the sight. With a large ceiling stretching meters above him, the chamber could have housed all the villagers of Pittance. Carved into the far wall were three huge gray faces. Two women on either side of a man. They were so detailed, Finn nearly expected them to move and talk in booming voices. Instead, their eyes remained peacefully shut as if in deep undisturbed sleep. Their defining feature were their opened mouths. Waterfalls poured from them: out into canals running along the length of the floor. Across the ceiling, three upside-down empty trenches mirrored the canals, giving the room an anesthetic balance.

In the middle awaited the scarred face of an older man with a long beard, scraggly eyebrows, and an elegant crown. On his crown rested the shape of a star. His mouth was releasing a slow gush of lava: the source of flickering light. The hot liquid fell at a calm pace, pouring into the middle canal and running along the floor. Finn walked to where the canal ended and leaned over to look for where the lava went. Underneath his feet at the edge of the canal was a grate where the glowing liquid disappeared. He gazed to the right, where one of the female faces rested. Finn walked closer to examine.

SUNRIDER

The woman was older, but beautiful. Her long hair was carved in such a way, it seemed to sweep around her face with thin wisps trailing on the edge of her lips. Flowers dotted her brow like a natural wreath. She had long lashes and laugh lines, indicating a happy youth. Finn jolted in recognition. The woman... the way she looked—so similar to the girl from his dreams. In fact, she could've been the dream girl's mother.

In wonder, he took a few steps closer. From her mouth poured out fizzing water letting off a white mist. The shushing sound came from it. Hitting his skin, mist crystalized into frost. He wiped at the cold coating and studied the water more carefully. Ice chunks glazed the top, floating along the canal. Just being near the water sent Finn's teeth chattering. He knew if he were to try and drink it, his mouth would freeze shut. He backed away, rubbing his arms to bring warmth to his body.

The woman on the far left had short, chin-length hair, strange slanted eyes, pronounced cheekbones, and a narrow face. For a crown, she bore a thick crude circlet. Spikes came from it and covered her closed eyes. From her mouth poured out a viscous dark liquid. It shimmered and wove not like fluid, but like black snakes made of smoke. As he approached her, the pungent smell he'd detected earlier grew stronger. Nearing the canal, Finn's nose crinkled. It was heavy; like the odors released from chemicals used to clean gems from beneath the Crust. *Acidic.* He didn't dare step closer. Who knew what sort of demise would come for whomever fell into *that* liquid.

He stood at a distance from all three and examined the room as a whole. Suddenly, it clicked into his mind. The three faces: they were the faces of the last survivors in the tale, one from each race. The man must have been the Seraph, the woman with the flowers Nature-kin, and the female with the narrow face a Forsaken. The chamber was some form of temple or shrine dedicated to them. Was this the place Finn would receive a wish?

"Hello?" he called out, his voice echoing in the room. He immediately regretted saying the word. After many uncounted millenniums, the room resting undisturbed, he'd been the one to break the spell of silence. The room began to shake.

Finn's eyes grew wide. Cave-in? He crouched, splaying his hands out. Instincts and years of practice in the mines took over. He spun in place, bringing his shirt over his mouth and nose as filter in case of dust. He sprinted for the exit but was too late. With a boom, a partition that'd camouflaged into the wall slammed over the tunnel, closing it off. It was a trap. Finn was stuck in the room!

The rumble grew louder and Finn spun, trying to find an indent to hide beneath. There was nothing. He looked up, expecting the ceiling to collapse. Instead, it lowered in a controlled movement. He stopped, looking about in confusion. Where were the falling rocks? The dust? The collapsing of the room? He was answered with a patterned grating, the noise similar to the turning of pulleys. *Mechanical.* The roof of the chamber was going to crush him. The story had lied. It'd tricked him into coming here and dying. Were the people of Pittance sacrificing him? Was he to be made a ritual for three ancient dead entities? No, that couldn't be it. There was no way Miriam and Piscus would do such a thing. Or would they? How well did Finn know them?

It was a test—like the stream.

Finn gritted his teeth, trying to comprehend what the room wanted from him. He studied the faces once more, the canals, the liquids, the open mouths. Open! He had to swim one of the canals and through one of the stone mouths. But which one?

He looked at each face. Ice-water, lava, or acid. He would die with all three. The ceiling moved closer and closer, the meters dropping. The trenches carved into the roof would clamp against the canals on the floor, forming closed tunnels. He had to choose one before they shut. Already the stone carvings were covered past their eyes, their features crushed flat by the block ceiling. Their noses were soon to follow. Then the rest.

Finn paced and huffed, his heart bouncing against his chest. He then remembered the Star-Child bracer. He was immune to heat! He wanted to hit himself. Finn ran forward, reaching the edge of the middle canal. He stared at the molten liquid. What if the lava had an enchantment to it? Or a curse? There was no time to question. Already the ceiling was pushing against his head, forcing him to crouch. He sucked in his breath. It was insane, absolutely insane. He was about to dive headfirst into lava. And he did.

Keeping his arms and legs together, he fell, smashing into the thick liquid, remembering with regret that he'd just bought his new clothes. Unlike water, he didn't sink right away. Instead, he hovered halfway above the surface and slightly beneath it. It was as if the liquid was trying to decide whether to accept him or not. Like in the Slaglands, there was no horrible burning sensation, but a stagnant cool touch. Stream water evaporated off him in one large hiss. His clothing erupted into flames, burning into ash and exposing him. Blackened fiber flew in spirals around him, trapped in the hot air, slowly disappearing into nothing from the heat. Finn thanked the heavens at least he'd left his satchel and gems back at the inn.

Finn sank into the lava. Fearing he wouldn't burn but simply drown, he splashed about, trying to right himself into a standing position. His feet carved downward into the liquid and he squinted as to not blind himself in the glow. The heat cooked the air, thickening it to a point where he could hardly breathe. If only he had Miner's Pumice with him. His toes found bottom and he stopped sinking, the lava coming to his chest. Above, the ceiling let out a massive boom as it shut, closing him inside the tiny tunnel created by the conjoining canals.

Right away his lungs overworked themselves as he gasped in the limited air. It didn't burn his lungs, but instead left him feeling as if he was breathing soup. He had no time to lose. Sloshing forward in the lava, he struggled to make for the distant light marking the exit. Now instead of looking like a mouth, it resembled a hole at the end of the canal, spewing liquid. Lava hit his face and splashed into his eyes. He rubbed them, feeling grit beneath his eyelids. In what had to have been the most dangerous situation he'd ever been in, Finn laughed. He felt dizzy. The ridiculousness of rubbing lava out of one's eye—as if it were nothing more than a casual act—seemed so preposterous he couldn't help but snigger. He stopped, scolding himself on disobeying the cardinal rule that'd been drilled into him since a small boy: when running out of air, don't do anything stupid to use it up faster.

Approaching the end of the canal, lungs heaving, he stopped. All that was left was to cross beneath the flow of lava, submerge beneath the liquid, and crawl through the stone mouth. Knowing if he wasted even a second longer he'd suffocate, he dove in.

It was heavy and the weight of the flow smashed into his back, forcing him to his knees. His arms wove about, churning in the thick lava. He couldn't open his eyes, he couldn't resurface, and he couldn't breathe. He was going to die!

Pushing with all the remaining strength in his body, he forced his legs to propel him forward. His pulse beat in his head, vibrating in his veins. His lungs compressed, causing a ring to sound in his ears and forcing his throat to swallow at nothing. His arms felt at the smooth walls within the mouth of the face and he guided himself forward. There was an incline to his step. He was moving upwards.

With a *whoosh,* his head broke through the surface. Spiraling arcs of lava flew about. Yellow rivulets trickled down his face and he opened his mouth wide, gulping air. He coughed, choking on liquid. His arms broke free and he grasped about him, feeling for an edge to the pool he was in. Touching dry stone, he gripped it and pulled himself from the sludge. The lava hissed and crackled, dripping off him and onto the stone. Wiping his eyes clean, Finn retched, spewing out his breakfast of bread and milk.

Shivering, he crawled forward to a clean patch of ground and collapsed. He lay there, waiting for his heart to settle down. Once calm, he wiped the remaining lava off himself. Already most of it had dried, forming a rock crust on his skin. He examined the room.

The new chamber was much smaller, possibly the size of a house. Lit by the lava he'd escaped from Finn was able to see about him. Three pools rested side by side against one wall, each containing a liquid from one of the three stone faces. Finn stared at both the ice and acid-filled tubs. He knew he'd made the correct choice. If he had dived into either of the other canals, he would've died.

Opposite to the pools was a tunnel continuing forward, but apart from that, the room was barren and inanimate. No walls moved, no noise echoed out, and all was still. Finn walked along the tunnel with trepidation, worried a new trap would spring, catching him unaware.

Ahead, a more natural light flashed out. He drew closer to it, wondering how sunlight could reach so deep into the earth. Abruptly, the passage came to an end, facing a flat stone wall. The light came from a small circular hole in the center. Puzzled, Finn drew near and peeked through. His naked body shivered in the cold cave.

Beyond, was what Finn could only describe as a magical garden. Sun beat upon a grass lawn leading to sinewy trees interwoven with ivy and moss. Dark bush leaves stretching as wide as a man grew through the patches of thick jungle vegetation, forming walls of green. Finn couldn't recognize a single plant; each as exotic as one could imagine. Yellow sand formed winding paths between the trees, none seeming to lead to anywhere in particular. Large narrow rectangular stones carved with circles seemed to grow from the soft grass in sagging angles. Birds fluttered about and

Finn adjusted his gaze through the small peep-hole to try and follow their movements. They held all the colors of the rainbow and some seemed to have human faces. Far back between the brush, Finn could see the silhouette of something tall and with a long neck. The creature wiggled as spikes protruded from its head, then retracted. With loud crunching footsteps, it disappeared, not giving Finn a chance to make out detail.

He continued to examine in wonder, forgetting where he was and what he was doing. From the path directly in front of his peep-hole, footsteps sounded out. A form came from beyond the forest. Stepping forward, an ancient bent woman left shadow and stood in the light of the lawn. Her long thin hair waved as if in a breeze and her light green eyes shimmered. She had so many wrinkles that it was difficult to discern her features. Yet Finn recognized her from both the stone face in the large chamber and from his dream. She smiled at him.

"Welcome SunRider. I've been waiting for you."

for the cult

16

—Circa 5,122 E.E. (Economic Era-The 17ᵗʰ Era): Stones roll down Mount Pluhm and a voice growls out across the night air, heard for kilometers around "Myza-baen! I curse your passage out of this world! May your travel to the next life be choked by the tail you have cut from my body! I curse you!" The voice was never heard again and no more rocks ever rolled down the mountain. Brave explorers who've summited the top of Pluhm have never found the source of the voice but did come across the skeleton of a two-headed man. —

The ancient tomes told her much. Methods of extracting information from the strongest of warriors, the languages of shadows, stories of demons circling the dark between the stars and beneath the trenches of the earth. Glorious dark knowledge—forbidden to her, but not for long. Soon, she would be privy to all the temple's secrets. For now, she would have to disobey orders and read more than she was supposed to.

Wahala flipped another page in the skin-bound book. Whether it was human skin or animal, she didn't care. She was too engrossed in the words written by a long-dead Queen who'd traveled into the Land of Light for knowledge many centuries ago. In the Queen's travels, she'd found a dead Star-Child. The corpse had told a story of war, but the details of the Queen and the events of the time were not discussed. The priestess had surgically removed the Star-Child's bracer and experimented on it. Wahala read a passage.

Scraping the remaining flesh from the device only confirmed my theory: the bracer biologically altered the body, changing the subject into something altogether not human.

Notations:

>Segments of the bones in the left arm have meshed with the device. I believe the longer one wears the bracer, the stronger the fusion. The first few months, it only clings. But as the months turn to years, bone and metal merge as one.

>In addition, bone material shows more of a glossy nature instead of porous. Speculation: flexibility? Bone tensile strength? His unique ability?

>All signs point to the bracer giving the wearer powers different to what we know as natural or magical: otherworldly.

>Upon using forbidden necromantic spells and performing acts of ritualism, I have effectively created a crack on the bracer. The effort has nearly killed me. I am now in recuperation. I fear there is not enough gold in all the Kingdom of Rot to fix me.

Wahala flipped the page, but the writing only guessed at the dead Star-

Child's possible powers. There were no more references made as to how the Queen had damaged the bracer—neither was there any more information on the ancient generation of Star-Children that'd long ago been chosen. How had they died out? How had they been erased from history?

"No!" Wahala hissed, turning more pages. She was unable to find any more clues. Marking the spot, she set down the book and swept her arms across the thick study desk; tossing quills, papers, books, and artifacts across the temple's library floor. Three days back and still no answer. She stood and paced, fuming. There was a way to destroy the bracers; some form of spell or some dark art. It had to be within the prohibited books. The library door opened and Salastine stepped inside. Wahala nearly threw a book at him but stopped herself.

"I apologize." the man said with a bow. "I didn't mean to intrude upon your studies, my leader."

Wahala waved a hand, her thoughts unshared. Her mind was so preoccupied with Star-Children it took her a while to realize Salastine was still waiting. "What is it?" she asked.

"We're ready for you."

Wahala froze as a mixture of emotions ran through her, coursing inside her skin like maggots feasting on flesh. Fear and excitement battled for dominance. It was time. "Lead me." she stated. Salastine handed her a torch, bowed, and opened the door, disappearing into a dark stone hallway. She followed, her boots clacking on the hard floor, dust tickling her nose.

Through passageways and stairwells they walked in silence, Wahala's skin shivering in anticipation. They passed black rooms where chittering rang out and shadowed forms moved. They hurried through the plague floors, where magical bubbles surrounded them, holding back the shambling dead corpses of festered men and women. Their ancient eye sockets followed Wahala's every footstep and their emaciated dried hands opened and closed, reaching out. Wahala and Salastine wove around the Lung Chamber, where thousands of small tunnels ran from floor to ceiling. Little eyes stared out from each one, blinking and casting red light. Deeper and deeper they went into the massive temple, into its bowels. Approaching a thin, but tall rectangular passage leading into a hallway, Salastine stopped, taking her torch. He turned to her.

"Only you may continue this way."

He indicated for her to move forward and Wahala stepped past him. She walked in confidence without a word—the dark was her true and only lover; although she knew Salastine wished it was himself. It was in the way emotion seemed to arise to the surface of his otherwise blank face every time she was near him. It was in the twitch of his lips when she bore her gaze at him. How long had he admired her from afar before he'd finally stepped forward and introduced himself to her life? She clasped her hands together. Knowing Salastine held feelings for her could prove a great advantage. Already plans formed in her head on how she could use the man.

The hallway was pitch black and alone without a guide, she had to stop, allowing her eyes to adjust to the dark. Once they'd accustomed to a point where she could see a few paces around her, she continued. Minutes passed and the passage narrowed to the length of her shoulders yet grew taller and taller. The ceiling could have been a kilometer above her head for all she knew, lost in the dark where no light hit. She stopped and looked up, hearing leather sliding on stone. She squinted, barely making out movement. What was up there?

There was a wet slapping sound as something dropped down. At first Wahala thought it to be a rope, but when she saw the suckers and the moist liquid dripping like saliva, she jumped back, covering her mouth in alarm. More tentacles dropped from the unmeasured height above, hanging about her. She could hear the rumble of wet breathing. There was a long and harsh sniff. The tentacles grew still, freezing in place. A tendril of thought entered Wahala's mind, working its way through her like an animal tossing aside documents. It wasn't a sapient thought, but a magical force. Wahala gasped and grabbed at her temples; her eyes watered, her memories shuffled without her consent, old recollections were pried and pushed away. As quickly as it had invaded, the force left, with only the lingering scent of satisfaction staying behind.

Wahala blinked and rubbed her face, sitting up from the ground. She'd fallen and hadn't noticed. The silhouetted tentacles didn't move. She stood and approached one with hesitation, bringing her hand out to touch it. It was stone. She stood there for a while, contemplating the phenomenon. Had she been tested by the temple itself? If so, she had been found worthy of Queen-ship. She bared her teeth in a vicious grin and moved on, even more confident the path she was to tread was the correct one.

She stepped out into a circular room. Two hooded figures awaited her there. Walking into the chamber from another passage was Salastine, also wearing a black robe. Mal'Bal had allowed her to take three cult members, so Wahala had obviously chosen Salastine. She allowed the man to pick the other two, only asking he chose the most loyal to her cause. What Mal'Bal wasn't aware of, was instead of returning home only to bring back more gold for his campaign, Wahala was also fulfilling her own agenda: knowledge and power.

The chamber Wahala stepped into was peculiar. In fact, it was a shallow indoor pond. Rising out of the warm water in the center of the room rested a stone slab big enough for a human to lay upon. The torches set against the round walls gave off a red light, layering them in somber ambiance. No one spoke as Wahala sloshed over to the stone slab. She took off all her clothing, exposing herself to the cult members. Her golden knees glinted in the dim light. She didn't blush, nor did she care that they stared at her. The ceremony had no place for carnal thoughts.

Taking her black, shoulder-length hair and putting it into a bun, she dropped herself onto the slab, laying down. Her three followers walked forward. One put hands on Wahala's feet and another upon her brow. Salastine placed his upon her soft smooth belly. Wahala watched him to see if his attraction to her would distract him. It didn't. She was pleased.

"*Where light cannot live, in the core of the dark.*" Salastine spoke. "*Within the abode of pain we gather.*" His voice was whispery, yet it resonated with strength. The room hummed as it detected the spell. Far beneath the temple, massive Apex gems powered by thousands of sacrifices shook at the bottom of underground lakes, responding to the chant.

"*For the cult, always for the cult.*" the two others echoed back.

"*Where fester spreads and blood is wine, part of death we become.*" Salastine continued.

"*For the cult, Always for the cult.*"

"*Za shavazol dë culathas. To nothing we transcend.*"

"To nothing I shall transcend." Wahala spoke. Salastine nodded.

"*Where base elements meet: darkness, water, stone, and magic; we gather for high ritual.*"

"*For the cult, always for the cult.*"

"*Gav-da, meî-deoth, shavazolum, baj-uah. A leader has been selected.*"

"I have been called. I shall accept." Wahala answered. Salastine nodded again.

"*Give all to us and we shall give all to you, Wahala-zah, lady of shadows.*"

"I give all for the cult."

"*For the cult, always for the cult.*"

"*By this we pledge alliance to thee. Mudah. Vindisca. Meî-bith.*"

SUNRIDER

The three cult members pulled out ceremonial scythes from beneath their black cloaks. They glinted, sharp as snake fangs. The room thrummed. The walls shook and ripples rode outwards from the stone slab which Wahala lay upon. Her breathing intensified and the spots where the cult members had touched her grew abnormally hot. The three cut gashes into the crooks of their elbows. Each approached her, dripping their blood into her open eyes and mouth. She drank the hot fluid; a symbol of accepting their loyalty. She blinked and red tears ran down her face. From now on, they and all those who pledged themselves to her would sacrifice limb and life at her command.

"The ritual has been accepted. We now ask for your devotion, Wahala-zah."

"For the cult, always for the cult."

"I accept. Take from me what is required."

Wahala closed her eyes and clenched her muscles, feeling energy seep into her from the stone slab touching her bare skin. It electrified her bones and arched her back. This was the moment, the final step in the ritual. Her mouth opened and she let out a shrill scream as her blood boiled. She could feel a strange change within her—a purple-hued leviathan awakening and sinking into the depths of her core. It was as if necromantic energy had come to life and had taken her for a host body. Her golden kneecaps were frozen and sent an ache that twisted her mind. The cult members leaned over her, their scythes lowering to her chest.

"Depravity and ruin, wash through our souls. Take away the light. Leave us embraced within the void."

"FOR THE CULT, ALWAYS FOR THE CULT!" Wahala screamed, feeling her throat tear from the strain.

The scythes plunged, cutting into her chest: piecing between ribs, digging, reaching for their target. Surgical cuts. Blood ruptured from her chest. Her cry intensified and her body shook violently. Water splashed in waves, turning red. The room resonated with thousands of voices. Blades sank deeper. Thirsty. Hungry. They found her heart. They bit and clawed, eating the organ. Removing it.

Wahala's consciousness slipped, but not before witnessing Salastine bringing forth a golden object from beneath his hood. It already beat in time to her blackened veins, excited for its new housing. Salastine lowered the golden heart into her chest.

"Now you are our Queen priestess, rightful ruler of the cult."

The library doors opened and the three cult members entered the room bearing empty trunks. Wahala swept in after them, her cloak flapping as if in an invisible breeze. Her breathing was heavy and her head felt hollow. She grabbed at the wall. "Take the oldest books. I want their secrets. Their words shall be mine to command." she rasped, her voice wavering.

Salastine approached her with a smile, bowing and kissing her hand. He treated her gently, respecting her state of weakness. She allowed him the gesture. "My Queen, soon you will have the necromantic knowledge of all Queens before you, along with their acolytes and scientists."

She smiled. "Yes, soon I'll know."

"Know?" Salastine asked.

"Know how to stop a Star-Child. Soon, I'll know how to destroy Mal'Bal."

The handsome man grinned and left her to her thoughts. Their belongings were quickly packed and the group navigated through the temple to the Trophy Room. The room was a large long rectangular chamber with thousands upon thousands of golden limbs mounted on the walls. The long space went on and on for what seemed to be well over a kilometer. Arms, legs, digits, torsos, every type of extremity from ears to chins were proudly displayed. Above each inorganic part was a name written on parchment and tacked onto the stone wall. The names served to tell of each appendage's previous owner, long passed into the void after death. But the limbs—the gold itself—was far more than one person's alone. They were imbued with the strength of all their ancestors.

Wahala and her group respectfully chose parts and put them into a cart. They pushed the full cart, needing all four of them to do so, and took the parts to the end of the room where a large blackened vat leaned against the wall, side-by-side with an urn. Both were as large as houses. Stairs led to the vat's rim and below it was a press with a mold. The three men took the limbs up the stairs and dropped them into the vat. Wahala approached the urn, where a spigot faced her at eye level. Near to it, a bucket hung from a hook. She took the bucket and turned the spigot. With a hissing sound, what looked to be gray ash poured out into the container. She shut off the flow when she'd taken enough. She fingered the contents within the bucket. How many of her ancestors lay at her fingertips? In her hands had to have been a conglomerated mix of over a thousand cremated corpses.

She climbed the steps to the top of the vat while the three men went back for more limbs. At the top, she looked inside, seeing that the golden parts were already melting. Massive heat hit her skin and she cringed, shying away. Although there was no fire to liquefy its contents, the vat glowed red and yellow, defying logic. Ancient magic still flowed strong through the ancient artifact.

Wahala tossed the ash into the vat, honored that the strength of those before her would be imbued into the recycled gold. How many ancestors were part of her kneecaps, part of her new heart? Four more carts were deposited into the vat. Once all the contents were melted, the men worked the press, forming bars of gold. Wahala sat on the ground, her body tired and still recuperating from her ritual.

"Rest." Salastine called out, waving a hand. Sweat poured from his handsome face. "We'll wake you when we're done." Wahala nodded, too tired to argue, and closed her eyes.

A long time later they retrieved their steeds, attached them to their wagon, and left the temple. The animals brayed and bucked, foam coating their mouths and gems dotting their foreheads. Salastine took a chart with calculations showing the directions in which the waves of the dead were traveling. He charted a course back North into the Land of Light, working quickly as they knew the scent of human and animal would draw the undead in from hundreds of miles. Once charted, they mounted their beasts and rode as hard as they could. The horses, twice the size of Lenovan steeds, snorted and foamed, their muscles strained as they pulled the heavy gold. Wahala looked to the gray barren horizon. Beyond it awaited Mal'Bal, continuing his siege against all life.

She chuckled to herself. Finally, the first steps to overthrowing the renegade leader were in place. Soon, they would abandon their foolish quest to end all life. Maybe then the cult would find its path, perhaps spreading their tradition beyond their borders. There were many opportunities for growth in Lenova after all.

through the bird's window

17

—*Heed now and perk your ear, for the song of the Ralain the Swordmaster, m'dear. With a swish and a twirl he cut the moons, and with a stab and a jab he formed desert dunes. Naught might nor speed could best his skill, all armies and beasts Ralain would kill. 'Til one day Ralain met the Shade of De'Mort, in battle, in love, the both did court. With a hiss and a swipe they kissed and fought, from Lenova to the Southern Kingdom of Rot. On beyond those aster-purple spines, that blocked those dead lands from our verdant pines. Ne'r to return, the watchmen said, they' gone to die facing the dead. Believe the words that come from my mouth, that on wintery nights a sound haunts the South. Of Ralain's blade finally breaking, and of him and the Shade last breath a-taking. —*
-*song unknown, date unknown*

The ancient woman moved slowly, as if time bent to her will and would allow her as long as she needed. Her bare feet trod on soft grass and her arms extended as if to embrace Finn, even though it was impossible through the rock wall. He watched her from behind the peep-hole, wondering again how sunlight hit a place so deep underground. The woman smiled, her face crinkling up.

"It's called *the Bird's Window,* love."

"W—what is?" Finn asked, stumbling over his words.

"The hole which you see me through. It's only a glimpse to where I reside. Not here, but somewhere else altogether."

"Where is that?"

She laughed softly, her voice frail yet melodic. "A place where Spring never ends and animals stay babies forever."

She sighed and looked at him with the eyes of an examining practitioner. How she could see him so well while on the other hand he had to squint one eye shut to peer through to her? Startled, he covered himself and blushed. She tapped one bent finger against her cheek and pursed her lips. As she watched him, a squirrel ran up her leg and perched on her shoulder. The little animal turned and also stared at Finn, mimicking the woman before scampering away. She sighed, looking pleased. Whatever she'd seen in Finn, she'd liked.

"Oh one who's footsteps are guided by fate! Behold Walker of Flames! The Unchosen! Truly the stars watch you as closely as bees do a flower! Well met, Finn SunRider! Well met indeed!" Her words rang of power and her chest puffed out. Behind her, birds took flight, chirping in songful delight. Finn didn't know what to say. He'd not expected to find this at the end of his quest.

"Who are you?" he asked, suddenly feeling the need to act respectful. "How do you know me?"

She shook her head and her flowing white hair danced. As her hair moved, Finn caught glimpses of grapes, leaves, and small red berries. They were woven-in like decorative beads. She crouched and plucked a flower with bell-shaped petals. She drank from it, a little golden drop escaping her lips and falling to the ground. The woman smiled in contentment.

"So long have I been witness to the changes of Lenova, young hero-to-be. For many centuries I have watched these lands grow darker. But now, I've been given hope! To talk to you will be sacrifice, but sacrifices are part of what makes Lenova exist."

She wiped at her eyes and in surprise, Finn noticed silver tears dripping from her cheeks.

"I am Lady Tuliah, last of my kind, Grower of Berries, Sparrow-Speaker, Crown-Bearer to the Trees, Witness of Lenova, and Nature-kin."

Finn took a step back, stumbling over his feet. It was as if he'd been hit by a log. His arms shook. The story was true. The three elder races. The great war. The last Nature-kin had spoken to him.

Tuliah laughed. Finn could hear her from beyond the wall as if she were only a pace away. He hurried back to the Bird's Window and peered through. Tuliah was crouching in the grass, feeding strawberries to a white-pelted boar. The creature squealed and nuzzled his head against the ground as if embarrassed. It scampered off into the brush and the elder stood.

"SunRider! How I've longed for the day to meet you, or I guess anyone to be honest."

"Meet me? Why me? I'm nothing! You—you're Nature-kin! You must be...be..."

"Very old." Lady Tuliah finished, chuckling. "Yes. I feel it. Believe me."

The knowledge she possessed. Witness to Lenova's history for countless years. Any scholar on Lenova would give all they had to spend five minutes with her.

Lady Tuliah yawned. "Why you, you ask? Lots of reasons. Mostly because talking to squirrels grows quite boring. Thank the roots you had enough brains to cross the stream! I'm glad that the one to reach this far is one who is so resilient. You were an idiot to run into the center of the Slaglands but was also too stubborn to die there. There's nothing special about it, you just ended up being the one who stumbled into something far bigger than yourself. You've become part of a great cycle! Fate, destiny, sheer luck... blah, blah, blah. It doesn't matter. What matters is that you're here!" She approached the peep-hole until all Finn could see was the light green of her left eye. It glimmered at him and he felt lost within its depths. "You heeded my call quickly too! Not as dense as I imagined you to be— nope, not at all! I've called plenty others, not that many seem to be able to even hear me. You'll be surprised at how many Lenovans don't even dream!"

"Your call?" Finn stuttered.

"Yes, twice! Once physically and once mentally! Didn't you dance with me at the festival of Lith-Lamma?"

Finn jumped. He'd danced with a beautiful maiden that night. His cheeks flushed. He'd thought the girl attractive. But she wasn't young at all.

Tuliah laughed. "I still got a hop to my step, don't I?" She frowned and tapped her lips. "Granted I wasn't really there..."

"Wait, so I was dancing by myself? In front of everybody?" Finn yelped, feeling his cheeks grow even hotter.

"I suppose so!" Lady Tuliah said with a giggle not appropriate for her age. "But everyone was drunk anyways. I doubt they'll remember!"

Finn put his hands over his face, shaking his head. He could hear the elder woman laughing uncontrollably on the other side of the wall.

"If—if you had seen your face as I had! Dancing about and gyrating with no one near you, your rear bouncing along like two lopped potatoes in a sack!'"

Finn groaned and shook his head again. He heard a thump come from through the Bird's Window. All went silent. In curiosity, he peered through. Tuliah was on the ground rolling in mute laughter, her face red. The elder shimmered as if behind a mirage. At times Finn would see a budding Tuliah, at others, the elder.

"Y—you l—l—looked like a d—duck who'd been hit by a s—stone! Couldn't even call it dancing, could w—we? Wobbling and s—shaking your arms like you were having a seizure!"

Finn hit the wall. "I never danced before! Don't mock me! I thought you were supposed to be a pompous wise sage, not some perverted garden-tender!"

His words made Lady Tuliah laugh even harder. Finn huffed and waited for her to settle down. She wasn't at all like one would think an elder should be. She quieted and stood, sighing in contentment, and approached the peep-hole.

"I apologize, SunRider. I'm just happy to be able to talk to someone." She pointed at him. "As a young orphan boy, the mine supervisors gave you the name of SunRider. Do you recall why?"

Finn shook his head, perplexed.

"When you were brought in, along with many other orphans of the Crust, your little face stared at the sky with a grin. Tiny and hardly able to walk in a straight line, you found the reflection of the sun beaming onto the dirt through a glass wind-chime one of the supervisors kept. You hopped the lines of colored light back and forth, giggling as you did so. Thus they called you SunRider. But perhaps your name will mean so much more—or nothing at all. It's your choice!"

"How—" Finn stammered, "how do you know all this?"

Tuliah looked on to a part of the garden Finn couldn't see. Her eyes were faded and suddenly, she seemed ancient. "It's a burden and a gift all the same—vision and long age granted by Lenova itself. Last of my race, am I." Her face grew sad. "What people we were! Our palaces and cities! One with nature! Would put the villagers of Pittance with their tree-homes to shame, yes it would. The culture and history we held, all lost to hate and fear."

She stared off into nothing for a long time. Her words hit Finn hard, as if Tuliah's emotions were invading him by force. He was hollow, as if his existence had been taken from him, only leaving an ancient sadness. Tuliah snapped her fingers and Finn blinked the feeling away. "We don't have the time for moping! I'll soon be gone!

"Gone?" Finn barked, "Are you and the other two elder race survivors not immortal? And where are they? Shouldn't they be here with you?"

Tuliah gave him a small smile. "Such large questions for one so young. They would take much too long to explain in detail. Know this: The Seraph has long passed into another realm. The quiet Forsaken left for lands far South beyond Lenova, pregnant with twins. It was a foolish hope, for the call of the beyond reaches out. The elder races are not to stay; our cycle is over." Tuliah pressed against the Bird's Window. "We became stuck in the cycle of repetition. What happened to us has happened many times before."

"What do you mean?" Finn startled. "What happened?"

But Tuliah was shaking her head. "No, perhaps it won't occur in your lifetime. Much else comes first. Many quests, adventures, and battles. Prophecies, bah! I hate prophecies. Reveals too much you know. Takes the choice out of a man's heart, it does. I can give you one. Perhaps it'll even speak truth, but you don't have to listen to it. There's never been a prophecy that was always correct. Goodness, there wasn't even anything saying whether you were going to make it all the way to me or not. There's never been a *chosen one*, you know that right? No such thing. SunRider…

there are so many paths to take…" She leaned in. "Did you know that there's a possibility that one day you could lose all your limbs and tend to sheep for the rest of your miserable life? There's also another one about you drowning in an ocean, one with you becoming a rich map-maker, one with you dead from the Clover's Flu, one with you as the King of Lenova, one with you activating your bracer, one with you losing the bracer… and so on. You see? Its expectant of me to give you something. Guiding words perhaps. I can do that, I can. I just don't think you should put much thought into a set future. Does any of this make sense to you?"

Finn, dumbfounded, shook his head.

"Of course not. You'd have to be a seer to understand. Ugh, well I'll give you a prophecy. You know, back when my people were around, we had plenty of heroes too. It seemed every one of them had a prophecy about this or that. Most of them died or were maimed attempting to fulfil them."

Finn closed his mouth and chewed on his cheek. "So why give me one? I won't know what to do with it. I mean, am I even supposed to be someone special?"

Tuliah's face softened and she clucked. "If I could reach you I would kiss your forehead in a blessing, young one. Everyone can be special and a hero. But… you could also walk out of here and die of constipation. There's no glamor to it. Do what you want with your life, but at least hear this—not a prophecy, but guiding words:"

Her face grew abnormally still.

> *"From breeze to storm, we pray must rise a child!*
> *With a path made long, a journey made wild!*
> *Evil seeks to change all we hold dear,*
> *Will one save us, protect us, take away our fear?*

RAFAEL HOHMANN

"Glory or ruin, Lenova shall observe,
Lords and Kings to whom shall you serve?
Will one stop the curse, or will one see it done?
It's all unpredictable in the long run.

"Destroy monsters and men, choose to live or to die,
Choose whatever you want, to walk or to fly.
Confront beasts made of stone, Gods made of gold,
Through trial's hands, shall a warrior be mold!

"Let all hear the call,
each to answer or deny,
Some will choose to save Lenova,
Others to let it die.

"From breeze to storm, we pray must rise a child!
With a path made long, a journey made wild!
To follow their feet, forward through death,
And whisper the Name with a final breath.

"When earth comes to life and all shall be lost,
A power awakens, but at sanity's cost.
Remember the dream: a world uncollapsed,
A divine prediction not given, but just a perhaps.

"Men become Gods, and Gods become dust,
All in false vision they'll put their trust!
With a path made long, a journey made wild!
From breeze to storm, we pray must rise a child!

Tuliah collapsed to the grass, heaving. Her eyes bulged and sweat poured down her face. Finn pushed against the rock, his heart hammering. "Lady Tuliah! You're ill!"

She didn't reply, but rested, her body shivering as if in the depths of a cold. When she rose, she looked much older and paler. "See?" she snapped, frustration twisting her face. "Visionary guidance could mean anything! Or goodness, nothing at all! Quite worthless!" Finn opened and closed his mouth. "Do you remember the words?" she huffed, quite irritated.

"Yes! They're burned into my mind!"

Tuliah slumped, panting. "Now see them erased from it."

"What was that? What did it mean?" Finn exclaimed, feeling strange energy course through him. He wanted to run, to jump, to swim to the ends of the earth.

"An old fool's meandering predictions." she croaked, eyes fluttering. "They tell of potential events to come."

Finn shivered and stuttered. There was so much to ask her, so much to know. He was so confused! But Tuliah was shaking her head and backing away from the Bird's Window. She looked very old indeed. "My time's up, SunRider. The yonder calls to me."

"Wait!" Finn shouted, pressing his face to the rock wall so hard he scraped his cheeks. "Don't go! What do I do? I—I don't understand! Am I supposed to do something special?"

Tuliah gave him a sad smile and silver tears coursed from her face. "Do what you want. Be a hero, a farmer, a martyr, a rebel. But please SunRider, take care of her. Take care of Lenova better than we did." Tuliah's emotions swept into Finn and tears flowed from his cheeks as well.

Tuliah began to fade into the brush. The sunlight hitting the garden grew dim. "I almost forgot:" she whispered. "The tale's promise of me granting a wish. Bah, what a load. I'll tell you this, only half that historic story is true. I cannot grant you the power you seek in your bracer. Only you control that. I shall give you something else. Your kind nature toward your friend changes him. Return to existence, SunRider."

She was nearly gone now, her green eyes all that was left, twinkling between tall leaves. The room was darkening. "Even in the yonder I shall remember you, Finn SunRider. Well met. Well met indeed."

She was gone. Through the peep-hole Finn saw nothing but a black empty cave. It looked undisturbed since the dawn of time. He backed away, his mind trying to process what'd happened to him in the last hour. He wiped his face free of tears and muttered the strange guiding words she'd shared under his breath. It held no meaning, or did it? Should he even listen to it? But truly, for Lady Tuliah's sake, he would consider their counsel.

He turned, in a hurry to return to the surface. Instead of finding the tunnel he'd come from, he found a plain oak door. In puzzlement, he grabbed the iron knob and pulled it open. Beyond, was the room with three faces. The door itself was the mouth to the middle face; the Seraph. Instead of canals full of liquids, only flat floor met him. He stepped into the room, marveling at the magic.

Near the tunnel leading outside, Finn found a mound of clothing waiting for him. They were his clothes, no longer burned to ash. He smiled and thanked Tuliah under his breath, putting them on. In his pants pocket, there was a lump. He fished inside and pulled out a glass bottle made in the same shape as the flower Tuliah had drank from. Within, he could see an amber liquid sloshing about. There was a note attached to the bottle and Finn read it.

For when speed is of the essence.

He put the bottle back into his pocket, treasuring it more than he ever would the gems he'd taken from Nozgull. He stepped back out into daylight, looking back to the magic chamber for the last time. Seconds after walking back into the forest the rock mound was gone, all traces of the ancient ruins vanished. Pittance's legend was completed. Had he used up the wish?

Finn walked to the water's edge and pushed through the cattails, admiring how little the sun's position had changed. On the opposing bank, none of the villagers, nor Piscus and Goblin, were to be seen. Finn turned around and walked backward, washing the crusted lava from his skin and reaching the other bank. Step after slow step, he returned to a quiet Pittance.

return to pittance

18

—Circa 5,607 E.E. (Economic Era-The 17th Era): Finn SunRider hears wild tales of the wonders of Lenova from new miners. The excitement and desire to explore the world seeds within him and never lets go. —

With Tuliah's words heavy in his ears, Finn approached the center of town. The outer streets were empty, as if the people had gathered in one location. Turning a corner to face the grass field where the night before festivities had abounded, Finn came across all the citizens. Looking both agitated and nervous, they moved in place, gathering into hunched groups. Finn could hear them talking in hushed voices. In the middle, Piscus and Miriam stared at Goblin, their eyes wide and their mouths open. As Finn drew near, the crowd noticed him. They turned to face him, growing silent one by one. The air became heavy with a sense of reverence and Finn's spine tingled. Piscus, Miriam, and Goblin saw him. They froze, resembling the statues surrounding the village.

For a moment, no one spoke. Finn bit his lip, worried he'd done something wrong. Had by crossing the stream, his actions offended or angered the villagers? Had he been too brash? Too quick to rush into the water?

"StreamCrosser."

The word vibrated in the silence, even though it'd been whispered. But it was more than a word—it held power. A title. Soon, others repeated it like a chant, *directed at him.* A few villagers even reached out, touching his wet clothes; feeling the stream water run off him. Miriam came closer, the other elders gathering around her like a cloak. Her face held a childish wonder, mixing with her aged wisdom.

"Finn, by all that binds and surrounds us, I can't believe it! In my lifetime... I never thought... Did you make it to the other side?"

Finn thought of his experience in the underground chamber of the ancient races—how personal it'd been. "I did." he stated with hesitance, careful with his words. He didn't think describing every detail of what'd happened would be wise.

Miriam nodded in acceptance. "Did our stories hold true? Tell us if our culture speaks truth."

Finn looked about at the villagers. They stared back, awaiting his answer in earnest. Warmth overcame him. These people had accepted him, welcomed him in, and treated him with kindness. "Maintain your faith, it's all true." He shouted the words out, hoping all would hear. It was a sudden reaction, like a wildfire spreading across a dry field. All about him, smiles ruptured. Wide grins claimed the faces of each villager as they turned and hugged each other, patting their neighbor's backs and wiping away happy tears. Miriam embraced him. "Please, will you share at least a portion of what lay beyond?" Her words stilled the people and they listened with ears perked.

Being the center of attention made Finn's knees quiver. He'd never experienced so many stares. Licking his lips and fiddling with his hands, he cleared his throat. "The three races existed. This village has been watched and protected by the last of the Nature-kin. She's been pleased with the people you've become. She—she's now gone, but her love for each of you could be felt. Her name was Lady Tuliah. Her final wish was that Lenova wouldn't follow the path her people or the others took. She wished for a time of peace. That—that's all."

All about him, the villagers shed tears. Their beliefs were proven true. So moved were they by Finn's words, some fell to the ground as if in prayer. Finn didn't know how to continue. Instead, he stood there, feeling strange, as if he'd intruded upon something far bigger than himself. Tuliah's name was spread about, spoken with such love and holiness, it reminded Finn of a child snuggling with their mother. Miriam grabbed Finn's hands fervently, her smooth palms holding him tight. Her face was deep with gratitude, welling with joy.

"As speaker for Pittance, you have done a great thing for us today Finn StreamCrosser. A stranger to our customs—yet you risked your life on the belief of our stories. You've verified what we couldn't." About them, the villagers were nodding. Piscus and Goblin looked stunned. Miriam continued. "We'll never forget your bravery! Your name shall be sung each year at our festival of Lith-Lamma, a part of a new tale: Finn StreamCrosser! Can you not feel it? The rejuvenation of our spirits? The energy seeping from the ground?"

The villagers cheered, hugging and dancing around each other. Again, the name *StreamCrosser* was spoken like wind carried through leaves. Finn was overwhelmed. He didn't know whether to bow in thanks or to raise his hands in the air. Of all reactions to what he'd done, he'd never expected this. Piscus and Goblin ran to him and both patted him in turn. A voice spoke out.

"Finn! Finn!"

It was a happy, higher-pitched voice full of excitement. There was a strange accent to it—a smooth chirpy sound. Finn looked about, turning his head to find who'd called for him. Suddenly, ice shot through his veins and fire wrapped his head, causing his mouth to drop open. The voice... it'd come from none-other than Goblin himself.

Goblin, his darker skin and brown short hair sparkling in the sun looked at him with the eyes of one reborn. He stood taller, as if a year older, and glowed with health. Finn remembered Tuliah's words back in the cave: *I cannot grant you the power you seek in your bracer. Fate controls that wish. I shall give you something else. Your kind nature toward your friend changes him.*

Lady Tuliah hadn't been able to grant Finn's wish, but had still given him something of value: the miracle of his friend's voice.

"Goblin! You speak!" Finn shouted, grabbing the boy by the arms.

"I-speak! I-speak!" Goblin repeated, bouncing up and down. The two ran around each other, laughing and acting like fools. Piscus clapped and danced as well.

"Finn, my friend!" Piscus chortled. "Why didn't you tell me you'd play the hero? We could have gone with you! You're a sly devil, you! Look what you've done—the impossible! Accomplished a task none have succeeded in all of time! By the Nature-kin's growth! Magic has restored Goblin's voice!"

"You-healed-me!" Goblin stated at incredible speed, his words coming out without pause. "How'd-you-do-that? Was-it-your-wish? I—I-can-talk! I've-never-been-able-to-do-that! My-throat-tickles-when-I-do-this! Cat-dog-fish-tree-bird-life-death-food-milk-bread-honey-home-flower-crystal..."

"Make him stop!" Piscus fake-moaned, holding his ears shut.

"He's no longer human, but a monster! Alas, my hearing!"

Finn laughed in wonder. It was as if he was in a dream. Who knew by one action, so much could be the result? He listened as Goblin recited every word he could think of, clapping his hands each time he pronounced one correctly. Around them, the villagers were pressing in, asking about Lady Tuliah. Miriam and the elders did what they could to form a barrier.

"Finn," Piscus said with sudden seriousness, grabbing his shoulder. "May I ask this: what *did* happen beyond the stream?"

Finn stared at the horizon, over the tops of the trees. Clouds rolled by, the greatest of explorers, eternally moving into the unknown. *With a path made long, a journey made wild...*

"Much happened, Piscus. Much." He faced the older man. "I must move on. I can't stay. I have to follow my feet, that much I know."

Piscus removed his hat and gazed into Finn's eyes. The man studied him for a while without saying anything. He smiled. "I feel history writes itself around you, Finn StreamCrosser. Lenova holds its breath when you speak. What I would give to be young and follow with you, wherever you may journey! Whatever you learned beyond the water, keep it safe and don't share it with anyone but the most trusted of companions. Don't even tell me. What you've learned is sacred. I can only advise you to follow it. Follow it closely."

Finn accepted Piscus' words. They reflected the man's kindness, understanding, and goodness. Gratitude swelled within Finn. "Thank you Piscus."

The man put his hat back on. "I take it you mean to leave today?"

"Now, if I can." Finn replied. Piscus grinned. "Then let it be so but allow me to fill your bags with food. I'm sure the villagers would kill me if I let you leave without enough supplies to feed an army. Look at them—already they adapt to the news you've brought." The villagers were gathered as one, talking with brows furrowed in concentration. Miriam left one of the conversations and approached them. "Already so much is changing." she told them, excitement entering her voice. "As we speak, many of the villagers are now planning on traveling across Lenova to spread the word. Missionaries, they say—Tulian Missionaries—after Lady Tuliah, of course." Miriam bowed to Finn. "We owe everything to you." She left them, returning to her people.

"You-make-waves-Finn." Goblin spoke, words coming out so fast it took Finn a while to process their meaning.

Piscus ordered two villagers to return to his inn and prepare bags for both Finn and Goblin. The men hurried off, each shaking Finn's hands and grinning broadly. The thought of leaving Pittance so soon saddened Finn. In the small time he'd been there, the village already seemed like home. He worried for it. With rumors of Star-Children walking the lands, how soon would one of them stumble across this peaceful place? Mulling over Star-Children, he turned to Piscus.

"Piscus, I must share with you a secret."

The man tipped his head respectfully. Finn could tell the innkeeper's curiosity was nearly overwhelming him.

"Do you remember where you found Goblin and me? The exact location?"

Piscus' face changed to confusion. He nodded. "Yes. I do. What's this about?"

Goblin stared at Finn in questioning as well. Finn knelt on the ground near a patch of dirt. With his finger, he drew a rough path from which Goblin and himself had traveled. Using lines for the trail, squiggles for the trees, and a circle for the destination, Finn traced a picture. "Follow along like this and head here." He pointed to the circle, growing solemn. "Treat the place with respect. What you find there will represent my previous life—its death-spot. I won't be upset if you bury it all. All I can ask is that you take care of it. I trust you Piscus. What I do is dangerous.

To show you this location could mean you much harm."

"What lies in the forest at that location?" Piscus asked in caution.

"A vast sum of evil wealth." Finn whispered. Goblin stiffened, now knowing exactly what Finn was talking about. Finn licked his lips and erased the map with a wave of his hand. "But what lies beneath that wealth is what truly matters. I won't tell you what it is out loud, but you'll understand when you see it. You're not a man of greed. I believe you'll care for it without using it."

Piscus' face became one of deep contemplation. He opened his mouth, then closed it. He did so again three more times. Finally, he pulled off his wide hat and scratched his head. "By grace and grass! What are you involving me in, boy? Shall I end up thanking you or cursing you once I find this mysterious *wealth*?"

Finn smiled. "Both. But you'll understand why I tell you this. I need friends whom I can trust Piscus. You happen to be one of those."

"I take it there's much importance to this?"

"Yes. No one else can know or find what lies in the forest. It's already risk enough that it's been left alone this long. When you return to the village, do so by night, when no one can see you."

Piscus studied Finn. The innkeeper recognized the seriousness of the request. He patted Finn's shoulder. "Don't worry StreamCrosser. You can trust in me 'til your dying breath. You've earned this old man's loyalty."

Finn's shoulders relaxed. Nozgull's bracer would be safe in the care of Piscus. He knew the man had enough sensibility not to wield it, nor leave it where the world could find it. Soon after, the two villagers returned with their possessions and bags brimming with food. Goblin once more recited every word he could think of, enjoying the sound of his own voice. Piscus sighed and stretched his arms. Around them, birds flew, chirping and spinning in the air currents. The villagers of Pittance danced.

In the distance, the Stream of Fate continued its confusing journey.

"Do you know where you'll be going?" Piscus asked.

"No." Finn replied. "I'll follow my feet. I'm sure they'll lead me to where I'm meant to be."

They were silent once more, hesitant about saying goodbye. They'd known each other a short while yet had taken like a nephew to an uncle. It was strange to Finn. Already in the small time he'd explored Lenova, he felt as if he'd lived a lifetime.

"May your adventure bring you much happiness young Star-Child. The people of Pittance will miss you, I'm sure." Piscus said.

Finn gave him one final nod and turned, facing the road out of the village. The villagers approached him and Goblin, saying their own goodbyes. Miriam planted a kiss on their foreheads and gave Finn a small bottle of milk; a joke to that very morning when he'd first tried the beverage.

They walked away, leaving behind laughter and music. As the trees swallowed them and he pointed himself Eastward, Finn swore he saw a brief glimpse of someone familiar in the crowd. It must have been his imagination—he knew she was gone—yet maybe, just maybe, a set of green eyes twinkled in amusement, following his footsteps.

lands of wonder and awe

19

—Circa 1,055 R.E. (Resurgence Era-The 2nd Era): The city of HighFurl shakes for three days. A strange sound can be heard below the ground and ancient words whisper out from under the rocks. Upon the fourth day, the earth beneath the city collapses and the land is swallowed up. Thousands of holes appear all over the terrain. Two-hundred years afterwards, courageous humanoids seeking to mine for treasures settle in the terraformed land and rename it Kar. —

Now that Goblin could speak, Finn was finally able to have a decent conversation with his friend. The only subject not discussed was Nozgull, as every time the name was mentioned, Goblin went quiet. As for his life, the boy wove a tale much different than Finn had expected.

Goblin had come from a vast group of traveling gypsies. His

people numbered in the thousands and traveled the plains of Lenova, living from the land, performing for money, and trading foreign goods. Goblin described his people like moving cities: swarming across plains, setting up oceans of tents overnight, and within days, leaving on whim.

Goblin, like the rest of the gypsies, was raised by their entire people. He'd only met his parents once, seeing them briefly at a tribal gathering. They'd shared a few words and moved on. Goblin was alright with it. The whole tribe were his parents—equal teachers.

His people often spread out into smaller groups, separating to various citadels so as to not compete for commerce. After a few weeks of trade, they'd all reunite. Being under the age of sixteen, Goblin hadn't been allowed to sell, but instead had been forced to stay behind in the plains with the other children and learn the various arts of the gypsies. Unlike many of the other boys, Goblin was terrible at sleight-of-hand and thievery. Instead, he became a passionate cook, learning to make meals from the simplest ingredients.

"So how did you go from a life of travel to landing at the mining outpost?" Finn asked in curiosity, jealous of his friend. The boy had done so much traveling.

Goblin's face saddened at the question and for the first time in over a day, he went quiet. With a sigh, Goblin opened up. "It's-a-hard-story-to-tell." he began.

Finn listened as Goblin explained one day being placed in a small tribe calling themselves the Whey-Weavers, a group specialized in selling seeds and plants. Loving food, he'd been happy with where he'd been assigned. Goblin told Finn of campfire nights under blanketing stars and sitting on vast plains, listening to talk of incredible trades and foreign animals.

The Whey-Weaver tribe arrived at their final city and the adults went forward to trade while the children and elderly stayed in the fields and set up tents. Two days passed and the adults didn't return. It was unusual, Goblin described, for the adults only traded in the day and came back to camp at night. The gypsies didn't have the money to rent rooms at an inn. But as the hours passed, no one came back.

Goblin's eyes glazed over. "We-waited-and-waited. Three-days-later-a-group-of-many-men-approached-our-camp. I-could-see-that-they-wore-our-clothes-but-were-not-our-people. It-was-then-that-the-elders-told-the-children-to-run. Unknown-to-us-the-town-we'd-entered-had-been-ravaged-by-a-large-group-of-bandits-the-week-before. The-adults-had-all-been-killed-and-had-all-they-possessed-stolen-from-them. Learning-that-we-were-out-upon-the-plains-the-bandits-came-for-us."

Finn clenched his hands.

Goblin went on to describe his flight across the plains with his fellow children. Behind them, the elders were slaughtered. Trailing in their wake and grabbing at their heels, the bandits followed. One by one, the children were caught, until at last only Goblin and two others remained, uncaptured by hiding in badger dens. But thirst and starvation drew them out and Goblin was seized by the evil men. The group of Whey-Weavers were no more.

Greed consumed the men and all they could think of was how to make profit from the boys. After days of marching, the children were sold to slavers. Goblin told of weeks passed inside a wooden cage side-by-side with twenty other children. He'd gotten sick with a fever and didn't remember much of the journey.

The slavers made their way to the Crust, where they sold the children to the supervisors, who had no qualms dealing with criminals. Last to go, Goblin was placed in the outpost Finn had resided in. He'd been made a cave-diver and the rest of the story, Finn knew.

Goblin assured Finn he'd made his peace over what'd happened. He patted Finn on the back. "Fate-works-in-strange-ways. Without-those-events-I-would-have-never-met-you. I-never-would've-faced-a-vat-worm-and-lived. I-never-would've-seen-the-power-of-a-Star-Child-and-lived. I-owe-a-lot-to-you! Even-my-voice!"

Finn snorted. "You owe me nothing. Without you, I wouldn't have had the motivation to leave the Slaglands. My body would still be out there, eaten by sand and sun."

Time passed and they walked on, telling more stories of their lives and deepening their friendship. The forest grew scarce and transitioned to grassy slopes and meals from Pittance were shared under clear skies. It was a peaceful few days of travel.

They traversed farms and passed houses, sharing the dirt path with worn crop-growers and men who lived off the land. They finally came upon their first large city: a stone-walled farmer's-market of a place called Wyrmroost, full of callous-handed workers and strong-jawed vendors.

Finn and Goblin used a small amethyst from Nozgull's pouch to replenish their food supplies. On their travels, the food from Pittance had all but gone, leaving but two dried apples. On a cobbled street they broke bread with a beggar, feeling sorry for his weakened state. In thanks, the beggar told them of rumors he'd heard.

"The king and House Royal do us no good." the man croaked. "He's up far above the rest of us on those massive floatin' islands of Lyria. He don't care much for us ground-walkers here so far below 'im. They say he keeps his armies and men on those islands, guarding his palace and all those other rich nobles and their Houses. Only his Paladins are sent to the grounds below."

"Paladins?" Finn asked.

The withered man nodded. "Yes, Paladins! Star-Child hunters!"

Finn's heart jumped. "You know of Star-Children?"

The beggar cackled. "Finn SunRider, right? Everyone knows of the Star-Children! They wander the lands and take over citadels with their magical powers. Some say a few of them can kill with a wave of their hands! Can you believe that? But others say good'uns walk about as well, protecting the people. They gather somewhere, but I don't know if much o' that's true."

Finn stuttered over his words. "And of the Paladins? Why did you call them hunters?"

The beggar sniffed. "The king—he's so desperate to gain a bracer for himself. Ooh he was angry when they fell from the sky, choosing common men. It was a downright insult to 'im when he wasn't picked. So desperate is he to gain one, he sends out Paladins to capture a Star-Child and take their bracer by force! He's tried to bribe other Houses with vast treasures for a bracer. Everyone knows that at least a couple of houses 'ave captured a Star-Child or 'ave one working for them as their champion. It's all hush-hush but I'm certain House Glover and House Phure have Star-Children working for them now. Paid in the dark to do their slimy bidding."

"But the bracers can't be stolen by force," Finn stated, speaking without thought, "they can't be removed!" He froze and bit his tongue, chiding himself. The beggar gave him a funny look and went to stare at Finn's arm. Finn hid his hands inside his food bag, pretending to rummage for a tart.

"You know much about them Star-Children for one who claims he doesn't!"

Goblin gave the man a slice of bread and the beggar's suspicion dissipated.

The beggar nodded. "The king knows they're hard to remove. He has his Paladins carry scissor-like weapons. Arm-Bitters they call 'em. Slip through skin and bone all surgical-like. King will have his way no matter what, I guess."

Finn shivered. "Has he killed a Star-Child yet?"

The beggar laughed out loud. "I doubt it! Based on what I've heard, Paladin bodies dot the land like rocks in a field! I bet it's drivin' our generous king mad! Hope it rots in his bones, I do! Serves 'im right for not caring for us humble folk. His late father was much better. Too bad he drowned in some swamp."

Finn and Goblin thanked him and stood in preparation to leave. The beggar stopped them.

"Last warning for you good men: careful out there if you mean to continue your journey! They say something dark moves from the South. Many cities have disappeared or grown silent. All trade has stopped in that direction. Rumor spreads of a Star-Child with an army, killing and destroying. Others say it's a demon horde, finally arising to finish off this wretched land."

The beggar's words made Finn hesitate. There were powers out there far beyond what he'd seen. By the stories alone, they sounded far worse than Nozgull. He tried to imagine someone more evil than the EarthBreaker and it made him shiver.

As they walked away, Finn forgot to cover his bracer-donned arm under his cloak. The beggar spotted it, his yellowed eyes growing wide and his mouth hanging open. Not knowing how to respond, Finn pulled free a gem from his pouch and tossed it to the man. "We aren't all evil." he told the beggar.

The beggar caught the treasure, gripping it tight enough that the veins on his hands bulged out. There was a strange gleam of both wonder and respect in his eyes. The man bowed, "*SunRider*." and ran down the street.

"Come-on. Nothing-good-can-come-from-that." Goblin stated.

Finn nodded and they hurried out of town, crossing a plaza and losing themselves between the many trading carts and crowds of traveling people. Soon, they'd left Wyrmroost far behind, still moving East, deeper into the heart of Lenova.

On their travels, Goblin mentioned something to Finn that made him startle. "I've-been-having-these-dreams-at-night."

"What about?" Finn asked, turning to his friend and adjusting his travel bag.

"It-doesn't-happen-all-the-time-but-once-in-a-while-I-see-this-woman."

Finn laughed. "Oh, so it's one of *those* dreams."

Goblin's face flushed. "No! There's-this-old-woman-that-stays-in-the-background... guiding-me." Finn thought of Lady Tuliah. "She-smiles-and-whispers-to-me-yet-I-can'-tell-what-she's-saying. I-feel-comforted-though. Strange-isn't-it?"

"What color are her eyes?" Finn asked.

"I-don't-know. I-can-never-see-her-clearly. That's-a-strange-question-to-ask."

Finn waved a hand dismissively, ending the conversation. It could be Tuliah, watching from some distant plane of existence, or it could be wild food-induced dreams. If it was Tuliah, why would she visit his friend and not him? Had he not a special connection with her?

Their exploration of the land continued and one night, Finn took the time to scratch out Tuliah's words on a stretch of parchment he'd once used to annotate ore veins in the mines. Using a piece of charcoal, he recorded the entire prophecy. During the process, Goblin finally asked him what'd happened beyond the stream. Knowing if he couldn't trust his friend, he couldn't trust anybody, Finn told him of the secret underground chamber, the lava canal, and the Bird's Window. Goblin listened, mesmerized by the story. Afterwards, Finn read the prophecy and the two had fun trying to guess its meaning.

"Here she says, Evil seeks to change all we hold dear/Will one save us, protect us, take away our fear? What do you think she means by evil?" Finn contemplated, "Do you reckon she meant the Star-Children?"

"What-if-she's-talking-about-the-king?" Goblin asked. "He-hasn't-exactly-been-caring-for-Lenova." He nudged Finn's shoulder. "Remember-what-she-said-though-none-of-this-could-even-matter-or-be-correct."

Finn snorted. "But then why tell it to me in the first place?"

Goblin sighed. "Does-it-look-like-I'm-an-all-knowing-seer? To-me-it-seems-more-like-a-warning-of-the-potential. It-could-still-be-useful."

Finn shrugged in agreement. "Well what about a curse? It talks about that too."

"No-idea-what-that-could-be." Goblin shrugged. "I'm-more-focused-on-the-fact-that-you-danced-with-an-ancient-entity. Was-it-love-at-first-sight? What-drew-you-in? The-wrinkles-or-the-white-hair?"

Finn put away the parchment and rolled his eyes while Goblin roared in laughter at his own joke. "Funny. Go to bed." He lay on his sleeping mat and stared at the sky. "Maybe I'll pray for Tuliah to remove your voice." he whispered under his breath. "That'll teach you."

"What's-that?" Goblin asked, yawning.

"Nothing." Finn responded.

The following day, they stepped back out onto the highway from the hidden grove they'd slept in. Even though it was early in the morning, people already walked the road carrying belonging or pulling carts. Finn and Goblin joined the crowd, allowing traffic to guide them. They were passed by rich nobles sporting various house emblems and riding white steeds. Their many belongings trailed behind them in wagons pulled by teams of oxen. Soon they came to a wooden signpost stating they were approaching Kazma, a city Finn had never heard of. As well as citizens, many trading caravans passed them, some heading the other way to the rest of Lenova. Finn asked a stranger why the crowds were so large. The woman explained that Kazma was one of the larger trading centers of Lenova; in fact, it was the capital of business. Many rich company owners and merchants lived there. She told Finn the city's layout was—literally—*magical.* Feeling curiosity and excitement grow within himself, Finn picked up his pace, nearly dragging Goblin along.

As they walked, they continued to hear rumors of Star-Children and dark forces brewing in the South. Yet mixed with the foreboding words were songs and lute-music. A passing entertainer sang a tune about a horse with no legs to the great amusement of a group of children. There was so much culture and so much to experience. Finn was more alive than he'd ever been.

They topped a steep hill and beheld an incredible sight. Ahead of them was the citadel of Kazma. But Finn couldn't even begin to comprehend what he was seeing. At first he mistook it for a mirage, but after rubbing his eyes, deemed it real. The citadel was in fact, *two* circular cities; one just happened to float hundreds of meters above the other. Finn imagined a plate hovering above another plate and it was the only description that came close. Goblin grabbed at his arm, gasping.

The ground-planted city had a massive gray wall, thick as a house, running in a circle around the condensed space. Casting a massive shadow about the land, the second city—floating above the other—was made of a yellow rock carved with arches and large runes. Finn speculated that perhaps the runes were what kept the city up, but none of it was explained it to him. *True magic.* Never had he conceived such power could exist in Lenova. How did people live their lives within such a place? How could they ever think it as a normal existence?

Drawing near to the phenomenal location, Finn could better contrast the two halves. It was easy to see the floating city was a richer, cleaner, and a better-put place compared to the ground. The bottom city resembled more of a stone fort, full to the brim with compacted buildings and claustrophobically stacked homes, forming man-made canyons. There was a strong distinction of class and wealth. Those rich lived high in the sky, while the poor and common lived on the ground.

How would it be like to wake every morning and look outside, seeing that even the bottom of the floating city was cleaner and nicer than where you lived? How could one even reach the floating half? He couldn't see any form of stairs leading upward. As if in answer, when he was but a kilometer away, Finn spotted a cylindrical tower rising from the center of Kazma, connecting the two halves. It was like the axle between two sideways wagon-wheels.

As they approached the massive gates to the ground city, Goblin and Finn were compressed shoulder-to-shoulder within the thick crowd. Above their heads and hanging over the archway, flags with the silhouette of a black water-scorpion and the motto *To Cherish our Keep* fluttered in the breeze. Overworked soldiers carrying silver spears attempted to control the flow of commerce, but due to the volume of people moving about, Finn and Goblin made it inside without being harassed by the armed men.

Immediately, their senses were assailed by shouts and loud talk, voices overlapping each other in waves that made their ears ring. They were pushed and shoved as citizens of Kazma went about their daily lives. The rich, with lifted chins, were escorted by walls of dim-eyed guards heading toward the connecting tower. It seemed as if they were trying to spend the least amount of time on the ground as possible.

A green-skinned man riding a large dog moved by and a flock of saddled red birds locked behind stable doors fluttered in a panic. A mousy girl set a round table in the middle of the street and offered palm readings. The smell of meat and sweat was strong, and food vendors preyed on people's hunger, dangling seasoned chicken legs in front of faces. A group of young boys laughed far above and jumped the gap between buildings, their feet treading on air over the crowd. A baby cried and three minstrels were booed off a crate. Finn gripped his satchel of gems tightly, worried for pickpockets. Five stories up, a woman leaned out of a window and dumped a bucket of dirty water down a sloped roof. The water trickled all the way to the ground where a gathering of street cats and mangy dogs lapped it up.

Goblin froze, reached out, and grabbed Finn's arm. He looked to have all his muscles clenched at the same time. Finn followed his gaze and went still himself. Panic fluttered in his stomach and he fought the urge to run. It was like a cold finger was running down his back.

Directly in front of them were rows of market stalls. Other stalls were stacked above, with wooden catwalks running between, crisscrossing and overlapping. If one stared straight up, it was like looking at a cobweb of bridges, pathways, and hanging clothes. Goods and artifacts tempted shoppers, bringing profit to the sellers. Glowing pendants passed hands and feeble boneless mice wobbled in small glass bottles. Everything one could think of was being sold: armor and spices, weapons and pets; even plants.

Shopping at a second-floor stall, ahead and above, were a boy and a girl. The girl had a lithe frame, leaf-brown hair braided into a ponytail, and close-fitted leather clothing. Finn thought her beautiful. The boy, maybe in his early twenties, had long blond hair flowing free to his waist. He held a jovial grin: a troublemaker's look. But what stuck out the most was what rested on their arms. Both were wearing Star-Children bracers.

moths and honey

20

—Circa 5,612 E.E. (Economic Era-The 17th Era): A young girl by the name of Sia is taken to the Crust to work in the Hub. She meets Finn SunRider but for a brief moment, saving him from a severe beating against a supervisor. He thanks her as he wipes the blood from his face and they are never given the opportunity to speak again. Sia watches SunRider from afar, in love with the boy. Months later, Sia is pushed out of a high window by her master for dropping his drink. Her body would have lain on the desert ground for days if not for SunRider, who risked his life to sneak away from his cave-diving shift to bury her. Wild flowers now grow on her grave, the only green vegetation as far as the eye can see. —

Finn crouched in the middle of the street. He forced Goblin down as well, causing passing citizens to give them strange looks. They moved to a nearby vending stall where a man with an impressive mustache and a heavy brow claimed his many collections of moths were, in fact, tiny monsters. They wove through the crowd gathering around the vendor and hid behind a stack of crates. Finn and Goblin peeked over the boxes and watched the Star-Children—they were young.

For some reason, Finn had imagined all Star-Children—apart from himself—as grizzled adults with poor hygiene. Sitting on a crate inside a jar beside Finn's head, a moth fluttered in agitation, as if annoyed Finn was hiding beside it.

"It's true! They're smarter than you think!" the vendor was saying, his mustache bobbing up and down. He pulled out a glass bottle holding a fat wide bug with purple wings. "The matriarch moth controls 'em, telling the rest what to do! They took the lives of four of my men before I was able to capture 'em and plead a bargain with the lot! They like honey, you see. So I goes and tells the matriarch moth, *listen here, if you let me keep you around, I'll feed you honey and let you rest fat and content the rest of yours lives!*"

"You talking to bugs now, Quinta? You've gone daft, you have." someone yelled.

The two Star-Children were now bargaining with a trader for a crossbow. The girl was pulling out coins while the boy paced around the second-floor catwalk, looking annoyed and bored. Unlike Nozgull, they weren't flashing their powers and killing everyone. Neither were they acting rude or...evil. The people about them seemed to notice the bracers, yet only gave them space. They didn't run or scream. Why were these two different? Could perhaps Finn have been wrong? Were the metal bands they wore not Star-Children bracers? No, Finn was sure they were. He had stared and fiddled with his own bracer enough times to know what one looked like. Near his head, a moth buzzed angrily, as if telling him off. They were unusual creatures. Instead of gray or brown, they had bright blue fur enveloping their bodies, giving them a puffy appearance.

"Now these babies aren't your typical pet." the vendor kept talking, "They'll live for dozens of years and even bring you good luck! Ah bet if one'o you were to buy a moth from humble ol' me, you'd find coins on the road, your ol' lady will be healed from 'er bunions, and you might even keep your teeth 'til you're fifty!"

"Too bad you didn't find them sooner Quinta! Maybe you'da kept some of your own teeth!"

A couple of people in the crowd laughed, coming closer. Others, those with more sense, rolled their eyes and walked away. Someone bumped the crates where Finn and Goblin hid and a jar smacked Finn on the nose. The moth inside hummed even louder, the noise now sounding more like high-pitched swearing. Above them, between the many stacks and stories of vending stalls reaching high into the air, the two Star-Children were finishing their purchase.

"Ey! Don't crowd about too much!" the vendor Quinta said nervously. "Matriarch here don't like being hassled!"

"You say they're smart? You say they're monsters? Looks to me like they're hairy moths painted blue!" someone yelled.

Many few citizens looked to the stall and Finn pushed himself farther back into the shadows, trying to hide. "Shut up!" he hissed to the blue moth near his face. The moth froze and drew close to the jar wall, as if peering at him. It shook, as if angry.

"Stop buggin' us!" Vendor Quinta was yelling. "If you're not here to buy, get out! You're all makin' her angry!" The man patted his bottle. Inside, the wide purple moth was moving in circles. "Don't listen to 'em matriarch! They're fools!"

"You're the fool Quinta! Let me see that bottle!"

"No, you can't!"

Near Finn's head, the blue moth was smashing itself at the jar, as if trying to get to Finn. Goblin was grabbing onto his shirt and pointing to the Star-Children. The boy and girl were walking away with the crossbow they'd bought. They stopped, staring curiously at the commotion coming from Quinta's vending stall.

Blast it! Why had they chosen the worst place to hide in all of Kazma? Finn gritted his teeth, trying to cover his bracer. So far, the Star-Children hadn't noticed him.

There was a crash from the front of the stall. Finn glance over. Quinta was yelling at a fat man with a blacksmith's apron while on the ground between them, the glass bottle lay smashed open. The wide purple moth was fluttering around their heads.

"Now you done it! Now you made 'er mad! We're all doomed I tell ya! I need honey! Anyone 'ave any honey?"

The crowd was laughing at the poor vendor as he scrambled about. The purple moth suddenly dove for the blacksmith.

"Hey! What's wrong with your bug? Leave me alone!"

The moth dove for the man again, a strange bell-like sound coming from it. All around the stall, the many hundreds of jars containing bright blue moths shook. Quinta stopped, a look of horror coming over his face. Scores of people were now watching him.

"M—matriarch, what're ya doin'? C—calm down and I'll get you some honey. What's that? No! He's not a jerk! He doesn't—no, don't attack 'im!"

The purple moth dove, hitting the blacksmith on the face. Quinta tried to catch the moth, but it slipped between his fingers. The blacksmith sneezed and grabbed at his nose, which started swelling.

"Wad you dud to mhe? De moth makin' mah node shwell! Wad you dud?"

Another bell-like ring came from the moth and Quinta dove for the ground, trying to shout a warning. With an explosive shatter, all the jars ruptured and hundreds of blue moths flew free. They swarmed the place, spinning in a furious cloud. Every time they brushed against someone, they left behind welts that swelled to ridiculous proportions. The jar beside Finn's head burst and the angry blue moth dove at him. Finn ducked and rolled away from the crates. Out of the corner of his eye, he saw the two Star-Children spot him. Even worse, his bracer was exposed.

"We chose the wrong stall!" Finn groaned, untangling his cloak from around his neck. Around him, people were screaming as blue moths led by their matriarch dove and attacked the crowd. Goblin moved to help but the angry blue moth which had tried attacking Finn hit the young man on the ear. Goblin howled, pawing at his face.

"It-got-at-me! It-got-at-me!"

Already his ear was swelling to thrice its size.

"Get honey! Get some honey!" Quinta was screaming, trying to cover his own head. "Matriarch, this wasn't part of the deal!"

Finn had to throw himself backward into a stall full of felt hats as the vengeful blue moth came at him again. People were running about, ducking and dodging as swarms of moths fluttered against their exposed skin. The blacksmith was wailing and hiding under a cart, half his face looking like the world's biggest pumpkin. Quinta shot past, yelping and holding his butt.

"How'd you get in mah trousers? No way! No way!"

The poor vendor's rear was now large enough to stretch out his brown pants to their limit. If there happened to be a moth in there, it was surely squished. Finn didn't know whom to be sorry for. Quinta tripped into a horse's trough and splashed foamy water everywhere, soaking his mustache.

The tightly packed market turned into a scene of chaos. With only small alleys and stacked layers of catwalks to maneuver through, the citizens of Kazma were finding out the hard way how difficult it was to escape an angry swarm of moths. Stalls were overturned, crates and barrels were tipper, food and goods flew as men and women yelled and fell over. Trapping his attacker with a hat, Finn allowed a quick glance to the second-floor catwalk. The Star-Children were gone. He looked about in a frenzy, spotting them marching down a set of stairs his way, disregarding the moths. They had serious looks to their faces. He couldn't fight two Star-Children at once. He jumped away from the hat stall, grabbing Goblin's arm.

"Come on! We have to run!" he screamed.

Goblin nodded, his right ear sagging and flopping like a sheet of parchment. The two of them dodged through crowds of flailing citizens, ducking and weaving as moths buzzed about. Quinta was nowhere to be seen and the market was being commandeered by the bugs as everyone vacated. They smashed through a pile of hay and ran past a whimpering vendor with fingers swollen to the size of sausages. Cutting to the right, they turned down an abandoned alley barely wide enough for one set of shoulders. Grunting, they squeezed their way forward past stacked brick buildings and piles of garbage, feet stomping over centuries of mush. An alley cat yowled and shot between their legs, disturbed from his nap. Finn watched it run toward the market area, get hit by a moth, and immediately spin in place with its tail fat and swollen. It shot past them again, dashing the other way. But catching Finn's eye, more movement entered the alley. It was the two Star-Children. They were giving chase.

Led by the girl, the two moved forward, eyes narrowed. Finn shoved Goblin ahead and tipped over a box to block the passage. They burst out into yet another alley; one running perpendicular to them. Reaching the opposite end, they found no means to continue. Finn and Goblin smashed their hands against the wall and turned, facing the approaching forms. The girl stopped, folding her arms. Her face was serious and ready for anything. The long-haired boy stepped beside her, flicking his blond locks and bringing up his crossbow.

Finn didn't know what to say. How were he and Goblin to die? Would they be tossed in the air? Smashed by an invisible force? Would one of the Star-Children freeze them in place?

"Nice bracer." the boy commented. His voice was confident and full of mirth, as if he'd cracked the greatest joke ever. The girl didn't speak at all.

"I—I like yours also." Finn replied, sweat running down his palms. Goblin, holding his floppy ear, shook in place. Finn was sure his friend was remembering his terrible week spent as Nozgull's prisoner.

"So, what now?" Finn asked.

The boy shrugged. "That depends on you. Are you gonna run—or fight?"

Before Finn could reply, the alley cat with the swollen tail dropped from a catwalk above, landing on the boy. With a yelp, the boy let go of his crossbow and tried to pry the cat free. Instinct took over and Finn darted forward, diving for the weapon. He slid on his belly, grabbed the bow, and aimed it at the girl. She didn't bat an eye.

The boy tossed the cat away and wiped at the scratches on his face. He was irate and bedraggled. "Well great, my looks are ruined! If I find that cat, I swear I'm gonna make it eat its own insides!" He didn't seem to care that Finn held his weapon. Instead, he turned to the girl. "I'm still handsome, right? I still look attractive?"

The girl, even more beautiful up close, gave him a dry look. "Shut up, Altin."

The boy faked injury and grabbed at his heart. "You kill me Leeya! I need your approval!" She ignored him and instead pointed to Finn's arm. "When were you chosen?"

Finn bit his cheek and his finger nearly squeezed the trigger. Would the bolt hurt her? Would she dodge it?

"I wasn't chosen. I found it."

"Ha! Found it?" the boy—Altin—spit. "You were walking the street and *stumbled* across it? Hey Leeya, remember when we *tripped* over our bracers while grabbing a bite to eat? How *convenient*."

"I really did." Finn mumbled. "It's a long story."

"Leave him be Altin." the girl sighed. "He's not a bad one." She turned and faced Finn. Her face was perfect. And her eyes... they were strong—full of courage. "What's your name?"

"Finn." he stated, lost in the girl's gaze. "What do you mean I'm not a bad one?"

The girl—Leeya—pointed to Goblin. "You walk with equals, not subordinates. You haven't killed anyone, nor attacked us."

The boy snorted. "Bet he doesn't even know his own ability."

The insult hit close, making Finn's hands clench tight around the crossbow. The boy was right; he couldn't even activate his bracer. Heck, he wasn't even officially a Star-Child. He pointed the weapon at Altin. "What are *your* powers?" he asked.

"Oh, he's got some fight, thank goodness for that!" the boy teased. There was a metallic *snick* and before Finn knew it, Altin's bracer activated, separating into four segments. They slid along his skin and wrapped around both ankles and wrists. The movement was smooth—the boy was experienced. The bands were plain metal, a carved feather on each one. Before Finn could fire the bolt, Altin was in the sky, soaring twenty feet above him. He was a bird taking flight, flipping backwards with ease. The trigger was pressed and the crossbow hissed to life. The bolt bit through the air where Altin once stood. Twisting in a loop, Altin curved around them and dove behind Finn, tackling him. Finn went down hard, dropping the weapon and losing his breath. His arms were pinned behind his back.

"Run Goblin! They'll kill you!" Finn shouted.

His head was smacked. "We're not going to kill you, stupid. You're not even worth our time."

Altin stood, allowing Finn to get to his feet and spin to face the Star-Child. He raised his fists. "What did you do? How did you do that?"

Altin laughed. His teeth were straight and white. "It's my power. When it's hot I can fly, when it's cold the suit grows dense. Bet you're scared senseless now, huh? Haven't met anyone like me, have you?"

The girl pushed Altin away with a sigh. She motioned a finger toward Goblin, who was half-in and half-out of the alley, his eyes panicked. "Come here boy, we won't hurt you. Altin," she stated, looking to her companion, "you're only an Accessory. Don't go boasting your power when you couldn't even face a Half-suit."

"Half-suit? Accessory?" Finn asked.

"You're fresh Chosen, aren't you?" Altin remarked, walking over to pick up his crossbow.

"I told you," Finn said in annoyance, "I found the bracer."

"Accessories and Half-suits are terms used by the Star-Children as names for how strong we are." Leeya explained. "The more a bracer wraps around you—the more there is of it on you—the more powerful you are. Accessories like Altin only have small segments of their body covered by their bracer. They're the most common. Half-suits are rarer and more dangerous. But the deadliest are Full-suits. I don't know how many of those there are—not many, maybe one or two. No one's encountered one and lived."

"They're practically legend." Altin added. "I doubt they even exist."

"W—what are you?" Finn asked Leeya.

"She's an Exception." Altin interrupted, wiping dust from his weapon. "A unique case."

"What do you mean by that?"

Altin scoffed. "Exceptions—very rare. Only seen her power once. I tried to boast about it and she punched me so hard in the face I awoke hours later. If you wanna talk about her power, don't do it with me."

Finn's head spun. Accessories, Half-suits, Full-suits, and Exceptions. So many terms. So much he didn't know yet. "You won't hurt me or my friend?" he muttered.

"We're not one of those wild Star-Children wandering around killing and taking over places." Altin scoffed. "What, you think Kazma would let us in here without a fight if we did something like that?"

"I apologize." Finn bowed his head. "The only other Star-Child we've met was one of those wild ones. He destroyed our home and killed everyone."

Altin's eyebrows went up. "Had a little Star-Child battle, did you? How'd you beat him? Was he able to use his bracer? Bet you stabbed him while he was drunk."

Again, Finn grew angry at the cocky older boy. What did he know about what Finn had been through?

"He must have been a Half-suit. Killed a thousand men right in front of my eyes. I ran away but came back later and... well he died."

Altin laughed but Leeya kept a straight face. She watched him as if she was studying a book.

"He just... died?" Altin chuckled. "Gosh, what a power you have there, mister Star-Child! Will you be so kind as to show it to us?"

Finn bit his lip, ignoring the jibe. The girl came forward and Finn stepped back. She was by far more intimidating than her partner. If he were to battle Altin, he would hold his own for a while—but this girl... there was something about her that emanated fierceness. She could fight.

"Come," she said, "bring your friend also. We have much to converse about. Perhaps you'll join us for lunch?"

The beautiful girl stood so close to him, he could smell her hair. It was the strong scent of cinnamon and another spice... something sweet. Was he being invited to talk with two Star-Children? He felt something strange in his gut: a sense of destiny he hadn't felt since talking to Lady Tuliah. Here he was, facing two powerful humans who weren't about to kill him. He hoped it stayed that way.

Far above them on a catwalk, Quinta rolled a large barrel of honey. The man popped the lid and grabbed at his swollen rear, stepping back as swarms of moths dove down and feasted, finally leaving the citizens alone.

class distinctions

21

—Within Castle Allÿn lies a secret hall of past Kings, where their likeness is carved from a special soft marble and set within niches against the walls. Kings who lived through times of war hold the very-real weapon that they once took to various battles: the GoreBirther, Izmianduur, the Deliverance, and so on. Rumor abounds that there is another hall for the kings too infamous and unworthy to stand next to their ancestors. King Tipidus the Second has sworn to those closest to him that on stormy nights, pale forms fade in and out of existence within the two dark passages. —

Receiving a tour by two Star-Children was a strange phenomenon. Finn felt he should be fighting, running, shouting; yet they walked like four relaxed companions. Although intimidating at first, Altin and Leeya were innocent—Finn couldn't sense any foul intentions within them.

SUNRIDER

Like Finn, Altin was new to Kazma as well, having merely arrived five days before. Leeya, who'd been born and raised in the Upper-District, the local name for the floating city above them, pointed out places of interest and led them about. As they passed a half-cobbled street, Finn overhead a drunkard yell out, "The Upper and Lower Districts are the head and the ass. You guess which one yer standin' in!" Finn, Goblin, and Altin all laughed, although Leeya stayed solemn.

The city was under the loose control of House Crookshanks, whose House Lord lived far away in another land. Either by laziness or lack of care, he saw fit for local smaller noble families without legalized houses to run the city and maintain it. The fact Leeya was a part of a 'noble' family by Kazman definition was made more interesting as she seemed to be the only member of the Upper District who was content with being on the ground, rubbing shoulders with 'commoners'. It could have been Finn's imagination, but Leeya seemed to despise the haughty attitude her fellow classmen displayed.

Lucky for Goblin, Leeya knew a practitioner who had a quick-cure for swelling. She took them to a small white shack where a line of weary moth-stung citizens already waited. When it was their turn, a calloused woman rubbed thick ointment onto Goblin's ear and bandaged it, telling him by late evening, it would be healed. As they left the shack, the line of victims had doubled and despite having been told to leave it alone, Goblin pawed at his bandages like a cat with its head stuck in a shirt.

Kazma was by all definition, Lenova's hub of business. Everywhere Finn looked, documents and contracts were being signed, properties were bought or sold, and companies were created or shut down—either legally or by force. Prolific men and women with silk robes and jewels on their fingers sat and talked, discussing stratagems and industry. Threats and arguments broke out, all in level tones and with half-lidded eyes. Like too many predators stuffed into a small space, businessmen paced around each other, as if sniffing out for weakness. Those who could be taken advantage of—were.

There was a distinct difference in attitude between the local workers who lived in the Lower-District versus the rich business owners of the Upper-District. While the simple humble folk laughed, yelled in anger, or complained in frustration, the upper-class showed little-to-no emotion at all. In fact, many had mastered a stone-faced look so well, they were unreadable. Leeya was a daughter of two business owners who'd decided it would be beneficial to partner up both as companies and in a relationship. She held the stoniest face of all. Finn was certain a man on fire could run around a corner screaming and Leeya wouldn't even bat an eye. It made her both intimidating and mysterious.

"So, is there love between couples in Kazma?" Finn asked. "I mean, if relationships are only forged because they help two companies grow..."

"Is marriage not a business deal?" Leeya responded. "For example, if you and I were to marry, would that not be the conjoining of our ideas, our abilities, and our potential growth?"

"Uh..." was Finn's reply, no longer focusing on the question he'd asked but instead turning away to hide his red face. Goblin passed by and poked Finn's side with a wink, whispering, "Looks-like-you-want-to-start-your-own-business-right-now."

They squeezed and wove through narrow spaces between buildings. Each time Finn looked up, vertigo hit him. Houses and shops were stacked upon each other, sometimes lining up, other times overlapping and forming tunnels. They leaned over him, appearing as if about to tip over. Finn imagined some giant child playing with blocks, and without care, building his own chaotic city.

Adding to the claustrophobia was how packed the Lower District was. Thousands of voices intermixed and became a single hum. Foot-traffic clogged every path and alley. Finn finally understood the purpose for the thousands of catwalks crisscrossing above him. He knew without Leeya they would have been lost within seconds. They climbed a set of stairs, walked through a stone tunnel to a tower, and reappeared out in the open, four stories higher. Even at that height, buildings towered about them. Finn counted at least nine layers of catwalks above him.

Deeper in the city, luminescent crystal lampposts were spaced between every five stores—Finn found that Kazma measured distance by shops instead of meters. Three stores left and five stalls up was a horse stable, while six shacks below and one shop to the right was an accounting firm.

The Upper-District was smaller in circumference than the Lower-District. Hanging far above them, it cast a circular shadow across the dense heart of Kazma, leaving only its edges bathed in sunlight. The torches and crystal light-posts stayed lit day and night, a permanent blue and orange glow across the expanse.

"How-do-people-live-in-these-conditions?" Goblin asked out. "Condensed-and-poor-and-with-no-light?"

Leeya shrugged. "Such is the way of the world. They do what they can to survive."

Altin gave Goblin a strange look and Finn was sure the golden-haired Star-Child was wondering why Goblin spoke in such a funny way.

The deeper they traveled, the closer they got to the central tower connecting the two districts. The structure was huge, possibly the thickness of an entire city block. Finn frowned, a question coming to mind. "Leeya, how does Kazma work? How does the Upper-District float above us? Surely that singular tower can't support it all by itself?"

"No, it cannot." Leeya concurred. "The Neck only houses elevators. Did you perhaps notice the many runes carved into the outside walls of the Upper-District as you approached the city?"

"The huge symbols each the size of ten houses?"

"Yes. There's a magic flowing through them, keeping the Upper-District floating. They're powered by the DozDum Organ, three hollow pipes running at angles down the center of the Neck. Buried in the ground far below the Lower-District—the Ass, as so eloquently put—" Goblin snorted and Altin let out a giggle. "lays an ancient power source. That power source vibrates the DozDum Organ, which sends out a signal bringing energy to the runes. We don't know how such feats exist. Kazma's an ancient place and has been around far longer than us. After we eat, we'll go through the Neck to my family home. You'll see the DozDum Organ then."

Altin scoffed. "History, architecture—how dull!"

Leeya looked over her shoulder at her loudmouthed companion. "It's boring to you because you're ignorant." Finn turned his laugh into a hacking cough, doing his best to keep a sincere face. Altin was in a sour mood for the rest of the tour.

At last, they arrived at a small restaurant. It was wedged like a knob on the center of a stick, jutting halfway out from a leaning tower of colorful brick stores. They were given a balcony table with an incredible view toward the center of Kazma. In his wooden seat, Finn put his bracer-donned hand on the brick ledge, feeling a small breeze hit his face. They were up far enough that they were able to escape the sticky heat of the cramped bottom levels.

The sun lowered in the sky and its bottom peeked beneath the Upper-District. The entirety of the Lower-District was bathed in a warm light that wormed between alleys, throwing a vibrant orange glow across skin and stone. The view was more stunning than Finn could have imagined. Kazma lay sprawled before him, its central tower—the Neck—only a kilometer away. White birds flapped lazily far above and to the distance, cawing out a merry tune. It must have been one of the two times in the day where the lower citizens of Kazma were privy to the sun: once during early morning and once in the evening. Able to see in detail the conglomeration of homes and alleys, Finn couldn't help but sigh in contentment. The simple dream of exploring Lenova felt so real now that he could witness such incredible wonders. The large city was a vast contrast to the simplicity of Pittance. It was an even larger contrast to the Crust, where there was little life, and what there was moved in sluggish anguish.

A waitress with scaled skin and almond-shaped eyes approached and Leeya ordered four Bantu flowers. Finn had no idea what the dishes were, but wanting to further his experience in Kazma, was willing to try whatever food was placed in front of him. Knowing Goblin's hunger, he was sure the boy would have been fine regardless of whether Leeya had ordered a goat's head or soft bread. Altin though, complained.

"Flowers? We're going to eat flowers? Let me guess, to drink we'll have some river water? Maybe for desert we can munch on some tree bark?"

"Why-are-you-so-negative?" Goblin asked him. "You-should-be-thanking-Leeya. She's-paying-for-your-meal."

Altin turned his sour look to the younger boy. "Why am I so negative? More like why are you so weird? Can't you speak properly?"

"Well-before-I-couldn't-speak-at-all-so-it's-an-improvement."

Leeya nodded her head. "You must both share the stories of your travels. I am much curious."

"If-you-share-yours-as-well." Goblin replied.

Leeya agreed. Before any of them could begin, the waitress returned with four plates. Upon them were massive steaming flowers, their large purple and green pedals splayed open. Examining the dish, Finn looked to the center of his flower. In the middle, where the filaments or seeds should be, was a cupped puddle of dark brown liquid. In puzzlement, he watched as Leeya tore a piece of pedal from her flower and dipped it into the liquid. She put it to her mouth, chewing without any sign indicating whether it was tasty or bad. Truly, trying to read her expressions was an impossible task. Finn was not the only one who watched her. Both Goblin and Altin studied her as well, trying to determine how to eat the dish. Finn copied Leeya and tore a piece of his Bantu flower. He dipped the strange-colored pedal into the sauce and put the whole thing into his mouth, chewing down. His eyes widened as the taste of smoked meat hit his tongue. It was as if he was chewing on a well-seasoned lamb's chop, a dish he'd only sampled from a drunk supervisor's plate back in the Crust. Finally seeing a reaction to the food, both Goblin and Altin dove into their flowers as well. A server came by with a pitcher of water and everyone but Finn accepted a drink. He had little thirst.

Unlike Goblin, who swallowed his meal faster than a vat-worm ate dirt, Leeya was a meticulous eater. She carefully tore small sections of pedal, folded them in half, and dipped into the sauce which gave the meal such a smoky flavor. Trying not to look like a choking pig at his last meal, Finn attempted to copy her. It was a difficult task. His stomach howled for him to crunch the entire dish into a ball and stuff it whole down his gullet, which comically enough, was what Altin was doing himself. No longer was the Star-Child complaining about flowers, instead he was insistent not one single morsel escaped him.

"I was chosen nearly three months ago." Leeya began, pausing the meal and wiping her lips with a cloth. "Strolling at night in the Upper-District, I was coming home late from my father's employment. I remember the stars shone bright. The bracer landed in front of me, as if the heavens themselves were granting me a gift. I couldn't be one to turn away from such an honor. I donned it and passed out, seeing strange flashed of faces and sounds."

Finn startled. Did all those who put on the mysterious bracers receive hallucinations? Leeya continued.

"Once I awoke, I ran home and told my parents. Using our resources and network of informants, we searched for information. Realizing I couldn't take the bracer off, I knew whatever had transpired would decide the entirety of my future, from now until my death.

"We received word others had been granted bracers as well. Some who used their new abilities went insane, either by the bracer or by the potential for power. Stories of evil Star-Children—the name given to us—spread forth. Cities demolished. People enslaved. Populations slaughtered. The nobles of Kazma are raised to not have fear. Yet I worried using my power for the first time would turn me like the rest. I didn't want to cause harm.

"After a month of meditating, I was able to activate my bracer. The power surged through me and festered in my mind—I couldn't control myself. I don't remember what I did that night. When it was over, my room was in tatters, the rose gardens near my home was no more, and my parents were injured. I had taken a wooden club and attacked everything around me. It was only my subconscious discipline that spared my parents. But after First-Use, it was far easier to maintain control. Apparently the rampancy only happens once."

Finn had so many questions. "So to activate the bracer you need to meditate for a month? And you said you can't control your First-Use? But what about the man I fought? He was rampant, but on purpose. It seemed as if he had full control of himself!"

Leeya held out a hand to indicate Finn should take a pause. "Calm yourself."

Finn shoved another bite of Bantu flower into his mouth. Leeya continued. "For your first question: no, meditation isn't the direct way to activate your bracer. Each activation is dependent upon the wielder. I must maintain a calm mind to activate mine. Granted for me and my upbringing, that's an easy task. For Altin, he must feel a surge of confidence to activate his."

"You spew secrets as if they were nothing more than trivialities." Altin mumbled, cheeks bulging with Bantu.

"If it were a secret," Leeya sighed, "you shouldn't have come to me with your tail between your legs, begging for advice and revealing all about yourself."

Altin growled, swallowing. "I didn't come to you with my tail between my legs *begging*. I was merely excited to meet another like me. It's unfortunate—if I had known how much of a square you were; I would have kept going without revealing myself."

"Yet you stay at my side." Leeya replied. Her words shut Altin up and the young man blushed. Finn had a feeling Altin thought Leeya beautiful as well. Leeya faced Finn once more.

"To answer your second question: it does seem First-Use is uncontrollable for all Star-Children. Depending on the strength of your mind, you might be able to maintain a sense of awareness—but more than that seemed impossible. During First-Use, your power is at its strongest. It will never reach that level again."

Finn thought over Leeya's words. If he figured out the trigger that activated his own bracer, he would have to do so in a time and place where he could be alone. He didn't want to run rampant in public.

"How's it like to wield an ability?" Finn couldn't help to ask. "Do you grow tired using your powers?" Leeya furrowed her brow as she thought of a way to describe it. "It's like running a long distance, but in your mind. A… mental use of stamina that translates into physical exhaustion."

"What-about-your-First-Use?" Goblin asked Altin. The Star-Child rubbed his jaw and stared out over the balcony toward the setting sun. "I don't want to talk about it." He stayed silent and the group turned away from him, feeling a sense of awkwardness. Something had happened to him, perhaps something bad. Wanting to break the spell, Finn cleared his throat. "Altin, where do you hail from?"

The handsome Star-Child seemed to come back to life and scoffed. "Lyria, Lenova's floating capital." Surprise ran through Finn. Altin had lived in a similar situation as Leeya, floating above the average populace. "The floating islands of House Royal?" he exclaimed. "Isn't it magnificent there?"

Altin pushed his empty plate away and laughed. "It's a prude kingdom full of laws and fake bravado. Those rich and blind Lyrians can't see past their daily drama and coin purses. Don't even get me started on the soldiers and guards."

Remembering what the beggar back in Wyrmroost had told him, Finn spoke up. "Doesn't the king send out Paladins to claim a Star-Child's bracer? Was it not dangerous to be there?"

Altin grew dark. His complexion reminded Finn of the look miners took on when speaking of the Crust overseers. "Yeah. Even now he hunts us for a power that doesn't belong to him. He's a coward and a lazy lout not fit for kingship. I escaped Lyria with but a small batch of soldiers chasing me. Four other Star-Children in the neighboring island of Ephyria had been chosen around the time. They were all in rampant First-Use, destroying entire neighborhood blocks. A section of the island broke free and fell—thousands went with it. The king sent his Paladins to put a stop to them. Last I heard, his Paladins all lay dead. I think they managed to kill one of the Star-Children, but his body fell the four kilometers to the vast SeaLake below, lost for eternity. The other three escaped.

"I flew and fell my way to the ground. After two months of wandering about, I made it to Kazma where I met Leeya."

Finn was left speechless. There was so much happening around him. So much involving the Star-Children. He'd been thrust into a story far bigger than himself.

"To answer your last question," Leeya spoke, "if what you say is true and you faced a Star-Child who controlled his chaotic powers yet still killed, then you fought an evil one. One of the many that allowed their new abilities to control them instead of the other way around."

"How-do-you-know-all-this?" Goblin asked.

"Like I said, through my parents we have a long network of informants. Now I must ask both of you your stories."

Finn studied the wooden grain on the table, trying to determine where to begin. Taking another bite of his depleting meal, he started back when he'd first met Goblin and worked his way forward through Pittance and entering Kazma. Once he was finished, their table lay empty of food and in a state of silence. Altin, who at first pretended to not pay attention to the story, now faced Finn with a look of suspicion and what could have been slight respect. It was as if he was having an internal struggle of whether to believe it to be true and whether or not to be rude about it.

"Although you may not have use of your bracer, you are one of us." Leeya stated. "If you wish to, you may join us in our journey."

"Journey?" Finn asked.

"We travel to Jakitta, a city near the shadow of Lyria. Rumor spreads all Star-Children who mean no harm gather there as a coalition."

"Truly?" Finn asked in wonder. "Why so near the king when he desperately wants a bracer?"

"Some say they plan on overthrowing the king. Others say they plan on bargaining with him. Some say they only gather there for convenience, not caring one way or another if the king comes with all his armies or not. It's not like many would be foolish enough to fight a mass gathering of Star-Children."

"Could-the-rumors-of-a-coalition--be-lies-spread-by-the-king-as-a-trap?" Goblin asked.

Leeya shook her head. "No. My father's informants are smarter than that."

Finn thought of the prophecy. It could all be relevant or not at all. In the end it was only him and him alone that could make his choices. He decided to follow his gut.

"I'll go," he told Leeya, pointing to Goblin. "but only if my friend can come as well."

"What? What's he gonna do? Cook for us?" Altin jeered.

"Sure." Goblin shrugged. "I-like-cooking."

Leeya ignored them. "Very well Finn. But when we arrive at Jakitta, the coalition may not approve of him."

"If that's the case, Goblin and I will leave." Finn replied with determination. He knew joining with the good Star-Children might reveal more about his destiny, maybe even help him gain power over his bracer. But he would not—could not—leave Goblin. If they denied his friend, then they denied him as well.

They stood from the table and Leeya left six bronze coins as payment. She led them back outside into the orange-hued city. They moved from catwalk to bridge, back to catwalk, and through various tunnels. Finn's body clenched every time he walked across open catwalks far above the ground. Having only known the depths of caves, open height was a new experience for him, and one he didn't much like. He imagined having Altin's power. How long would it take Finn to become comfortable with flight? Probably never.

They turned down a wide bridge, weaving through people and carts. On the other end was an opening into the Neck. Three other roads connected to the spot—the central streets of Kazma. Leeya went on to tell them like the four roads leading to the Neck, there were also four gates leading into the city from the four directions of the compass. Finn and Goblin had entered from the Western gate, the smallest and least busy of all entrances. Finn recalled how packed it'd been when he'd first gone in Kazma and scoffed in amazement.

They entered the cool shade of the Neck and up close, Finn could recognize the purple material as obsidian. Above the entrance, a large number five had been painted, indicating the floor. Walking across colored tile and moving around oxen-pulled carts, the group passed elaborate stairwells and steel platforms where people gathered into groups. Finn watched as one of the platforms launched up, carrying three carts and a dozen aristocrats to the next floor. Nearby, pipes hissed steam, indicating pressure. Finn assumed it was steam—used in an ingenious fashion—that brought life to the elevators.

Inside the Neck, Finn was able to confirm his estimations of how wide it was. One could fit an entire city block within the massive tower. Finn examined large intricate murals painted onto the walls using white and yellow tints. They weren't art as much as business logos and slogans: McKinley's Domestic Tools. Bontiff & Sons.

At the center of the room were three metal pipes running from floor to ceiling at a slant. Air-holes the size of children—round at the top and flat at the bottom— were cut at waist-level into the pipes. They vibrated, giving off a low thrum, and making Finn's bones vibrate when he got too close. They were the DozDum Organ pipes Leeya had talked about, keeping the Upper-District floating for uncounted years.

Leeya took them to an elevator platform crowded with rich civilians. Seeing three Star-Children coming toward them, people respectfully—or fearfully—made room for them. Leeya told Finn and Goblin they would be going to the top.

When the elevator came to life and the steam pipes planted against the wall behind them hissed, Finn clenched his muscles. He expected to be jolted, but the elevator moved smoothly. They passed floor after floor, painted numbers scrolling by in red blurs. After leaving the twentieth floor, the platform entered a long shaft with no more openings. Crystal lights built into the walls whizzed past and Leeya explained they'd moved above the highest levels of the Lower-District. The only floor left was far above them—the actual Upper-District itself.

Anticipation made Finn bounce in place as the minutes rolled on. He was about to step foot onto a floating city. Slowing and coming to a stop, the platform left them on a wide hexagonal pavilion with a stained-glass dome ceiling. There were no walls, but instead they were greeted with cobblestone paths winding between grass fields, bushes, and fruit trees. The green landscape was colored by the see-through ceiling above and the warm sunset. Birds flew about and the rich strolled the well-maintained paths. Villas and houses topped verdant hills, showcasing large areas of free space. The air was colder at their higher elevation but not enough to be uncomfortable. Although Finn doubted there were ever any foot-traffic problems, it was not all open land—he could see various clusters of tall business buildings made of pink marble. The Upper-District lived a far better life than the Lower-District. It was grandiose, but Finn held a bitter taste in his mouth. He'd grown up in poverty. His limestone hut with cave-diving gear was all he'd owned. The Lower-District— knowing what was above them—lived in the literal shadow of wealth. They knew the injustice of the world as Finn did.

Leeya led them down a path and they followed, marveling at the sights. Finn looked back once more at the Neck's pavilion, watching as another elevator rose to the top, depositing a new group of upper-classmen. Nearby, the Dozdum Organ Pipes rose from the middle of the hexagon, connecting to egg-shaped stones housed within golden mesh cages. He imagined a massive egg beneath the Lower-District where the pipes connected. Where had these strange artifacts come from? Had the Nature-kin created them? Or perhaps the Forsaken?

Leeya took them to a beautiful neighborhood where multiple

homes faced each other in a circle. Leeya's home resembled a horseshoe in shape, with the door in the middle. What was odd, was one half of the house was painted blue and purple, while the other half was painted silver.

"What's with the color scheme?" Finn asked.

"I asked her the same question when I first got here." Altin jumped in.

"They're the colors of my parent's businesses. The house is two variations, yet it is one. It's symbolic for their mutual partnership."

"So they only married for business?" Finn dared ask.

Leeya seemed unbothered by the question. "Of course." was her reply. "As are all Upper-District marriages. It's called a merger, and it will bring them both greater profit. Having me was also planned. One day when they're gone, their businesses won't fall to a board of committee members, but instead will be solely ruled by me. I will then have a higher status in the community and have more power and influence."

The way she described the lifestyle of Kazma made Finn feel lost in a new world. Marriage for profit and not love? Were these people emotionless? Yet as Leeya said the words with a monotonous voice, Finn detected a hint of sadness there, as if Leeya wasn't wholly committed to the tradition. Perhaps she wasn't devoid of human emotion.

"What-do-your-parents-do?" Goblin asked.

Leeya gave a courteous nod. It was a pre-calculated gesture, as if when talking about business one was supposed to act polite. "My father lends money to new companies while my mother helps businesses with their taxes. As you can see, their joining was beneficial. We are quite well respected by House Crookshanks. The House Lord and he have been in good terms for nigh a decade."

She led them into her home, a place so clean, Finn doubted he would be able to find a single speck of dust. It was exactly as he imagined it to be: white walls with elaborate paintings, fanciful furniture, and glossy floors. Everything had a place, everything had a sense of precision.

Leeya took them to one end of her home where she put them in separate guest bedrooms. A maid and butler came forward, bringing fresh linen. They offered to take the boy's clothes for wash in exchange for clear shirts and pants. While they changed, Leeya told them from beyond their doors that her parents wouldn't be coming home from their jobs. They had living quarters at their office, which they stayed in six days of the week. She spoke with no emotion. Finn was at a loss. With a society built around only money and occupation, how could familial relationships work?

That evening, they made the decision to leave for Jakitta in two days' time. While in Kazma they would relax, explore, and buy whatever supplies they might need. The maid and butler returned with their now-clean clothes, dried by super-heated steam pipes. Marveling at both city and the two Star-Children with them, Finn went to bed wondering what lay in store for them next. Goblin took off his bandage, revealing a healed, normal-sized ear. He rested in a bed across to Finn, falling asleep and possibly dreaming of Lady Tuliah. In the other guest room, Altin retired to his quarters. Leeya stayed in the living room, staring at her fireplace and thinking thoughts no one would ever know.

Kilometers away to the South, Wahala rode her horse, still pulling at the gold-filled wagon. The beast whinnied, begging for rest.

She'd traveled many days from the Kingdom of Rot and its temple to catch up to Mal'Bal's campaign. She came to a stop and unsaddled herself, stretching her aching back and relishing in the blessed pain. Salastine unhitched the wagon and started a campfire as the other two cult members hunted for dinner. The sun disappeared, leaving the land dark—

but that was alright. Wahala had followed Mal'Bal's path of destruction across Lenova and knew where she was. Only a little farther North the Lich-Lord prepared his army and rested, ready to lay siege to their next target: Kazma.

the dozdum drop

22

—There was a woman at the edge of the stream last night. Now I know that may not sound special or anything, but she was on the other side, the side no one has ever been to! How did she get there? I attempted to call out to her, but my voice caught in my throat. The scene was far too beautiful. There she stood, in a beam of white-blue moonlight, staring at the sky with such a sad face, as if waiting for someone who would someday come. —
-secret childhood journal of Miriam, daughter of Mirtle, leader of Pittance

Hands grabbed Finn, shaking him awake from peaceful slumber. He surfaced back to reality, confused and foggy. Leeya and Altin were both in his room.

"Awaken Finn! We have a problem!"

He rubbed his eyes and yawned. "Wazematter?"

Altin and Leeya looked at each other but didn't say anything. Their expressions made Finn come to his senses quickly. Something was wrong—very wrong. On the other bed, Goblin sat up as well. Finn could hear voices coming from beyond the bedroom window. He saw torch light flickering by and knew it was the wee-hours before sunrise. People were moving past the house. By the sounds of it, there were many.

"Grab your belongings. We must hurry." Leeya commanded.

Finn threw on his cloak and boots then strapped on his belt with its hanging pouches. He made sure Lady Tuliah's vial of amber liquid and his broken miner's goggles were stored at his side. Following Goblin and the two Star-Children, he ran out of the house. He was right, the sky was black and dark-blue: right before sunrise. Dark forms walked past them, wearing long shimmering night-robes glinting with jewels. It was the many rich of the Upper-District, moving through the manicured grass. They all walked in the same direction, whispering words Finn couldn't catch. What was going on? There was a sense of urgency all about. A feeling of fear—terror even.

Leeya led them into the crowds. Beside him, Goblin sniffled and put on his feathered hat Piscus had bought for them. Finn wrapped his cloak tighter.

"Did anyone receive notice of this? How'd they appear?" a voice asked. *"Did no one see them march toward us?"*

"They must have come through Sodomona."

"Then Sodomona's no more."

Leeya increased her pace. She was fast and for Finn to keep up, he left the rest of the crowd far behind. The torch and crystal-lit landscape gave no indication an emergency had happened. Above them, the glass dome glinted in orange firelight. All Finn could tell was Leeya was leading them to the Southern edge of the floating city.

They passed an empty garden, a waterfall trickling a melodic greeting. They walked a long quiet cobblestone path and neared the edge of the city where a chest-high wall protected the citizens from falling to their deaths. Finn was surprised to find many people already gathered there. They all leaned over the wall as if trying to see the Lower-District far below. Finding a clear spot, Finn and his group looked over the edge as well.

Finn was confused about what he saw. In the vast blackness that was the pre-dawn land, there was a large field of fire. He stared at the distant swathe of flickering light. Could someone have set the surrounding lands of Kazma ablaze? Three-quarters of the land seemed to be writhing in... torchlight. It hit Finn like a boulder—he was staring at torchlight. He looked left to right. If that were true... then below them stood an inconceivable number of people.

"An army." Altin answered for all of them.

Finn's heart hammered in his chest with both awe and horror. An army? What was an army of such magnitude doing outside the walls of Kazma?

"*Is it the king?*" someone asked.

"*No. He has no qualms with us.*"

"*They came from the South.*"

"*Aye, I heard rumors about a darkness spreading from there.*"

"*Some say civilians of Metés and Vestés are part of the army. Why have they turned on us?*"

"*Can we defend ourselves against such a force?*"

"*We don't have to. The Lower-District can deal with it. Just shut down the elevators and we'll be fine.*"

The words shocked Finn. It seemed as if the people of the Upper-District were more curious and agitated than afraid. They felt safe in the sky. Their attitude toward the Lower-District was disgusting. Were they going to leave their fellow citizens to fend for themselves far below?

"We have plenty of food and many gardens. Send out a bird asking assistance from the House Lord and the King."

"If they send anything at all, we won't see forces arrive here for at least a month."

"We can hold out for a month. Perhaps bargain with the enemy. We have eloquent tongues."

"Hmm, if we're lucky the army will clean the vagabonds from the streets."

Finn bit his lip, fighting his urge to not scream at the people. How dare they not care about the Lower-District? Were they heartless?

The sky lightened as the first rays of sun broke over the edge of the horizon from their left. Suddenly, detail could be made out. Indeed, far below was an army of immense proportions. Individual people couldn't be made clear because of the distance but Finn swore there were mounds mixed within the mass, like living rocks. Everyone grew quiet as they beheld what lay below.

A conch horn blew. It was low and long, ringing for an eternity. Other horns joined with the first until the sound seemed overwhelming even from up in the sky. The noise cut out and there was a stillness in the air. Would they send out a spokesperson? Would the army demand terms of surrender? Would anything happen at all? Sweat poured down Finn's brow, yet he was cold.

The sound of ocean waves crashed out, low at first, then louder and louder. It was the sound of thousands of voices screaming. The army was charging Kazma. Leeya spun about. None of the other Upper-District citizens were doing anything but staring. Their faces held concern, but not much else.

"Gather weapons!" Leeya roared. "We must assist those below! Those whom have strength in their body, hurry to the Neck! We can't sit by while our brothers die!"

The citizens frowned at her. None of them moved.

"Leeya, what are you saying? We're safe here." one of the men commented.

"Exactly." another added, "They have their own soldiers. If we go down there, we risk dying. We have more to lose than they."

Finn couldn't take it. These people were like the supervisors at the mines. They couldn't care less if an underling died as long as they lost no money. It was all about power and wealth. He took a step forward, his body vibrating. "Listen up!" he screamed. Everyone turned to him.

"If you love your land, your homes, and your families; take arms! No more hiding behind the backs of the common! You *must* make a stand! Prove you're worthy of your wealth, rank, and power! Below, the Lower-District dies protecting you! It's not their duty! Their duty is to themselves! Yet they fight because they must! Where is your honor? Your justice? Where is your courage? Are you not men and women of Lenova? Raise your weapons! Fight!"

The Upper-District civilians wobbled in place, discomfort running through their features. Had he got to them? Had his speech worked? It seemed as if at least a few were considering his words. One of the men stepped forward. He was handsome, with raven-black hair and a finely-trimmed goatee. His clothes were elaborate and well-adorned.

"Our duty is to ourselves and our businesses. Without us, Kazma is nothing! We must stay safe. Our coffers can't be plundered. We won't fight—we've already sent men to shut down the elevators." He spoke nonchalantly, without care.

Finn opened and closed his mouth, stunned. Around him, the citizens nodded in agreement. Goblin shook with rage. Even Leeya, one of the Upper-District herself, looked shocked at the decision.

Altin jumped forward. "Cowards!"

The people winced and stepped away from him, expecting the

Star-Children to attack.

"We're better than this." Leeya stated, her face flat and emotionless. "Father, I thought you were better than this."

Finn's eyes bugged out. The man that'd turned the people against them and argued against Finn's speech was non-other than Leeya's father. The man didn't show any emotion. Instead, he looked away, facing back to the horizon. He didn't reply to Leeya; neither did she stare at him.

"Come on," she told Finn. "We must hurry. We have to get to the elevators before they're shut down."

"So-we're-still-going-to-fight?" Goblin asked.

Leeya faced him. "We must act with logic. We have to learn the enemy's purpose: who they are, what they want. If there is a diplomatic solution, I shall take it. I *am* the only Upper-District member who seems willing to do so."

Finn worked his jaw. "Right. Let's move!"

They ran from the ledge, weaving through the crowds of the rich. Finn expected someone to try and stop him—a hand to reach out and grab him—but no one did. They only gave him a look of disapproval. Many didn't care, but instead watched the rising sun. Finn's last glimpse of them was of a large crowd back-lit by the early morning light, no one moving to help. The vision would haunt him forever.

Led by Leeya, the group sprinted at full speed toward the center of town. Winded, they approached the DozDum Organ pipes and the three egg-shaped objects connected to them. Running across the hexagonal floor toward the nearest elevator platform, Leeya grabbed a lever sticking out of a mechanical control board. She pulled the lever, but nothing happened. Leeya swore, an act opposite of her composed nature—a sign of emotion.

"They've turned off the steam. We have no power to the elevators. We're too late."

"So-we're-just-going-to-sit-here-and-listen-to-the-battle-below-us?" Goblin asked.

Altin pulled at his long hair in frustration. "This doesn't make sense. Why are we even being attacked?"

"What-do-we-do?" Goblin asked Leeya.

The girl's eyes showed a sudden lack of confidence. There was nothing that could be done. Finn looked to his broken bracer, thinking back on his dream of exploration. He was supposed to be a Star-Child. He was supposed to see Lenova—perhaps even protect it; not watch it be destroyed. Why couldn't he use his bracer when he most needed it? What would trigger a power? Of all times and places where a special ability could be useful, now would be the best.

Finn paced back-and-forth, gritting his teeth. He neared one of the DozDum pipes and kicked at it. His toe throbbed and he hobbled back, nearly falling into the hole where sound and wind blew out. The thought clicked in his head: the organ pipe, the vein of the city—it ran at an angle to the Lower-District. *And there were holes in the side of the pipe. Holes the size of a child.*

"Get over here!" he yelled to his group. They came running forward, worry on their faces.

"What is it?" Leeya asked.

Finn pointed to the pipe. "Can we all fit through there?"

"No way!" Altin said, shaking his head and backing away. "I can't believe you'd even think of something that stupid."

Leeya's face was once more stone. "We can. It's our only way down."

"We're going to die." Altin groaned.

"Most-likely." Goblin agreed. "You-first-Altin."

"He's right. Altin, activate your power. You'll go first." Leeya commanded, taking charge. "If we slide too fast, you can control our descent by holding us up."

"I'll be crushed at the bottom by all of your combined weight!" Altin shouted.

"Do-you-want-to-stay-up-here-and-do-nothing? Are-you-not-a-Star-Child? Were-you-not-chosen-by-the-heavens-themselves?" Goblin remarked.

Altin spun on the boy, snarling. "I can barely understand you, numb-mouth! You have no idea what you're talking about! Have you ever been in a battle? Have any of us? Do you think the attackers will be intimidated by a little boy with a lisp?"

"I'm surprised out of all of us, you're scared the most." Finn growled.

Altin howled in annoyance and pushed past them. He grabbed the edges of the thrumming pipe, then froze with hesitation. His breathing was ragged. He shook his head. The pipe was barely wider than him. If at any point the tube grew narrower...

"What of the other holes on the way down?" Altin asked, his bracer sluggishly coming to life. The dark armor pieces slid along his body and wrapped around his ankles and wrists. They moved slowly, as if Altin was having to force fake confidence.

"Best to keep your arms and legs tucked in." Leeya responded. Everyone gulped.

"And if we can't slow down?" Altin asked again as he fit his legs through the tight opening. He wiggled his body until he was holding on to the edge of the hole, only his head peeked out at them. The older boy was wincing, whispering, "*We can't control this. We don't know what could happen...*"

"There's no time for this." Leeya sighed. She moved forward and shoved Altin down. The boy lost his grip, and with a scream, was gone. Leeya turned to Goblin and Finn. "May we live through this day." With a lithe, smooth movement, she slid her body through the tight cavity and fell.

"Being-chased-by-a-vat-worm-sounds-nice-right-about-now."
Goblin commented. He too jumped through the hole. Before beginning his
rapid slide, Finn heard his friend grunt out, "What-a-tragedy. And-I-just-
learned-to-talk."

Finn was left alone to calm his heart as best he could. He hadn't
been able to save his fellow miners from Nozgull, and by himself he
couldn't stop an army. But he'd changed in his journey so far and he had
two Star-Children to help him. He might yet live. He wiggled into the pipe,
his body expertly moving into the tight space.

Inside, the magical thrumming of power was deafening. His entire
form vibrated and his muscles complained. He struggled to maintain his
grip on the edge of the hole. His boots slipped and slid, finding little hold
in the steep angle. It was dark in the tunnel and with the little space he had,
he couldn't see below him nor pull out his goggles. He couldn't even hear
the voices of his fellow friends. The pipe was only warm to him and he
thanked his bracer under his breath. He worried the others were being
cooked alive as they fell.

Finn let go and his stomach lurched to his throat. He remembered
Leeya's words, wrapped his arms around himself, and tightened his legs
together. He shot down in the dark, clueless as to how fast he was moving.
The pipe's hum became a shrill whistle biting at his ears. The angle was
ridiculous. There was no way he would land alive at the bottom.

His feet caught up to something below him. He'd reached Goblin.
His friend pressed into Finn's legs as if the boy was slowing down. Was
Altin beneath them, using his power to slow their descent? He could
faintly hear what sounded like a strained scream.

Suddenly a light flashed by to his right. It was a quick blink. The
first hole—the organ's opening at level twenty. Finn tightened up, terrified
one of his body parts would stick out at the wrong time and be amputated.
Goblin's speed decreased even more, pushing into Finn. Another opening

passed them, and another, the flashing lights giving Finn a quick glimpse of those beneath his feet. Leeya was holding on to Goblin's legs. Altin was directly below her, arms straining to push against their weight. The feathers carved into his bracer armor glowed with blue energy and blood marked his face. They were thrown into the dark again.

More openings came and went to either side and they slowed even more. Finn felt some of his stomach return to its proper location. He put his feet out, pushing his back against the wall, hoping to help Altin. His added friction brought him to a slow slide. With a jolt, he came to a stop, nearly crushing Goblin between himself and Leeya. He held his own weight, pinning himself in place.

"What's going on?" he yelled. He had to shout to be overheard through the pipe's humming.

Leeya yelled something back but it came as a muffled grunt. Finn could see light below him but Goblin and Leeya were both in the way. Had they made it to the bottom floor?

Leeya crawled through the light and was gone. Goblin slid down and disappeared as well. Finn released the pressure in his hands and feet, coming to a stop against Altin, who floated between him and a blackness leading only to the depths beneath Kazma. Beside them was an exit. Altin groaned and Finn took the hint. He pushed out of the child-sized space, falling to cool tile floor. Goblin and Leeya, both covered in sweat and red skinned, helped him up. By the looks of them, the tunnel had been hot after all.

Altin collapsed through the pipe, gasping. His armor contracted and re-solidified as a bracer on his wrist. The blood Finn had glimpsed earlier leaked from a large gash on his forehead, matting his blond hair.

"What happened?" Finn huffed.

"I landed on him while going too fast." Leeya responded.

"Had to slow us somehow, right?" Altin replied with a cough, rolling over onto his back. He too was red from the heat within the organ.

"So-did-we-make-it?" Goblin asked. "Are-we-on-the-bottom-floor?"

"Listen." Leeya replied, standing.

They perked their ears. Screams and shouts came from all around them. As they turned in place, surging crowds of people burst through from all four openings into the massive room. Men and women ran toward the elevators, flipping levers to bring the platforms to life. None of the elevators moved.

"They aren't working!"

"The cowards above us left us to die!"

"What are we going to do? Our soldiers and guards can't hold against the invaders!"

Leeya raised her arms and walked to the crowd. "The Upper-District locked us out. There's nothing we can do. Those who wish to flee, leave by whichever gate isn't being attacked. Those who wish to fight, gather your weapons!"

The people yelled and shouted in response, their voices intermingling into a cacophony. Many panicked and sprinted away, taking family members with them. Some sat on the ground with mouths opened, stunned. But a small few drew swords and shields; others pulled spears. They looked at each other with terror, knowing they had no choice but to take a stand.

There was a moment of chaos as citizens made their choices. The crowd surged and twisted within itself and people pushed each other out of the way, running outside and disappearing down the alleys.

Altin grabbed a passing form. "Wait! Who attacks us? Can we reason with them?"

The citizen shook his head, trying to break Altin's grip. "It's a Star-Child! He leads men made of gold and an army of monsters! We can't kill them! Kazma's doomed!"

The man broke free and ran. Altin turned to them, his face pale. "A Star-Child."

Finn shivered.

"One of the Chosen runs rampant." Leeya spoke, her words slow. "Perhaps the rumors of darkness moving through the South have been true all along."

"What-do-we-do?" Goblin asked.

The group went silent for a moment.

"We're Star-Children." Leeya spoke. "We've been granted a higher power. This is my home and I will not flee. I'll find this Star-Child and fight him myself. If he can't be reasoned with, he'll die."

She turned to Finn. "You don't have your power yet. Neither has your friend been granted a bracer. You may leave. We'll meet again in Jakitta as we planned if all goes well."

Finn had a sudden surge of loyalty toward the people around him. It was as if Lady Tuliah was patting him on the back. He thought of his friends in Pittance. What if the attack had been there? Who was to protect those who couldn't fight such evil? Energy coursed through Finn's body. He might not have access to his bracer or even be a true Star-Child—but he would fight for Lenova all the same. For Kazma. It was *all* his home.

"I'll stay." he said, his voice unwavering.

"I-will-too." Goblin stuttered, looking at Finn. "I'll-do-what-I-can."

"I guess I can't run away by myself." Altin smirked, wiping blood from his face. "Would be bad for my reputation, you know."

Leeya smiled at them; a genuine reaction. Finn staggered. The emotionless girl was suddenly the most beautiful person he'd ever seen.

"Then let's fight." Leeya confirmed with a nod.

the battle for kazma, part one

23

—The secret to the hygiene of a Mockingtoad is through harvesting the tattooed marks on their backs. The faces that form like inked artwork on the reptile's body may have features that are stretched and disproportioned to incite anger upon those that come across them. Remember: it's only a defense mechanism of theirs. If you are brash and rush to attack bare handed, merely touching the toad will price you with a fast-spreading rot. You will soon lose your fingers. But if you are careful and can collect the easily-shed skin while wearing leather gloves, you can sunbake the thin membrane to remove all toxins. What you will have left is almost a parchment-like picture of strange faces. It is said that in the city of Kazma you can sell the art for a pretty penny. —

-Excerpt from The Care of Mysterious Lenovan Beasts, page 14

Leeya led them over catwalks and past tunnels, guiding them through the city. Light peeked over the walls, bathing the entirety of the Lower-District in yellow. It wasn't the only light: distant buildings were on fire.

Jumping from one catwalk to another and hopping a trickle of water forming a small waterfall off a roof, Leeya took them to a weapon shop wedged between two vendor stalls. Although many citizens ran the other way, no one tried to prevent them from looting the small store. Altin, having left his crossbow in Leeya's home, was forced to find another one. Leeya took a spear and handed Finn a sword with a sheath. Goblin found a falcata that fit him just right. Armed, the four returned to the ground floor and ran toward the Southern gate where the army was invading.

Finn had no idea how to wield a weapon. He doubted Goblin knew as well. If they were to cross enemies, there was no way they'd come away unscathed. He pulled his blade free. It was heavy in his hand. Leeya motioned for him to sheathe the weapon.

"Wait until we meet the enemy. I don't want you tripping and impaling yourself."

"What, you can't take me seriously with this?" Finn asked, doing his best not to wink at the girl. He was sure Leeya would have broken his spine if he had.

"You look like a blind man brandishing a log." was her only reply.

Finn put his weapon away, blushing. Unlike him, Leeya held a weapon with confidence. Finn had a suspicion Leeya was an expert with a spear. Altin himself looked at home with his crossbow. It irked Finn. Was he the least experienced of them all? He hoped he didn't make a fool of himself in front of Leeya. He hoped he didn't *die*.

They turned down an alley and came face-to-face with a nightmare. Ahead of them was the massive South gates to the city. It looked as if soldiers had attempted to lower iron bars to block the entrance, but something had smashed through it. That *something* was right in front of them.

At first Finn assumed it to be a pile of rubble from the destroyed buildings—then it moved. It jumped forward, swiping out at a group of spear-carrying soldiers. Their chest-pieces caved, they flew backward, dead before hitting the ground. Other soldiers shot arrows at the creature, but they bounced off its stone body. It rose to its full height of ten meters, roughly resembling a man. Civilians screamed and ran away. Soldiers held up shields. But the monster had no mercy. It swiped and hit, crushing and smashing anything that moved. Blood painted the street. From over Finn's head a blur shot out, the size of a cart. A bolt embedded into the creature's chest and it fell apart, showering the area with rock. Above them on a catwalk, two soldiers pulled back on a large portable ballista, reloading it.

But with the creature out of the way, the gate was exposed. Battle cries rang out as a mass wave of black-cloaked figures rushed in, holding scythes and whatever form of weapons one could conceive. Many of them had golden limbs. The soldiers of Kazma paused. What sort of odd army was this?

The invaders clashed with the guards like two clouds conjoining. From Finn's right, a door burst open and thirty soldiers poured out, brandishing swords and shields. More ran across the catwalks, launching arrows into the enemy. Leeya pointed out a group of intruders climbing a set of stairs. She charged toward them and Finn followed, Goblin and Altin at their tail, not wanting to be left behind in the bloodbath. Finn's group chased the six attackers up the stairs, watching in horror as soldiers were pushed off, falling to their deaths with bloodcurdling shrieks. Catching up to the cloaked figures as their backs were turned, Leeya struck. She was a blur of movement, leaving Finn behind to draw his sword.

The hooded figures turned to try and stop Leeya, possibly attack back, but she gave them no chance. She ducked a scythe swung for her head and jabbed her spear forward, stabbing it into the thigh of one man. He howled and Leeya tipped the spear, unbalancing him. He fell three-stories into the middle of the battle below. She turned, propping the spear over her shoulders and jabbed out, using the weapon's length to her advantage. The other five tried to step forward and grab at the spear, but she bobbed and wove, timing her attacks and leaving them with cut hands. An arrow pierced one enemy through the chest and he toppled over the side of the catwalk. Finn looked up, seeing Altin floating a few meters above him. He reloaded, a confident snarl on his face.

In the open space below, a voice shouted out. "The Star-Children fight for us! We're saved!"

The soldiers of Kazma cheered, their valor renewed. Finn watched as Altin zipped about in the air, launching arrows and tackling men off high perches. Leeya finished killing the group ahead of them and engaged another using a ladder to get to their level. Perhaps the battle would not be lost.

There was a yelp behind Finn and he turned. Goblin parried a slash from a hooded figure who'd snuck up behind them. The man had a golden nose and fear reflected in his eyes, as if he preferred to be anywhere but Kazma. He swung with the scythe, visibly inexperienced with the weapon. Goblin blocked and was pressed back, closer to Finn.

Finn didn't hesitate, knowing if he were to kill, it would be justifiable. He had lives to protect. He darted forward, holding his sword like a lance. Goblin had fallen backwards and was scrabbling for his weapon, unprotected. The man loomed above his friend, about to strike down. Finn jumped in front of him and stabbed forward. His weapon smashed into the man's chest, cutting through thin cloth, skin, muscle, and glancing off bone. It slid between two ribs and Finn lost his hold as it moved up, piercing the attacker's heart.

Merely a few finger-lengths away from the man's face, he made eye contact. The man's fearful eyes wavered for a second more, confusion and uncertainty running through them, then he was falling backward. Finn slid the blade free from flesh and the body collapsed. Something bubbled inside Finn—a mania tottering on the edge of coming free. He remembered the training back in the Crust and stilled his breathing. He tripped back but stopped himself, tightening his muscles so to not shake. He had to continue fighting. He turned and lifted Goblin to his feet. The boy gave Finn a nod.

"That's-got-to-be-the-millionth-time-you-saved-me. How-much-do-I-owe-you-now?"

"Too much." Finn replied.

They ran back to Leeya's side. Bodies pilled around her, and far below, others lay broken and prostrate. Blood covered her spear all the way to her hand and smeared across her face and clothes. It gave her a fierceness that made her terrifying to behold. Altin landed nearby, pulling a broken arrow-shaft out of his shoulder. He gritted in pain and blood oozed from the wound, yet he winked at them.

"You lot suck at fighting. Too bad you're not more like me, huh?"

At first, it looked to be as if Kazma was winning—possibly even pushing back the robed invaders. Then, when all seemed to be going in their favor, there was a lull in the battle below and they stared down. From beyond the smashed gate came a towering monster of a man. The enemy stepped away from him, showing terror toward their own ally. Something primal and cold crawled through Finn's belly. He had seen the inside of a vat-worm. He'd ran from Nozgull's wrath. He had come within a centimeter from death in the Slaglands. Yet this being emanated a far worse threat. A sense of absolute doom. Hopelessness. A panic clawed at Finn's throat and put ice in his veins.

The man was made of gold from the neck down, an inhuman form stranger than all other creatures of Lenova. His face was hidden, covered by a dark wooden mask with thousands of eyes. He was naked, no features carved into his golden body to detect his gender. Only his stature identified him. Finn could tell he was bald and could see black pulsing veins running from his scalp to beneath the mask, where his face was. But worst of all, he bore a bracer. He was the Star-Child.

Words from the prophecy came to him. *Evil seeks to end all we hold dear.* Something else came to him, something far more disturbing: a flash from a vision, the screaming face of a golden man; a glimpse given to him from when he'd donned the bracer.

Finn's knees gave out and he fell to the wooden catwalk, shaking and struggling to see straight. Goblin and Leeya bent to help him, concern written on their faces. This wasn't right. That man...that monster...they were all in mortal danger.

A cocky soldier charged forward with a yell, swinging his blade. The Star-Child was a blur. He grabbed the sword with one golden hand and snapped it in half. He pounced, seizing the soldier's mouth with both hands and ripping his jaw clean off. He dropped the corpse and lifted a blood-soaked arm.

"*Vetis-fin.*"

His voice beneath the mask was the hoarse whisper of death itself. There was a shimmer and his arm wiggled strangely, sagging and stretching. The gold meshed and molded, forming a lance. He jabbed forward, cutting through armor like water, impaling four other soldiers.

"*Ginda.*"

His arm liquefied and returned to normal, dripping gore. Everyone backed away. *Magic. No—necromancy. This man could control the dark arts.* A massive bolt whizzed out toward the Star-Child. Before it hit him, something jumped in front. Catching the cart-sized blur in mid-air was a puppet as thin as a walking-stick, limbs like sharpened edges. It landed and its dagger-thin fingers walked along the missile, feeling it. The bolt, as large as a man, seemed as light as a feather in the creature's grasp. It dropped the useless projectile, staring at the ballista with a blank, oval head. It had no eyes, mouth, or nose. For all Finn knew, it could be staring at him.

"Kill them all." the Star-Child spoke. It was a trigger sentence. All about him, the cloaked invaders came back to life. They screamed obscenities and rushed the overwhelmed soldiers and guards of Kazma. Men were slaughtered left and right.

The puppet launched forward, climbing walls with all four limbs like a spider. It landed on top of the ballista and decapitated both operators before they had a chance to react. With a quick heave, it tipped the engine-of-war over the catwalk, crushing the men below. It moved as a blur, disappearing deeper into the city. Finn could hear screams come from where it'd gone. On the ground, the Star-Child stood with his arms crossed in the middle of the chaos as battles were fought all about him, none daring to draw near. Men writhed on the ground, holding stumps where limbs once were. Blood sprayed like loose water and gurgling cries filled the air. The Star-Child was saturating—*bathing*—in the horror.

Finn observed the powerful man. The figure studied the Upper-District, bending his neck all the way back to take in the whole of the floating city. Although Finn couldn't see his face, he imagined the man held a wide smile. Below his mask, the bottom of his jaw was moving. The man was reading the massive ancient runes carved into the Upper-District's walls. Who was this being who possessed necromancy, had a golden body, a terrifying mask, the bracer of a Star-Child, and knew ancient languages? The man looked to the center of Kazma where the Neck soared above all other buildings and connected the two city centers.

A hand grabbed Finn's shoulder and shook him. It was Altin. The older boy's eyes were wide with terror. "We must move! We can't stop this!"

Altin grabbed at Leeya and Goblin; both mesmerized by what they saw below. "Run!" he shouted into their faces. The group came to life.

They turned and fled the South gate, Leeya taking point as she wove and ducked her way through narrow alleys and catwalks. Behind them, the screams and the moans of dying Kazmans followed their footsteps.

Leeya smashed through a wooden door and Finn found himself back inside the restaurant where he'd been first introduced to Bantu flowers. Altin closed the door behind them and they sat in chairs, panting.

"What-do-we-do? We-can't-possibly-stop-that-man." Goblin gasped. The boy was shaking.

"I've never seen anything like that." Altin added, rubbing his head. "He can't be defeated."

There was a crash and they all spun to face Leeya. She was faced away from them, leaning against a counter. The noise had come from a ceramic cup she'd thrown. Again, she'd shown emotion. It unbalanced Finn. "We can't let this happen." she hissed. "We can't let that man take this city." She turned, eyes sparkling. Her bracer glistened as if about to activate. Finn wished it would have—he'd yet to see her ability or even know what it was. Leeya picked up her spear and pointed it at them. "The fleeing citizens were rushing toward the Eastern gates. It looks as if the Northern and Western passages are on fire. I believe East is the only way out, but I guarantee soon the entire city will be surrounded. Leave. Get out of here with the rest."

Shock jolted Finn. What was Leeya saying?

"This is my home." she spoke. "I must protect it until I'm dead. You have no such loyalties. Get out and live."

Fear and stubbornness battled within Finn. He'd promised Leeya he would stay. He knew there were people even now dying around him, dying like the miners in the Crust had. Yet the image of the golden Star-Child wouldn't leave his mind; the ease in which he'd killed, the way he stood amid the chaos as if content—as if he relished pain and death. A familiar terror entered him. It was the overpowering sensation that had nearly swallowed him as he ran into the Slaglands, leaving Goblin to Nozgull's hands.

"No!" he shouted. The terror itself was doing something to Finn. Making him stubborn, or perhaps remind him that friends were not made to be left behind. "I won't leave, not if you stay." Something warm was unfurling in his chest, a radiant, yet frail confidence.

There was silence in the restaurant.

"Finn... you hardly know me." Leeya whispered.

"It doesn't matter! You won't face this alone!" He pulled out his sword and brandished it. "If we die, at least we die giving time for more citizens to escape the city!" He turned to Goblin and Altin, expecting them to be backing out the door. Instead, they held their place.

"You're-right." Goblin spoke. His cheeks were flushed and there was a strange look to his eyes. "We-can't-cower."

Finn turned back to Leeya. "I believe I know where the Star-Child's going. We might be able to slow him. Maybe stop him."

"Where?" Leeya asked, her eyes not leaving Finn.

"He's heading to the Neck. I believe he means to go up to the Upper-District."

Leeya stood straighter. "Then we must be quick. I know the shortest way to get there. If we do this, we do it as companions. As friends."

Finn nodded, hoping he hadn't lived all the way to this point just to die. Altin and Goblin approached them and there was a sudden sense of bonding between all four. Something unbreakable. Fate.

Wahala saw the smoke from a kilometer away. Leaving Salastine behind to guard the wagon of gold with the other two cult members, she rode for the South gate of Kazma. Pouring through three of the four gates were the entire forces of Mal'Bal. They'd grown great in his campaign. She watched as a dozen stone golems broke a new hole into the city wall and slaughtered the people within a home. Another group of golems threw citizens from the tops of the wall. Their bodies plummeted like flaying rain.

Most of the city was in full retreat and many of the soldiers now only guarded the Eastern gate, escorting civilians out. Mal'Bal was letting them run. What the Lich-Lord was up to?

Her horse charged beneath the ruined South gate and she called out to a cult member. The man pointed toward a distant purple tower, rising from the middle of Kazma.

"He goes there, my Queen!"

The man called her by her new title. A loyalist. She hoped there were far more if she were to overthrow the cult's current leader. But for now, she would assist Mal'Bal—her plans had to fester for a bit longer as she adjusted into her new role.

She rode her horse forward toward the tower, spotting Mal'Bal's creepy puppet following her from far above, running on all fours across the rooftops. It was covered head-to-toe in blood. Apparently, it'd been having a good time. She smirked, wondering if there were any poor fools holding out at the tower. If there were, they would be met with an ill demise indeed.

the battle for kazma, part two

24

—*And now that we have left land and taken to sky, upon the wings we have sown on our shoulders, the lives we once had now seem so distant and strange. As quickly as we flap, our memories of who we were fade quicker. I hold my sister's hand and my father's arm. Both look up and not down. Their eyes already show no sign that they recollect that we were once Lenovan. Our entire town glides around us, pushing higher and higher. At first the children were shouting in joy and glee, twisting around us in the air, their mothers chiding, the fathers commanding. But now we are all silent, a cloud elevating onwards. Higher and higher we go. I no longer remember my name nor how I got these wings. Who am I? What am I? The hands I once held no longer touch and the people I once knew as family are no longer familial. I have lost sight of them among the crowds of others. We all gaze up with mouths open, straining to breathe the thin air.*

We must go higher. Why do I write this as I fly? Was I a scribe of some sort? What does that title even mean? Our whole town… What is town. What me be? Me no more. I go higher. I am sky. I am air. Wing. Flap. Higher. Higher. High. I see whole world. —
-Abandoned journal found in the middle of the GrassPlains of Faanda.

Finn entered the bottom floor of the Neck, feeling as if he'd been there only an hour before—which he had. No one waited at the large tower. All the crowds that'd rushed inside it before were now gone, leaving the block-wide space empty of any movement. It was suddenly eerie.

His friends prepared for the fight that was sure to come. Altin strung a new bolt onto his crossbow, having scavenged a large quiver from a fallen soldier. Leeya checked her spear's wooden shaft for any cracks and jabbed out with the weapon, practicing. If he lived through the day, Finn would have to ask her how she'd learned to fight so well. Goblin swung his falcata as best as he could, more like a child with a dagger than a teen with a sword.

They centered themselves near the DozDum Organ pipes and tried to calm their breathing, not speaking to each other but instead mentally preparing themselves for whatever might come.

A few moments later, echoing footsteps sounded out as a figure entered the tiled chamber. It was the Star-Child himself, alone and with no troops to back him. He held his arms behind his back in a regal pose. His body demanded an air of confidence. He showed no fear, as if he could care less whether four faced him or a thousand.

"Here we go…" Altin whispered.

The man stopped a hundred meters away from them. He watched from behind his carved mask, breathing like a wild animal. The Star-Child grabbed his mask, setting it on the floor. Finn faced the enemy as he truly was.

The man bore strange features. His eyes were slanted, nearly snake-like, yet widened crazily, showing tiny pinpricks where his pupils were. He grabbed at his face and rubbed it, muttering of too many visions to interpret. Finn suspected the man was insane.

His face bore a linear jaw and a wide neck, yet was also foreign, pale as if he'd lived in darkness. The many veins Finn had seen pulsing along the man's scalp also ran to his eyes and mouth. It gave Finn the sense he was facing an undead, one who'd long passed into the void yet refused to leave the land. Even at their distance, Finn could tell the man stood a chest and head taller than them—a monster.

"Bracer wearers!" the man hissed in pleased amazement. "I heard there were more—quite a surprise. Now I finally meet some." His voice was strange—there was a cutting accent to it. He looked genuinely happy to see them. "Tell me younglings, do you fear death? Or love it?"

Finn's stomach churned as the man laughed. "Ah, Lenovans. You're all the same." He spread his arms and paced. "You should join me, not oppose me."

Finn startled.

"What?" Altin stuttered.

"Don't deny me. It would be foolish." The man chuckled. "My devotion is far greater than yours. No matter your answer, I'll get things my way." His eyes bore into them.

Finn had no idea what the Star-Child's power was. He could possibly snap his fingers and break all their bones. He held to his sword with more force.

"Why do you attack us?" Leeya asked. "Is it First-Use? Does your bracer control you?"

The man smirked, then clucked. "Stupid girl. Look up to the void above you! Don't you see the futility of life? Mortal bodies corrode. We. Don't. Last! This world is not meant for us: for those that expire. Have gratitude for the pain I bring your people! I am your savior. I make you *feel*. I remind you of existence and take it away, ending your insignificance! Help me bring in a new dawn; a time of anti-life. Help me bring meaning to this world."

Finn had no idea what the man was talking about. He spoke of life and death as if it were nothing; as if reality was an abomination.

"Leave Kazma and we might let you live." Altin replied.

The man laughed again. "Let me live? I live and die by my choice." He spread his arms. "You've made your choice then."

Finn clenched up.

"Behold and face your end! I am Mal'Bal! Lich-Lord! The Golden Agony! Ruler of the Kingdom of Rot! Your bodies will fester here for generations, symbol to your weak ideals! All about you I shall pile the corpses of children and babies! I'll end the evil you call life before it begins! I'll single-handedly stop the tide of birth and death! Your lands will be desolation!" He spat the words out, his face growing red with passion and his eyes wide with madness.

The words rang in Finn's head. This man was the embodiment of everything Finn was against. This Mal'Bal would stop Finn's dream. He would crush all he loved. Everything within him rejected the man's words. He couldn't stay quiet. "No!" Finn shouted, walking forward.

"Finn!" Goblin hissed but Finn didn't stop. He continued to move toward the man.

"Your delusions of death are lies! Your beliefs are wrong!" Finn pointed to the Star-Child, feeling burning hot, as if he emanated heat himself. "This will end now!"

The man had frozen, his face stuck in an unreadable position. Finn stared up at Mal'Bal, breathing heavily, passion flaring. Mal'Bal's golden body glinted in the morning sun. He twitched. "You." he spoke, his words barely controlled. "What's your name?"

"Finn SunRider."

"SunRider. Your caring for the world will only lead to disappointment. You will not find satisfaction in the temporary. I—I'll enjoy your death above all others."

As he said the words, movement came from their far right. Entering the Neck from another opening, a cloaked woman emerged. Her eyes were narrow and her skin pale: she was one of the invaders. Behind her, the Golden Puppet followed, crawling on all fours. Like Mal'Bal, the woman held herself in a way that boasted authority. Was she the Star-Child's partner?

"Wahala." Mal'Bal purred. "Right on time."

He made a motion with his hands and the puppet ran to his side, standing at perfect attention. Finn studied Mal'Bal. He controlled the creature. Perhaps through the power of his bracer?

"Master. I apologize for interrupting you. I'll leave if you wish to kill them yourself."

Mal'Bal shook his head. "No, no, Wahala. Look at them. They wear bracers like mine. They're special."

The woman's eyes grew wide. She looked at each of them in turn, her shoulder-length hair flapping as she spun about. Finn guessed her to be in her late twenties, maybe early thirties. Clearly Mal'Bal was the one in charge—perhaps she wielded no special powers of her own.

"Star-Children!" she hissed. "Master, they might be dangerous!"

Mal'Bal shrugged and indicated for her to pull out her weapon. "Nothing we can't handle." he purred.

Wahala dropped her black robe, revealing a bandage-and-leather-wrapped body. She was skinny. Mal'Bal frowned at the sight and the two invaders made strange eye contact. Was there more going on than Finn realized? From behind Wahala's back she pulled out a wicked-looking scythe. Finn's heart beat faster. He'd been expecting the group to face the

Star-Child alone, but now there were others involved.

Mal'Bal turned to Finn and sighed, scratching his nose. The move was casual and of one who seemed bored. He waved a hand and both the puppet and Wahala came to life, running forward toward Finn and his friends. The group jumped, readying their weapons.

"For Kazma!" Leeya shouted.

Altin's bracer glowed and in a split second he shot straight up, barely dodging out of the way as the puppet leapt with incredible speed and height. The creature spun and twisted in mid-air, its limbs rotating and grasping, trying to snag Altin's feet. It dropped back, landing on all fours. Immediately it blurred forward, smashing past Goblin who was thrown across the floor. The puppet ran toward the nearest wall and climbed, digging its fingers and elongated toes into the obsidian like it was clay, losing no speed or momentum. Thirty feet up it jumped out again. Altin twisted and performed an uncontrolled loop to avoid being cut in half by sharp arms.

The woman—Wahala—threw her scythe at Leeya. It spun, moving so fast it formed a blurred disk. Leeya swung her spear like a club and the scythe was knocked out of the air toward the puppet. Yet the puppet, its eyesight unreadable, rotated its upper body as it jumped, grabbed the weapon with one extended hand and slashed it toward Altin. The boy, having dodged out of reach, didn't compensate for the weapon extending the scope of the creature's attack. He screamed as blood spurted out from across his chest.

"Altin!" Finn shouted.

Wahala pulled out two more scythes, sheathed on her legs. She rolled on the floor and popped up in front of Leeya, surprising her. The two began a furious dance of combat across the vast room, grunting and shouting as they attacked and parried.

Altin smashed into a wall, leaving a blood-stain, and fell to the ground, crumpling into a heap. The puppet landed and rushed toward his victim to finish him off, scythe poised for the fatal blow. A falcata hit the scampering monster across the head and it paused. Its body moved slowly, turning to Goblin, who was standing back up. Now weaponless, Goblin was vulnerable—a perfect target. The puppet rushed back the other way like a bucking horse in a mad three-limbed charge, its one free arm holding the scythe. A bolt hit it across the back and again, the puppet paused. Behind it, Altin was wobbling to his feet, a confident grin on his face. His shirt was red with blood. In his hands, he reloaded his crossbow.

"Did you already forget me?" he spoke. "Maybe without eyes it's hard to tell, but you only left a scratch."

The puppet rotated, turning to face the armed threat. It crouched and spread its limbs, crawling slowly on its fingertips and toes, arching its back. It moved in an unnerving way, accessing Altin with a cocked head. Without warning, it was a blur of speed, bounding forward. It focused on Altin and no one else, leaping up and slashing out, attacking with an unstoppable fervor. Altin dove sideways and took off into the air, panic written across his face. The puppet climbed a wall, spun and swiped, yet Altin dodged the attack.

"SunRider!" Mal'Bal shouted. "You stand there gaping and forget the true threat!"

Finn spun, raising his sword and expecting an attack. Instead, he was shocked to find Mal'Bal hadn't moved from his spot. From behind the man, the entrance to the bottom floor of the Neck exploded inwards, showering the room with obsidian and tile. Ducking through the opening was a massive figure—a humanoid shape with a tall cylindrical head. A wooden golem. The monstrosity had to have been twice as large as the stone golem which had attacked the South gate. Mal'Bal laughed as the creation stepped over him and moved toward Finn, its feet shaking the ground.

Altin had flown through an open elevator hatch in the ceiling and the puppet had followed—neither were in the current battle, having taken their personal fight elsewhere. Leeya saw the golem, yet she could do nothing to help Finn. She clashed with Wahala, the strange woman managing to drive Leeya back, keeping her on the defensive. The Kazman girl was doing everything she could to block Wahala's blurred movements. Wahala pressed the attack, chopping bits off Leeya's spear and cutting the girl across the face. Finn saw sweat dripping from the scythe-wielding attacker and knew she was running out of momentum, losing her energy. If Leeya could hold out a little bit longer, she could win the fight.

That left him with Goblin—who'd picked up his falcata—to face the large wooden golem and its master: the Star-Child Mal'Bal himself. The golem swung a massive oak arm, the dark wood knotted and covered in branches. Finn ducked and rolled backward, wondering how such a beast had been created.

The golem's lopsided head—a tree stump with roots hanging like a beard—shook and let out a noise sounding like a forest creaking in a fierce wind. It brought its two arms up and Finn barely managed to roll to the side as the monster smashed its limbs against the ground, splintering tile. Goblin ran to Finn's side, lifting him to his feet. They threw themselves behind an elevator control station and rolled away as it was crushed by the creature. Steam burst out, hissing and spluttering.

"We-have-to-fight-it-outside!" Goblin shouted above the noise. "If-we-stay-here-it-will-corner-us!"

Agreeing, Finn sprinted toward the nearest exit, Goblin close behind. The golem gave chase, its legs extending in wide steps. Behind them, Mal'Bal followed, walking with a calm smile on his face. Outside, Finn ran over a bridge, up a set of stairs, and across a long stretch of catwalk, stopping on the other side. He'd had no choice but to leave Altin and Leeya behind to fight their own battles. He raised a hand to halt

Goblin, who would have kept running.

"We-must-continue!" the boy pleaded. "It-will-kill-us-if-we-stop!"

The golem ducked beneath the destroyed entrance to the Neck, crossed the bridge, and went up the stairs, each long step coming closer. It stepped foot onto the catwalk and the structure groaned. The monster moved again, bending the narrow platform under its large weight. Behind it, Mal'Bal waved his hands forward, either goading or controlling the monster onwards. It took another step—now halfway across. If it came any closer, it would bend down and crush them into paste.

"Finn!" Goblin screamed.

The catwalk shattered, exploding downwards as Finn had planned. The golem let out a haunting cry and collapsed into the falling debris, breaking through the roof of a house below and disappearing from sight. Dust rose into the air and the platform Finn stood on shuddered. Far beneath their feet, another smashing noise sounded out, and another. The monster was still alive, struggling in the tight confines of the alley floors. Finn looked to the other end of the newly-formed gap. Mal'Bal was nowhere to be seen. Had he fallen?

"Come on!" he told Goblin, "Let's find our way around to one of the other bridges. We have to return to the Neck and help out the others!"

They ran across a small stone path and slid down a rope to the level below. In the distance, they could see citizens and soldiers fighting against Mal'Bal's forces. Finn spotted Quinta, the crazy vendor, charging a score of robed figures. He brandished a stick as a weapon and around him, swarms of blue moths converged on the enemy. Finn could hear screams and Quinta's shouts. "Kill! Kill! Kill! Protect the city, Matriarch!"

Leaving the scene behind, Finn sprinted through a house, finding a dead-end. Both him and Goblin were forced to hop a window to continue deeper through the city. They landed in a large clothing store with wooden shelves boasting nightwear. The dark room was lit by torches, bathing the place in red light. Like many of the other buildings, this one was abandoned due to the attack.

"If-we-go-through-that-door-we-might-find-stairs-leading-up-to-the-plaza!" Goblin suggested, pointing to a nearby passage.

Before Finn could concur, the floor exploded, throwing them across the room. Finn smashed against a wall, crying out in pain. His head vibrated and he couldn't see straight. He attempted to stagger to his feet but tripped and fell back down. Smoke, there was smoke in the air—something was on fire. The torches! The torches must have fallen onto the clothes and wooden shelves. A haunting moan rang out and suddenly the entire room shifted, tilting to the side. Finn rolled and bounced, smacking into furniture and screaming in shock. He fell through a hole in the floor, landing in the store beneath. The place was so full of flames Finn couldn't tell what it had once sold. And being immune to heat didn't prevent him from choking on the thick black clouds surrounding his head.

"Goblin!" he coughed.

Something moved in front of him. Bursting out of the flames came the wooden golem, its body swallowed by uncontrollable fire. It sounded as if it were shrieking. It writhed about, flailing its arms and breaking everything in its path. Finn tucked and dove, dodging falling beams and burning branches, backing into the depths of the room. He spotted Goblin leaning against a shelf. His friend looked dazed and held his mouth open, unable to take in enough oxygen. There was a crash as the golem came for them, a hairsbreadth behind Finn. In desperation, Finn tackled his friend and—without planning to—broke through a window, falling outside. He landed on a wooden platform between two bookstores, losing his breath. Garbage sacks and clothes tangled his feet.

Behind them, a section of towering stores exploded outwards and the golem reappeared. Debris and furniture rained around them and into the depths of the city. The golem ran to them, crackling and popping as flames ate its body. It'd lost an arm, leaving only a red-hot stump in its place.

Finn untangled himself and jumped to his feet, running for his life, Goblin at his heels. Spinning down an alley and turning a corner, they came to a bridge leading into the Neck's pavilion. Far inside, he could see Leeya still battling Wahala. The alley behind them was ripped open as the golem rushed through. It stretched out its remaining arm as if to crush them, its shoulders grinding against the walls. Half its head was crumbling off, black and red wood turning into coal and ash. Its chest was cracked open, exposing a glowing green gem for a heart. It was dying.

Finn and Goblin ran away, once more entering the shade of the Neck. Behind them, the beast gave chase, so close Finn was afraid Goblin would catch on fire.

"Split up!" Finn roared out and Goblin complied, dodging to the right. Finn took a sharp left and the monster followed, going after him. Ahead, a bloodied Wahala beat Leeya to the ground with a closed fist. The two women were gasping for air, equally matched. Finn ran past Wahala, screaming. She looked up in time to be bowled over by the golem. Wahala flew backward, head cracking against the ground. She rolled to a stop, robes smoking. Her body didn't move.

The golem's legs caved inward, its knees breaking, no longer strong enough to support its own weight. With a final howl, it went down face-first. Its body burst into chunks of burning wood; snapping, shattering, and flying about. Splinters buzzed through the air, embedding into skin. The scorched gem heart shattered upon impact with the hard tile, pieces sliding all over the room. There was silence. Finn fell to his knees gasping. Nearby, Leeya stood up, groaning and rubbing her ribs and cheek. Goblin walked over to them, trying to catch his breath.

"We-did-it! It's-dead!" he said.

There was a thump behind them and they turned, finding Altin.

Blood leaked from dozens of cuts on his body and he walked as if drunk—yet he still had a crazy smile to his face. "Lost it." he panted. "The puppet's up somewhere on floor eighteen."

"Impressive."

They spun in place, hearts jumping to their mouths. Finn was already clenching his fists, recognizing the voice.

Mal'Bal strolled forward, looking as if he'd awoken from a nap. His gold body moved smoothly, each joint adorned with a green gem like golem's heart. He was human, yet something else entirely. Something...wrong. An abomination.

"I guess I'll fight you all myself."

The words had barely left the man's mouth when he was upon them, a blur of movement so fast Finn could hardly follow. The Star-Child punched Altin across the face and there was a crunch of bone. Altin shouted and fell back, blood bursting out of his nose. In the same movement, Mal'Bal spun and kicked Goblin in the chest, sending him flying.

Leeya jabbed at the man with her spear, yet Mal'Bal wove to the side like a snake, not even needing to parry. Finn dove for his sword, which he'd dropped when the golem first attacked. As he grabbed it, something collided with his chest. It was as if he'd been hit with a battering ram. His ribs cracked and suddenly he was airborne. He hit the ground rolling, coughing, and half-unconscious. Mal'Bal had merely kicked him. His vision blurred as he sat up, holding his stomach. There was a flash of light from where Mal'Bal fought Leeya. Finn cleared his eyes and beheld a magnificent sight: Leeya had activated her bracer.

It was unlike anything Finn had imagined. Every time he'd seen a bracer activate, it'd split and moved, settling on various sections of the body. Leeya's on the other hand, did more.

As Mal'Bal swung his scythe at her, the metal of the bracer

hovered over Leeya's body, barely kissing her skin, and covered whatever spot was being attacked. *Like a living, moving shield.* The round plate-sized piece darted to her neck, blocked the blow, and dove to cover her knee. So that was the power of an Exception. No wonder she couldn't be classified like the other Star-Children. She was no Accessory, Half-suit, or Full-suit. This was a fluid, adaptable, armor.

Mal'Bal stabbed and slashed, creating complicated patterns, leaving the afterimage of strange lines in the air. Yet no matter how quickly or skillfully he attacked, he couldn't cut Leeya. On the other hand, Leeya could attack back without worry of being injured. She gored Mal'Bal over and over, her spear cutting divots into his golden body.

"Duna-vel-meyoh!" the Star-Child screamed.

Leeya's spear sunk into Mal'Bal's leg, his appendage becoming liquid. Mal'Bal tipped over, unable to support himself.

"Bek-mull!"

The leg hardened, trapping the weapon. Mal'Bal rolled and the spear shattered, its head trapped in Mal'Bal's body. The man spoke more strange words and the spear-tip dropped out. He stood, panting. His eyes gleamed with what seemed to be pleasure.

"WORTHY!" he roared, face split into a wide grin. Spit flecked his lips. The man looked to the ceiling. "Break the organ."

It took Finn a second to realize whom the man was talking to. He followed Mal'Bal's gaze. In horror, he saw the Golden Puppet drop from the elevator opening and land by the DozDum pipes. Finn recalled what Leeya had told him. *There's a magic flowing through the runes, keeping the Upper-District floating. They're powered by the DozDum Organ.* A cold claw of despair grabbed at Finn's soul. So that's why Mal'Bal had made his way to the Neck. He wasn't interested in capturing Kazma for himself. He wanted to destroy it off the face of Lenova. He was going to drop the entire Upper-District on top of the Lower-District.

"No!" Finn screamed, picking up his sword and running toward the puppet. Goblin and Altin stood as well, charging the creature. Leeya shouted a war cry and attacked the Star-Child with her fists. Mal'Bal laughed hysterically, letting her blows bounce off his chest.

The puppet cut into the thick metal pipes, its sharp arms biting deep. It used its arms like axes, its fingers like prying blades. Hacking off a piece, it turned and threw it at Finn, who ducked and tripped, nearly falling on his head. Altin tried to grab the monster's legs but the puppet kicked him away, hitting Altin's already injured face. He collapsed, unmoving. Behind them, Leeya screamed as Mal'Bal liquefied his arms and stabbed at her from various angles. Leeya's suit was only able to block one attack, leaving her right side open. Mal'Bal's sharpened hand jabbed through her skin, near her hip. He splayed his fingers, tearing her flesh. Goblin twisted in place, changing his course for the Lich-Lord.

Finn, still running to the puppet, threw himself, and slid across the floor. The move was a surprise to the puppet, for it didn't react in time. Finn skidded between its spidery-thin legs and stabbed up, sliding his blade between where the right leg met pelvis. His sword cracked against a gem serving as a joint and his weapon shattered. Yet the move did something to the creature. The puppet spasmed, writhing and twisting upon itself, its appendages lashing out. It smashed into Finn, and his left arm—the one with the bracer—dislocated as he was crushed against the DozDum pipes. With face pressed against the metal, he could detect a large change of vibration in the magical structure. The hum was far more sporadic, as if losing strength. He moaned in pain but was unable to break free. The puppet continued to twist about him, as if without control of its limbs. Another section of the pipes was cut. Above them, a titanic groan roared out. How had the evil Star-Child known the secret to the Upper-District's magic?

Goblin rushed Mal'Bal, who loomed over Leeya with bloodied

hands. The girl was crawling backward, holding her side and gritting her teeth. Her face was pale, as if she was losing consciousness. Finn tried to break free to help his friends, but the puppet continued to pin him.

Using a chunk of burning wood from the fallen golem, Goblin jumped in the air and hit the Star-Child on the back of the head. The crack was heard across the chamber. Goblin's makeshift club shattered and Mal'Bal fell to the ground, landing heavily. Goblin fell beside him, sprawled on his back and losing his breath. *Had he done it? Had Finn's young friend taken out the evil man?*

Leeya was unconscious, her hand falling away from her injury. Blood leaked out freely. Altin was moving, his body turning over. The puppet threw Finn to the side and sliced one final time, cleaving the DozDum pipes in half. Mal'Bal turned around on the floor, holding a glowing shard from the dead golem's heart. Finn was falling, hitting tile, opening his mouth to scream, eyes widening. Altin was rising. The pipes were shrieking. The ceiling was shaking. The puppet was twisting in place.

Mal'Bal stabbed Goblin through the chest.

Time froze. Finn couldn't hear anything. About him, pieces of the ceiling rained, shattering against the floor, forming craters. The evil Star-Child rose to his feet and kicked Goblin to the side. He was no longer grinning. His eyes met Finn's and their gazes locked.

We're not through yet, you and I. Someday, we'll meet again. The words weren't spoken but felt. Fate coursed through them both. Visions of the future. Their bracers glowed, as if acknowledging each other. Two swords raised in salute, ready for a distant duel.

Mal'Bal spun and ran toward Wahala's fallen form. He picked her up with ease and grabbed his mask, dodging around collapsing obsidian. Three golems appeared near one exit and hoisted their master. Before Finn could shout, the Star-Child was gone, whisked away, leaving behind the afterimage of gold.

An arm pulled Finn up—Altin. The boy was blinking blood from his face.

"We must run!" he was bellowing over and over.

They sprinted to their fallen companions. Finn's dislocated arm dangled freely: useless. As Altin reached Leeya and picked her up, Finn dropped beside his best friend in the whole wide world.

Goblin's eyes were closed. Waves of blood soaked his shirt and he didn't move. Gone. Finn screamed his throat raw, feeling heat emanate from him unlike anything he'd ever experienced. Rage hotter than the Slaglands wanted to tear free, wanted to consume him, *control him.* But he couldn't. Not yet. Not now. He had to escape. He had to take Goblin with him. He couldn't leave him there to be crushed by the collapsing city. With adrenaline rushing through his veins, Finn lifted Goblin with one arm, holding him over his shoulders. His body shook, wanting to collapse, his legs threatening to give out. He gasped, gritted his teeth, adjusted his grip, and raced after Altin.

He didn't know how he had the strength. Didn't even care. He only focused on putting one foot in front of the other. His steps were a monotonous droning chant. *Escape. Escape. Escape.*

He ran across catwalks and bridges, citizens and enemy alike fleeing around him, shouting in terror. Behind them, the connecting tower caved inwards, throwing debris and dust across half the city. Shrieking stones, the size of city blocks, spun in the air and fell, smashing and rolling around them. Entire streets were obliterated. Towers containing homes and businesses collapsed against each other, flattening people in the alleyways like two doors closing shut against a bug. Finn ran faster than ever before, his lungs working to a point of near bursting. Goblin's body bounced and slid along his back, tottering on the edge of falling off. Finn could see the distant Eastern gate—the only free exit. Crowds surged toward it, fleeing for their lives.

Altin changed his course toward a nearby stable where horses buckled and whinnied, terrified. Citizens were grabbing at them and jumping on their backs. Men fought men for a chance at the animals, neighbors and family turning on each other, fear blanching their faces. In the confusion, Finn and Altin found a gap to the back of the stables. Behind a shut door were two forgotten plow-horses: a gray filly and a brown mare. Putting their friend's bodies across the animals, Altin and Finn hopped on the saddles. Finn had never ridden a horse before, yet instinct took over. Following Altin's lead, he grabbed the reigns and whipped them. The beast took off at full sprint, pushing through the crowds and back into the streets. Panicked citizens grabbed at Finn's shirt and he verged on toppling off.

Breaking loose, they made it to the main alley and rushed through the Eastern gate, tearing out of Kazma. Around them, people cried and shouted, running with arms outstretched, reaching for life as if it was escaping them. Within under a minute it happened.

The Upper-District broke apart, tipping and coming down with a haunting roar. The walls which held the carved runes imploded: the destruction of a powerful magic spell, the death of a city. With the boom of finality, the Upper-District hit the ground and Kazma was obliterated. Earthquakes forced the ground into a bounce, splitting earth. Waves of dust swept out like curtains across the land, turning Lenova into a place of shadows.

upon the ruins

25

—*The practice of cannibalism was purged, city by city, throughout the first millennium of the Economic Era. Either by sword or diplomacy, the King and his men went forth putting a stop to the primitive act. Placing trade routes and teaching agriculture, the King helped civilize vast lands across Lenova that were once wild and had been so for thousands of years.* — *-Lenovan Economic History Vol 4, page 457*

A ll was still. The world no longer moved nor battled itself. The sounds of collapsing rock and the screams of death no longer rang out. Blood on skin had caked dry, forming thick crust. Thirst had been intensified, demanding with more strength. Body had no energy, but instead screamed as every muscle contracted, tightening into spiraled knots. Wahala opened her eyes.

Smoke and dust clotted the air, darkening the noon sun. She'd been unconscious for a while. Surely the battle for Kazma had finished and since she was still alive, the cult had won. Yet... she was still alive. Why was that? Had she been saved? Heavy footfalls answered her and she turned her head, feeling her hair drag along debris. She was laying on a collapsed street. A shadow hit her face and covered the sun. She blinked. It was Mal'Bal. She croaked, her chest and lips trembling.

"You live." his voice spoke out, "by my decision."

Wahala tried sitting up but her body refused to obey. It twitched and rolled on its side, flopping like a food sack. In a move she didn't expect, Mal'Bal crouched and lifted her head and neck, propping her on a flat stone. He gazed into her eyes and they stared at each other. She was sure her weakened state shone clear to him. In turn, he was unreadable. His eyes reflected only controlled madness. Mal'Bal stood and turned away, looking about him with a sigh. Wahala studied the rubble: Kazma was no more.

Rock and mortar collected in mountainous mounds, forming vast landscapes of broken buildings and collapsed infrastructure. Pylons and wooden catwalks stuck out at odd angles like broken bones protruding from skin, pipes were intestines displayed for the air. Debris the size of city blocks formed cliffs, latticed with holes where tunnels and homes once were. Massive segments of the Upper-District lay in radical angles, leaning precariously, threatening further collapse. Much of the Lower-District lay far beneath them, crushed and pushed into the ground, forming a layered nest of destruction. The air was choked with the smell of dust. Wahala looked to her left, where a beautifully designed fountain from the Upper-District still poured water at a weakening trickle, mysteriously having survived. Throughout the ruin, golems near and far lifted boulders and walls, searching for people, useful objects, and whatever else Mal'Bal had commanded them to find.

Wahala's vision blurred in and out and she winced as strange whistling filled her head. She hoped the wooden golem that had knocked her down had met with an ill demise.

"Gather into groups of six. You'll each be assigned one of my creations." Mal'Bal spoke to someone beyond Wahala's sight. "Round up the fugitives of Kazma. We must replenish our armies, after all."

"Wise you are, oh Lich-Lord." the voice of a cult member spoke out, "Having left the Eastern gate free, you protected your investment of lives. I hope plenty see sense in joining us instead of choosing death."

Mal'Bal grunted. "While you're out, hunt for those within our army that used the opportunity of battle to run from me. Kill them. Cowards don't deserve life."

"Yes, master. As you wish."

Wahala listened as the cult member's footsteps retreated. Another approached Mal'Bal. He was a new recruit; one they'd picked up from a small village nearby. The man rung his hands nervously.

"Lord, the golems have excavated the remains of the Neck. They've found a deep hole leading to the belly of the earth. It's all that's left of the pipes. Near to it lays your puppet-servant."

"Good." Mal'Bal purred. "I'll have the golems bring my child to me. Use the hole to dispose of all the bodies."

"We mean to stay here?" the new cult member stuttered.

Mal'Bal backhanded the man, sending the cowering figure rolling down a pile of rocks. "Don't talk back to me, you're only here to receive orders." the Lich-Lord spoke, voice calm like a father disciplining a son. "But yes, we do plan to stay. For at least a while."

Wahala's mind struggled to hold on to the slipperiness of reality and focus on what was happening around her. Mal'Bal was putting a pause on his campaign and gathering new troops. What was his reasoning to slow down? Losing momentum could be fatal to them. What if the king sent out his armies?

"Only one more of you may approach me. I have other business to attend to." Mal'Bal commanded.

Was there was a line of cult members around them, waiting for their turn to talk to the Golden Agony and request guidance? How long had men and women been walking past Wahala, looking down upon her weak unconscious form? How humiliating. From the corner of her eye she saw twelve men approach Mal'Bal. They weren't in black robes. Instead, they wore an assortment of torn ragged clothing. Many had missing teeth and earrings dangling from their lobes. They were dirty and unkempt.

"Mighty Star-Child," one of them spoke. "we're but common highway robbe—scavengers. We're honored to be in your presence." His voice was hesitant and stank of failed praise. Mal'Bal didn't reply so the man continued. "Please, great one, master of all, destroyer of kingdoms, accept us into your fold. We have much to offer your cause."

"You wish to be enlisted?" Mal'Bal asked. The man dipped, his companions doing the same.

"Yes, oh yes! We're great as a unit, stealing the very lives from under the nose of our prey without them noticing. We know the lands round about and can pose as fugitives, drawing in your enemies."

Mal'Bal was silent for a while. The tall cult leader kept his arms folded and he studied the group. "I assume you ask for payment in return?"

The robber bowed his upper body so low it threatened to tip. He waved his arms like windmills, making his appearance even more ridiculous. "But only a small fee m'lord. Naught much more than one gold piece per week."

Instead of beheading the lot of them as Wahala would have predicted, Mal'Bal swept his gaze over her injured body and focused on her face. "While you were back in our homeland, did you gather gold?"

Wahala had to refocus her mind before nodding her weary head.

"Y—yes." she croaked. "I brought some."

Mal'Bal turned back to the band of highway robbers. "You may join." he spoke with a wave. He waved again, dismissing the crowd. Wahala heard many footsteps recede as people dispersed upon the Lich-Lord's command.

"You let them steal from you?" Wahala rasped. "Their price is far too steep for what they offer."

Mal'Bal smiled, not looking at her, but instead to the horizon. The reaction was strange, a far transition from his usual behavior. "They will serve their purpose. And when they've done so, they'll either be dead by my campaign, or by my hands. They are fodder. When they lay broken, I will loot my gold from their corpses and return it to our coffers. They don't know it, but they've sold me their lives for nothing." The leader sighed. "Other thieves, murderers, and crooks have asked me this. I've denied none. For that, Wahala, I am wise."

He motioned to the destruction. "Behold their stupidity. They didn't even know the language carved above them, telling me exactly how their precious city worked."

Wahala furrowed her brow. *She* hadn't known the meaning to the runes either. How had Mal'Bal known? How many languages did he speak?

He turned to her and crouched, resting his arms on his knees. His face was pensive. It terrified Wahala. He was so… controlled.

"Oh, my dark butterfly." he whispered, licking his lips. "You've done it, haven't you?"

Wahala's heart smashed against her chest. Her golden heart. It could feel the power from Mal'Bal's necromancy prodding at it— scrutinizing. He could sense it.

"What did you do within our temple, Wahala? What forbidden rooms has my little snake slithered into?""

"M—master?" Wahala choked.

"Answer the question, Wahala."

The control in his voice, his half-lidded stare… what had come over the man? Wahala had never felt more vulnerable in her life, had never felt as close to death. She knew she couldn't lie to him. She knew he was too cunning, too alert, to be fooled. Had he known all along, since the beginning, what her plans had been? *Had he known of her intentions before she'd known them herself? What was his scope? His vision?*

Mal'Bal sighed and motioned with a hand. A smaller rock golem came forward. It wrapped its oblong arms around Wahala and lifted her with no effort. She hissed in pain as her body was moved. Her muscles coiled and tightened even further.

"You've betrayed me, Wahala." Mal'Bal spoke. "Usurper. Heathen. Heretic. Fearful of change. *Queen Priestess.*"

When he said the words, Wahala closed her eyes. She'd been uncovered. There'd never been any chance. Perhaps Mal'Bal was too powerful—too knowing—to ever be stopped. She had Lenova as an example to her master's ferocity and strength. He was a force of nature. He was the embodiment of death. The only question remaining was in what method would she be executed.

The golem walked and Mal'Bal kept pace, strolling beside her with his arms behind his back. The crunching of their feet rang out as they traversed the ruins of Kazma. They passed by a human arm sticking out from beneath a stone. Blood caked the entire area. Wahala, one who'd seen gore all her life, suddenly couldn't stomach the sight. She looked away, into the bosom of the golem.

"You wanted my power. You wanted me gone. Why?" Mal'Bal asked.

Wahala, knowing there was nothing left to lose, scoffed. "We've walked with, tamed, and fought monsters; yet they all pale in comparison to you, Mal'Bal. You've changed our ways! You've spat upon all we stood for! You ended our traditions! Your birth killed your mother, the last Queen and within the twenty years before another could be chosen, you killed all the acolytes—the possible successors."

Mal'Bal barked and let out a small smile. "With growth comes change, Wahala." His gaze roamed over her. "The Queens were weak. They had no vision. You were one of the many too fearful to accept that. You couldn't adapt. Now, you must face your consequence."

Wahala gulped and clenched her jaw. They left the ruins of Kazma and walked the vast plains of tents that were home to Mal'Bal's forces. The cult taught that death was glory: a release from futile existence. Wahala would return to the void, cease to exist, and finally be at peace. No matter what happened, she would accept it. She would be noble in her martyrdom.

The golem crouched as they entered a large hexagonal tent. It was Mal'Bal's gore tent, where he'd birthed the Golden Puppet. The golem lowered her onto the red-stained canvas floor, leaning her against the tent's central supporting pole. Mal'Bal entered after her and closed the tent flap. She was bathed in warm darkness. The sweet, sickly smell of decay overwhelmed her senses, pushing its way down her throat and churning her stomach. It overpowered her and made her dry-heave. She pushed with her foot at a bent spinal-column resting nearby. Mal'Bal walked behind her and crouched, pulling a rope from beneath his robes and binding her arms together, tying her to the pole. He went to her legs and tied them also. Up close, the man reeked of rot, his smell equal to the tent. Tiny bits of putrid flesh clung to the small crevices and joints of his golden body. Had he been bathing in corpses?

"What is this?" Wahala asked, feeling feverish. Her abs and her lower back clenched and unclenched.

"Prepare yourself, little Queen. I'll make an example of you to the public. They'll see what happens when someone second-guesses my leadership."

Then Wahala saw the depths of Mal'Bal's eyes, beyond the carefully-layered wall of tranquility: a chasm of pure black. Mal'Bal took the persona of a demon, a terror, a God. He was in absolute control. He held Wahala's feeble fate in his hands. Body vibrating in time with her burning muscles, Wahala faded into the dark, her last vision being of the Lich-Lord standing and smiling down at her, his grin growing wider and wider until it split into a chasm, swallowing her up.

an idealist

26

—The creation of lead dentures allowed many in Lenova to have full sets of teeth once more and helped promote a greater practice of oral hygiene. House Regilus spent years assuring that the weight loss and joint pain many felt soon after implanting lead dentures was due to old age settling in. But the populace caught on that lead poisoning was rampant among the elderly. Threatened with the termination of their House, the nobles of Pania invented Soot-Shine, a charcoal-based drink with magical properties that nourished and cleaned teeth. There were no ill side-effects apart from occasionally black-stained teeth. The inventor of lead dentures was pulled out of his home and buried alive under all of his rejected product, leaving a slimy mess of saliva and toxic metal for the cleaners of Pania to deal with the next day. —
-Excerpt from The Evolution of Baser Lenovan Technologies, page 88

Finn, holding his reins with his one uninjured arm while balancing Goblin on the horse, slid sideways, tipping toward the dirt road rushing beneath him. He jerked back up, his body as weak as a bag of liquid, bouncing and wiggling with no sense of control. His chin hit his chest and his eyes fluttered as he tried to stay within reality. The pain in his body had faded, which Finn took to be a bad sign. He could no longer feel his chest where Mal'Bal had kicked him. Neither did his dislocated left arm send jabs of electric shards into his brain, telling him something was wrong. Blood soaked his leather pants and matted the horse's mane and saddle—Goblin's blood. The flow had slowed, which meant truly, his friend was dead.

The emotions that'd drowned him since the collapse of the Neck now sucked all the energy from him, leaving him a husk that could blow away at the slightest breeze. He didn't know how to feel anymore. Was it rage or sadness leading him on? Or perhaps the memory of his friend, smiling at him as he returned to Pittance?

"I-can-talk! I-can-talk!"

Tears welled in Finn's eyes and he sobbed, his vision blurring to nothing more than smeared color. Fear ran through him for Leeya, where to his left, she lay in the same position as Goblin, carried by Altin, who fared worse than Finn. Both Star-Children bled from multiple wounds, yet Leeya, whose side had been torn open by Mal'Bal's hand, looked to be dead as well. The only sign she was alive was that blood continued to flow from her wounds, indicating her heart was working weakly. But for how much longer?

Altin turned to Finn. His face was so covered in dried blood, his featured were masked, making him nearly unrecognizable. His left eye was swollen shut and the other was blood-shot.

"Finn." the boy croaked. "There's a commotion ahead."

Finn blinked the tears from his face and focused on the road in front of them. They were approaching a group of people blocking the path. Horses grazed nearby, their coats covered in sweat. The half-packed luggage strewn on the road indicated they were Kazman survivors. Among them were three soldiers, their armor battered and scratched. Finn and Altin were forced to slow their pace.

The three soldiers held between them a cloaked figure. Finn's tired eyes widened. The figure was dressed in black. It was one of Kazma's invaders. The soldiers beat at the man, punching his head and stomach. The figure tried to block the attacks but was kicked to the ground without mercy. Around the group, civilians cheered and spit at the cowering form.

"Please!" the cloaked man begged, "I ran away before the attack began! I had no part of it!"

"He lies!" one of the civilians shouted.

"Why'd you do it?" a soldier asked, smashing a stone against the man's foot. The cloaked figure howled and grabbed at the broken appendage.

"Stop!" Finn croaked, not able to take the sight. He was tired, so tired of seeing pain. The people finally noticed him and Altin. They gazed upon them and someone whispered out *"Star-Children."*

"I see your kind still lives while our families lie beneath the rubble of our once great city." one woman spoke, the spite in her voice surprising Finn. Why was she directing her anger toward them? "Should you not be back at what remains of Kazma, fighting for us? What good is your power, oh Chosen?" She spat on the ground in front of them. The others around her nodded in agreement.

Beside him, Altin barked out a laugh. "We could be asking the same of you, cowards. If your families lie in Kazma, why are you so far from them? Did you leave them behind?"

The woman froze and her eyes flickered in pain and fear—with embarrassment.

"What are you doing to this man?" Finn asked one soldier, indicating with his chin to the prone figure holding his mangled foot.

"Interrogating him." the soldier growled. "And you better move along and not interfere."

"Or what?" Altin asked, his one open eye shining with anger.

The soldier took a step back and swallowed. "You look half-dead."

"And do you think that gives you an advantage? Do you plan on fighting me?" Altin hissed, his voice low.

The soldier bared his teeth. "Be on your way then. We've already been hurt enough by your kind." He turned and kicked the form on the dirt. "And his *cult*."

Cult? Was that what Mal'Bal's forces were? It made sense to Finn—the robes, scythes, strange deformations and replaced golden limbs...

"I told you!" the man cried out, "I was forced into service! I hail from Sodomona! It was join or die! I left before the battle! I didn't kill anyone!"

"You joined them!" the soldier shouted. "You *are* one of them, then! Do you see us wearing robes? We're not like you—easy, bendable, weak-hearted! Again, I'll ask you: why attack us?"

"It wasn't me!" the man groaned. "It was the Star-Child, the Lich-Lord Mal'Bal! He travels the land and ends all in his path! He has no mercy nor no end!"

"What does he want?" another soldier asked. The cult member winced as a blow was aimed for his side.

"D—death! Only death! He doesn't care for power or money!"

"All tyrants care for power and money!" a civilian yelled.

"How'd he do it?" the third soldier asked, crouching in front of the cult member and pulling out a knife. "How'd he destroy Kazma? Tell me or I'll cut off your face!"

The robed man exploded into tears. "I don't know! I don't know! All I heard was he understood the runes carved on the Upper-District! He knew the ancient language as if it was his own! He knew of the DozDum pipes! I left before the army charged into your city, I swear!"

"He lies!" one of the civilians shouted. "His scythe is caked in blood!"

The cult member shook his head vigorously. "No! No! The blood's my own! I fell upon the weapon as I fled! It wa—"

His voice was cut short as a bolt stabbed through his right eye, ending his life. His body flopped to the dirt. The soldiers jumped back, pulling out swords as the civilians shouted in fear. Finn spun in horror, turning to Altin—who held his crossbow, his body shaking from anger and exhaustion.

"This was taking too long. We must pass through. Where's the next town?"

One of the soldiers dropped his sword and raised his arms to the air, his eyes full of terror. "E—EldenBurrow, lord. 'Tis only three more kilometers East of us down the path."

Altin nudged with his chin. "Move." They did, giving Finn and Altin a wide berth. Finn, speechless at what had transpired, followed. They cantered forward, their horses whinnying in complaint. Behind them, the group of Kazman citizens watched them leave.

"You killed him!" Finn spoke, working up the words.

"So?" Altin replied, his voice calm and his open eye focused forward.

"You didn't have to do that! He said he wasn't part of the battle! He wasn't even trying to attack us! That wasn't self-defense, it was murder!"

Altin was quiet and picked up the pace of his horse, putting one hand on Leeya's neck to check her pulse.

"ALTIN!" Finn shouted, nudging his horse to move faster and catch up.

The Star-Child scowled. "We care for our own Finn! Only our own! You can't trust people! You can't let them in—you just can't!"

Finn clenched his jaw. "Your tone was a lot different a few hours ago when we fought to protect Kazma!"

Altin spun to face him, his expression one of fury. His long blond hair swirled around him. "AND LOOK AT WHAT HAPPENED, FINN! LOOK!" He motioned to both Goblin and Leeya.

Fresh tears left Finn's his eyes. His friends… "We were chosen, Altin." He spoke the words through gritted teeth, his body shaking. "We were given this power to protect Lenova, all of it. Don't say the words. Don't make their deaths meaningless."

"Their deaths *are* meaningless." Altin whispered. The sentence was a punch to Finn's heart. His mind reeled into darkness. Oh Lady Tuliah, what do I do?

"You're a fool and an idealist, Finn." Altin spoke the words as if they were poison. "You have fanciful visions of heroism and bravery. Of saving Lenova? Give me a break. We can't save Lenova. *You* can't save Lenova. No one can. Focus on what we can do. Focus on bringing Leeya to a healer before she too, is gone."

Altin forced his horse into a full gallop, leaving Finn behind. With his best friend's body resting against him, Altin's words lingered in Finn's heart.

Within the hour they spotted EldenBurrow. It was a small city comparable to Wyrmroost, where Finn had talked to the beggar. Its small stone walls boasted no strong defense and the people inside wore humble clothing and lived in sad wooden homes with thatched straw roofs. Mud coated the streets and light rain pattered the area, adding to the gloominess of the place. EldenBurrow looked to be a city heavily taxed by the king, where only those too poor to move, stayed. It was a place that left the taste of ash in one's mouth.

Finn and Altin were not the first fugitives of Kazma to arrive. Already, nearly a score of Kazman civilians clustered around the center of town, shouting warnings of Mal'Bal and frightening the local populace. In a cold gray alley, Finn and Altin found a healer. The woman and her daughter sucked in their breaths, shocked at their state. They brought both Goblin and Leeya indoors while Finn assured the woman's husband they weren't bad Star-Children who would cause them harm. While the healer called for help from the rest of her family, Finn promised he'd pay whatever price she demanded. The healer sent off her daughter for supplies and had her son fetch clean linen, bandages, and hot water. As her husband and Altin set Goblin and Leeya onto the kitchen's wooden table and bench, Finn did what he could to be of service.

The healer and her family went to work, wiping away blood and mashing ingredients together to salve the wounds. Needing to focus, she sent Finn and Altin out of the house. Altin disappeared, taking their tired horses with him. Where he went, Finn didn't know. After a long time, the healer's young boy came out and sat beside him on the wet wooden steps. He stared at Finn's dislocated arm where the bracer rested. The boy must have been no older than eight. His eyes were deep and discerning and Finn couldn't tell what thoughts were running through his young child mind.

"What's that?" the boy asked, fiddling with his woolen vest.

Finn was startled. The boy didn't know of Star-Children. His parents must have kept the fact from him so to not scare the boy. "It's…"

Finn stalled. How to answer such a profound question? "It's a symbol."

"Of what?" the boy asked.

Of what indeed. Finn was regaining the sensation of pain in his body and he winced in agony. Both him and Altin had refused to be attended to until the healer had taken care of their friends.

"Well, it can be a symbol for power." Finn said.

"What kind of power?" the boy probed.

Finn rubbed his face with his one good hand. "A noble power or a bad power. A confusing power. It can symbolize heroism. Or a monster. *Fate.*"

"So why do you wear it?" the boy asked. "What's the symbol to you?"

The question rattled Finn's bones and he opened and closed him mouth, eyes going wide. The power the question had was overwhelming. Why *had* he donned the bracer? What did it stand for? He remembered one of his first talks with Piscus on the way to Pittance; Piscus had yet to trust him at the time.

"I didn't want to be a Star-Child." he had whispered to the man. *"I only put it on to give me the power to protect my friend."* Piscus in turn replied: *"Then you're a special case, Finn. An Unchosen. A boy who wants power for righteous reasons. Words hard to believe."*

"Why do you wear it?" the boy asked Finn again.

To protect my friends. To protect Lenova. Altin's words of foolish dreams were pushed away and replaced with an image of Goblin.

"I wear it as a reminder of a dream." he said the words with a quiver.

"My father tells me I should follow my dreams." the boy responded.

"Your father's wise." Finn choked. "We should all follow our dreams."

"Are you going to follow yours?" the boy asked.

Before Finn could reply, the house door opened and the healer stepped out. Sweat hugged her pale brow. She wiped her bloodied hands on her apron and mentioned for Finn to come forward. Finn jumped to his feet. "What is it?" he asked.

"I've stabilized both of your friends."

"B—both?" Finn spoke the words with dry lips. Goblin...

"Yes, but unless you can find someone who can perform miracles, they'll perish before the end of this day. They breathe for only a while longer."

a race to jakitta

27

—In 3,775 E.E. Lord Yuggu halted his siege of Divundar to celebrate his birthday. He invited everyone in the land and promised by the name of his mother that all those that came to revel, he would forge an alliance with. It was to his utmost surprise when the non-warlike people of Divundar, the very people he'd been sieging, showed up, holding Yuggu to his word. Soon after, Yuggu befell into misfortune, falling off his horse and breaking his neck. His people, leaderless, fell into the control of the Divundar, who without losing a single man, had defeated their enemies. —
-Excerpt from Strange Lenovan Facts of Flight and Fancy, page 3

The healer took Finn inside of her home and they approached Goblin together. The boy was shirtless with bandages wrapped around his chest. Upon examining his friend up close, Finn could see shallow breathing. His body trembled. There was still hope.

"A gem shard of some sort is embedded within his heart. I can't remove it without killing him. Each time his heart beats, the gem shifts, tearing his insides. Time, I'm afraid, is not on his side."

"H—how does he live?" Finn asked, choking on the emotions welling within him. "Should the injury not have killed him immediately?"

"I don't know. There's something to the gem shard, some form of magic—something that gives him…life." The healer's words were hesitant. Even she couldn't guess at what Mal'Bal had done to Goblin.

Finn pointed to Leeya. "How does she fare?"

"Not much better. The wound in her side runs deep into her organs. If she doesn't receive some form of magical help, her internal bleeding will kill her."

"I have no magic." Finn admitted. "I can't even use my bracer."

"Then we must ride to Jakitta." a voice spoke out. "The Star-Child Coalition might have someone who can help us."

Finn turned. Standing in the doorway was Altin. The older boy had a grave face. "I traded in our horses for fresh steeds. I swiped one of your rubies for them."

The Star-Child threw Finn his bag of jewels. Finn caught the bag, irritated. Where Altin had learned to steal from under people's noses without being caught? Finn hadn't even been aware his wealth was gone.

"You must let me mend your injuries before you leave." the healer spoke.

Finn and Altin both were sat in chairs. The healer tended to Finn's side and arm while her husband and daughter tended to Altin's face and the large slash across his chest. When the healer grabbed Finn's bracer and pulled on his arm, straightening it and turning the bone, he let out a yowl of pain. His arm popped into place and the terrible tension he'd been feeling went away, replaced with an angry soreness. It still hurt but was far more manageable. He flexed his hands and bent his arms as instructed by the healer.

"You'll have full range return within a week." she told him.

After checking to make sure he didn't have any internal bleeding, she wrapped tight bands around his chest, causing him to cringe and his breathing to come in gasps. He was told the cracked ribs would take longer to heal.

When both Altin and Finn were ready, they took their unconscious friends outside and strapped them to the horses Altin had bought. The black beasts were strong, fresh, and had been trained for long-distance galloping. Finn gave the healer a thumb-sized diamond, telling her to give her family a better life. With mouth agape, the woman spluttered out a thank-you, overwhelmed by more wealth than she'd seen in all her days.

Finn and Altin took the horses and rode them hard, continuing their journey East beyond EldenBurrow and toward Jakitta, twenty kilometers away. As they left the sad muddy city, the rain picked up, soaking the land. Finn, who had Leeya on his horse this time, pulled off his cloak and wrapped her in it to keep her dry. Altin begrudgingly did the same for Goblin. Freezing and with wind biting at their skin, they charged forward, gambling the Star-Children Coalition would have someone who could mend grave injuries.

As water slapped Finn's skin and wormed into his mouth, he checked on Leeya's breathing. It was shallow and harried. He swept wet strands of hair from off her beautiful face and goaded the horse to move faster. Finn's anxiety grew, only matched by his exhaustion as the day matured, then darkened. The rainfall chilled and his teeth chattered. Altin, having not said a word to Finn since they left EldenBurrow, leaned lower and lower on his horse to a point where he was hugging both Goblin and his steed's mane. Soon, Finn did the same, trying to share what little body heat he had with Leeya, whose lips were turning blue.

Darkness deepened and soon Finn had to rely on his horse to continue forward as he couldn't see anything through the rain. Holding tight to Leeya and trying to hide his face within the crook of his elbow, he didn't notice the distant lights at first. Drawing near, he recognized them as lanterns hanging from a tall wooden wall resembling the entrance of a fort. Their horses, gasping in the weather, slowed to a stop in front of the structure. Altin's horse approached from Finn's left, by luck having stayed at his side the whole unguided journey. Altin was unconscious upon the beast, his body sagging and arms hanging limp.

"Help." Finn croaked. "Open the gates!"

He repeated the words louder and louder, but the storm overwhelmed his voice and his vision darkened. Shivering, Finn loosened his hold on Leeya, slipped off his horse, and fell against the wooden barrier. He croaked out again and smacked his fist against the thick door— a large swinging gate. He did so again and again, his chest struggling to work. He faced the dark clouds and water washed over him, taking him into a land of gray fog. Beyond him, there was a creak as the entrance to Jakitta opened and multiple Star-Children walked out. They loomed over him, their bracers glinting in the lantern light they brought. Finn closed his eyes.

the bite, the sting

28

—*Circa 5,614 E.E. (Economic Era-The 17th Era): Fourteen-year-old Finn SunRider secretly gathers food and water to attempt an escape from the Crust. Going near hungry for two months and often passing out from weakness by his second work shift of the day, he is able to salvage enough meager supplies to last him a week. He hopes to climb the cliffs behind the Hub, where easy foot and hand-holds can be found. Two days before he makes the attempted escape, adult miners looking to tease Finn and relieve their anger kick in his hut, collapsing the walls and exposing his stash. The men forcefully steal the supplies and eat it in front of Finn. Finn holds a stoic face until after they are gone. When finally alone and only accompanied by the echo of mocking laughter, he sobs and finally releases his hope on ever being able to escape the Crust. Soon after, he moves to an empty hut at the edge of the limestone fields, where less men live and no pranks are done. He talks of leaving but never seriously considers escaping the Crust again until Goblin is brought to the camp two years later. —*

The greatest of tortures was the waiting. Wahala sat in the muck and filth that was Mal'Bal's gore tent and listened as beyond the heavy canvas, men and women screamed. Mal'Bal was changing what had made them a people. He was creating a new race, tribe, and religion. He was ritualizing Lenovans. With her preparing for her death, Mal'Bal was forced to take on Wahala's responsibility to graft golden limbs to ritualized bodies. She hoped he withered away his energy doing so.

All she'd known since birth—the stories of her land, of the honor and glory brought to those who'd fought and sacrificed for their ways, her own mother a High Acolyte to the previous Queen Priestess—gone. She could say Mal'Bal was her older brother—not by blood—but by their mother's relations. By that, the betrayal was that much stronger.

She remembered as a small child her mother walking her through the temple halls, guiding her past the dangerous rooms where small unescorted children would be eaten, and telling her stories of older days.

"Wahala, it was an honor to be in the Queen's presence. Her regal stance, the way her masterful eyes roamed her people, and the necromantic power she wielded... She was a fair leader. Stern, but traditional. Ungiving to weakness. Ritualisms were made only upon initiation into adulthood and as advancement in rank. We would herd the dead into massive groves and there we'd watch as the Queen Priestess summoned purple flames, consuming the monsters by the thousands, releasing them into the void. It was an honor to walk in her shadow, Wahala. But her son... given to her as gift by the earth... he is but a curse."

Wahala blinked away the fever from her eyes and adjusted her bound arms. Visions of her tattoo-faced mother, marked with the symbols of an acolyte, swam about her.

The child-version of herself tugged at her mother's robes and half-ran to keep pace with her mother's long strides. "Do you not like Lord Mal'Bal? I don't like him either. He's too tall. Also, he doesn't participate in the ceremonies."

"The young lord is readying his pounce, Wahala. Be wary of him and don't stray too near."

"Why mama?"

"He reeks of rebellion. Until we've finished our twenty-year preparation and chosen a new Queen, don't listen to his doctrines as so many have. His words have a blasphemous bitterness to them."

Wahala's mother took her into their three-roomed chamber and put her to bed, rubbing her cheek with one finger. Her love for her daughter was only rivaled by her love of the cult.

"Stick to the traditions as closely as I have, Wahala. Perhaps one day you'll be an acolyte yourself." Her mother's words made Wahala smile. "And perhaps you'll be the next Queen Priestess mama!"

Her mother stiffened but the young Wahala could tell the woman had been pleased. "Perhaps." she shushed, leaving the room. Wahala fell asleep, unknowing to the fact that an hour later, a teenage Mal'Bal, having learned forbidden secrets only meant for the Queen Priestess, ritualized his entire body and swept through the temple-city with his loyal followers, assassinating all the acolytes, including her mother, thus putting an end to a millennium-old way of life.

The next day, Mal'Bal proclaimed himself ruler of the cult. And who was to stop the man with the golden body? He was the son of the dead Queen Priestess, first offspring to a leader since the beginning of their history. Perhaps the earth had wanted him to lead. Perhaps it was the land telling them it was a time for change. Naïve and foolish, Wahala soon came to accept the way things were, forgetting her mother's words, and instead believing the false lies told her by those older than her: her mother had been a heretic, had wanted to defy the land itself.

Mal'Bal was cunning and made changes slowly, corrupting more and more. The ones who spoke out found themselves dead and only the hopeful quiet lived on to remember the old days. Wahala was entranced and manipulated like all the others. But… something changed her. Upon her moment of first ritual when she cut off her kneecaps, the memory returned—the acolytes, the traditions, the way of life stolen from them. With it came the creeping worm of thought: Mal'Bal was not their leader, never had been. And within Wahala's heart came the flurry of emotions. Wrong, wrong, wrong. They were doing everything wrong. They had to return. They had to go back to how it was or surely the cult would perish. The culture. The history. Her people. Her mother.

The gore tent's flap swept open and Wahala wiped at her tears with her shoulder. She calmed her face and steadied her pose. Mal'Bal entered the tent holding his Golden Puppet in his arms as if carrying a son. Wahala shivered. For all intents and purposes, the Golden Puppet *was* Mal'Bal's son, his heir. Perhaps far in the future when all life had been eradicated and the cult replaced with anti-life beasts, they would be led by the spider-like monster. The puppet itself looked badly damaged. Dings and deep scratches ran along its body and one of its legs hung limp. Its head took in the room slowly, as if the creature was tired and Mal'Bal was a father getting it to sleep. It was such a macabre scene that Wahala's bowels clenched. A second figure followed Mal'Bal into the tent, one which Wahala didn't recognize.

It was an elder woman, bent with age and with silver hair tied back into a frayed bun. She put her hands over her mouth and nose, hesitating at the entrance and looking at the dried blood and old viscera with horror. She was clearly not a member of the cult or a newly added.

Mal'Bal set down his creation with a sigh and the puppet leaned itself against a pole. It looked to be staring at Wahala, but she couldn't tell. To her, the scenario might have been the strangest one she'd even been in. There was the powerful Lich-Lord, her tied and injured, an old Lenovan woman, and a broken puppet made of gold—all staring at each other.

"Berula, you shall care for my puppet and for this woman. You'll do so with all your skill. If I'm not satisfied with your work, I shall delicately peel off your skin and staple it back inside-out, leaving you alive in your agony."

Mal'Bal spoke the words slowly, placing emphasis on their weight. The trembling woman nodded vigorously.

"Y—yes." she spoke, not daring to say more than one word.

Mal'Bal crouched behind Wahala and undid her knots. Wahala's heart leapt like a frightened rabbit and her pained muscles clenched once more. Was this it? Was it finally the end? But Mal'Bal had assigned the old woman to care for her—yet, that could mean care for her corpse...

Mal'Bal took off the ropes binding her legs and pulled Wahala to her feet. Grabbing her by the nape with a giant golden fist, he forced her forward out of the tent. Stumbling and with blood rushing through her pinched veins, Wahala hissed in discomfort. Sun hit her eyes and she blinked, staring at the ground so as to not walk about blind.

"You bring back slaves?" she asked.

"We've captured most of Kazma's fugitives." Mal'Bal replied. "Those who haven't ritualized and joined the cult have been pressed into servitude cooking food, cleaning tents, healing, and doing other jobs."

Wahala laughed, feeling delirious. "You grow soft. I thought you reveled in the killing of those weaker than you."

Mal'Bal chuckled, a worrisome noise. She was sure he would have flown into a fit of rage.

"Wahala, today will be a wonderful day."

Wahala wrapped her arms around herself, battling the fear in her chest and mind. She uncrossed her arms and straightened her back. No, she was Queen Priestess—she wouldn't cower. Let her go to her death with dignity.

Mal'Bal noticed her change and he let out a soft laugh. He led her to a large clearing in the middle of the multitudes of tents making up the army's camp. All about them, thousands of cloaked figures stood row upon row, silently watching. Intermingled were thousands more in civilian clothes, bleeding from cut limbs. *New recruits*. Around them was another group numbered in the thousands. They were bound and broken, shivering in their misery. Slaves. Mal'Bal finally had a formidable force large enough to threaten even the king of Lenova himself.

The only noise heard in all the camp came from the crunching footsteps of Mal'Bal and Wahala. She could see in the middle of the clearing two thick wooden poles jutting out of the ground. They each held two ropes. She knew what they were for: to bind her hands and feet, stretching her out between them. When they drew near, Mal'Bal changed his grip, using his massive strength to toss her through the air. She smashed into the dirt, fighting with all she had to not cry out. Let the people see she wasn't a coward or a weakling. She was a Queen, their true Queen.

Mal'Bal picked her up, tearing off her robe and exposing her skin to cold crisp air. Only her womanhood stayed covered by leather and bandages. The Lich-Lord tied her to the ropes. As each limb was secured, she became a human "X", strained to her bodily limit. Finally, Mal'Bal raised his arms to the air, walking circles around her and facing the crowd.

"Behold!" he shouted, his deep voice booming across the land. Without his own clothes, his exposed golden body glinted in all its splendor. "The heretic that would usurp me!"

The crowd stirred.

"My assistant and supporter! A backstabber and a fool!" Mal'Bal pointed an accusing finger to Wahala's face. She straightened her chin and locked her jaw, unblinking.

"She entered forbidden rooms within our holy temple and there she ritualized, calling herself Queen Priestess!"

Mal'Bal spat the words yet Wahala couldn't help but let out a small smile. She watched as many of the original cult members stiffened and their eyes widened. Instead of having to gain support in secret, telling others of her rank by whisper, Mal'Bal had done her work for her, loudly for all to hear.

"There are no more Queens! The old ways are dead! Her actions weaken us and corrode my work!" Mal'Bal stopped his pacing. "And now she must be punished!"

There was silence. Mal'Bal made a motion with his hands and six cult members walked forward, a large barrel carried between them. By the way they strained, the object must have been heavy. The panic within Wahala shook and buckled, trying to break free. What was Mal'Bal going to do to her?

The barrel was dropped beside Mal'Bal. Wahala could hear something sloshing inside. Smoke and heatwaves shimmered from the edges of the lid. Her panic worsened. A seventh cult member walked forward, presenting a long and terrifying whip with multiple strands, covered in barbs and glass. So there would be pain after all. Her toes curled.

Mal'Bal pulled the whip across his hands, dragging it along his palm. The whip's sharp edges grated against gold. Loudly, he spoke necromantic words to the object. With her knowledge of necromancy she was able to understand him.

"*Sheath of magic, cover this weapon. Make it unburnable.*"

Had her status of Queen Priestess granted her the ability to hear the necromantic words in an understandable form? If so, it was a power kept secret from even the temple's forbidden books.

Mal'Bal pulled the lid off the barrel and a thick cloud swirled away into the air. Within the container Wahala could see melted silver. Its glossy, near-white surface bubbled like a slow beast surfacing a swamp. Mal'Bal dipped the whip into the fluid and held it there. Wahala's legs gave out and she sagged into the ropes. Mal'Bal grinned, the mask of calm finally gone. His eyes widened and the pulsing veins on his face grew. His breathing intensified with unbridled excitement and spittle flecked his lips.

"The Lenovans say twenty-five lashes is a terrifying punishment. But we're different from them, are we not Wahala? We revel in pain. We *love* it. Let's not worry about numbers, shall we?" The crowds shuddered and leaned back. "Leaders suffer for their people, Wahala. They agonize over them. You accepted your false calling—so remember, *you wanted this*."

Mal'Bal pulled the whip from the barrel. It dripped sizzling silver onto the dirt, where it boiled and danced across the sand, turning it into glass. Wahala's muscles betrayed her and they shook without control. This was not like the sacrifice she'd made of her knees. The pain had been brutal but quick, the wounds mended within minutes—same with her heart replacement. This… this would last.

Mal'Bal circled her once more, faking a lash, trying to get her to cry or flinch. Diving into her willpower and mastering it with only the ferocity of her mind, she didn't make a sound, nor did she recoil. With no warning, as he passed behind her, Mal'Bal struck.

The whip cut across her back, carving in and sending melted silver across her skin. It burrowed though tissue and muscle, *into her bones*. She heaved, her face opening to the air and her eyes rolling. Her hands grabbed at the ropes and her fingers spasmed wildly. She nearly swallowed her tongue. If all the pain she'd ever felt combined as one, it would still not live up to the one lash. The bite was so strong she didn't have the power to make a noise. She didn't have the means to show her weakness. Her bowels loosened and she didn't care.

Mal'Bal circled to her front, facing her. Her knees tried knocking together but were stretched too far apart. He looked at her with contempt, madness playing across his face.

"Already you shake, Wahala." he teased, "We haven't even started yet." Wahala dropped her head. She couldn't do this. She couldn't survive one more lash, much less however many more Mal'Bal saw fit to give her. Her life was at his mercy—and the man had none.

"Say thank you to me." Mal'Bal whispered, his voice sing-song.

Wahala giggled, her teeth chattering. The silver droplets stung deep within her and the smell of burning flesh lingered in the air.

"I bring you sensation." Mal'Bal spoke, "I bring you feeling. Once you've passed into the void, you'll have nothing. I scar the memory of sense into you. Say thank you to me."

Wahala worked up the mental fortitude and shot her head up. She laughed in Mal'Bal's face, her eyes as wide as his.

"Thank you! Thank you so much, oh Lord!" The words came out ringing with spite and pride. She was the Queen Priestess, rightful ruler of the cult!

Mal'Bal scowled and lashed across her front. Wahala gasped and danced in her ropes. Yet she didn't scream. Mal'Bal whipped her again and again and again.

"Say thank you to me! Show me your gratitude! *I* am your leader! *Yours!*"

Slash. Slash. Slash.

"Thank you, Lich-Lord! False master! Defiler of truth!" She screeched the words, masking agony for irony and confidence.

Mal'Bal grew restless and dipped his whip into the liquid once more. He whipped her with a down-stroke and Wahala went deep into herself, burying her consciousness far below layers of mental barriers. They broke one by one with each lash. She knew she should be dead from the pain or the shock, but something in her kept ticking—kept feeding her the smallest of energy. *The power of the Queen Priestess.* But… perhaps she wanted to die. The emptiness would taste so fresh…

"She's not your leader! Look upon her weakness! Look upon her cowering form! What has she done for you? Nothing! What is her name to you? Nothing! Where are her supporters? Why don't they speak out?"

Wahala found Salastine's face in the crowd. His eyes brimmed with fury and his fists clenched and unclenched. He looked about ready to step forward and attack Mal'Bal, but he didn't. No one did.

Slash. *Burning. She was burning alive.* Slash.

"Say thank you to me for your pain! Say thank you to me for being your guiding savior!"

"Thank you, oh grand falseness! Thank you!"

Slash.

Wahala, it was an honor to be in the Queen Priestess's presence. Her regal stance, the way her masterful eyes roamed her people, and the necromantic power she wielded… She was a fair leader. Stern, but traditional. Ungiving to weakness.

All that had been, all that could be: halted and defiled by Mal'Bal. He was no member of the cult. He was a *Star-Child.* The whip was dipped once more and Mal'Bal went insane, hitting her over and over mercilessly, his face a mask of fury and uncontrolled emotion. He missed multiple times, striking dirt, no longer aiming. He was the one screaming while Wahala stayed silent, her body now only wiggling. There was no more pain. All had faded into a dull drone of movement. Silver, tickled with light, rained around her. Her wounds didn't bleed. They were closed off by the melted metal.

Finally, with a howl, Mal'Bal tipped over the barrel, pouring silver across his legs and dirt. Throwing the whip with disgust and kicking the container away, Mal'Bal rushed forward and grabbed Wahala's head between his hands. He shook her face and screamed, his only organic body-part red with anger.

"I AM YOUR GOD AND YOU'VE BETRAYED ME!"

He motioned for a scythe and a terrified cult member slunk forward, cowering beneath his mad leader and giving him his weapon. Mal'Bal took the scythe and decapitated the man with one blurred stroke, kicking the body to the side. The crowds shrunk back, jaws hanging open. The Lich-Lord faced Wahala once more, blood dripping from his face. His tongue darted out and licked at it.

"DEATH IS MINE TO GIVE! YOU DON'T GET THE PLEASURE OF AN END! ALL IS MINE! MINE! I AM LEADER, YOU'LL BE BUT MY PERSONAL SLAVE, A REMINDER OF HERESY!"

The curved blade slashed across her ribs, opening her chest. Wahala gasped faintly. Tossing the scythe to the ground, Mal'Bal plunged his hand within her. Maybe the crowds were screaming. Maybe it was Mal'Bal. Maybe she had finally caved and it was her. Mal'Bal tugged and pulled and there grew a terrible pressure from within herself. The wet squelching noises shook her form and the tart scent of carnage stank the air. Mal'Bal stepped away, holding her golden heart in a crimson grip. Were the crowds fighting among themselves?

Wahala was hollow, empty, cold. Her heart still beat, magically transferring life to her even out of her body. But life or not, her spirit and mentality couldn't hold itself together. Pieces crumbled and broke, falling away into dark puddles of incomprehensibility.

"Less than gold." Mal'Bal wheezed to himself, one hand holding her heart and the other rubbing his scalp. He walked back and forth in front of her, looking at the ground with bulging eyes. "Less than gold. She's less than gold. Just a butterfly. Less. Lower. Silver. Prove it."

He dropped her heart into the spilled pile of liquid silver. With his foot, he rolled the magical organ around, coating it in the new metal. Rage shrieked out from many. Others though—they cheered. The people were raising weapons to each other, arguing. Salastine had half-stepped into the clearing, face red. The man struggled with himself, then was gone. Wahala smiled. Good—Salastine had to keep his beliefs a secret. He could continue without her, perhaps choosing another as Queen.

Robed figured were pulling back hoods, swinging weapons. Were they infighting? One tried throwing a rock at Mal'Bal and was disemboweled for it. The movements became blurs of color. Wahala was going now, she was sailing into a storm of frozen shadow. She was so cold.

Mal'Bal lifted her now-silver heart. "A SYMBOL! LESS THAN GOLD! LESS THAN ME! BENEATH ME!"

Then he was approaching, his face filling the entire expanse of the world itself. His eyes danced and spun around her, expanding and contracting. He was putting her heart back into her chest and speaking strange words of necromancy. Words of binding and adjustment. Of healing. His punishment was worse than death. It was the taking away of her martyrdom. Mal'Bal's head poured sweat from the strain of using so much dark magic. Her chest was closing and her skin tugging, pulling itself back together. Mal'Bal looked about ready to pass out himself.

Wahala grinned, last bits of breath leaving her lungs. The void had opened its mouth and she was falling through it. "Thank you, oh leader. Thank you for the pain. I *will* remember it."

Wahala opened her eyes, once more greeted by the smell of rot. The gore tent. She couldn't move. It wasn't that she was bound, it was that her mind didn't seem to be working properly. The thoughts didn't travel to the muscles. A face faded into view: the slave Berula.

"You awaken!" she croaked, her voice wobbly with age. "After a month I thought you gone forever! Don't move. You still have weeks upon weeks to heal of such wounds as these."

Wahala's lips twitched. She tried speaking but only small gasps escaped her. She finally formed words. "A…month?"

"Rest." the old woman spoke. "Rest now."

Berula disappeared and reappeared with a small bowl of paste. When the elder's fingers touched Wahala's skin to apply the medicine, Wahala fell back into the fogs of darkness.

RAFAEL HOHMANN

salt

29

—Circa 5,612 E.E. (Economic Era-The 17ᵗʰ Era): Lady Tribalyn of House Phure takes a pleasure ride on her personal boat. Although the SeaLake looks calm and her men are confident, the tides turn as a massive storm overtakes the water and threatens to pull the boat down. Strange beasts surface, armor-plated and with tentacled eyes, jaws large enough to swallow the boat. Gripping onto the boat's railing and shrieking for help, Lady Tribalyn spots a lone man rowing across the waves with a merry whistle. The unknown stranger winks at her with no fear in his eyes. Taking a spear and blowing into a conch-horn, the sailor draws the lake-beasts away from Lady Tribalyn's boat. She is unable to see much in the darkness, but as lightning flashes across the sky, casting purple hues across the wild water, she briefly makes out the sailor spinning a spear and twisting a curved blade. One of the beasts rolls dead in the waves and

another is sinking with a screech, impaled in the mouth. Lady Tribalyn's boat is pushed away from the scene and she never sees the man again. —

Finn opened his eyes to a log ceiling and the scent of fresh bread. He was tired and his body complained of weakness, but his arm and his ribs held no pain. He sat up and examined himself. He was wearing a soft tan shirt and thick warm leggings. His travel clothes were draped over a nearby chair. His pouch of gems, broken goggles, and Lady Tuliah's elixir were untouched. Faces stared at him from through a window near his bed. They were people he didn't recognize. They scowled, eyes narrowed with suspicion, then were gone, replaced by dim sunlight behind gray clouds.

"First to rise, you are. That be a testament to yer health."

The accented voice came from the end of the room, where from an open door, a strange man entered bearing a tray of food. It was from the tray that the smell of bread came from. He presented Finn a loaf and a bowl of chunky stew brimming with caramelized vegetables, potatoes, and melted cheese.

The man had long, black curly hair pulled back into a ponytail. From his ears dangled yellow hoops and a scar ran from his stubbled, tan chin to his scalp. He wore a strange dark-blue overcoat, its popped-up collar casting his lower face in shadow. Upon putting the tray in Finn's lap, he presented a gloved hand for shaking. Finn could make out a bracer glinting beneath his coat sleeve. *Star-Child.*

"I be called Salt, for a salty ol' dog am I."

"Finn."

"Fin? Like a fish fin? Perchance you're a sailor?" The man's voice sounded hopeful.

Finn shook his head. "No. Just Finn for Finn's sake."

Salt sighed. "Damn, that sullies my trousers, Finn-for-Finn's-sake. I've yet to meet another ocean-prowling, scally-scrubbing, swell-swaddling mother-of-none among all these ground-trotters."

The edge of Finn's lips curled in a smile. The man's strange clothing and exaggerated facial expressions were disarming. The way the man spoke made Finn want to laugh. This Star-Child wouldn't hurt him.

"I miss the sea, I do. Anyways, so who might ye be, Finn? Are ye friend, or be ye a foe? Ye near sent us into a battle-flurry. We thought we were being attacked. Took all the trust I had to allow ye inside."

"Friend, not foe." Finn replied. "My group and I come to seek shelter with the Coalition." Upon remembering Goblin and Leeya, Finn jerked up. Salt tried to hold him down. "Blast it, boy! The ship ain't sinking! Calm yerself!"

"My friends! Do they live?" Finn spluttered.

Salt patted Finn's knee, grabbed the loaf which had flown down his blue coat, and handed it back to Finn, tearing a chunk off for himself. "They're getting the same treatment ye did. They'll all live."

"They will?" Finn choked out in relief. "How?"

"With nearly a hundred Star-Children, we have quite the variety of powers, Finn-for-Finn's-sake. Yer friends' wounds will mend like the hearts of the many wenches I've left behind."

"Nearly a hundred you say?" Finn spluttered. That many Star-Children—and all of them good? Finn wanted to dance.

"Where do ye hail from Finn?" Salt asked, his tone becoming serious. "And don't worry, my friend. It would be best if ye told me the whole story—without leaving anything out. Ol' Salt the Sea-dog here is as reliable as the tide." He leaned in and took a sip of Finn's soup. "Even tell me the bits about yer bracer-vision."

Finn was shocked at how blunt the man was. They'd barely met and already Salt was asking him to explain himself. How could he yet trust any man well enough to speak of his bracer? Or even more so, the vision that had come with it?

"Let me see my friends and tell me your story first, then I'll consider telling mine."

"Finn, yer a stranger to us. Ye could be attempting to kill us or gain dominance over the Coalition. Yer not the first Star-Child to come into Jakitta, riling us up, thinking they're clever."

"I came under no false pretense." Finn argued. "Plus, you have power over my friends. I seek no harm to you or your people."

Salt smiled and tapped a finger against his nose. "Yer name precedes ye, Finn. I merely jest."

"You already know me?" Finn asked in confusion.

"Know *of* ye. Them Tulian Missionaries go around the land, speaking of a righteous Star-Child who crossed some stream or other. They sing happy praise of one called Finn. Unless there's another bracer-wearer with the same name, I take it to be ye."

Finn didn't know what to say. The people of Pittance spoke of him? Had he made that much of an impact with them?

"How have you gotten word from Tulian Missionaries?" Finn asked.

Salt winked. "My Star-Children come from all across the land. They have connections. I have connections. We have support from a few Lenovans—not many, mind ye, but word gets around. So ye crossed a stream huh? Ye sure yer not a sailor?"

Finn shook his head. "Is it enough to earn your trust?"

Salt chuckled. "It wouldn't have been enough but for the stories of three Star-Children who fought to try and save Kazma. Some hate ye for not actually saving it, but many recognize yer attempt."

Finn again was at a loss for words.

Salt beckoned him to stand. "Come, I wish to show ye Jakitta. Don't mind the others. Many are hostile to those they don't know. With word of ye spreading, some may treat ye with even more unkindness."

"I thought the Coalition was full of friendly Star-Children."

Salt scoffed. "About the only reason we don't kill each other is due to me bein' so handsome. The others can't get enough o' me appeal. If I was but a common, ugly man such as yerself, Jakitta would be a lake of blood."

Finn stuffed a large section of bread into his mouth, not knowing how to react to Salt's comment, and left the room after the man, stretching his legs. He noticed his boots had been replaced with comfortable loafers. Out of the door, Finn found himself outside, breathing in misty air. Around him were dozens of moss-covered log cabins. In the distance, Finn could see a small grove of dark-green spiky trees. Near them was a large dip in the ground—as if a hole had been dug. He could hear shouts and laughter coming from within it. A dark-skinned man wearing lenses on his face walked in front of them, leading a goat to a nearby cabin. Salt pointed to the cabin and nudged Finn.

"In there lies yer pretty friend. She's being healed now."

"What's with the goat?" Finn asked.

"That man there, Petreamus, is a Star-Child with a unique power. He was the one who healed ye. He's already taken care of that long-haired blondie too, but the other two—they need more mending."

"How did he take care of us so fast?"

"He sacrifices animals in place of yer friends. The injuries are passed from human to beast. Don't ask me the science of it, there is none. It's a terrible thing, it is. Us Star-Children have war powers, Finn. Seems even the healing is meant for hurting."

Finn closed his open jaw. He'd never imagined such abilities to exist. "Will he be able to take care of Leeya and Goblin?"

"That be their names? Well, he better find some mighty big animals for them. I heard the worse the injury, the more exuberant the sacrifice. Told me once, he did, of a time someone near to him was clean-cut in half—don't know how or why. He took a team of Convoy Bears as sacrifice—mind ye, they be large beasts. It didn't work so well. The bears all died and so did the individual. At least he tried. Guess ye can't heal all injuries, right?"

"That doesn't make me feel any better." Finn groaned, gritting his teeth.

"Oh. Sorry about that."

"May I see them?" Finn asked. But already Salt was shaking his head. "Ye may see the blondie, but not them other two. They need to be left well enough alone for now." Salt paused. "Say Finn, that younger boy... he ain't a Star-Child."

Finn grew defensive. "He's my friend. If you kick him out, I'll leave with him."

Salt nodded. "Loyalty. I can respect that in a man. If the boy—Goblin—lives, he can stay as long as he's beneficial."

Finn smiled, calming down. "Good. I didn't want to choose between the two."

Salt led Finn around a group of cabins, some were small homes and others large dorm-like bunkers. Few of the buildings were made of stone and clay; the majority of Jakitta was wood. Between smoke-spewing chimneys he caught glimpses of the tall fort-like walls of the town. Had Salt been the first to find him outside, drenched in the rain?

Salt scratched his stubble. "I was a merchant sailor. Still am, deep in my heart. I roamed the SeaLake beneath Lyria and its many vast rivers for nigh on twenty years. I was near shore on a small skiff, fishing solo for Pepper-Guppies. Mind ye, them dimwitted fish only come out at night to feed on moonlight—strange animals they are. Suddenly my boat exploded, throwing me overboard into the waves. Something had crashed through the vessel, sinking it and taking me with it. Shaking my head, dazed, and with my fishing pole halfway up my—"

Salt paused and looked sideways at Finn. "Well, it's best to not go into details. But anyways, t'was a bracer. I had been chosen."

"You were made a Star-Child." Finn spoke.

Salt huffed. "That I was. And soon enough, so were many others all across the vast reaches of Lenova. Rumors of powers running rampant spread across the land. Uncontrolled death. I couldn't allow my world to fall apart. I formed the Coalition as a means to bring in as many Star-Children as possible before they turned wild. We try to get them before they first learn to use their power. That way, when they go stir-crazy from First-Use, we can guide and coax them back into normalcy. Sadly, there have been many who've fought or turned on us. Yet we still spread the word throughout the lands in hopes those like ye and yer friends will show."

"Those that fight you, or those who become rampant, what happens?" Finn asked.

Salt grew somber. "We do the only thing we can. We end the threat. Whether they be Accessories, Half-suits, or Exceptions. Thank the waters we haven't faced any Full-suits. I'm sure we could perhaps defeat one, but I might lose most of the Coalition."

A question burned in Finn's throat. "And what of their bracers?"

"Perceptive ye are, boy. I think I like ye! Follow me."

Finn was led across the camp and toward the only building in the area made of stone. It was small—no larger than his old limestone hut. Pulling open the thick door, Salt presented a set of stairs leading into the dark. Brimming with curiosity, Finn followed after Salt, the door behind them closing. All became dark except for a soft glow at the bottom of the stairs. Leaving the final step, Finn entered a room where two Star-Children stood side-by-side, each holding a sword. They were both exactly alike. Their height, weight, and even looks were identical. The only difference were their weapons. One sword's blade was white and the other black.

"A beaver has a rudder, making him a better boatsman than I. Yet I shall profit more. Why?" Salt spoke.

Finn cocked his head in puzzlement. The twins didn't blink, nor stare directly at them.

"Your rear won't ache after half-a-day of sailing." the twins stated, their voices monotone and whispery, like the echo of ghosts. Finn shuddered when they spoke yet wanted to laugh at their response. They nodded to Salt and stepped aside, revealing another door. Salt clapped and chuckled.

"I love when ye boys say that!"

Salt led Finn through, leaving the two eerie twins behind. Finn made sure to stay close to the sailor. Closing themselves in the room, an empty place apart from a wooden chest, Salt winked at Finn.

"What was up with that?" Finn asked the man.

Salt snorted and grinned. "Just a witty little phrase I came up with as extra security. Ye never know when someone's going to mimic yer looks. Lenova's a strange place."

"They didn't look so happy with the reply they had to give." Finn commented.

The remark made Salt hold his stomach and laugh. "I know boy! That's the best part about it! Couldn't get those two to say anything more than yes or no, so I decided to humor myself. They don't have both feet on the deck, if ye know what I mean."

"What do they do?" Finn asked, creeped out by the twins.

Salt became serious. "They be Exceptions. It may not look it, but them swords are their bracers."

Finn spun about but the door was already closed, hiding the two men. "Their powers were active?" Finn asked.

"Always active. They never turn it off. Perhaps that's the reason why they act so strange. No one knows. We don't even have their names.

The others, they call them Justice and Punishment. Ye don't want to be on their bad side. Loyal though. They fight all evil with unbridled passion, they do."

"What are their powers?" Finn questioned.

"They fight united; each move in perfect synch—as if they can read one another. Ye get hit with the white blade, then the black blade in the same spot, you immediately die. Doesn't matter if yer wearing armor or if they merely tapped yer toe. They fight so well and so quick, most don't even have time to draw their weapon before they're touched by the swords."

Finn licked his dry lips. "And you said they're on our side?"

"On the side of righteousness. I figure if I were to ever abuse my power or hurt the innocent, they'd come after me. Dreaded be the day."

Finn wondered if the twins fought Mal'Bal, how the battle would fare. Another thought entered Finn's mind: Mal'Bal had never activated his bracer in front of them. Was he an Exception? Was he perhaps a Full-Suit? Finn felt he knew the terrifying answer.

Salt approached the wooden chest and cracked open the lid. He stared at Finn with a cool, calm, and friendly smile. "Now don't ye turn on us Finn. Don't ever turn on Lenova. For if ye do, especially after seeing this, I'll have to personally kill ye myself."

The words were spoken calmly and in a friendly manner, but they dripped with the power of a man who could keep promises. Finn froze, yet not in fear or offense. Here was one who'd seen a lot of Lenova and fallen in love with it. His conviction to protect the land was strong.

"If the day comes, then by all means, lop off my head." Finn replied.

The man smiled. "Now that we got the friendly banter out of the way, behold: each sea-dog has a treasure chest full of loot."

Taking a step forward, Finn examined the container. He gasped.

Within, was a small pile of bracers. Eleven in total. Dried blood coated them and dimmed their reflective glow. Each one was strikingly similar yet held small unique differences. One was wider. Another longer. One had the carving of a star and another the carving of a snarling cat standing on its hind legs. One even had small blunt spikes sticking out from its edges.

"These came from rogue Star-Children?" Finn asked.

Salt nodded. "We've had our share of run-ins with those who believe they are new gods of Lenova. The end result is clear: we're no gods, Finn. It's blasted difficult, but we can be killed. Petreamus removed these from the arms of the corpses. Some had begun to mesh with bone, others only to muscle and skin."

"Why don't you put them on? Gain even more power?" Finn asked, the idea sounding so instinctual. With multiple bracers, one could be invincible. Salt laughed.

"If it were simple, the chest would be empty and all evil would be long defeated. What yer talking about is becoming a Prime-Child."

"Prime-Child?" Finn whispered, furrowing his brow.

"Yes, only a theory. But if a Star-Child were to wield multiple bracers, he'd become something beyond mortal, beyond what even we are, become...a new thing. But, as is with a lot of theories, it seems an impossible task."

He rolled back the sleeves on his arms. Upon one arm was his bracer. The other arm though, bore a brown and purple scar running around Salt's wrist.

"It was nigh unbearable to keep it on for longer than a split second before it slid off, leaving a beauty-mark. The emotion and chaos that came with it was impossible to overcome. It was as if my bracer and the other were fighting, using me as the battleground. My mind was so overwhelmed, it's a miracle I'm not in some cabin, drooling like a sun-fevered sailor lost at sea. It seems it would take a willpower far greater than my own—greater than any can attest to. As far as I know, there are two other Star-Children in this camp who've had previous encounters with rogues, killed them, and tried to wear their bracer. They bear the same scar. Some higher power has made a rule against wearing more than one. Perhaps it's the same entity that makes these blasted things rain upon us and scuttle our ships."

Finn was bummed. In his mind, he'd pictured putting on one of the spare bracers and gaining a power he could activate. Perhaps because his bracer was ancient, it no longer worked.

Salt closed the chest and sat on its lid, folding his arms. "And now yer story."

Finn bit his lip. Salt deserved to know the truth. He was fighting for everything Finn believed in. He began his tale with the day he'd escaped the vat-worm. Salt constantly interrupted, asking all sorts of questions. Many were of Finn himself. How had working the Crust affected his views toward slavery and power? What could be improved? What did a vat-worm look like? The man was as much of a scholar as he was a sailor. Every little detail interested him and at no point did he act bored. When Finn told of Nozgull's attack at the mining outpost, Salt listened with upturned eyebrows.

"We've heard of the name EarthBreaker. He's a dangerous fellow. Half-suit, they say."

Finn told Salt of escaping into the Slaglands and finding his own bracer in the heart of the crater. At that point, Salt took heavy interest. He seemed to stop Finn at every other word, asking a multitude of questions from how each rock looked to how each experience was felt. The fact a bracer hadn't fallen from the sky in front of Finn, but he'd found it in a land unexplored in hundreds—if not thousands—of years, made the mystery that much stranger.

"So ye be an Unchosen."

"What do you mean?" Finn asked.

"Well, Unchosens are ones who've managed to kill a Star-Child and take their bracer for themselves. It's a rare occurrence. Only way a human's been able to kill a Star-Child has been through deceit, poison, or assassination. Yer the first to have *found* a bracer. An ancient one at that."

Salt grabbed Finn's arm and examined the bracer. He read the word carved on its edge. "*Akuun*. No idea what that means."

The implications that there'd been Star-Children long ago quieted both Finn and Salt. Why had no records been made? As far as Lenova knew, Star-Children were a new thing—yet Finn's bracer proved otherwise. Sometime long ago, another generation had been chosen. None of them were alive or had been talked about. What had happened to them? Where were their records? How had Finn's bracer come to be? And the biggest question of all: where were the bracers coming from?

Finn continued his story and Salt listened patiently. When Finn told of how he'd defeated Nozgull, Salt laughed loudly and clapped his hands. "Served him right! Poetic justice, that is!"

He asked Finn what had become of the rogue Star-Child's bracer and Finn told of Pittance, Piscus, and the Stream of Fate. After much convincing, Salt finally accepted Finn's actions of entrusting Nozgull's power to Piscus. Under Finn's circumstances, there had been little choice. Salt promised that once he could spare the men, he would send a couple of Star-Children to Pittance to retrieve the bracer and bring it back to the Coalition. He told Finn to write a note that could be handed to Piscus to assure the man all was well but warned him that it could very well be a long time before they were given the opportunity to take the bracer.

When Finn got to Kazma and Mal'Bal's attack, to his surprise, Salt didn't look shocked. The sailor sighed, rubbing his face slowly.

"Aye, there were rumors about an army from the South moving its way across Lenova. We were also made aware of its leader, a Star-Child

Full-suit."

Finn had been right. Mal'Bal *was* powerful. "Why have you not done anything against him?" he asked, trying to not let anger creep into his voice.

"Don't overestimate us, Finn." Salt sighed. "Many of us are only now adjusting to our powers—to learn control over ourselves. Many have no fighting experience whatsoever. As a group, we could take down a few Half-suits, Accessories, perhaps even Exceptions—but a Full-suit leading an entire army? That's something that takes preparation. Think on it: what if we had already attempted to engage Mal'Bal? Ye spoke of him fighting yer group without even using his ability. He tore ye apart. He has necromancy, a body made of gold, followers that would die rather than face his wrath. If he killed our men, took our bracers and gave them to his own people, where would we be? Where would *he* be?"

"But Kazma…" Finn started.

A look of terrible pain came over Salt. The man leaned over and stared at the ground. "I have failed my land." He spoke the words quietly. "I put the Coalition above Lenova."

They went quiet for a long time, listening to the creaking of the timber walls.

"I'm surprised a former slave is going against Mal'Bal." Salt spoke up.

Finn narrowed his eyes. "What do you mean?"

"Many slaves have joined Mal'Bal's cult as revenge against what Lenova has done to them. All they have known from the land is misery."

Finn shook his head. "It's not Lenova itself, but evil men that do the enslaving."

Salt shrugged. "In Mal'Bal's perspective, he must see that we are the evil and he is the light. Many former slaves see it that way as well."

Finn stopped, unable to find a clear answer to Salt's comment.

"It's..." he began, "it's more complex than that. I can't explain it, but everyone in the world believes themselves the good guy. That's just how we are. I'm certain no one believes themselves wrong and then relishes in the fact."

Salt leaned in. "So...are ye a good guy?"

Finn shrugged. "I hope so, but I can't control the way others might see my decisions. What I mean to say..." Finn stopped. This topic was heavy. It was making his head hurt. "I must be set in my belief that I'm good, because to stand up to the stubbornness of those who do true evil, I have to have an iron will. I can't let myself doubt the choices I make. I can't afford to. I'm good because I'm a reflection of the choices I make, not just because I say I am."

Salt pulled back, and suddenly Finn felt as if he'd been tested. "That's a very wise answer." Salt whispered.

"But no matter what other slaves might choose or think, we can't let Mal'Bal destroy Lenova." Finn spoke, his conviction quivering in his throat. Salt nodded. "We'll face him, but there's still much to prepare. Will ye help me Finn? Will yer friends stand with ye and help as well?"

"If it means getting back at Mal'Bal and saving Lenova, then yes." Finn replied.

"Then we must train. All of us." Salt spoke, his voice resonating with determination. "We've been given word Mal'Bal has paused his campaign. We don't know why, but we'll take advantage of it like a sailor with fair wind in his sails. And when Mal'Bal moves, so shall we: to war."

Finn's heart beat quickly, responding to the dark words and the anticipation of a fight.

"To war," he responded, "and to a safe Lenova."

There was a knock on the door and one of the twins opened it. Standing at the passage was the bespectacled Star-Child with the power to heal through animal sacrifice. He greeted Salt and Finn with a curt nod.

"Sir, there is a complication with one of the patients—the younger boy. It's urgent."

distant and alone

30

—*It is a common misconception to believe that shape-shifters are born the way they are. In fact, shape-shifting is a randomly occurring genetic disease so rare, that never in recorded history has there ever been more than three alive at one time. The disease is said to first show symptoms of existing at the age of twelve. Some of the symptoms include are: an allergic reaction to metal and leather, the eye's pigmentation lightens and darkens as the sun rises and sets, and the absolute incapability to sing any song, as the vocal cords tend to loosen and tighten, giving the victim an ever-changing voice pitch.* —

-Excerpt from Strange Lenovan Facts of Flight and Fancy, page 52

Finn and Salt were escorted out of the underground chamber. Behind them, the two twins closed the door and followed their movements with unblinking eyes. The Star-Child healer led them outside and brought them to a small cabin near the edge of Jakitta. He stopped at the doorway, his face grave.

"He's still not awake. He won't be for a while. It took close to every animal in Jakitta to bring him back." He looked to Finn. "Your horses are alive, but I've given them to the twins as replacement. Their steeds were old and I used them as sacrifice." Finn was shocked. So much death for one person. It was a barbaric power that made Finn question the true purpose of the bracers, but it was also a testament to Salt's integrity— a steep payment for one whom Salt had never met before. The healer continued. "The girl will be alright. She had difficulties as well. She's not…whole but will awaken within a few days."

"Well, what's this complication you speak of with the boy, Petreamus?" Salt asked.

The Star-Child, Petreamus, opened the cabin door and led them inside.

The cabin was warm and a nice change to the chill weather. A small fire cracked in a hearth. Dried herbs hung over the flames and gave off strange smells that calmed and relaxed the muscle. Laying in a bed near the fire was a form: Goblin. Finn hurried to his side and knelt. A blanket covered his friend all the way to his chin. Goblin's face, no longer a healthy brown color, was pale and seemed drained of blood. His breathing was labored and without pattern, yet he looked better than he had the night before out in the rain.

Petreamus lowered the boy's blanket. A lump entered Finn's throat. Goblin's chest was healed, blood no longer coated his body. In the center, in the middle of his ribcage, a green nub jutted out. The gem shard, heart of the wooden golem, hadn't been removed.

"No matter what I did or how I used my power, I couldn't pull it out without killing him. Whatever it's doing, it is a part of him now. Feel his skin."

Finn put his hand on Goblin's chest. Near the nub it was tough and hard, like rubbing a stone. He moved his hand over toward Goblin's shoulder. His skin was soft there. Whatever had transpired radiated from his chest and came to a slow halt.

"Ye spoke of a golem, controlled by Mal'Bal." Salt commented. "Its heart—is that it?"

"Part of it." Finn replied, worried for his friend.

"There's something magical about this." Salt contemplated. "Perhaps Mal'Bal stabbed him on purpose, not with the intent to kill?"

To Finn's surprise, Petreamus nodded. "I believe so. This type of wound should've killed him, but when he was brought to me, it was as if his body was in a state of hibernation—awaiting healing."

Salt sighed and folded his arms, a stern look reflecting in his eyes. "What has the evil Star-Child done?"

The question was an open-ended one, left lingering in the air. Finn's mind raced, thinking of the golden man, of the golem, and of the heart. Of Star-Children powers. He recalled Nozgull's control over gems.

"Perhaps…" Finn began. Salt and the healer turned to face him. "I know what Mal'Bal's power is."

"Well, spill it." Salt coaxed.

"Mal'Bal controls an army of golems. They follow his commands mindlessly. The wooden golem died when its gem heart shattered. What if Mal'Bal can imbue life into gems and create the beasts?"

Salt was silent for a long time. He sighed and faced Petreamus. "Gather two Star-Children. Assign them to guard this cabin. Inform me at once when the boy wakes. He's not to leave this building or leave yer sight. If anything unusual happens, ye let me know immediately. As far as we're all concerned, this boy is under probation."

"Wait!" Finn shouted. "Are you saying you mean to keep Goblin prisoner in here?"

"Yes." Salt confirmed, his voice hard. "We have to maintain security."

"He's my best friend! He's not some monster! He's not going to turn into a golem!"

Salt motioned for the door, indicating Finn should leave. "Use yer common sense boy! I know ye have it! Mal'Bal's clearly done something to Goblin, whether intentionally or not! We can't take a risk he'll awaken and try to slaughter us all, infect us with some strange disease, or spy for the Star-Child!"

"He wouldn't do that!" Finn argued, refusing to budge from beside Goblin's bed.

"Can ye be sure?" Salt asked, calm but serious. "Look Finn, I know a Star-Child with the ability to detect ownership over items—useful for sensing poisons and tracing assassination attempts. Perhaps she can tell us whether the shard piercing yer friend's chest belong solely to him or to Mal'Bal. We'll be able to know its intentions: whether it's a freak accident or not. Either way, ye need to leave the cabin."

"Then go get her! I'll stay here until then!"

"No." Salt spoke, unmoving. "She's not here, I have her off scouting for new Star-Children. She won't be due 'til three weeks' time."

Finn licked his lips, suddenly angry at Salt. "We came here as free men, and we'll be treated as such."

Salt grabbed Finn's shoulders and pushed him firmly to the door. "And if I leave him free? Surely the other Star-Children will hear of his condition. The guards and the lockdown are as much for our safety as it is for his! Do ye want to find his mangled corpse in the middle of Jakitta? Until we trace the ownership of the shard, ye are banned from this cabin."

"What!" Finn shouted. His anger for Salt doubled, if not for the fact the man was speaking sense. Finn knew his stubbornness and friendship were blinding him. But one stern look from Salt quieted him. If Finn acted out, he could be kicked from the Coalition.

"Alright." he submitted with a sigh, freeing himself from Salt's grip and leaving the room. Outside, Finn folded his arms and watched his breath turn to mist. Salt came and stood beside him.

"Ye have a great opportunity Finn. There are nearly a hundred Star-Children here. Ye haven't activated yer bracer yet. This is an ideal place and time to learn how to do so. Speak to the others and watch them. Perhaps that'll give ye clues to yer own potential. Attempt to focus on yerself while here. Yer friends will all be fine. Goblin will be fine."

"And what will you do?" Finn inquired.

Salt ran a finger down the scar marking his face. "I'll do all I can to learn of Mal'Bal. Where he came from. Who he is. Perhaps plead with the king to work with us, instead of against us. Ye will not be seeing much of me."

Finn was startled. "And who will I train under? I want to learn to fight."

Salt laughed. "We are a group of equals, Finn. I may be the head of the Coalition, but I am far from a superior to any of ye. My only job is to guide. We train each other—everyone going around and passing along their skills and craft. I've seen it grow and unify many of us into a unit."

"And where will I be staying?" Finn asked the Coalition leader.

"In the same cabin ye awoke in. We have plenty of homes. The locals were slaughtered by three rogue Star-Children, leaving behind many empty rooms. The twins, myself, and a few others took care of them and established base here. It's how I got m'scar. Jakitta's a reminder of what we could become if we were to submit to our powers."

Finn shifted uncomfortably.

"Let it remind ye as well, Finn," Salt spoke gravely before turning away and walking off into the mist, again rubbing at the pink line on his face. "that we walk a fine line between heroes and demons."

Finn didn't see much of anyone in his first day at Jakitta. Salt was the last one to speak to him, leaving him to fend for himself. Instead of wandering around, Finn returned to his cabin where he ate his small meal and slept the rest of the day away. The following morning, he awoke to see Altin wandering the village with two Star-Children. He ignored Finn, brooding and whispering with wild-looking men. His feelings hurt, Finn followed them from a distance, watching as they made their way to a large field. There Finn bore witness to the majority of the Coalition. Scores of bracer-wielding forms fought each other with a variety of weapons, hand-to-hand combat skills, and powers.

Near one corner, a large crowd had gathered with shouts of excitement. Finn stopped following Altin and veered to see what the others were watching. Making his way into the crowd—drawing cold stares from many—Finn walked to the edge of a wide pit. It was the same pit Finn had seen the day before, hearing strange noises come from it. The hole was perhaps ten meters deep and at the bottom, two people fought.

A man and woman, both with bracers activated, rolled on the ground, punching at each other with ferocity. The spectators shook their fists, shouting words of encouragement and advice to whichever Star-Child they were rooting for.

"*Rush her Cion! Crack open her chest!*"

"*Antina, jab at his eyes! He can't hit what he can't see!*"

The two fighters separated, panting and snarling. They walked in circles along the edges of the pit, facing each other with hunched backs. The woman, Antina—whose suit covered her arms—fake-dodged. The man stumbled and snarled. The crowd jeered and laughed. The man, his suit forming pauldrons melded into a yoke-collar behind his neck, bashed his fists together, lowered his head like a goat, and dashed forward. His body was a blur, moving at inhuman speed. The woman dove to the side, but the man grazed her, and she launched sideways, bouncing along the dirt floor. It looked painful and the crowd groaned. The man smashed into the wall, causing the ground to shudder. He peeled himself away and shook his body to clear the dust from his skin. Finn watched in interest, wondering what their powers were.

The woman got into a crawling position and stayed there, stunned and disoriented. The crowds yelled at her to get up. The man lowered his head again, but the woman wasn't facing him. She slowly pushing at her knees, huffing as she stood back up. The man tightened his body and launched forward, charging at her exposed back. With no chance of escape, she was hit dead-on, bent over the man's yoke, and tossed into the air. She spun four times and slammed into the ground with a grunt. The crowd hissed. Was the battle over? The man hit into the wall of the pit again and pulled himself free, showering the ground with loose dirt. He turned and lowered his head. This time, Finn paid closer attention. Before each time the man—Cion—charged, there was a moment of hesitation: a build-up. The man had to suck-in energy before shooting forward, as if released from a bow.

Cion's chest expanded and his muscles tensed. Finn smiled, believing he now knew what the Star-Child's ability was. The woman rolled over and raised a hand. Water droplets pulled themselves free from the ground around her, like upside-down rain forming into a glistening wiggling sphere. With a flick, it flew at the man's face. The man stumbled back, spluttering and wiping at his eyes with thick fingers. When he pulled his hands away, another ball was formed and hit him. He howled and wiped again. The woman struggled to her feet, pain shaking her body.

The man activated his power and charged blindly, missing the woman and slipping in the water. He bounced and skidded at high velocity into a wall, getting his shoulder armor stuck against a stone. The crowd cat-called and yelled even more. The woman smiled up to the people, waving like a celebrity. One Star-Child blew her a kiss and she launched water at him, dousing the crowd. Many laughed.

Cion broke free, lowered his head, and roared forward. The woman was able to move away, but Cion stuck out an arm, clotheslining her. She went straight down, her head bouncing off the dirt. Yet to Finn's surprise, she immediately got back up, her face masked by fury. When the man turned, she clawed her fingers and crouched. Cion charged.

Antina raised her arms to the sky and thousands of water droplets rose from the dirt. She flattened her palms and the water froze, floating in place. Cion, unable to stop, ran into it. The unmoving water slashed his exposed skin, cutting furrows along his limbs. There was a flash of light— a gleam so bright Finn shielded his eyes. It was followed by a deep rumble. Thunder? Finn cleared his vision to see Cion standing rigid in the middle of the pit, shaking violently. Throughout all the thousands of water droplets, lines of light ran at incredible speed, forming a spiderweb of lightning that enveloped the Star-Child. Antina lowered her arms and the water dropped, the electricity disappearing. With it went Cion, crumbling to an unconscious heap and leaving the air with the smell of ozone.

The crowd erupted into cheers and money exchanged hands. Star-Children brought out ropes, tying them to posts and climbing into the pit. They awakened Cion and helped both fighters up. When a drowsy Cion went forward to shake Antina's hand, she raised her chin and turned away.

Up close, it was easy to see that many members of the Coalition were barbaric—fierce. As often as they acted friendly, they also lashed out. It was as if they were part of another species—another race. Finn imagined them as wild animals, barely kept in check. He had a feeling if Salt hadn't put forth great effort into bringing these people in, Lenova would have already been in ruins. If left to their own fates, or if led by another... Finn shuddered. But a few in the crowd held themselves in check, keeping calm and gazing out with half-lidded eyes—they were the ones with strong mental control.

Now that the battle was over and the two contestants had left to tend to their injuries, many noticed Finn. Some nodded, yet many scowled, staring at him as if he were a nuisance. Finn backed off, feeling vulnerable and unwanted. He was as Goblin must have felt when he'd first came to the mining outpost: he needed someone to guide and help him out, yet the only person, Salt, was gone.

"*It's one of the new Star-Children.*"

"*Is he strong? He doesn't look it.*"

"*He's probably an Accessory. Bet he hasn't activated his power yet.*"

Suddenly, Finn wanted to be in his cabin, alone and drawing no attention. Turning and leaving, the words of the other Star-Children following in his wake, Finn hurried off.

As the days passed, Finn was more alone than he had ever been before. At least as a cave-diver, he'd not known the pleasure of friendship. Now with the experience taken away, he was left a shell. He had expected Altin to have stuck with him, especially after what they'd been through, but instead, from the moment Altin had awoken, he'd done everything he could to not associate himself with Finn. In fact, he spoke of Finn as if he were handicapped, telling the other Star-Children Finn merely found his bracer and had no power, making him an outcast and not a true member of the Coalition. From that moment on, Finn was shunned left and right. It was as if the Coalition was waiting, expecting him to slink off into the night and disappear. They wanted him gone. He didn't belong.

Finn's desperate desire to learn drove him to ask a lone Star-Child, who sat watching a distance sparring match, how to activate his bracer. The wrinkled older man turned his head and his glazed eyes met Finn. Immediately Finn was assaulted with the desire to throw-up. He had no chance to ask anything else as he stumbled away into the bushes, gagging and trying to not fall over.

After a lonely meal in his cabin—food mysteriously appeared in baskets in front of each home every morning, a power Finn attributed to one of the Star-Children—Finn went outside determined to find Altin and the group he spent time with. He had to develop his potential. He had to learn to fight. Finn had grown so desperate in his solitude that he'd taken to watching bouts from a distance and then trying to copy the moves within the secret confines of his room.

He met Altin lounging under a tree with two other Star-Children. When they saw him approach, Altin looked away as if embarrassed while the others gave predator smiles. Finn felt it best to speak first. "May I train with you three? I want to learn to fight."

"Heard you're not one of us." one of the boys spoke. "You wouldn't be able to keep up."

"Bet you'd die practicing." the other said. "Why don't you bring me some food? Maybe if you get me something nice I'll teach you not to cry." The boy laughed at his own stupid joke.

"Just get out of here." Altin spoke in a cold tone, a far-away look to his eyes.

One of the Star-Children opened a large pouch at his waist and whistled. The bag wiggled but nothing seemed to come out of it. Suddenly, it was as if Finn had been pelted by multiple small sharp rocks. He grabbed at his arms and jumped. Red lines were already forming. The boy whistled again and this time Finn swore he saw near-invisible tiny blurs come from the pouch. Again, he was struck across his skin by what felt like many rocks. They stung and left a horrible itching sensation. Were they bugs?

Perhaps some form of projectile? Finn backed away and the boy whistled again. Hit a third time, Finn was forced to run away while peals of laughter followed him.

After a week of horrible neglect, Finn stalked Altin late into the evening, waiting for a chance to catch the long-haired older boy alone. He wanted to meet with Altin at a time where the other Star-Children weren't around to influence him. As Altin went back to his cabin to sleep, Finn blocked him off, stopping in his path. Altin paused and eyed him coolly.

"What do you want?" he asked.

"Why are you being this way?" Finn asked back, trying to not show how hurt he was by Altin's actions.

Altin shrugged. "Why do you assume we were ever friends, Finn? We stuck together because we were outcasts. I was forced into the situation and so were you."

"But after fighting together, escaping Kazma, making it here—don't you care?" Finn hissed, anger creeping into his voice.

"We're not the same, Finn. You don't belong and we all know it. I finally found a place for myself. Unfortunately, you happen to be in it."

"I've never wronged you!" Finn fought back.

Altin clenched his jaw. "So? Life's tough! Get used to it! When an opportunity to grow stronger comes by, you take it!"

"And you don't think I'm trying to seize this opportunity?" Finn snapped back.

"I'm not talking about you!" Altin growled, walking past and forcing his shoulder into Finn.

Finn was left alone in the darkening path, watching as someone he'd assumed was his friend walk away. That night he had nightmares of swirling faces: outpost miners and Kazman citizens moaned at him, asking why they'd died.

Leaving his cabin late in the afternoon, the idea of leaving swirled through Finn. He struggled to fight it away.

He'd only seen Salt twice since the day they'd first met. Both times, the man appeared to train the Coalition on battle drills, using Star-Children that'd once been part of militaries to help teach. With Salt's hands-on-deck discipline and his loveable humor, he controlled the crowd as a shepherd to sheep.

Because Finn had no practice, he stuck out like a gem in a vat-pig's slop. His marching, his weapon holding, his stance—were all atrocious and earned him quiet laughs from the others. Altin, guided by his new friends on how to do the exercises, did fine.

As each day passed, Finn's loneliness grew stronger. So when he left his home one morning and saw Leeya limping outside, Finn nearly shouted for joy. He ran as fast as he could to her side, shocked at her weakened nature. Her beauty was still there: her hair was back in its ponytail, side-swept and with slight waves, her lips were still elegant lines, and she wore her same dark leather clothes—but her skin was a tone paler and her eyes were carefully guarded. A cloud surrounded her and she barely acknowledged Finn's presence.

She'd lost her home and family.

Finn's throat contracted. She'd already been an emotionally-closed person; with the fall of Kazma, how would she react?

"Leeya, I'm pleased you're awake." He spoke the words cautiously. "For a while I thought that I—I mean we—had lost you."

Leeya studied her surroundings. "Is this Jakitta?"

"Yes." Finn replied, keeping his pace slow to match her.

"It's less than I imagined." she stated flatly.

"Leeya… I'm so sorry about what happened." Finn spoke out, feeling pain for her. He knew exactly what she was going through. He'd seen Nozgull destroy the mining outpost within minutes. His hand moved forward to grab her arm and he forced it to stop and lower back down. "How are you?" He knew the question was stupid yet didn't know what else to ask. She was silent for a long time.

"Mal'Bal's wound has made me infertile."

Her words froze Finn in his tracks and he stumbled. Leeya's slow walk and hunched shoulders spoke volumes: a cry for help—yet there was no show of emotion. Finn wanted to rush over and hug her. He wanted to fix all that'd happened. No one deserved such loss. No one deserved to carry such a burden. With it came rage: rage for all Mal'Bal had done to Lenova and to them personally.

"I'll kill him." The words escaped his lips without permission. Leeya stopped. She turned around and her eyes blinked.

"We'll kill him together."

The statement brought a strange sense of bonding over them, two emotionally hurt forms standing alone, yet not.

"I swear to you Leeya, I'll stay by your side and fight until we've righted the injustice done to us." The promise came without waver.

Leeya nodded, as if her mind was still far away. She shuffled off and Finn joined her. Together they walked side-by-side, silent and united.

the shadow in the bed

31

*—Lords and Ladies bow and twist, learn thy fancy and flick thy wrist.
Bend at waist, praise thy dancer, enjoy your night free from the
necromancer. The Golden Tyrant cannot see, the defiance within me.
Lords and Ladies bow and twist, learn thy fancy and flick thy wrist. —
-Secret dance performed by the many slaves of Mal'Bal, tune sung quietly
late in the night as cult members sleep and enslaved couples dance,
remembering better days.*

Something was burning within Wahala. Something that festered. Rage
gripped her with more power than the pain from her torture. Her
humiliation. Mal'Bal had made her a symbol to the entire cult. *The Star-
Child.*

She screamed and howled as Berula wiped her wounds and picked at excess silver with small tweezers. The noise escaping her haunted the camp and rang out across Kazma's ruins, echoing through the ears of her people. Her shouts of agony made them cower and fear her. She was the scarred witch in the gore tent. The shadow of a failed coup. She was the disgraced Queen Priestess. Silver-Heart. Her noises must have been music to Mal'Bal's ears, a lullaby to help him sleep at night.

"Don't move so much, Lady Wahala. I'll end up stabbing your skin if you don't hold still." Berula chided as she dipped her instrument in a bowl of warm water to clean the blood.

"What skin?" Wahala spat, her eyes gripped shut. "Touch me again and I'll split your bones in half with necromancy!"

Yet Berula went back to work wiping and prodding, doing what she could to fix the ghoul that'd once been Wahala. Berula didn't flinch at the words and Wahala didn't follow through with them. They both knew why. Wahala needed Berula and Berula needed Wahala: both to live.

"I'm almost done." Berula commented. She dug her tweezers against a mound of hardened metal that'd lumped above her tailbone. Wahala screamed again, her wails going through the thick tent canvas, shaking the poor Kazman slaves and new recruits.

"Alright. That's all I can do." Berula spoke, standing away from Wahala's cot. "The rest must mend with time. Your muscles are still far too frayed to allow you to stand. Here, let me bring a mirror for you to see the improvements."

"No!" Wahala groaned, rocking back and forth. "I don't want to see again! I don't want to!"

"Lady Wahala, it's far better than it was. Once the scabs heal, all that'll remain are the silver stripes running across your skin. It'll be an exotic beauty."

"Don't try to comfort me! I'm no fool! I'm a monster! Look upon me!" Wahala shrieked the words, trying to lift her head. The motion was far too difficult and she sank back. Berula walked away.

"See? You can't stand me! Fear me, Berula!"

The slave came back with a mirror. She clicked her tongue at Wahala and shook her head. "We must both accept the state of life we're in Wahala. Don't speak like that. You sound like the Lich-Lord."

The words froze Wahala with her mouth half-open. Berula held up the mirror and Wahala's reflection stared back. Facing her was an alien gaunt face. The black storm of sorrow and fury rolled behind shadowed sunken eyes. Her cheekbones stuck out like knives and her once-silky hair looked as if it could crack like dried twigs. Silver stripes glowed on her skin, running in lines along her entire body. Scabs, bruises, and blood blisters pocketed every segment of her, yet there was no scar where her abdomen had been torn open. *Where Mal'Bal had violated her with his golden hand, reaching, reaching, plucking out her heart. Her once proud beautiful golden heart. Now silver. Below gold.* She was a monster, hardly resembling the Wahala that'd once been.

"*Hide me.*" she spoke in the ancient necromantic language; words she'd learned in her temple studies when she'd disobeyed Mal'Bal. Her malformations disappeared behind clean beautiful skin. Her face was no longer skeletal. She was beautiful. But the eyes... the eyes didn't change.

"Lady, don't use magic!" Berula gasped. "You need the energy to recuperate!"

Wahala let go of the spell, her consciousness threatening to leave her. It was no use. There was no point in hiding how she looked; who she was: the last of an old tradition. She'd let her mother down. No, the dream wasn't her mother's anymore. It had been hers.

"Get me water." Wahala hissed.

Berula disappeared, her feet treading on the red flood of the tent. She reappeared with a cup. The old woman held Wahala's head while she drank.

"Too bad we don't have any of the duck I can smell outside. It seems some of the cult members have found another of Kazma's food storage facilities. Do any of them grow their own crops or do they sweep the land like a plague, taking all nourishment and growth with them?"

Berula's question was worded in a way that made Wahala sound as if *she* was no longer part of the cult. An outcast. An individual in the same status as the Kazmans.

"At home, we have animal farms and crops grown underground, lit by glowing lichen. We're not simple barbarians with no skill or culture." Wahala's words sounded distant to her, as if she spoke of another people.

"Do they dance, sing, love? I don't think I can imagine it." Berula asked, facing the tent flap.

"We're raised strict. But there are times…" Wahala winced and gripped the edge of the cot, a wave of pain washing over her. When it subsided, she continued. "when we celebrate our strength. Our race. Our ancestry and history." Wahala's voice cut out as she again thought of the past. Mal'Bal had cut it away from them. Gone: gone were the traditions and the way of her people. *Star-Child.*

"We laugh and we love and we kill. We were a family overcoming the danger of the Kingdom of Rot."

The elder smiled softly. "What dark names you have. Was it all Mal'Bal?"

"It was him that brought us to this accursed land, Lenova." Wahala spat the words.

Berula became somber and looked away, perhaps into the depths of her mind. "If not for him… If we'd known of your people so far to the South in the deadlands… perhaps friendship instead of war…"

Wahala scoffed. "We're not ones who ally themselves with the blind. Your people hold false beliefs and praise omnipotent beings in the sky that don't exist. There's nothing more than pain and death. It's final and perfect."

"But you laugh and love." Berula spoke, a gleam to her eyes. "We're not so different after all."

"We're nothing like each other! Blasphemous, weak, trash! You're all a waste of resources! Your children are slugs, squelching in their filth! The women are squabbling crows and your men are easy to shatter! You all deserve death!" Wahala's rage smashed over and over against the old slave but Berula didn't waver, nor did she grow angry. Instead, she gave Wahala more water when she went into a coughing fit, mid-rant.

"You'll see, Lady Wahala. We can become friends and we can stop this suffering. But rest now, I must leave to tend to Mal'Bal's puppet. The Lich-Lord had demanded it cleaned."

Wahala couldn't reply. She didn't know how to react to Berula's courtesy. Instead she fell into a deep and restful sleep.

Wahala was shaken awake. Berula stood above her, concern on her face. "Quickly, awaken! You have a secret visitor!"

Wahala blinked her eyes. An outline of a male form could be seen from beyond the tent wall. It hovered there as if halfway ready to run at the slightest sound.

"Salastine?" Wahala croaked.

"Yes, my Queen." the voice whispered back.

Wahala smiled, her excitement rising. "You live! Did Mal'Bal not kill those loyal to me?"

"Many of us live, my Queen. We are a shadowy people. In fact, Mal'Bal's actions have given us far larger numbers than we could have ever dreamt of."

"Then where are they, Salastine? Only you speak to me, no others draw close. How come I have neither heard nor seen your people since Castor?"

"*Your people,* my lady. They watch from afar. They are cautious—too aware of what would happen if they were caught. They wait for you to prove yourself to them."

Wahala made the move to argue but Salastine stopped her. "Don't worry. After the assassination, your supporters will flood to your side."

Something stirred within Wahala. Something she thought she'd never have again. *Hope. Frail, easy-to-shatter hope.* Yet she held herself in check. It was too soon to think about what could be, far in the future. Mal'Bal was strong and growing stronger every day. She was lower than the weakest member of the cult. She couldn't influence anyone, much less her entire people. She couldn't fight Mal'Bal herself either—that was an impossibility. Neither could she openly do anything without inciting Mal'Bal's suspicion—perhaps causing more torture. She was stuck in a cot, prisoner and slave. There was nothing she could do but think. Already her frail hope was crumbling.

"My Queen?" Salastine called out.

What could she do then? She couldn't *think* Mal'Bal to death. Neither was she yet strong enough in her necromantic ways to fight him with magic. She didn't know enough. Wasn't experienced like Mal'Bal, who had—against all rules and regulations—studied many forbidden books from the day he became cult leader until now. Yet an idea hit her. One risky enough to not cause another torture, but execution. The thought led to another and another, until sticky webs of a plan emerged—a means to winning; played from the shadows, manipulated through cunning, worked over by patience. Wahala smiled wide and she knew the action must have been horrifying. But it was alright: her scabs would heal. *So would the cult.*

"Salastine. I need you to remain low." Wahala spoke with whispered control. "Play the humblest of servants and the most loyal of cult members."

"Y—yes, my Queen."

"What's Mal'Bal up to?"

"He awaits your recovery so as to use you publicly as his servant. He'll shame your title and status! I can't bear to think of it without wanting his blood! He also sits within the middle of Kazma, wearing the All-Face mask all day—*your* rightful artifact! I'm afraid he's trying to master its power and bear witness to all possible futures. Lenova's armies are sure to come and he wishes a perfect campaign. But the mask isn't for him. It wasn't meant for anyone but the Queen Priestess. It warps his mind and carves furrows into his thoughts. I'm afraid he grows madder than ever before. He's never been fit for leadership but with his growing insanity…"

"Continue." Wahala whispered, shocked at the news.

"He allows the fear of himself to hang over the people to prevent disobedience or rebellion. But many question why we are still here in Kazma. They whisper of vulnerability. Of doom. Some have run home without plan. The ones who haven't been caught and executed will surely die at the hands of the dead. They need groups and maps to survive. Others now say Lenova, not the Kingdom of Rot, is the land of death."

Time was running out. Soon her people would be nothing more than an echo of what they once were. There was no choice but to attempt the dangerous plan.

"Salastine, do you still have the books I brought from the temple?"

"Yes Queen. I've hidden them in the remnants of a safe, deep within a Kazman house."

Wahala closed her eyes. "Bring them to me. We'll meet again soon. I'll send Berula as our means of communication."

"When Queen?"

"Soon. But don't grow inpatient. We'll have our revenge. We'll rip the cult back from Mal'Bal's cold dead fingers."

"How?" Salastine whispered. "His golden body, his Star-Child suit, his necromancy… how can we kill one who can't be hurt?"

Wahala smiled into the dark of the tent, her eyes closed and full of visions of a bright future. Her dark plan swirled and crept like a snake beneath black rocks. Berula leaned in, curious as well. Wahala was alright with telling them. They had as much reason to want Mal'Bal dead. They could be trusted. She sighed and words flowed out like spoiled honey. A weakness—she'd thought of a weakness to the Lich.

"We shall poison him."

development

32

—Between wild beasts, monsters, raiders, slavers, and disease, many children of Lenova are left homeless. While many are adopted or cared for in orphanages, others die by the various dangers of the land or end up in the Crust, forced to work to the bitter end. —
-Excerpt from Statistical Population Counts, published by House Royal

A Star-Child glanced at Finn from the corner of his eye and Finn clenched his fists. He focused on his meal of oat paste. Across from him, Leeya ate without emotion, ignoring all else. Having lunch outdoors—in Finn's opinion—had been a bad idea.

"They judge us all day and night." Finn huffed, taking a big spoonful and swallowing it faster than he intended. The sooner he finished the meal, the sooner he could get away from the demeaning stares of others.

"Let them." Leeya replied in a monotone. Immediately she shut down again, no longer talking. Finn knew she was hurting. Even stoic Leeya had emotions buried deep within her. To Finn, her quiet was a call for help, a silent plea stating something was wrong.

"Perhaps she hides her weakness behind her pretty looks."

The voice came from behind them, sudden and unexpected. Finn turned to see Altin approach with the two other Star-Children he'd been so fond of hanging around with. The two brutes were like the miners in the Crust: strong, but too dumb to control their mouths. Even now with Leeya awake, Altin hadn't returned to their side. Instead he chose to stick with those that had no respect or civility.

"Why does she frown? Is the oatmeal not to her standards?" one of the Star-Children mocked.

"Altin, does she not hail from Kazma? Let me guess: Upper-District? No wonder she doesn't talk to us. We're far beneath her grace!"

"Perhaps." Altin spoke, eyes down.

Leeya didn't respond but continued to eat her meal. Finn though, shot up from his seat, rage flowing through his head.

"You made him angry!" one Star-Child laughed with a snort, his flat upturned nose making him look like a mole. He was the one who had chased Finn away with his bag of invisible projectiles.

"What's he doing? Protecting the girl?" the other Star-Child mocked, a tall individual who could've passed for a scarecrow. "Well Altin, your friend looks like he wants to fight!" Behind them, others paused their meals. They sat back in front of their cabins and stared with looks of amusement.

"He's not my friend." Altin snapped, spitting out the words.

Scarecrow poked Finn in the chest. "You haven't been doing a good job of protecting her. Have you seen her city? Looks like you let her down. Get it? It all came down?" He sniggered and mole-face laughed. Altin shifted and clenched his muscles.

Before Finn could scream at them, a blur hit the tall Star-Child. *Leeya.* Everyone jumped in surprise. Scarecrow flew back and crashed into the ground, his head bouncing against a rock. He gasped in shock but had no time for anything else. Leeya was on top of him, raining furious blows too quick to be dodged or blocked. Her cupped hands clapped his ears then smashed against his nose, breaking it. Leeya's face was a stone: her eyes mere pinpricks.

She closed her fist and punched the man in the throat. He convulsed and let out a croak, trying to roll over. Yet Leeya, with expert skill, pinned his body with her knees, preventing him from escape. Mole-Face shouted in anger and rushed her. Finn jumped him, his weight pushing them both down. Landing on the Star-Child's back, he didn't waste time. His blows were desperate and badly aimed. Although targeting the back of the head, plenty of his punches grazed neck or struck shoulder muscle.

Finn was tackled from the side and sprawled to the dirt, his chin scraping against a pebble. He was rolled over and hammered square in the jaw, the blow so hard Finn's teeth clacked together and his skull reverberated. Another blow landed against his cheek, then jaw again. It was Altin, his face a mask of anger. Finn tried to copy Leeya's move, aiming to punch Altin's throat. Altin ducked and Finn missed, sending a knuckle into Altin's left eye. Altin howled and reared back, grabbing at his face. Finn sat up and backed away, grimacing in pain and holding his own wounds. Then Leeya was there, her bracer activated into a protective metal plate, sliding along her body in blurred speed. Little pings rang out from the metal, yet Finn didn't see anything hitting them. Mole-Face was using his bag of invisible projectiles. Leeya uppercut Altin and as the boy tipped backward, she guided him down with a sharp stomp of her boot, leaving an imprint on his forehead.

She spun about—ducking in an arc—and sprinted for Mole-Face. The Star-Child backpedaled, sweat on his brow. He let out quick whistle bursts, his bag wiggling as unseen objects shot out. As she drew near, he threw out a right hook to clip her across the face. Leeya caught his wrist, spun under it so she was at his side, and used her free hand as a bludgeon, smashing his elbow and bending it the wrong way. He stopped whistling and shrieked along to the crack of bone, looking on in horror at the white protruding from his skin. As quickly as the fight started, it ended, leaving Finn and Leeya standing in the middle of a dirt-scuffed patch with three groaning forms.

Finn stared at the beautiful girl in awe. Behind her still face was a storm of conflict. To show emotion would break the code that made her a member of Kazma, yet just the same, not showing emotion meant a lack of caring for what'd happened to her home. Perhaps in her mind, either choice was a dishonor. Finn recalled how she'd told him in a flat voice of the permanent damage caused by her run-in with Mal'Bal. *Infertility.* Why had she told him? Why had she spoken of it without any emotion? *A silent cry for help.* Leeya was cracking at the seams.

Altin rolled onto his side and spit out a glob of blood. The other two Star-Children were both unconscious. The spectators from the other eating tables approached with caution, giving Leeya plenty of space. Many had looks of respect and others, of fear.

"*Untamed.*" someone whispered.

A voice shouted for Petreamus, the Star-Child healer. The crowd gathered around the fallen forms and stared, none bending to help. Finn approached Leeya with a slow step. "We might both get kicked out for this."

The female Star-Child from the arena—Antina—passed by. "I doubt it," she spoke, overhearing them, "there's been worse fights in

Jakitta."

She narrowed her eyes at Leeya. Up close, Finn noticed her skin seemed to swirl with translucent shadows as if she'd been created from clouds. He had a feeling she wasn't entirely human. Finn had heard of other races existing in Lenova. He thought he'd even seen some in Kazma. The Star-Child continued talking. "You brawl well for a female. Most women here are more accustomed to washing clothes than snapping bones. Where'd you learn to fight?"

"Where did you?" Leeya asked back, turning the question around. Her eyes were still narrowed in battle fury and Finn worried she might lash out at Antina.

Antina, talking as if to someone calm and collected, shrugged. "My family was poor. My sisters wooed men for money. I chose to fight them for money. You have good skill. I wonder how you would do against a seasoned opponent."

Leeya grunted, unwilling to reply. Taking it as a sign that the conversation was over, Antina smirked and disappeared down a path among the pine. Leeya deactivated her bracer and examined the bruises forming on Finn's face from Altin's attack. She showed no sign she cared about Antina's comments.

"Thank you." Her words were clipped and quiet. They startled Finn. Before he could reply, she continued. "It wasn't enough. You'll have to do better. You must learn to fight—not only with fists, but weapons. It's time I train you."

After Leeya pressed a Star-Child for information, they were told of a cabin reserved for weapons and training material. Many in the Coalition brought in a variety of armaments and Salt himself had added an assortment of gear taken from military training camps. Entering the cabin, Finn and Leeya were greeted by collections of swords, racks of spears, quivers and bows, axes and staves, full suits of armor, leather wrappings, and even a worn mace and chain with a dark crust on its handle—Finn had a suspicion of what it was. Immediately drawn to a large double-edged blade, Finn took a step forward only to be stopped by Leeya.

"No. You're not ready for that."

"Why not?" Finn whined. He hungered to go for a weapon.

Leeya inspected a dusty corner of the room. She rummaged along shelves piled with bulky clothing that looked as if untouched in a thousand years. She glanced at Finn and pursed her lips, gauging his height. She nodded, reaching for a set of thick leather garments. They were atrocious and marked with disturbing black smudges as if the previous wearer had left traces of mold behind. Written on a piece of cloth above the set and pinned to the shelf with a rusty nail was the title for the piece: *Old Heavy.*

"Oh come on!" Finn whined yet again. He swore he saw the faint echo of a smile on Leeya's face.

She pulled the garments free and let them drop to the ground. They let out a strong thump louder than they should've. Upon closer examination, Finn could see that the clothing—a vest, leggings, ankle guards, and bracers—had thick rectangular lumps rising from the material, stretching the stitching as if something was sewn into the pieces.

"What's with that?" he asked.

"You expect to clash blades and win fights, yet what happens when you come across someone who's faster than you? Or stronger than you?"

"I'll use my wits, I guess. Either that or die."

Leeya shook her head. "You can't rely on wits alone. You're far behind most warriors. Many have trained all their lives for battle, but maybe with this we can boost your progress. Put it on."

Finn walked forward, bent, and lifted the vest. He let out a groan. "It's as heavy as a horse! I won't even be able to run!" Leeya didn't reply but waited and Finn took the hint, donning each piece with a grimace. Once fully clothed, his body sagged under the weight. It was as if someone had hidden iron bars within each leather piece. Finn knew he looked ridiculous. Leeya studied the shelved weapons, moving past the heavier ones without a second glace. No maces, clubs, double-sided war axes, or pikes.

For a while she lingered at a box of knives and Finn prayed she'd move to the other armaments. If he walked outside wearing a leather suit looking like he was a toddler in his father's armor *and* while wielding a petite dagger, the Star-Children would keel over all across the camp, struck dead from laughter. Leeya continued on and Finn let out his breath. She selected a few staves, two spears of different length, some swords, and a green-tinged trident. She tossed Finn the trident and he fumbled before catching it. It was a strange piece and heavy on both ends. Immediately, Leeya pulled it away from his grasp, shaking her head. "No way. Not that." Finn agreed.

She had him try each weapon one at a time. Some, such as one of the spears and two of the swords, she took from him before he even had the change to properly grasp them. Others though, she let him swing and thrust: test out. In the end, it came down to a spear the length of his body and a bastard sword, which could be either used with one hand or two. Leeya had him alternate between the weapons, continuously asking him to perform certain feats. Some he could do with ease such as thrust forward with the spear. Other tasks though—such as sideswiping the sword with his right hand, switching to his left for a thrust, and using both hands for a downward stroke—were too difficult to accomplish properly. She continued this way for a while with both weapons, acting as indecisive as

Finn felt. He kept entering the realm of imagination, trying to picture how impressive of a warrior he could one day become.

In the end Leeya had him sheathe the sword, fasten it to his waist, and grasp the spear with both hands. Instead of picking one, Leeya had chosen for him to have both. "For longer-range combat and for close-and-personal." she spoke with a nod. Expecting to head straight out of the cabin and into the practice field, Finn was surprised when she took the weapons away from him and found their wooden equivalents instead. "If you think I'd let you use real ones right away, you're mistaken." she told him.

She rummaged through a stack of projectiles until she produced a quiver full of strange-looking arrows with large blunt tips. They could have passed off as fletched sticks with pebbles attached to their ends. She found herself a sturdy bow and motioned for the door.

Finn adjusted the hold on his own equipment. He detested the wooden fake weapons he'd been assigned. Made of dark solid wood, they were far heavier than the real sword and spear. Donned in "Old Heavy", Finn stumbled and dragged himself out of the cabin, following Leeya. Sweat already collected along his back.

She led him through mist—what seemed to be a common occurrence for Jakitta—and followed a dirt path. They found a secluded spot near an outer wall, far from any curious eyes. It was a section of the small town where no one had made the effort to inhabit. Signs of skirmish still remained from back when Salt had fought the rogue Star-Children that'd ravaged the place. Finn's eyes wandered over to a cabin where a massive vertical slash scarred one wall.

"You expect me to do all my training with this stuff?" he asked Leeya, tossing the practice weapons down and shaking his tired arms. He was already panting as his face scrunched in discomfort.

"I expect you to use them if you plan on standing any chance in a battle." Leeya replied.

"With all this, I'm practically carrying my own weight!" Finn complained.

"I thought you made me a promise." Leeya spoke shortly, her face as emotionless as ever. The words shut Finn up. He gave in, waiting for Leeya's instructions. She was right: he wouldn't break his promise; he'd defeat Mal'Bal. But the only way to even consider accomplishing such a feat would be to first know how to fight. From a lifetime of cave-diving, Finn knew he had a healthy body—although he was far from a muscular titan like many of the miners after years of wielding a heavy pickax.

Leeya pointed to two cabins on either side of them. They stood evenly between both buildings. "We need to develop your strength and stamina. Your body must become accustomed to strain and exertion. You need to become stronger if you plan on lasting a full battle. Some fights can go on for days. You'll run back and forth between the two buildings, touch the wall, turn, and run back to the other. Touch the other, go back, and so on."

"Until when?" Finn asked, already his stomach sinking, not looking forward to the exercise.

"Until I say so." Leeya spoke, backing away and removing her bow. She tested the string-pull and nodded in satisfaction.

"What's that for?" Finn asked.

"Motivation." Leeya replied with a gleam in her eye.

"Wait. You mean—" Finn began.

"You better run." was her quick reply.

Finn didn't hesitate. He jogged to the first cabin and tapped the wooden frame of one wall. The weights in the leather yanked at him, pulling on his muscles and messing with his balance. He jogged to the other cabin, his breathing already changing. When he was halfway between the two buildings, something bounced against his exposed neck.

He yelped, grabbing at the skin. *It hurt!* He stopped and spun to look at Leeya. Already she was restringing her bow. "Faster." she spoke in a monotone. "And pay attention to your surroundings."

She'd shot an arrow at him! It was a blunt practice arrow, but still! Finn resisted the urge to swear, instead running, not wanting to risk getting hit again.

The exercise was horrible. It was worse than lugging minerals from beneath the ground or a triple-shift in the mines. Never in Finn's life had he felt as if he was using every one of his muscles at the same time. Old Heavy tugged on his skin and rubbed raw at his joints, making each step forward twice as uncomfortable. Turning at one end and coming back for another round, Finn glanced toward Leeya. She had one eye shut and held her head cocked over the bow. Her hair fell over one shoulder, glinting in the sunlight. Her pink lips were pressed tight and her lithe perfect body straightened... *Whack!* Finn was hit in the forehead.

"Don't pay attention to me." Leeya barked. Finn stumbled backward, hands flying to his face as he yelped. He tipped and smashed down, the weights hugging the ground. Immediately Leeya was reloading. With a grunt, Finn flopped over onto his belly and pushed himself up, his fingers digging into soft earth. An arrow smacked into his backside. The pain was dulled by the leather, but it was enough to motivate him to move faster. His body groaned as standing, he ran once more. And that's how it went for the following hour.

Finn sprinted, jogged, tripped, hobbled, even at one point crawled—holding one arm over his face for protection. Every time he drew near the middle of the two cabins, Leeya would fire an arrow. Most of them hit, some missed. Thankfully the leather protected his skin from many of the shots—but occasionally one came through and stung him, leaving a deep throb that pulsed for minutes. When she ran out, Leeya would come forward and retrieve the arrows to begin again. It gave Finn reprieve and—shamefully—he used those moments to stop and suck-in as much air as possible, hoping the dizziness he was feeling would go away. He was embarrassed of his weakness and it was made especially worse with Leeya watching. When he was near collapsing, his limbs quivering and refusing his commands, his eyesight of one drunk or near-dead, Leeya held up a hand for him to stop. Finn fell to his knees.

"Are we done?" he panted, struggling through each word.

"No. I'm just hungry." Leeya replied. "This exercise has given me an appetite. We'll eat and return to continue our practice. There's plenty of sunlight left."

Her—hungry? Finn couldn't tell if she was teasing or speaking truth. Leeya had kept a stern face through it all, yet Finn knew she had to have enjoyed watching him suffer in the ridiculous suit. He didn't have the strength to complain. Instead, he staggered toward her cabin where at the front door awaited a basket of bread, fresh fruits, vegetables, and soup. As he ate, his stomach spinning in both greed and nausea, Finn again had the desire to meet the person whose duty it was to provide them food.

They shared their meal in Leeya's cabin, sitting across from each other at a wooden table. The door was closed but the window filtered in clear light, causing their glasses of water to sparkle. Finn drank very little, as the lack of thirst brought on by the bracer kept him hydrated for longer. Leeya didn't speak and Finn hoped the horrid smell coming from his armpits and back didn't offend her. Yet even in her stony quiet, Leeya seemed more at peace than Finn had seen all day. In the short time knowing each other, they'd developed some form of bond. Perhaps a friendship similar to what he had with Goblin, yet its own thing. How could he describe the variance? With Goblin, it'd been a friendship forged upon experience and survival—loyalty and jokes. With Leeya... and suddenly Finn came upon the answer. Although she didn't show it, their friendship had developed upon emotion: a loyalty of a different kind. And how quickly they'd been thrust into each other's lives. *Destiny*—a lot of the current events seemed to ring of it.

Finn adjusted in his chair, alone in the cabin with the beautiful girl. He wanted to talk to her. Wanted her to be more open with him. How could he get her to speak more? Get her to feel? They stared through the window, hearing the distant call of birds. The silence was there, but it was a comfortable moment.

When they'd finished eating, Leeya stood back up and indicated they should return to practice. Together they lugged the wooden weapons back out to the wall's edge in the secluded clearing. Leeya took the wooden sword and demonstrated a three-swing pattern, explaining each move, when and why to do it, and adjusting Finn's stance with her hands. Finn tried his best not to blush when she grabbed his thighs and moved them, widening his pose. He followed her commands, his body once again sweating under Old Heavy. A question arose in his mind and he couldn't help but ask it.

"Leeya, how'd you learn all this? To fight? To train?"

She took his wrist and changed its angle, pointing the sword a little farther out. Finn had nearly hit her on accident. "It was my passion."

Her words made Finn's chest jump. *Her passion.* She had desires. Something she cared for. Was she opening up?

"But weren't you being trained to become a business woman?" he asked. "Become the person in charge over two companies made one?"

Leeya stepped away from him and looked to the top of Jakitta's wall. "We were all born to do something; to become one thing. But yet...we weren't. There's always other paths." She pointed to him. "Cave-diver or Star-Child."

"You didn't want to follow in your parent's footsteps." Finn concluded. Leeya didn't reply. She acted as if Finn's words hadn't been spoken, but her muscles were clenched—barely noticeable. Finn pictured a young Leeya, barely tall enough to look over the wall of the Upper-District and see below at what lay beneath. The little girl wondered why her parents didn't show love. The little girl's eyes followed Kazman guards marching past her in the vendor alleys, their armor shining and imposing spears bobbing. Her parents would tug her arm, forcing her to look at shop counters, where money receipts and ledgers spoke of commerce, trade, and the life she was supposed to have.

"Who taught you?" Finn asked her.

"An old man." she replied, her words as soft as a whisper, her eyes dim. "A retired soldier who'd seen more battles than sunsets. Eyuro was his name."

"He taught you well." Finn praised.

"He's dead." Leeya replied and spoke no more of the subject. Instead, she returned their focus on sword swings and for the rest of the day Finn switched back-and-forth between his right and left hand until he was comfortable doing the move Leeya had shown.

Night came and they returned their equipment. Without Old Heavy, Finn was as weightless as moonlight. Walking home, Finn hesitated in front of Goblin's cabin, where the boy had been kept in solitary confinement. Salt had left a twin near the place ever since locking Goblin in. So far, Finn hadn't even seen his friend wake up, much less heard word of his condition. Yet tonight the cabin was guard-less. Leeya stopped and studied Finn carefully. He hesitated for only a second before jogging to the side of the building where bushes pile against a covered window. Leeya followed, her pace far calmer, and together they crouched between the leaves hoping no one could see them. Finn reached up and tapped one finger against the glass. Was he making a bad decision? He technically wasn't disobeying Salt. *He hadn't stepped foot at all into the cabin.* He was movement from within: the rustle of bedsheets and the soft steps of bare feet. There was a click and the window slid open. A face popped over the edge and looked at them.

Goblin beamed. "Finally-you-came!"

RAFAEL HOHMANN

unopening wound

33

—Circa 106 E.E. (Economic Era-The 17ᵗʰ Era): A strange brown smog sweeps over the Wooden Wall, encircling the thick forests South of the Table. All animals that breathe in the haze rush to the center of the forest where they begin to pile one atop the other, their skins, muscles, and bones meshing into an amorphous, horrid blob. The smog does not affect humans and no one is able to tell where it comes from. Eventually the smog dissipates and the blob comes apart, reforming back into the individual animals. Yet the animals no longer behave the way they used to. They stand still for long periods of time, as if distracted and oblivious to their surroundings. Predators no longer hunt after prey, regardless of how close they are one to another. Local hunters claim the meat from the animals has no taste and leaves them feeling quite ill afterward. Soon after, all animals vanish from the forest. All that is left are piles of bitter ash. —

-Excerpt from Lenovan Mysteries: Never Answered, Never Forgotten, page 133

"Goblin!" Finn exclaimed, the excitement in his voice difficult to contain within a whisper.

The boy grinned and noticed Leeya. His face mellowed. "I'm-sorry-about-Kazma. I-did-everything-I-could. I-hit-Mal'Bal-on-the-head-but-it-didn't-stop-him."

Leeya looked surprised. "You hit him on the head?"

"Yes-with-a-piece-of-the-tree-golem! It-knocked-him-down."

Finn could tell Leeya was impressed. "You're a greater warrior than I gave you credit for." She spoke the praise with a flat tone; but coming from Leeya, it meant a lot.

"Have you recovered?" Finn asked.

"Yes. But-it-required-much-sleep. I-dreamt-of-the-green-eyed-woman-many-times."

Lady Tuliah. "Did she speak to you? Say anything at all?" He probed the questions with the slightest hint of jealously.

"No. Only-sang-of-oceans-made-from-grass-and-lilypads-floating-among-the-stars. Finn…" Goblin bit his lip with a look of contemplation. "I-think-her-songs-were-protecting-me. Or-healing. Or-maybe-keeping-me-from-the-dark-edges-of-my-dreams. I-could-see-Mal'Bal-there-in-the-dark. Watching-with-a-mask-over-his-face."

The words silenced the group for a while.

"Goblin, what of the shard within your chest?" Finn asked with worry.

"Salt-brought-a-woman-to-the-cabin-a-few-days-ago. The-woman-was-a-Star-Child-Finn! Same-with-Salt! They-have-such-unique-powers!"

"Salt told you his power?" Finn asked in surprise.

"Yes. But-he-made-me-promise-to-not-reveal-it. He's-also-training-me-to-fight! He-comes-each-day-with-practice-swords-and-we-spar. I'm-getting-better!"

Salt was personally training Goblin? No wonder the man was never around. He was either out of Jakitta learning of Mal'Bal's forces or with Goblin, who he'd taken under his wing. Finn's frustration rose. Hadn't Salt kicked Finn out of the cabin *because* Salt didn't trust Goblin?

As if answering his question, Goblin continued. "The-Star-Child-woman-used-her-power-on-my-chest. The-ownership-of-the-shard-belongs-to-me."

Finn's eyes went up. Whether Mal'Bal had purposefully stabbed Goblin with the heart shard or not, his plans had failed: Goblin wasn't dead and not under Mal'Bal's control.

"When I last saw you, your chest was as hard as rock near the wound. It was spreading to the rest of your body. What was happening to you? And if you're alright, why does Salt keep you here?" Finn studied Goblin's neck and arms, the only exposed part of him. They looked normal.

Instead of answering, Goblin changed the subject. "What-of-you? Have-you-learned-of-your-bracer? Have-you-been-training?"

Finn lifted his dead bracer, flicking it with one finger. "It's as silent as the day I found it. Perhaps it's weaker than an accessory. Maybe it won't even grant me a suit, but only fire immunity. As for training," he looked to Leeya and tried not to blush. "Leeya's helping."

Goblin raised an eyebrow and Finn swore to himself that if the boy attempted to make a teasing remark, he'd tear out Goblin's voice-strings and leave him mute once more. Although Goblin let out a small playful smile, he didn't press the subject.

"Why is Salt training you?" Leeya asked, speaking up.

Goblin shrugged. "He's-taken-a-liking-to-me. He-said-I-remind-him-of-himself-as-a-younger-man. Sometimes-he-tells-me-inappropriate-jokes."

Finn shook his head. What sort of training was his friend receiving from the leader of the Star-Children? What sort of secrets was Salt sharing with Goblin that Finn didn't know?

"If the other Star-Children hear you're receiving special treatment, they'll grow violent." Leeya commented. "Perhaps some will even leave the Coalition. Salt's taking a risk on you." The words lingered in the air.

Finn knew there was more to Goblin's story than met the eye. Something had happened to his friend—something that'd sparked the scholar in Salt to stay and observe. From Finn's discussion with the Coalition leader, he knew Salt to have great curiosity about the world around them; a man far too similar to Finn himself. Noise from the street made both Finn and Leeya crouch lower. Peeking through the bush, Finn spotted one of the twins, the one called Punishment. He was making his way toward Goblin's cabin.

"We must leave." Leeya spoke.

Goblin nodded. "Go. We'll-speak-more-soon. Will-you-visit-me-again?"

"Every night if possible." Finn hissed.

Goblin gave one final toothy grin and disappeared, closing his window. Leeya and Finn crawled into the dark, away from the road and the approaching twin. They hugged the edge of the outer wall, keeping to the shadows. Passing a cabin, they heard booming laughter.

"Yes, his power is impressive, but have you seen the suit that forms around him? It's like a great metal loincloth! Of course I lost to him in the fight! I'd like to see you not fall down in laughter when a giant man-baby charges at you!"

Finn sniggered and moved on. Leeya, behind him, didn't even smile. When they neared Leeya's home and were far from prying eyes, they stepped out onto the road. Leeya stopped and turned to him with furrowed eyebrows. "You and Goblin, you're the closest of friends. You'd risk great danger for him."

Finn was surprised by her comment. "Him and I—we've been through a lot together in a short amount of time." Leeya stayed silent and Finn continued. "Before all this, I was alone in the mines. I had no one. No friends, no family. In the Crust, friendships are frowned upon."

Leeya gazed at him intently, her face showing the slightest hint of a flush. "Yet you befriended him."

Finn licked his lips, recalling the decision. It had affected his entire adventure. "No parents, no support, a dead-end future. I was to be a cave-diver until I died or transitioned to mining. My life was written and I was tired of it. It was dangerous and maybe even stupid, but I became his friend. He's the closest thing to family I could have. It… it gave me a sense of control over myself."

Leeya's face was changing, moving, struggling. "Family…" she whispered under her breath, as if to herself. "Now I know what you must have felt like all your life. Oh Finn, how it must have been for you…so alone. And now that I'm mutilated…" Her face was turning green, sickly. A terrible pain was seeping from her form. "I cannot have…I cannot…"

Finn spoke without thought. "You're with me now. I'm your family."

Leeya's skin flushed and her eyes scrunched up. She was clenching, her teeth biting together. Something happened. Something Finn never thought he'd see. Tears flowed from her face. She stepped toward him and they were close, very close. Then she turned and ran, taking the steps to her cabin two at a time. With one lingering flick of her hair, she was gone, disappearing and slamming the door behind her. Finn was left open-mouthed and alone. The distant booming laughter of a Star-Child mocked his puzzlement. Leeya had shown her feelings.

SUNRIDER

The following day, Finn met with Leeya outside of her cabin. Once more she was herself—calm and collected. Yet as they grabbed their gear and Finn donned Old Heavy with a whine of anguish, Leeya let out a small smile. Her braided black hair hung over one shoulder and the smell of cinnamon spice kissed Finn's nose. Her smile haunted his mind for the rest of the day.

Distracted, Finn tripped a lot during his run and lost count various times when preforming muscle-building exercises. Leeya shot him with practice arrows and with his mind still ensnared by the smile, the blows didn't hurt as much. When she drew close to help him with his sword swings, he tensed, thoughts wandering to those tears she'd shed, to how she'd fought Altin and the two other Star-Children, *and that smile.*

They moved on to the spear. Together, they practiced holding and throwing it. Leeya was still shut-in, but at one point when Finn finally managed to hit a tree stump from across the cabin yard, she let out another small smile and an approving nod.

That night, Finn visited Goblin once more. Leeya had gone on ahead and left Finn to spend time with his friend. Hiding in the bush underneath the window and speaking in whispers, Finn told the gypsy boy of what had transpired. Finn once more asked Goblin what about the shard and Goblin asked Finn whether he liked Leeya. Neither answered.

The days dropped by like the falling pinecones in the trees of Jakitta and Finn's training with Leeya continued without pause or rest. Runs grew longer, sword swings became complicated, and spear thrusts turned to spear twirls. Finn was by no means exceptional, but he did improve. He often remembered the fight with Altin and it spurned him to move faster, push farther, and become better.

A change came over Finn's body. Old Heavy became less heavy—difficult, yet not as much. His body grew and the exercise, hearty food, and sleep sharpened his reflexes. Occasionally, Salt gathered the Coalition for mass training. They would march out of Jakitta across fields of mud and rock until they were each left groaning in pain. Finn was no longer the first to tire.

Salt called out battle commands in a loud bellow, watching with eagle eyes for those who hesitated or refused to comply. "Move yer forsaken pimpled-rumps, ye sad-as-handless-thieves, sallow-skinned, spit-spleened festerjaws! Ye call yerselves Star-Children? Well, at least ye got the children part right! I've never seen so many complain over nothing! If ye were in my sea-ship, I'd throw the lot of ye overboard and train a crew of potatoes instead! They'd be more efficient!"

When a stubborn Star-Child refused to follow commands—rebellion gleaming in their eyes—Salt was immediately there, piling his insults upon the troublemaker with such speed and ferocity, the person would be left staggering back into line, nodding their head drunkenly. On those days Finn had little opportunity to talk to the Coalition leader. When Finn did try stopping Salt before the man disappeared, dark-blue cloak trailing in his wake, Salt would only provide quick chat, always hurrying out of Jakitta or interrupting Finn to speak with a messenger about delivering a letter to the king. Finn, frustrated enough to be blunt, voiced his anger.

"Where do you go that you leave us here to train alone? You—you never seem to take true charge! You're supposed to lead us, aren't you?" Finn felt like a little boy complaining to his father. Instead of taking offense, Salt nodded, suddenly looking out of place, as if a wall had come down for a brief second, revealing how the sailor truly felt. For a moment, Finn thought he saw a hollow frustration in Salt's eyes, like the look of a carriage driver with no reigns. One who had no control of where he was going no matter how much he struggled against the pull of fate. Then the walls came up and Salt had his cocky confident attitude once more. "That be true, Finn-for-Finn's-sake, it can seem like that. It is because I am in charge that my time is limited. There are many goals to accomplish—in addition to training—if we're to become proper protectors of Lenova." He grasped Finn's arm, feeling the new muscle growing there. He smiled a pleased crooked smile. "Yer developing. The book don't lie."

"The book?" Finn asked, his curiosity awakening.

Salt stiffened, eyes growing wide, then narrow. "Damn my loose sailor's tongue! Stupid, callop-brained, t—t—t..." he spluttered. "See, now I've gotten so upset I can't even properly swear!" With that, Salt turned and walked away, retreating into a conversation with a group of other Star-Children.

During the nights Finn and Goblin exchanged words on what they'd learned and pried each other's minds for secrets. Finn was impressed as Goblin described feats of battle against Salt and how both would bounce around the small cabin, exchanging blows. Goblin told of Salt's incredible speed and unmatched wits. Salt also engaged Goblin in battles of the mind, challenging him to answer complex riddles and battle situations. They went over scenarios such as what if the Coalition was trapped between two forces, or how does one save an entire army from volleys of arrows, and what subtle techniques can be used to negotiate hostages. Throughout it all, Goblin always refrained from talking about Mal'Bal's injury and the shard, leaving Finn tormented for answers.

More days passed and Leeya's smile, although rare, flashed in Finn's direction as he grew in skill. They began to spar, slowly at first. Upon those nights Finn would walk home sore and bruised, often with nosebleeds or swollen fingers. Altin, still spending his waking days with Scarecrow and Mole-Face, watched him from a distance with narrowed eyes and a disgusted frown. The blond boy who Finn assumed was a friend was perhaps gone or had never been there in the first place. Yet at one point, Finn caught Altin staring at their training longingly, the Star-Child having walked in upon one of his sparring matches with Leeya. Altin watched from afar, alone without the influence of others, and gave the feeling of wanting to join. But in the end, he slunk of into the shadows, and the next time Finn saw him, he was with Scarecrow and Mole-Face.

With Leeya's vast expertise, Finn was forced to use creativity to keep up with her. Once while spinning his spear above his head, he reached down and pulled his wooden sword free from its sheath, swiping up. It was slow and clumsy, but it still caught Leeya by surprise. At the last moment, noticing his change in form, Leeya activated her bracer and his sword glanced off her suit-covered chest. At that, she gave him the biggest smile of all, nodded, and called it a day. Both were sweaty and Finn, wearing Old Heavy, had a bad rash covering his armpits and upper back.

They ate a snack on the porch of Finn's cabin and watched as rain fell, bringing the common mists of Jakitta. Leeya, sitting close, nudged his arm with her elbow and pointed a chin at the landscape. "Your smell makes the sky cry in disgust. Perhaps tomorrow we'll switch to real weapons and retire the leather armor."

Finn was stunned. Not only had Leeya finally come around to allowing him a real sword and spear but *she'd attempted a joke.* Leeya had tried to be funny. A sudden flurry of emotion and disorganized thoughts ran through him. He stared at her soft lips and smelled the faint spice that came off her hair when she moved. His face flushing, Finn turned away and adjusted his seat, accidentally sticking one hand into a pile of dried bird droppings. He stuck his hand out in the rain and let it wash away the filth while Leeya wasn't looking. No, instead she studied an approaching form walking toward them, shirt and pants dark with water. Finn recognized the walk and shape. It was Goblin, free from his long confinement.

creating trust, creating death

34

—*Come Rose, Come Teeron, return home to me, I beg thout not stolen by Kindred Three. Watch children so closely, and lock thy home tight, late night the Brothers shall come within sight. Beware your abode not built far from village, for lonely home-dwellings shall surely be pillaged. Not by man, nor by raider, neither by beast, but by Kindred Three, approaching from East.*

A prayer: Please Brothers; take gold, take silver and spoon, but not my darlings. Please Brothers; take me if you must, but not m'tender starlings. A second prayer: Crack not their bones in thy malformed hands. —
-Common inscription found on wooden boards hanging above the doors in Urrimad

The tent flap swung open and Berula staggered inside, her body bent and strange, as if in pain. Wahala sat up, watching. The Kazman servant walked over the blood-caked canvas floor—crumbling it into red powder. Berula sat on her cot and grabbed a vial of thick fluid from a table full of plants, containers, mixing bowls, cups, and bandages. With a tremble, Berula downed the liquid and laid back. On her right hand, a bloody rag covered the stump where her index finger used to be.

"What happened?" Wahala asked.

There was a moment of quiet as the old woman winced. "I angered the puppet enough to make it lash out. I was only cleaning it as instructed by your leader."

"Yet you live." Wahala replied. "I'm impressed. One would think a slash from the Lich-Lord's child would bring death."

"How can you stand being in the company of such evil?" Berula groaned, removing the rag and getting to work on the injury with a dark-green poultice.

And that was the opportunity Wahala needed. "Do you hate him?" she asked the servant. "By his hand your city was taken, your freedom, and now your finger."

Berula was crying, not for her finger, but for the internal struggle within herself. Wahala wanted to smile yet she hid the emotion behind a quiet stare. The servant's optimistic belief was being questioned. The chance for peace between the cult and the Lenovans no longer looked as possible as before. Wahala was desperate for Berula to take the bait—to be convinced there was only one way to deal with Mal'Bal: Wahala's way. "Do you hate him?"

"Yes!" Berula sobbed, threading her stump closed, blood running down her arm. "Yes!" The woman was sagging, caving into herself in defeat. Wahala bit her cheek. *Good, now was the time.*

"We can end it together. End the evil you speak of." Wahala sang the words, picturing them as an enticing string working its way into Berula.

"How?" the elder gasped, finishing her stitching and wrapping it in a leaf.

Wahala pointed to Berula's work table. She'd been brought back from the brink of death by many tonics and poultices made there. "Use your skill for me—for us. Make a poison. Your opportunity to change the course of Lenova is at hand."

"What will happen if we do kill him?" Berula whispered.

The bait had been taken. Wahala reeled in. "We might finally get the glimmer of peace you've so talked about."

The servant didn't speak for a long time. Perhaps an hour passed, perhaps more. Then the words Wahala wanted to hear finally came. "What sort of poison?"

Wahala closed her eyes, the rush of future victory coming over her. "Something that can seep into the skin of his head. Nothing ingested could work, neither anything coating a dart or blade—that would require a battle, and there's none that can stand to him. Is there something we can put inside his mask? He wears the object all day."

Berula frowned, eyes red. "There are a few oils that can harm, some that can burn, but only one I know of that can kill. It is only speculation based on my knowledge of anti-venoms."

Wahala sat straight in her cot, hands like excited spiders. "What will you need?"

"Many of the plants can be found with ease, but the main ingredient, slime from a black Dikka Slug—that will be hard to come by."

"I shall have Salastine work closely with you. He or those he trusts can find your ingredients. How will the poison work?"

Berula shuddered. "It's rarely been made. The slug slime—upon contact with organic flesh—develops hair-thin strands of substance that bore into the body where they swell to the size of eggs and become acid."

Wahala's many silver scars rang with vile pleasure of the thought of such painful revenge. She imagined Mal'Bal awaking one day, donning the All-Face mask, and collapsing to the ground in pain, body shaking as he gurgled out his last breath.

"If you do this, you'll save us all, Berula. It is an act of desperation. A deed that must be done. *You* will save Lenova." Wahala purred out the words, thickening the praise and anxiety of the situation. "If this isn't done, Kazma won't be the only city to fall." Berula was shaking her head quietly, eyes downtrodden and mouth agape. "Now go and get me Salastine." Wahala commanded. "He is to deliver my books for study."

Wahala didn't expect Mal'Bal's visit. Her only warning was the scampering of metal digits moving over rocks and suddenly the Golden Puppet was in the tent, no longer bruised or battered. Mal'Bal entered after the creature, his body as powerful and strong as ever. Had Wahala forgotten his stature that quickly? Without the mask, Mal'Bal's face was exposed to the world once more. His organic flesh was paler than it'd been and the purple veins running across his skin now spread with greater definition: a spiderweb of lines curving from the corners of his features over his scalp. *But his eyes:* his eyes were far worse. Gone was any semblance of control over reality. The Lich-Lord's dilated pupils held a distant look—a look of a ship that'd passed over the horizon and seen beyond the edge of the world.

Wearing the mask for even a few moments should've killed him. It was not his to use, only Wahala's right as Queen Priestess of the cult. Yet the man survived wearing it at every waking moment. Perhaps it was because he was mostly gold or perhaps because he was the offspring of a Queen Priestess and the earth itself—a mystery which none had ever been able to explain. Either way, he was alive and had been granted the visions of future possibilities—paths which could be taken: failures or successes. Wahala could tell he'd seen much. It was in the twitch of his face muscles, the curve of his lips, the way he stared through her as if gazing into a star-field. He was no longer there. No longer the Mal'Bal she'd known, but something more—an evolution, crazier than ever. The only question remaining was whether he understood what the mask had shown.

"Wahala." he spoke in a whisper, as if tasting the air. Did the dried blood of the tent make him thirsty? The Puppet shivered in response to the voice. There were red dots on its arm—perhaps belonging to Berula, who was not in the tent but elsewhere, serving other members of the cult. "It's been long."

Wahala had thought on how she'd react when seeing the leader of the cult for the first time after her torture. At first, she'd planned on screaming at him, or playing coy and powerful, as if the pain had never affected her. Oh how she wanted to scrape her nails across his exposed skull and tear out his life. But she knew to act prideful would be a fatal mistake. No, she had to *play*. She had to act in a way that would undermine Mal'Bal. *The long game.* Yes, she had to sneak and slither on her belly, especially if she was to see him dead at her feet, poison leaking from his pores.

"M—master." she stuttered, eyes down. She clenched her shivering hands and pulled her legs up. The Lich studied her, his eyes there but not there. Where were his thoughts? Where was the dangerous purr that meant he was at an advantage, knew more than she did?

"You have rested for far too long, *little queen*. The cult wonders as to why your pained screams have gone silent—the music made them hide in their tents. They ask if you've become a shadow, traveling behind their cots in the night, widening your jaw in preparation to swallow them."

Wahala didn't reply but rubbed at a silver line running along her arm. A small tear came from her face and internally, she wondered whether she was pushing the act too far.

"We can't have you influence them, can we? They must see traitors do not pass on into martyrdom but stay as worms bathing in mud beneath my feet. You should be fully healed by now. Come, there are many who need tending to and there are many that need limbs replaced. You will not have any reason to study any more books—you know enough words." Mal'Bal pointed to the tent entrance and his cheeks quivered. "To think," he chortled softly, one eye faint, the other clear, "that I have a Queen Priestess as my personal servant!"

Wahala was surprised. Mal'Bal was still giving her the responsibility of ritualizing limbs. She had figured that he would never allow her to use necromancy again. Was he so full of pride that he still thought it a waste of his time to perform the magic himself?

Wahala didn't have to fake pain as she adjusted herself off her cot. Her frail body had dreaded the moment since she'd first awoken. The few scabs left on her skin cracked and secreted tiny dots of blood as her legs pivoted to the ground. Her feet found the soft leather shoes Berula had left for the occasion. Sitting up, Wahala prepared herself to stand. She clenched her thigh muscles and they responded dutifully, hesitant soldiers wary of their commands. With a pathetic whimper, she stretched out and bore her weight, standing without support. She wavered and the silver on her body glimmered. Deep within her chest, her coated-heart pounded without break in rhythm. *She was alright. She was strong.*

Finally came the moment she knew must be. The bitter acid in her voice was swallowed and it sank to her core, festering with malice. "Lord," she whispered, "I'll bear your will. I've learned lord, I've learned."

Mal'Bal's nostrils flared and his stance spoke of one who was half-listening to reality and half-listening to a tune hummed by another place. "Yes?" he stated, an invitation to continue.

"By my servitude will I prove my loyalty."

Mal'Bal nodded, a little of his old self briefly shining through as he gave a manic grin. "Your servitude is a given, Wahala. Be grateful I don't order you to drink my spit." Then he was distant once more. "I see a moving shape, Wahala. A titan shifting across reality and bringing its hunger and weight down upon life. There are Gods too—the mask has made that clear enough, yes. Gods of fire and air. They go in a circle around the shape, yes they do." His eyelids twitched. "It's something—something real, or something to be made real. All roads lead to it. All rivers, as if the subjects are the center of the world. We'll move again soon. I just need more. A little more."

Wahala had no words. Mal'Bal had always been unpredictable, his mood-swings as quick to change as wild ocean waves. But this was a new level of insanity and irregularity. He was one with the fog of his own mind, or the echoes left by the mask. Mal'Bal had fallen over the edge. Wahala knew only with time could she regain enough of his trust to allow for the fatal blow. But was there enough of him left to even recognize what was going on around them? It was a dangerous path she walked. One overreaching step and Mal'Bal would erupt. Then would come the whip. Then the silver. Then death.

Her eyes darted to beneath her cot where the earth had been dug up by Salastine. The books from the temple lay buried beneath the airy soil—many of them. She had already learned nearly a score of necromantic spells only privy to the leader of the cult. If only Mal'Bal knew she'd studied more than he'd asked of her... that she had learned words he'd kept all to himself, words that many of the cult could have used throughout their lives.

Had Mal'Bal seen a future where he died by her hands? Had the mask betrayed her? Or was he so far gone she was a blur to his eyes?

"Come." Mal'Bal spoke, turning in place. The physical movements seemed to awaken him.

She hobbled outside after him, the Golden Puppet following at the rear. Her steps were staggered and her eyes shut in the sunlight without her consent. So, this was what it was like to feel warmth once more... She was jealous of Salastine, who was off in the wilderness searching for ingredients to their poison.

Around them, the many tents of cult members, servants, slaves, and newly-inducted moved in the breeze. Men and women, uncloaked in the heat of the day, lounged around, looking bored or worn from too much rest. They were gaunt and some sickly. It terrified Wahala. Where was the order? Who was bringing in food? Surely the stocks of Kazma had depleted. Where were the hunting parties? The foragers? What remained of their supplies looked rationed. Truly Mal'Bal's halt had damaged the campaign. And what of Mal'Bal? Was he as Salastine had told, from day to night in the center of the fallen city, donning the mask? Did he not lead and command anymore? Why had his priorities shifted so drastically? It was as if the man was no longer a living being, but one of the golems he'd created: anti-life.

Some of the cult members kept busy, fixing armor and weapons, forging them as well. Others carved images into branches or stones depicting the Kingdom of Rot, reminiscing of the jobs they once held. Crypt-whisperers, cave-watchers, fungal-growers, canal-maintainers, explorers and scavengers—so many positions given up so Mal'Bal could realize his dream far away from home. So many that'd died on foreign soil.

The cult looked tired; a tired that sank deep into their bones. They needed motivation but there was none to be given. Wahala heard a song of the homeland as she passed a tent.

SUNRIDER

Heavy stone bury me down, down, down in the dark
Forms are a'moving outside.
The land is dead but we are not, down, down in the dark
Forms are a'moving outside.

Wahala wanted to clench her fists—but she knew better. Mal'Bal the traitor. *A Star-Child.*

He led her past the many men and women and they looked up, watching as if they bore witness to a ghost. There was a flicker of movement, Wahala herself barely caught it, but it was there. An older man held a fist over his heart, eyes solemn in her direction. *A tribute to her. A symbol. Silver-Heart. We know what he did to you and we despise him.* Wahala didn't know whether to nod or smile. It was respect they gave her, not the fear they reserved for Mal'Bal. She was distant and mighty in her weak submission—a true queen. Salastine had been right: there were those who still supported her. Their walk continued and others mimicked the symbol, doing it for a split second and only after Mal'Bal had passed them. It was brief and dangerous, but it was a show of support unlike Wahala had ever received.

They entered the rubble of Kazma and Mal'Bal led them to a tunnel made of fallen buildings where no light penetrated. They were swallowed by the dark and Wahala tread carefully, following the Lich-Lord for hundreds of yards. She caught glimpses of garden plants and crushed stalls. The tunnel had once been an open alley. At the end, a half-crushed wooden frame awaited them as entrance to a bank. Most of the building was flattened under meters of rock, but the central room remained. Dark cold tile reflected the few candles Mal'Bal kept lit. There was a consistent drip in the distance. All counters and desks had been broken or pushed to the side save for the central table where money once exchanged hands. Rancid bodies draped furniture and the smell of rot was strong enough to be a near-physical barrier. Wahala shoved her way into it, her skin shaking with lack of breathable air.

Mal'Bal sat at the central table and the Golden Puppet scampered off to lay with the dead bodies as a child would with a toy. The Lich-Lord interwove his fingers and stared at her. "Behind me in a crate you will find food. Prepare me a plate, servant. When you're done, soak a rag in alcohol so I may wash my body."

Wahala obeyed, every fiber of her being wanting to tackle the man and tear out his eyes. She found the crate and pulled out a plate which she set with fruits, vegetables, and a chunk of dried meat. She put the food in front of Mal'Bal and went back to search for a cup. In the crate was kitchenware and an abundance of preserved food that would've made the hungry cult outside rebel. She spotted a sharp cutting blade and froze. Mal'Bal was turned away from her. Could she do it? Could she move quickly enough? No. She knew it wouldn't work. Someway, somehow, Mal'Bal would catch her. She gritted her teeth and her chin quivered as she fought herself. A million scenarios of assassination ran through her head. And what if she didn't try now? What if this was her only opportunity? Her books came to mind: *And when inducted head of the people, many words shall be learned. Forbidden it is to use the energy of others to activate these spells. Words of power and construction. Words of control and destruction. Words such as gasta: which is to melt—used by every Queen Priestess to soften gold for ritualization.*

To soften gold.

Mal'Bal was gold; his entire body. She nearly spoke the word. It was upon the edge of her lips, tottering there. With Mal'Bal's cup in her hand, she stopped herself, grabbed a bottle of wine, and brought him the items. Nearly—nearly had she brought herself to death. Remembering the times in which she'd seen the man fight, liquefying and re-solidifying his limbs, she knew her limited, inexperienced control over the necromantic language couldn't stand up to the Lich-Lord's might. She would have the chance to say one word. Then Mal'Bal would speak *phrases*, more than she could understand or control. She'd be obliterated, without anything left to identify her body. He would cut her segment by segment and allow the puppet to enjoy the rest. She shivered and waited as the powerful master of the cult ate in silence. Beyond him she could see a sleeping mat in the far back of the room. Near the pillow rested the All-Face mask. The time would come. The poison was safe. The poison would grant her rulership.

Behind them, footsteps echoed out. Many sets. Mal'Bal wiped his mouth with a rag Wahala had set near him and stood. A small smile played on his lips. "I saw this." he chanted. "Yes, I saw this." His glazed look made Wahala shiver. The man was an otherworldly being.

Out of the dark came a cult member leading a group of eight strangers. When Wahala noticed their wrists, she patted her body violently, trying to find the scythe that was no longer there. Star-Children—eight Star-Children. The cult member stepped to the side and the men and women walked forward, bracers gleaming. When only five paces from the table, they stopped. As one they fell to their knees and bowed their heads. Mal'Bal chuckled and the chuckle grew to a laugh.

"Lord of the South. Lich. Star-Child." one spoke, addressing Mal'Bal. "We were wild with the hurricanes of power but now you have brought the perfect storm. There is none that can match your glory. We've heard of your dealings with the Southern cities of Lenova and even now bear witness to Kazma's ruin. Accept us into your fold, so we may drink of the blood of your enemies and receive Lordship under you—over the land."

Mal'Bal walked around the table and touched each on the forehead with one finger. Wahala watched on, eyes wide in terror. She hadn't expected this—no, not at all. The Lich-Lord held a huge open-toothed grin, eyes tiny smoldering coals. "Fight under me my *Ventri*—my power-thirsty.

RAFAEL HOHMANN

My Star-Children."

challenger

35

—Circa 5,616 E.E. (Economic Era-The 17th Era): Finn SunRider and Goblin of the Whey-Weavers meet Leeya SkyBorne and Altin, son of Dain. The moment is considered widely by many to be one of the most crucial tipping points in all the history of Lenova. —

Finn and Leeya stepped out into the rain to greet Goblin, nearly running to his side in excitement. The gypsy boy, wearing soft thin clothes, looked changed. A little taller, a little wider around the chest. His arms were more defined and his eyes perhaps perceived more, but his standard goofy smile was the same.

"You're outside!" Finn exclaimed, punching his friend on the shoulder. It was tough, like punching a wall. Goblin had been training hard under Salt.

"Good-to-see-you-too." Goblin laughed, looking Finn up and down. "It-seems-Leeya's-changed-you. You-no-longer-look-like-a-half-starved-shrew-with-a-flu."

"And you no longer look like a flattened cat sat on by the baker's wife!" Finn retorted.

"And-you-no-longer-look-like-a-dog-drowning-in-his-own-sick!"

"And you no longer look like a greased mule rolling down a mountain!"

The two of them laughed heartily while Leeya furrowed her brow. She looked to be confused by their greeting. "Do the two of you always insult each other like this?" she asked.

"Well-we-wouldn't-if-Finn-here-wasn't-so-ugly!" Goblin cajoled.

"Or if Goblin was smarter than a caved-in melon!" Finn fought back with a smile.

Leeya shook her head, her emotionless face not showing how bemused she was. "At-least-we-hadn't-attempted-to-insult-Salt." Goblin stated. "Imagine-competing-against-him!"

"He'd leave us spinning in place, floundering to make scene of the world!" Finn spoke, head nodding solemnly.

They stopped and wiped the rain from their faces. The weather was letting up, now only a soft drizzle. "Will you finally tell us what's going on?" Finn asked. "What of the shard?"

Goblin opened his mouth and from the arena a horn sounded. The group paused. Goblin grinned and walked in the direction of the sound, indicating they should follow. "Come!"

"But Goblin!" Finn protested. Already Leeya was jogging off after the boy and Finn had to hurry to catch up.

They moved past the many cabins as other Star-Children left their dry shelters and followed the sound. Many were already gathering around the arena, staring at a form flanked by the two twins, Punishment and

Justice. It was Salt, with his hands resting against his hips in a confident stance. The man's pulled-back hair dripped in the rain and the water made him look more alive than ever. Did the Coalition leader miss sailing on the SeaLake? Finn and his friends drew near to listen in. To his far right, Altin gave Finn a glare.

"Ye better stick yer ears out and hear my words, ye lard-gutted, jelly-legged trough-eaters!" Salt looked about. "I'm proud of ye all!"

Finn snorted and a Star-Child looked at him with a disapproving stare. Salt's way of giving out compliments was indeed unique.

"Ye have picked a more difficult path of control and nobility! Ye have honed yer skills and gained dominance over yer bracers! Some nearly went mad from it…" Salt stared at a newer Star-Child, who last week had used his power for the first time. The man blushed. The bracer had overwhelmed him and he'd run around, waving his hands and magically gluing people's limbs together. Someone finally knocked him out and Petreamus healed those injured. Thankfully after First-Use the Star-Child could control himself.

"As a graduation ceremony, I've decided to allow those of ye that choose to, to take turns going into the arena and challenging anyone of their choice to battle!"

Finn saw Petreamus the healer put a hand to his face and groan. Finn sniggered. He assumed the man was tired of using his ability. Poor Petreamus spent most of his day out setting traps and collecting small wild animals. At least whomever took care of the Coalition's food had a never-ending supply of meat to feed the Star-Children.

Salt motioned to the pit. "Go ahead."

Immediately Antina stepped forward, her chin out and her lips turned up in confidence. "I am Antina of the Flash and I challenge the Kazman, Leeya!"

The crowd muttered among themselves and Salt raised an eyebrow in surprise at how quickly the first challenge had been issued. Leeya narrowed her eyes and stepped past Finn. "Weapons or no weapons?" she asked calmly. She looked neither excited nor worried. "Fists and bracers only." Antina replied.

They moved to the pit and Finn grabbed Leeya's arm, hissing into her ear, "Watch out! She can summon water and lightning!" Finn pointed to the subsiding rain. "You must end the battle quickly!" She gave a quick nod and was gone, grabbing one of the ropes hanging over the pit. She dropped to the bottom, following Antina. Finn couldn't help but remember the strange woman's fight with Cion and how that'd ended. Goblin, not knowing anything about Antina, looked excited, anticipating an easy win for Leeya.

Salt raised a hand and the two fighters separated to opposite ends of the pit. Finn, having trained with the girl and accustoming himself to her techniques, could tell by the way Leeya posed herself that she was prepared to run at full speed toward Antina. The crowd leaned in. The skies quieted and rain no longer fell. Finn drew his breath, heart hammering.

"Begin!" Salt shouted.

Leeya moved as a blur, rushing across the enclosed space. Her speed was far greater than what she'd used on Finn during their sparing sessions. Seeing her in action showed how much Finn still needed to progress to reach her level. Antina crouched, her bracer activating, creating armor on her arms. Her eyes were narrowed, tracking Leeya. Focus worked through her every limb. She leaned forward, bringing her arms back and to her side as if doing a dance move. She brought them up, pointing forward. A lance made entirely of water flew out from a puddle. Leeya tucked and rolled beneath the projectile, coming to her feet in front of the woman. The water lance burst against the pit wall, chipping stone before exploding into droplets. Antina jabbed at Leeya's throat but the blow was dodged. They moved with a professional aggression that left the crowd—and Finn—gasping and open-mouthed. They were two ribbons spinning around each other, attempting to tangle but always pulling away to safety.

Leeya twisted around Antina and threw an elbow, trying to catch the woman's temple. Antina crouched, sucked moisture from the ground, and splashed Leeya in the eyes. Blinking rapidly, Leeya put one foot on Antina's bent knee and pushed off, jumping up as if running on air and wrapping her legs around Antina's head. The move was as quick as it was precise, boggling Finn's mind. Never had he seen one human climb another in a fight. Leeya leaned forward and grabbed Antina's stretched arm, pivoting her body. Both crashed down, rolling on the mud and separating. When they sprang back to their feet, Antina was smiling. It was as if the woman had been searching all her life for an equal and had finally found one.

They wasted no time and skipped forward, arms coming in from all sides, feet keeping their bodies moving so as to not get caught in one place. The first blow went to Antina, who hit Leeya on the mouth, but the following two—in rapid succession—went the other way, striking Antina in the armpit. Antina's left arm sagged, the muscles no longer working. Finn had seen what Leeya had done: she'd allowed Antina to attack so as to open Antina's defenses. The injury that Leeya sustained was a worthy exchange for what she'd done to her opponent. The fact that Leeya still hadn't activated her bracer only proved to point that she was being tactful, waiting to use her ability when she truly needed it.

Antina pushed away, trying to get clear but Leeya pressed the attack. No matter how quickly Antina moved, she couldn't recuperate from the first blows. Leeya had seized the opening, growing more aggressive and not leaving any room for Antina to breathe. Finn watched on in awe. Leeya not only had a natural talent for combat, but a talent for strategy.

Desperation showed in Antina's eyes as her back touched the pit wall. Finn knew she hadn't expected to be bested in a fight.

Leeya had never looked so beautiful as she did then and there. Her features were striking, like a goddess made of perfect lines. Her lips were slightly parted, as if she was about to smile yet held herself in check. She was so *alive*. Finn—and many other men in the crowd as well—were loose-jawed.

Antina let out a screech and a rumble shook the ground. Behind her, the wall exploded in three various places, pillars of high-pressured water cascading out and smashing Leeya against the chest like stampeding animals. Leeya was thrown back across the pit, rolling and tumbling. Antina let out another shriek, her eyes wide and her skin pale with exertion. There was a white flash and Finn was grabbing at his eyes, rubbing at an afterimage of jagged lines. The sound of thunder shook out, rattling his eardrums. He grabbed at Goblin's shoulder for support and slowly regained his vision. Was Leeya alright?

Antina was on all-fours, gasping. Her bracer was no longer activated and her injured arm collapsed beneath her, unable to support her weight. Water no longer shot out from behind her. All that was left were three holes in the wall of the pit and trenched areas of mud on the ground. Antina was spent, all her energy used in the lightning attack.

Finn spotted a form twitching in the mud. It was Leeya. She was laying belly-down, hair over her face, with one hand outstretched and protected by a floating plate of armor. A black star-shape discolored the metal. She'd tried to deflect the entirety of the lightning strike with her suit.

"Bad move." someone said. "Metal conducts electricity. I lived in the Grassplains of Faanda. Lots of storms there. We bury large metal rods in the ground to draw lighting away from the people. She did just that— became a conduct. Wouldn't be surprised if her insides were cooked."

Finn nearly swallowed his tongue. Was Leeya dead? Was she horribly injured? To Finn's shock, Leeya stood up. The crowd gasped. Even Antina, wavering in place, goggled. Leeya patted her clothes, examined herself and her hovering suit. The armor floated to her hand and slid along her skin, returning to her wrist. She looked to Finn.

"It seems my shield is invulnerable to all attacks. At least it wasn't touching me as it blocked the strike."

She spoke the words in monotone, as if already accepting the fact. Finn though, was amazed with the implications. Even if Leeya's suit didn't protect all her body, limited to the size of a plate, she could theoretically counter any form of attack, whether physical or elemental.

Leeya walked over to Antina, stomping and squelching over the mud. Antina tried to rise but her body didn't obey. She'd used all she had in a last desperate move. She could only lean back against the wall of the pit and wince, her chest heaving ozone-tasting air. Instead of punching her across the face or kicking her into unconsciousness, Leeya crouched and flicked the woman on the nose. Straight-faced she declared, "I win. Thank you for trying."

Finn and the other onlookers erupted into cheers. A few Star-Children went to help Antina climb up. When Leeya was out, Finn fought himself to not rush forward and give her a hug. Instead he grinned and winked. "Couldn't help but show off?" Leeya granted Finn the smallest of smiles and a nod, then her face was stone once more. But it was enough for Finn, who felt as if he were floating on clouds.

"Very good!" Salt was saying with a twinkle in his eyes. He nudged one of the twins who stood by his side. "She might even put you to shame, Justice!"

Many of the Star-Children looked to Leeya with a sense of respect, one even shouting for her to be named lieutenant of the Coalition. Finn though, noticed three that didn't cheer: Altin and the two untamed Star-

Children, Scarecrow and Mole-Face. Finn's eyes locked onto Altin's and the long-haired boy took a step forward, beginning to raise his hand. Was he about to challenge Finn? A voice spoke out—one familiar to his ears: Goblin. The crowd separated around him, giving the gypsy boy room. Everyone grew quiet, shocked at his words. Goblin cleared his throat and spoke again, repeating himself.

"I-am-Goblin-last-survivor-of-the-tribe-of-Whey-Weavers. I-challenge-both-Salt-and-SunRider-to-a-three-way-battle."

assassination

36

—*Many mysteries and histories of Lenova have been forgotten, lost, or destroyed. There are numerous cities whose origins remain unknown, various ruins and dungeons over a million years old, and riddles with answers left dead on the lips of skeletons long buried. —*
-postscript in Oddities of the Land, Oddities of the Mind, page 998

Zul'Ska, Seventy-Ninth Queen Priestess, upon the year of Festered Gold, do document my travels North. We've been four centuries confined to our temple ever since the blight, Teancus of the Meat, drew the swarms of husked corpses around our home. In his foolish attempt to breed our animals outside, he brought in the wandering dead from thousands of kilometers. Never had our people seen a swarm of such scale.

The dead have always moved in droves, tirelessly treading the *gray soil in loose armies. But after smelling our flocks…four centuries—four centuries wandering the uncountable hallways and corridors of our temple, not daring to walk outside lest we be torn to nothing. Their hands beat at our walls for so long, the noise became part of us. What blasphemy: only on the first day of the year is one chosen one to die at the mercy of the corpses. To die by their hands at any other time is sacrilegious, a blot upon our ancestry. We were therefore imprisoned.*

With the size of our home unknown, spreading far below us into the ground, there are still thousands of kilometers of hallways and passages left unexplored. Many a man and woman have dedicated their confinement to mapping the temple. Most do not return. I imagine their mummified corpses rest far in the dark beneath our feet, flies birthing on their cheeks. Four centuries of launching our flaming arrows and tar upon the waves beating on our walls. Millions, we must have killed millions. And now, after so many Queens have died without stepping foot outside, the numbers of the dead are small enough to once again control through necromancy. I have spoken the words which we didn't have the means to speak before. Pia-pun, abardeth fa-laram. *Return to your dark and your hunger. Not here, not here. And the other words:* Fugo-neh. *Burn peacefully.*

And now our people thrive once more. As I write, groups of explorers leave the temple and use ancient maps, travelling to the East, the West, and the far South Outposts. Lifetimes ago they contained records, storage, and small colonies. I doubt any of the colonies live. Without the temple's support, they would have fallen many years ago. I myself, in the interest of feeding our lack of knowledge, travel North, to lands uncharted, where the clouds thin out and break, exposing a sky with color we do not have a name for.

I Zul'Ska find myself walking upon plants. Here the land feeds itself and grows, still alive. It's a deep contrast to our home, a place transcended into its decay. Perhaps in a time far in the future when the sky has met the earth and all the dead have turned to dust, new life will rise from the rotted meat of our home.

Far-off to a grove of budding trees I spot a small village. It is spry and energetic and the families are fresh with the sweet air. I will speak to them cautiously, for their ways are not our ways, and greatly offend me.

I Zul'Ska keep away from the people of Lenova—as is what they call this place. We do not get along. They see life where we see potential for beautiful end. They believe and waste their energy making great strides in religion. Fools, there is but death. Many of them are afraid. They say something strange has come over their land—a threat from the sky. Bracers.

The text is too faded to read.

Here also the text is too faded to read. The only words made out are: *controlling the people, sweeping across, the battle rages on, many follow him and others follow the one who, the people establish a king,* and *powers from the bracers.*

I Zul'Ska have come to sit with one who stays out of the fight between the bracer-wearers and the Lenovans. He has a bracer but does not use its power. We don't like each other but have agreed that I shall use necromancy on the item to better understand its properties. This is a threat that can harm both our peoples.

I Zul'Ska return, bearing with me the bracer of a fallen Star-Child who's been killed in the battlefield. I've learned much, yet still know little.

RAFAEL HOHMANN

I miss the dark and the cold and do not enjoy the strangeness of this land and its culture. They are a fragile people and quick to put faith in others.

—Is it strange to say I trouble sleeping? No longer do dead hands beat at stone walls, the noise a drone in my ears, lulling me into my dreams—

The time spent with Dristan, the bracer-wearer who doesn't use his power, has given me insight. Using the most complicated of phrases in the necromantic tongue and sacrificing years of my life-energy for the research, I've found an odd anomaly within the soul of the pieces. It's hard to describe—as if the objects are attached to strings reaching out into the dark: somewhere not up or down, but somewhere outside of here—the Beyond Gate, a place farther than life and death. This terrifies me and I shall tell no one save for this journal.

I left the Star-Child and entered the battlefield to steal the sample which I have now, the entire arm with bracer attached is carried in my travel bag. I will go home and further analyze the piece.

-End of Journal-

Wahala closed the book with arms trembling. The information she'd gathered was far more knowledge than she'd ever possessed of her people's past, a murky shadowy history full of legends and little facts. She sat back in her cot, trying to not draw the attention of Salastine, who was working with Berula at the table, finishing the poison. They were carefully extracting the Dikka Slug's slime and mixing it in a wooden bowl. It gave the room a sour smell.

She separated her thoughts out like spreading papers across the floor. There had been Star-Children in the past—that was confirmed. There had been a great war with the Chosen, something that changed the entire political nature of Lenova—perhaps established their lineage of kings. The Star-Children were killable—that was a fact she particularly enjoyed. And there was some sort of ethereal connection with the bracers and something called the Beyond Gate. The name alone set Wahala on edge and brought anger to her throat. There was nothing after death. To see a Queen Priestess's words state of *something more* was sacrilege.

She clutched the ancient volume to her chest, the centuries-old book cracking like a fragile husk. This book—carefully stolen from Mal'Bal's belongings by Salastine—was now her most prized possession. How long had the Lich-Lord been holding this information, this history passed from Queen to Queen? What other secrets did he know that she didn't? Had he even read the books? Wahala had a hard time imagining the cult leader sitting in front of a fire and picking up a tome. Her thoughts would have continued if it were not for Salastine, who stood and faced her with a small smile.

"It's ready." he whispered.

Wahala's heart lurched. *The poison.*

Salastine licked his lips, pensive. He looked perturbed. Drawing close, he sat on the edge of her cot and stared at Wahala. She could tell there was a great longing for her in his eyes. Even scarred with silver stripes, the man couldn't resist her.

"I've never ritualized." he spoke. His words were true: not an ounce of gold covered his body and not a scar marked his handsome features. "Ritualization is for those deemed worthy by the Queen alone, called upon only on select days or special times. Mal'Bal might have changed our ways, but he's not changed me. I refused to cut myself in his honor."

The words brought shame to Wahala. *She'd ritualized for Mal'Bal once. Her knees were given up.* How foolish of her.

"I watched you when we were children." Salastine spoke, his eyes soft and full of emotion. "We were the same age but didn't meet. An irony, as there are only so many safe places to go in the temple. You'd walk by my chamber doors with your mother, the High Acolyte, every morning. I still remember the fire in your eyes. Even then I knew you were special."

Wahala felt a sudden vulnerability. Why was Salastine speaking to her like this? At this time and place? In the background, Berula stayed quiet, scraping the near-translucent poison into a small container with a lid.

"I was always a follower." Salastine whispered. "I followed the rivers underground as a boy, curious as to where they would go, I followed our traditional ways with dedication and joy, and I followed you with my eyes. And now, even after all we've been through—ever after Mal'Bal—I can finally follow you as my Queen."

His smooth, slanted cheeks were like stone, giving him a fierce expression. Wahala was overwhelmed. "So now I ask you permission to ritualize for the first time." From the pocket of his black hood he removed a large gold nugget the size of an apple and reached back, producing a cast in the shape of a hand. "This gold came from the limbs of my father. Will you allow me to cut?"

Wahala nodded and Salastine smiled through his fervor. He pulled out a scythe, inhaled slowly, and grew calm. He didn't make noise as he sawed off his left hand, not even whimpering as blood sprayed and soaked his front. He did it with a sense of pride Wahala hadn't seen since the old days when she was a child and bore witness to ritualizations done in front of the previous Queen. Salastine was the truest member of the cult Wahala had ever met.

She didn't allow his bleeding stump to leak for long. Putting the nugget into the cast she spoke, "*Fugo-a-gasta.*" The nugget superheated and melted, filling into the shape. Wahala's energy drained from her. It was a significant amount, but not enough to blur her vision with weakness. Before the gold could overflow the cast, Salastine dropped an Apex gem into the liquid and Wahala closed the shape with the other half of the mold. She spoke words of solidifying and words of flexibility. Once done, she pulled the golden hand free of the cast. Salastine brought out his arm, face pale with lack of blood. She finished the ritual by connecting the limbs, the Apex gem sucking life from organic and bringing it into the inorganic. Wahala fell back, her head hitting her pillow. Salastine was wide-eyed and open-mouthed, staring at his new hand with the joy of a child receiving a gift.

"*My Queen...*" he warbled.

"Is the poison packed?" Wahala choked out, her eyes already fluttering. She was still so weak. To think she'd performed the ritualisms for *all* the Lenovan recruits up to her torture.

"Here it is." Berula spoke, standing and hobbling to their side. Her face was pruned and she glanced to the container in her hand with the look of one who hated what she'd created.

"Then go." Wahala spoke to Salastine. "Prove your loyalty to me. Find a time when Mal'Bal has his mask off. Sneak into his room in his sleep as you sneak around the camp: with the stealth of shadows and the cunning of a scorpion. Use your new hand to rub the oil into the mask. We shall have our revenge. We'll finally return all to its proper place."

"And of the mask? When it's finished, you won't be able to use it." Salastine warned.

"It matters not. It's a worthy sacrifice if we're to kill the Star-Child Lich."

"And of the Star-Children that follow him and wander our camp?"

Wahala scoffed. "If we can kill Mal'Bal, we'll have no problem assassinating them as well. Worry over them after the Golden Agony lays writhing at our feet."

Salastine took the poison from Berula's hands. "I'll circle the camp like a vulture-snake, waiting for the perfect time to strike down. For you, my Queen." He gave one final look to Wahala, his face trailing the echo of another time, of another possibility. Wahala turned away and closed her eyes.

Wahala was awoken by an unfamiliar cult member. Mal'Bal had sent word she was to go and tend to the Star-Children. Rubbing at her eyes and still feeling the exhaustion of the ritual, Wahala reminded herself that until the assassination had been completed she had to remain the ever-so-humbled servant. Told the Star-Children rested from the heat of the day in a shared tent, Wahala stood, her weak body aching where the silver conjoined with her skin. She left the tent with dread, wondering what it would be like to interact with the eight *Ventri,* as called by Mal'Bal. Since the moment of their arrival, she hadn't seen them except for occasional glimpses as they walked past, laughing loudly and pushing at each other. They were arrogant—as if they owned the place. No one dared tell them off, for if they were anywhere near as powerful as Mal'Bal...well, death would come swiftly. Wahala had desperately tried to gather information on them through Salastine and others who worked under him, but all she'd accrued was that one held the name of Portious VoidGrasper, leader of the eight, and he didn't like the golems wandering the camp.

She found their tent, a dome-shaped abode draped in lavish furnishings plundered from the collapsed Upper-District. Upon entering, she was greeted with the overwhelming smell of perfume. Nearly tripping on a thick rug, Wahala forced herself to not sneer at hanging silk ribbons, elaborate vases, and the gem-laced furniture where laughing Star-Children laid back, covered in jewelry.

"Ah, the servant Mal'Bal promised us! I told you we'd be pampered for our support, didn't I?" a voice called out, in a rich snotty accent.

The Star-Children cheered and one threw coins into the air. The one who'd spoken—Wahala assumed it to be Portious—was lounging on a maroon sofa, swirling a cup of wine. He motioned the wealth in the tent. "Your people didn't dig deep enough to reach the largest of coffers and those dreadful golems could care less for money." Portious looked pleased with his own voice. "With our various powers, it would have been a crime to not take it for ourselves wouldn't you say, slave?" He sat up, staring at her in curiosity. "You're an odd-looking one, aren't you? I've only now gotten used to the golden limbs, but your silver skin—it's intriguing."

Wahala gave a brief nod, acting humbled. Internally, she repeated over and over the exact necromantic words to catch his flesh on fire—although the spell would kill her if she tried it. She didn't have the strength to achieve such a feat.

"This is wonderful and all, but when is Lord Bal going to continue his campaign?" one of the younger Star-Children spoke. He looked no older than twenty. "I want to fight! It's so fun when I make them turn on their own allies and strike each other."

"Oh hush little Simek." Portious cooed, his voice slathering the air in fake caring. "We'll bathe in the blood of the populace soon enough. It's only proper they learn to fear us. A noble lord can't subjugate rebellious citizens, can he?"

"I hope when the war is over and Mal'Bal rules the land he'll grant me control over the Opal Dominion. Do you think he'll do that, Portious?" another Star-Child asked out, picking at her teeth.

Wahala fought a snigger. Although a Star-Child himself, Mal'Bal had lied to his own, stating they could each be lords of their own kingdoms. They clearly didn't know Mal'Bal's true intentions of eradicating all life—including eventually their own. Observing the eight Ventri, Wahala couldn't help but see them as a group of spoiled brats. *Powerful,* but non-the-less childlike.

RAFAEL HOHMANN

Wahala was kicked in the back and tumbled to the ground. A few of the Ventri sniggered. Some didn't even notice, but instead played with their wealth. "Get me food slave. I'm hungry. Does this army have nothing to eat? You all look starved!"

It'd been the youngest, Simek. Wanting to disembowel him on the spot but staying her hand, Wahala stood and bowed deeply, speaking through clenched teeth, "Yes oh Chosen. I shall fetch food."

She left the tent—none of the Star-Children even noticing her departure—and walked to where the cult had set up a supply station. Men and women crowded around it, arguing and doing what they could to convince the station workers to part with some extra food. In the background, the many Lenovan slaves watched on silently, wishing they could come forward and beg but knowing they would be killed. They of all people looked the thinnest. A small Kazman boy, only skin and bones, stared at her silver stripes with dim eyes.

Wahala didn't have to push through the crowds to get to the counter—the people separated around her, staring with shameless fascination. She was the heretic branded by Mal'Bal. She was the Queen Priestess shunned and downtrodden. Many, but not all, put their fists to their chests and backed away, disappearing between the tents.

"I need food for our Star-Children guests." Wahala commanded. The station workers bobbed fervently and began to prepare her a package. They went to the large stack of crates behind the wagon which was used as the counter and rummaged for their better supplies.

As she waited, anxiety hit Wahala. *Tonight. It would happen tonight. Mal'Bal would be dead.* What then? What sort of rebellions would arise? Would the people immediately turn to her, uniting as one in loyalty? And what would she do? Would she take them straight back to their home? But what of the Star-Children—not only the Ventri, but all the rest roaming the land? She remembered her fight with the spry silent girl in

—(396)—

Kazma. She'd been powerful, that one. Was she dead? Mal'Bal had boasted to the people he'd killed four Star-Children on his own in the battle, but Wahala had the feeling the man was lying. *Star-Children.* Her anger toward those fiendish bracers roiled within her stomach and her lips pulled back.

Thinking they'd infuriated her, the station workers handed her the food and backed away, fear written across their faces. Wahala didn't comfort them but merely turned and stalked back to the Ventri tent, mentally preparing herself for a full day of abuse.

The day passed with such sluggishness and anxiety that whenever her hands weren't busy, Wahala bit her nails. The Ventri were the messiest people she'd ever met. They spilled precious food all over the floor and then, distracted, would step on it, laughing at one another's crude jokes. By the time they'd finished their meal, most were heavily drunk, and the others—moody. Trying to clean their mess was an endless task. Wiping seats and refilling their cups with wine only angered her. Being pushed, kicked, and pinched only stoked the fire of hatred she felt for Star-Children. And when one vomited on the floor after too much alcohol, she stared at the dwindling sunlight, thinking that soon, within hours, she would be in control.

By far, Portious was the worst of the lot. He was the biggest braggart, the vilest in his eating habits, and the most abusive. Occasionally he would try to trip Wahala for a quick laugh and at other times he would try to reach for her, his cheeks flushed and his breath bitter with wine. When that happened, she excused herself to light candles in the tent. The sun set and Wahala's pulse picked up. Surely Mal'Bal had returned to his chamber after a full day of wearing the All-Face mask. Soon he'd be asleep. She was sure at that very moment, Salastine was shifting through the shadows of the rubble, watching with the poison in hand.

Berula was nowhere to be seen. Wahala had glimpsed her earlier tending to a cult member's injury but that was all. No, for this final night Wahala was alone in her mind, waiting.

The hours passed and soon most of the Ventri were asleep. Only Portious and a fat Star-Child whom she didn't know by name were awake, singly softly about a wench with one leg. The night deepened and the air chilled. Wahala was on an island, staring out at the horizon, waiting for a sign. Her nerves were on edge and she'd altogether stopped caring for cleaning. Instead she sat in a chair, facing the outside with both hands wringing in her lap.

The camp had quieted in the night so when the scream rang out, it echoed freely between all the tents.

"DIED! SOMEONE HAS DIED!"

Wahala sat up so quickly, her chair fell backward, clattering to the ground. The Ventri awoke groggily, confusion squinting their faces. Tent flaps were opening and people were coming out, whispering to themselves. This was it. She'd finally done it! Wahala scoffed and jumped from the tent, running toward the edge of Kazma. She knew where to go even before the voice yelled out again that it was at Mal'Bal's chambers where the death had taken place. The voice, coming from a sentry, shouted out again, awakening the entire populace. Wahala was not the only one running, now many others sprinted forward as well, talking to themselves.

The Lich-Lord was dead?

Who had done it?

No, it couldn't be! It was impossible! The Golden Agony was invincible!

Wahala neared the entrance tunnel leading to the buried bank. She looked around for the body. Where was Mal'Bal? The mask? Salastine? A form moved in the shadows of the entrance and Wahala nearly cheered. She smiled and took a step forward, pushing through the crowds to get to the front. She was going to kiss Salastine—the man deserved that much for his incredible skill. But then she froze and without control of herself, fell to her knees. For the one who stepped out of the dark was Mal'Bal, grinning like a lunatic.

The crowd gasped. Immediately Wahala was at her feet again, pushing back. He hadn't seen her yet. No, no, no! The plan had failed. All that work!

"It seems my home had a snake." Mal'Bal spoke out, his eyes dim, yet bright. He stepped to the side and the people shouted. Behind Mal'Bal was Salastine's corpse, missing its head. Blood soaked the earth around it in a wide puddle. Still clenched in his new golden hand was the All-Face mask, poison gleaming from its inside. Something scampered from the dark: the Golden Puppet. In its limbs it held Salastine's head, clutching it softly like a toy.

"I have many eyes!" Mal'Bal roared. "And I have many ears! I *thought* I had many loyal!"

Wahala was shaking in place. No… not again… she didn't want to be caught again…

"It came as a surprise when I heard witnesses testify of two who plotted against me!" Mal'Bal cackled, kicking Salastine's body. He showed the mask to the crowd. "Poison!" he yelled.

The crowd muttered to themselves and seemed to collectively crouch lower to the ground. In his current mood, Mal'Bal could lash out at anyone. The Ventri were drunkenly stumbling toward them from a distance, dazed looks on their faces. Wahala was gasping, her eyes watering. Two plotters: Mal'Bal knew of her. And Salastine, poor foolish Salastine!

Mal'Bal was stomping forward toward her. It was over now. Wahala knew it. There would be no whip, no silver; only death. The cult would be the Lich-Lord's forever until the day he ended Lenova and turned on them, eradicating all life. She closed her eyes, but was pushed to the side, Mal'Bal brushing past her as if she was no more than a bush. Wahala's eyes shot open.

Mal'Bal shoved aside two cult members and grabbed a form, lifting her by the neck. Berula—the old servant had been hiding at the back of the crowd. Wahala couldn't speak. Berula croaked and struggled feebly. Mal'Bal brought her to the front of his chamber and raised her high, rage turning his face purple.

"I was told these two had been sneaking out, acting suspicious. *Collaborating*! Luck finally came when *this* one whispered of my death, thinking herself alone in a field but not knowing one of my golems hid as a mound behind her!"

The crowds turned in place, staring at each other. Mal'Bal used his golems as spies?

"DO YOU THINK ME STUPID?" Mal'Bal roared. Everyone jumped. In the blink of an eye, the cult leader's face relaxed and he stared at his Golden Puppet with love. "But we took care of it, didn't we? There is one whom I can count on." The puppet scampered side-to-side, stroking the hair on Salastine's bloodied head.

Mal'Bal turned to Berula, face still smiling. He relaxed his grip on her neck. Wahala knew what would happen—knew exactly what Mal'Bal was going to ask. Adrenaline roaring through her veins, she whispered out necromantic words under her breath: "*Still thy tongue.*"

"Was there anyone else in on the plot, Kazman?" Mal'Bal asked, his voice a deadly song. "Tell me and you'll be set free. You're no threat to me. Why should I harm you?"

Berula was opening and closing her jaw, unable to speak. She made no sound as sweat dripped from her wrinkled face. Her frustration grew and tears ran down her cheeks. She turned her neck, gazing at the crowd. She found Wahala, hiding behind another cult member. Their eyes met and Berula focused in as if pleading with her. *What of the peace we could achieve? What of all the time I spent healing you?* Wahala stared back, the hairs on the back of her neck standing on end.

"No one? Only you and him?" Mal'Bal hissed. "You won't say a word?"

Berula was fighting his grip now, her gaze in Wahala's direction unmoving. Mal'Bal's face turned to rage once more. He spun in place and stomped off, dragging Berula behind him. The crowds followed numbly, their eyes wide in terror. Berula was scratching at Mal'Bal's golden arm, her nails breaking. He didn't let go.

They walked to the center of Kazma's ruins, where once the DozDum Pipes had stood proud. All that was left was a black pit leading deep into the bowels of the earth. Mal'Bal stopped at its edge and pinned Berula with his foot. He was breathing heavily, his emotions unchecked.

"Oh servant, taste your own concoction." he spat. He smashed the mask over Berula's face. The woman writhed in agony, still without sound. Feeling the spell draining her energy, Wahala was forced to end it. Immediately muffled shrieks rang out across the rubble and the people winced, many looking away.

Wahala couldn't imagine the amount of pain Berula must have felt, having her face and internal head-parts melted by poison along with being assailed by visions of every possible future. Mal'Bal held her down, grinning manically. Eventually Berula stopped struggling and Mal'Bal stood. He grabbed her body with one large hand and tossed her into the pit, mask and all, gone from the world. The Lich-Lord's temperament changed and he smiled to them.

"The rot has been cut out." he spoke happily. "And I now know where we'll go next: into the dawn of anti-life, into the belly of the earth-destroyer."

Wahala fell against a rock, hollowed out. She was tired, very tired. The faces of her two conspirators were burned into her mind. Did Mal'Bal know she was involved? Or was he so far gone in his lunacy that the thought hadn't even crossed his mind?

"Go back to your tents." Mal'Bal commanded. "Tomorrow we pack and leave this place. The campaign continues."

the pit

37

—In all known records and accounts, no mortal has ever been resurrected. Neither has there been any proof of a valid way to achieve such a feat. The closest event in comparison is the strange developmental cycle of the people in the city of Crossover. Throughout time, the populace of Crossover has developed a strange resistance to illness and disease: when one grows too ill to recuperate, their body enters a state of incubation and their skin thickens greatly. After three weeks, they shed the skin-cocoon they have developed, their bodies now free of sickness and immune to whatever had ailed them. Footnote: Although able to survive even the most virulent of illnesses, the people of Crossover still die of old age. The oldest citizen in recorded history lived to the age of two-hundred and four. — -Excerpt from Development of Magical Cures and Secret Remedies, page 2

The shade within the fighting pit chilled Finn's skin. He stared at Leeya, who from high above, gave him a supportive nod. Tightening the strap around his waist from where a wooden sword hung, he readjusted the grip he held on his practice spear. Ahead of him to his right and left, both Goblin and Salt prepared themselves. Salt looked exited and blew kisses to the crowd. The man held both a net and a curious wooden sword shaped like a crescent moon. Goblin only carried a practice replica of a falcata, sticking with the type of sword he'd used in Kazma. The boy rolled back the sleeves on his shirt and Finn could see a large scar around one wrist. Finn frowned. Why was the scar familiar? The answer was on the edge of his mind.

Finn couldn't believe he'd been challenged—none-the-less by his best friend. Making the situation more ridiculous was Salt, who had happily accepted the three-way fight. It was a situation Finn didn't want to be in. He stepped in mud and pulled his foot free, feeling gunk enter his boot. In the pit was a perpetual smell of sweat and blood, as if the walls had trapped the residue of all previous battles. One advantage Finn had, was that without Old Heavy, the practice weapons felt light. It was strange to think three months ago when he had come to Jakitta, the spear and sword he now held had been clunky and awkward. Perhaps he stood a chance.

He *was* grateful the fight would be a no-powers-allowed brawl. With Salt being the Coalition leader, Finn assumed the guy had some wicked ability in store. Above them, Petreamus raised a hand. Finn tensed and bent his knees, weeks of practice with Leeya flashing through his mind. Stances, angles, which muscles to clench, which way to lean…

"Ready?" Petreamus called. The crowd cheered. Finn's eyes wandered to the scar on Goblin's wrist. No, his friend hadn't collected that in the battle for Kazma. In fact, it was a scar similar to the one Salt had. Finn startled. It was the scar of one who had tried to put on a second bracer. But that meant....

"Fight!"

Finn grabbed his spear with both hands, pointed it toward his opponents, and looped the tip in a circle. He remembered Leeya's words to never throw his spear in close combat unless it was necessary, but instead, use it to poke and prod. He had to let his opponents tire out and when the time was right, come in with the sword to finish the job.

Goblin charged him, twisting his blade back over one hand, then the other, switching his dominant side. Finn adjusted his stance accordingly and readied himself. Goblin was smiling at him, exhilarated at the chance to compete against his friend. Finn in return, couldn't help but to smile back. "Don't trip, vat-pig!" he called out. Instead of replying, Goblin twisted his body in an arc, ducking left-to-right beneath the spear, and broke through Finn's defense. He pushed Finn's spear to the side, coming close enough to hug. Finn was shocked. Goblin was incredible.

He backpedaled furiously, using his weapon to block a downward chop, and again to block a wrist-flick that caused Goblin's falcata to leap and bite in quick strokes. Finn could hear Leeya's training in his head and feel the old stings of his sparring matches. He crouched to one knee and rolled his spear, distracting Goblin's eyes. Then, popping the weapon up, he smacked Goblin under the chin. The blow was solid and had a lot more force than Finn intended, yet Goblin hardly seemed to notice it. Finn rolled away before he was struck across the face and jumped up, spinning his spear above his head in a wide loop and bringing it down. Goblin dodged away and suddenly Finn was falling to the ground, tangled in twisting confusing lines. Salt's net! His instincts screamed for him to move and Finn rolled away, tangling himself even more. A curved wooden blade cut across where he'd been. It was Salt himself, giggling like a young boy. Instead of continuing his attack on Finn, Salt leapt toward Goblin and they began a series of complicated moves too hard for the eye to follow. It was clear they knew one another's attacks.

Finn spat out mud, which covered every centemeter of his body, and struggled like a suffocating fish, desperately trying to free himself. By accident, he'd gotten both of his feet stuck through holes in the net. The tough string had twisted around his legs and over his face, cocooning him in a strange shape. He stopped, calmed his breath, and analyzed the knots in the net. Immediately he was able to detect how he'd been twisted up. With a few select yanks, he pulled himself free. He grabbed his fallen spear and shook the net in his spare hand.

Salt and Goblin were faced away from him, fighting around the edges of the pit, pushing forward and backing up. The crack of their swords rang out over the cheer of the crowds above. People were yelling at them, but in the heat of the moment, the words sounded like the cry of birds. Heavy sweat dripped from both sword-fighters. The heavy wooden weapons were getting to them. Finn on the other hand, felt as if he'd barely finished his morning stretches. He sent out a prayer of thanks in Leeya's direction for having tortured him with Old Heavy for so long.

Bounding forward, Finn came up behind them and tossed the net out. It spread open over the air and landed on the two, tangling Goblin's sword and Salt's head. Unable to stop their movements, the two drew close and were wrapped together. Finn readied his spear and jabbed, letting out a laugh of triumph. Salt though, wrapping his arms around Goblin, used the boy as a shield. Finn's spear hit Goblin's chest and the end shattered, numbing Finn's hands. Goblin, too busy punching Salt in the face, didn't even notice. Salt took the blows like a maniac, guffawing and sticking his fingers in Goblin's ears—who cringed and yowled. The fight was ridiculous and Finn didn't know whether to laugh or feel endangered.

Goblin was the first to break free. He came out of the net and kicked Salt away, worsening the knots that trapped the Coalition leader. The gypsy boy spun to swing a fist at Finn, but Finn pulled out his sword and jabbed it like a sting, aiming for Goblin's face. Everything he'd hit Goblin with had proved to not affect the boy in the slightest, but perhaps if Finn poked his eye… Goblin smacked the sword to the side so hard, it exploded into fragments. Finn stepped back, waving his arms. His mouth hung open. How had Goblin become so… strong?

His friend darted forward and soon they were launching fists and kicking out. Trained by Leeya on hand-to-hand, Finn fought with confident aggression, sliding around Goblin's basic moves and pounding him on the mouth. It was like punching a stone. Goblin advanced, and so Finn did the most desperate thing he could think of: he tried to copy Leeya's move when she'd fought Antina. When Goblin ducked a punch, Finn jumped up, putting one foot on Goblin's bent knee. Grabbing his friend's head and running up him, Finn spun and landed on Goblin's shoulders. He froze, shocked that he'd been successful, and let out a giggle. He put his fingers in his mouth, sucked on them, and stuck them in Goblin's ears.

Goblin yelped and threw himself backward. Finn tipped off, hitting the ground and losing his breath. Salt was suddenly there, bear-hugging Goblin from behind. Using the net, Salt tied the gypsy boy's arms back to his feet, leaving him immobile. Throughout it all, Salt yelled at them both.

"Sniveling, thin-armed babies! Wet-behind-the-ears, snot-swallowing, dense-skulled trolls! Yer rears are larger than yer heads! Yer not fighting, yer flirting! Weak plucked-chickens, crow-footed, soft-kneed, putrid-smelling…"

He continued, advancing on Finn, who didn't even have the chance to stand back up before Salt was dragging him by the feet toward Goblin and tying him as well. Laying back-to-back in the mud and incapable of moving, Finn felt Goblin shaking in fits of merriment. Finn knew he had lost, yet he joined in, a stupid grin on his face. Salt stepped back from his handiwork and wiped his muddied hands on Finn's shirt. He gave a nod and huffed, sticking his chin out. He winked at Finn and looked to the top of the pit where Star-Children were in danger of falling in from laughing too hard. Petreamus wiped at his eyes, face red. He waved a hand. "Salt wins!" Even Finn cheered.

The Coalition leader pulled out a small knife—this one with an actual blade—and cut them free. The three shook hands and Finn held on to them, refusing to let go. He narrowed his eyes. "You're telling me what's going on right now. I'm sick of waiting."

Salt looked to Goblin and nodded. Goblin smiled. "The-shard's-changed-me-Finn. It's-as-if-Mal'Bal-has-given-me-a-bracer-power-even-though-I-don't-wield-one."

Finn opened and closed his mouth. Goblin lifted his shirt and showed his chest. A small green nub stuck out from the center of his body. Around it, his skin looked leathery. "It-affects-all-of-me. Hit-me-all-you-like. I-don't-even-feel-it."

"That be true." Salt agreed. "He's one of us, yet not as well. We don't rightly know what to call him."

"But Mal'Bal's power…" Finn blurted. "Didn't we conclude it was to bring life to gems? How could he do this?"

Salt sighed. "We don't think he meant to Finn. It could be some strange phenomenon–a chance mutation—that came from the injury. Maybe it was a mix of many factors. Mal'Bal's power, the life imbued in the shard, Petreamus's healing… who knows. We have little knowledge of the bracers. Perhaps Goblin is an organic golem."

Finn opened and closed his mouth, finding it difficult to process his friend's change. He pointed to the scar on Goblin's wrist. "Talking about bracers, what happened?"

Salt snorted. "Well we figured if Goblin was going to stick around and be part of the Coalition, why not finish the deal and make him a Star-Child? It didn't work. Like those who've tried wearing more than one bracer, Goblin was unable to keep one on."

"But he doesn't have a bracer!" Finn argued.

"I know!" Salt spoke. "There's something far larger than we can understand happening to all of us Finn! Powers that make no sense are sweeping this land!"

Finn bit his lip, his mind racing. Goblin patted his shoulder. "It's-okay. I-like-being-tough-you-know. Not-like-I-was-happy-being-a-scrawny-nobody. Sorry-we-didn't-tell-you-right-away. We-had-to-test-out-what-I-could-do: see-if-I-was-going-to-turn-into-some-monster-or-stay-the-same."

"We can use this to our advantage." Salt spoke. "Goblin has no bracer, yet he has a power. Perhaps he will be a better emissary to the king than a Star-Child."

Finn had to admit what Salt was saying made sense. A voice called out to them from above, urgent and serious. "Salt! Pressing news from one of your runners!"

Salt frowned and ran to one of the ropes hanging down. Finn and Goblin followed, climbing out after the leader. Petreamus greeted them at the edge of the pit, surrounded by the entire Coalition. A young man stood beside the healer, breathing heavily. He was a messenger—Finn had seen Salt use them to learn of the happenings around Lenova, bringing back information of rogue Star-Children and sending letters to the king.

"Sir," the boy began. "Mal'Bal's forces are moving out of Kazma. They head North, already destroying the nearby villages, killing whomever won't join."

The Coalition murmured to themselves. Finn stiffened.

"That's not all." the boy said between lungsful of air. "Wild Star-Children are joining him. I've spotted them sir. They wander Mal'Bal's troops with bracers on their wrists!"

Salt was no longer playful, but as serious as one could get. There was silence in the camp as the Coalition awaited his words with bated breath. The sailor rubbed the back of his neck with one hand and his eyes flickered for a moment: showing sadness—perhaps a fatherly worry.

"Gather yer belongings. Gather yer weapons. We must end this before Lenova lays in ruins. We march now. We march for war."

march for lenova

38

—Circa 5,603 E.E. (Economic Era-The 17ᵗʰ Era): A competition of insults is held in the Raven's-Corpse Pub, hidden in the grimy downtown of the Opal Dominion. Men—and even a few women—step forward to face competitors. The objective is to display the most colorful, creative, and vulgar of insults. The crowd is made judge and the winner is promised free ale for the rest of their lives. After hours of competition, the insults grow more and more fierce and all believe Trogg the Itcher will take the prize. Confident, and having beat dozens before him, Trogg boasts to the crowd of his success. One man steps forward, nameless and carrying a swanky attitude that leaves the women fawning over him. He approaches Trogg and after clearing his throat, begins to insult him. Only exaggerated rumor is left to tell of what happens next. Some say the insults were so fierce that Trogg fell backward with an instant nose-bleed, eyes rolling to the back of

his head and teeth chattering. Some say the insults were so quick and vile that many in the crowd became permanently deaf while others went stark-mad. The only facts that can be confirmed is that mere minutes later the entire pub was on fire, an escaped horde of goats was running amuck down the alley streets, and a giant wheel of cheese was wedged over the doors of a nearby cathedral, twelve meters up. Trogg did not win the competition. —

After four days on the road, the Coalition was finally marching in rhythm, feet treading with the *thump, thump, thump* of synchronicity. Eyes forward as he'd trained, Finn focused on Salt, who moved ahead at the front of the battalion, riding on a gray stallion. The twins Justice and Punishment rode as well, using the horses Altin had bought in EldenBurrow. Occasionally, they would canter up and down the sides of the Coalition, checking for stragglers. To Finn's side, Leeya and Goblin marched as well, both with looks of vengeance and determination. Goblin offered him a waterskin and Finn took only one small sip.

Most in the Coalition wore no armor, planning to activate their bracers before the battle. The only ones who did wear armor were Finn—and surprisingly—Salt. Goblin had chosen to go bare-chested, hoping Mal'Bal would see his failed attempt. He assured Finn and Leeya any brute attack would bounce off him as easily as an apple hitting a tree. He told them weapons cut him, but the wounds would be shallow and none would go deep enough to hit a vital spot. In Finn's opinion, his friend's open confidence made him look far older and far more menacing than half the Coalition—in fact, many members glanced to Goblin with reverence and small smiles, as if more relaxed that the boy was on their side and not against them. Indeed, Finn's friend had grown up, yet was still the same—Finn was glad for that. A few pats to the shoulder even came his direction as Star-Children congratulated Finn on his fight. One told him she was eager to see his bracer come to life and Finn agreed, wishing the damned object would work.

One by one, Star-Children were asked to come forward and talk to Salt. They would walk beside the leader and listen as the man explained a variety of tactics for them to use when the battle started. Unlike traditional war strategies, the Coalition was to try a far more personal spread-out approach. With each Star-Child unique and powerful, Salt wanted them to apply their abilities in specific ways that would greatly improve their chances. Finn could tell the Coalition leader was new to the position of general, but Salt tackled the job with eagerness and energy.

The Coalition halted at Salt's command and the sailor jumped off his horse. The Star-Children took advantage and fell to their rears, resting. Petreamus, serving as Salt's right-hand-man, walked to Salt with a map in hand. The two sat on a rock and discussed their position in relation to Mal'Bal's march.

"We're here sir. Our last informant told us the cult heads this way."

"They're still ahead of us, but we're angling in from the East. Can we catch up Petreamus?"

"Yes. His forces are much larger than our own. I'm sure Mal'Bal knows we'll reach him soon."

"Then he'll have a strategy to counter us. What are his numbers?"

"Counting himself, nine Star-Children, over eight-thousand cult members, nearly a thousand robbers, bandits, and killers, seven-thousand newly-inducted into the cult, two-hundred golems, and almost twelve-thousand slaves. That's a force near thirty-thousand strong."

Those in the Coalition that heard the words staggered in place. The numbers.... the Coalition only had one-hundred! Salt sucked in his breath.

"There are reports that many are weak from malnutrition. It's hard to feed an army of such size, and it seems Mal'Bal doesn't care if

they drop dead in their march or not: he'll merely enslave and recruit more. If we consider that many of the slaves won't fight, we can perhaps expect eighteen-thousand or less."

"Sir, for us to win a fight of that magnitude, each member of the Coalition will have to kill nearly two-hundred a piece."

"We're Star-Children Petreamus. We can do the impossible. Remember what we fight for."

"Sir...this might be suicide."

Finn couldn't process the emotions running through him as he overheard the words. Sweat ran under his armor, yet he wasn't as exhausted as when he'd first worn Old Heavy. Was he going to die soon? He had no power, only adequate fighting skill.

"We need the king's support!" one of the Star-Children spoke out.

"It's pointless." someone else groaned out in chant.

"We fight for nothing!"

A fear took hold of Finn—but not for himself, no he'd accepted his own death since a young boy, each day stepping foot into the mines. The fear came from not having seen all of Lenova, from not having spent enough time with his friends. He looked about: Goblin was busy in conversation with Cion but Leeya was alone, yards away staring at the horizon. He hurried to her, standing by her side.

"Leeya..." he began.

"Don't." she spoke, her words hard and sharp. Finn was thrown back by her anger.

"I was just—"

"No Finn. Don't say it." she snapped again. She didn't look to him but kept her gaze elsewhere. "You won't die."

Finn was silent. Leeya had guessed his words. There was no emotion in her face, yet there was passion behind each quivering sentence.

"But if I do..." Finn started. "I—"

Again, she cut him off. "I'll never forgive you." Her back was rigid and her breathing shallow. Sunlight glinted off her hair and Finn could smell the cinnamon and spice. His stomach rolled. Where was she at that moment? Was she far-away? Or was she so close he could touch her? Embrace her? Finn's armor was both cold and hot, his bracer ticklish.

"Alright." he said with a slow nod. "I won't."

He turned to leave. "Stay." she called out. Immediately he was at her side again, so close they nearly brushed shoulders. They didn't speak after that, but instead enjoyed the break, not knowing if it was to be their last moment alone together.

The march continued and the Star-Children pushed with heavy hearts, but confident steps. They knew the end might come, but by the love of Lenova Salt had instilled into them, they moved without hesitation. Finn made a promise to himself—that he would at least reach Mal'Bal and wound him.

They were five days into their North-Western march, curving left to draw closer to the cult. By Petreamus's estimations, they were only a day behind, hounding at Mal'Bal's heels. Surely the Lich-Lord knew of the Coalition. They'd seen many horses take off from hilltops in the distance, hooded figures bent low over the animals. The cult had been watching their progression as closely as one could. At one point, Antina and Altin drew out both bow and crossbow, shooting arrows across the wide grassy expanse. Antina struck one of the spies in the spine, killing him. Salt examined the body and found a parchment with a rough drawing of their location and notes on some of their potential powers. Grimly, they moved on, now with weapons drawn in case of a trap.

The ground lowered in elevation, making marching easier. The grass grew taller, tickling their shins, and soon they were squelching in mud. After a while, they were wading through clear water up to their knees, green stalks rising to their waists. They were in a rice field as far as the eye could see. Finn took off the lower part of his armor, freeing his legs and giving himself more maneuverability. His travel pack took on more weight as he put the pieces away. Salt did the same from his horse. In the distance, they could make out a dark line straight across from them. Mal'Bal's forces, waiting. Yet the Coalition hesitated, because the line was a lot smaller than it should have been.

"I don't like this." Salt muttered, and Finn, a few paces behind, was one of the few to hear. Had Mal'Bal readied a trap for them?

"Drop your packs!" Salt ordered. "Weapons at the ready!" The Coalition obeyed.

Having no other choice, they continued to move, the water neither rising nor lowering. Closer and closer they drew, until individual sizes could be made out. There were three lines, stacked one behind another. Finn squinted his eyes. The first line looked human, bent and waiting. The second as well. And in the far back were golems. Many of them. One in particular seemed strange: jagged and awkward, like a massive porcupine on two legs. The golems rose above the water, each nearing the height of three men. But where were the tens of thousands?

When the Coalition was a hundred yards away, they stopped. Silence reigned out save for the chirping and buzzing of bugs. The sky was clear and bright, sunlight glinting off the water and reflecting into their eyes. The temperature was warm and delicious, yet the beautiful day only added a sense of morbidity to the moment.

Up close, they could now make out their enemy in greater detail. The front line was comprised of slaves, chained by the neck. Their metal cords ran back, tied to thick black collars worn by the golems themselves: a human wall of protection. Many in the Coalition swore and spat into the water around them, disgusted and horrified. By being tied, the slaves would be forced into battle whether they liked it or not. The men and women couldn't run away, nor turn and fight the cult. They'd been assigned their fate. Behind them, a large mass of cult members, slavers, murderers, and thieves awaited. In the center were the eight Star-Children Salt's spies had reported. But where was Mal'Bal? Where was the large army they'd been told of? The land was flat for at least twenty kilometers in every direction. There were no traps that they could see. Salt was swearing, enraged.

"Damn the rotten demon! He's left a portion of his army behind to stop us while he moves on! He doesn't fight us himself!"

Salt's horse whinnied and trotted a few paces forward. "COWARDS!" Salt bellowed. "WHERE'S YER GREAT MASTER? DOES HE RUN AWAY WITH HIS TAIL BETWEEN HIS LEGS?"

One of the Star-Children broke ranks and walked forward. He was portly and wore fine clothing. His black hair was slicked tight, as if pinned to the back of his head. The Star-Child spread out his arms, laughing. He carried himself like a nobleman. A golem stepped forward as well, its legs arching over the army and bringing itself to the front. It was the golem that from a distance had resembled a porcupine. Up close, Finn could see it for what it was and his stomach dropped. Mal'Bal had brought to life a new monstrosity, this one more terrifying than all others. With a green gem heart, the golem was wrapped by thick layers of metal wire—all of it tightly holding thousands of weapons. Swords, lances, scimitars, axes, and all sorts of sharp blades stuck out in every direction, twisted and knotted by wire. It had no slaves tied to it and moved like it was in charge. With a large rectangular shield for a face, it stood twice the height of other golems. The Star-Child that'd come forward didn't look pleased or comfortable standing by it. The man took one step sideways, sighed, and looked to them.

RAFAEL HOHMANN

"I am Portious VoidGrasper. I speak for the Lich-Lord, new God of Lenova. Mal'Bal sends you a message: Let's not fight. Instead, join us. Join us and keep your lives."

the redwater skirmish

39

—Hush now young child, and you shall be marked, with a prick to the finger, black ink your hand pockmarked. The sign of the snake you shall be, to strike for House Glover, bring fear for me. Young boys born for the Family shall be taught all to kill, how to remain silent, how to remain still. Forget dreams of peace and forget mother's embrace, sun-stroked days of dainty memory erase. You are now... Family. —
-Words too dangerous to disclose origin

There was silence among the Coalition. Finn and the Star-Children looked to each other with shocked expressions. Their feet moved in place, sinking in the marsh. A gentle breeze hit their faces.

"Think about it!" Portious called out, shrugging his shoulders. "No one here has to die. Not one drop of blood needs be spilled! Mal'Bal treats his Star-Children with the greatest of luxuries! The best food, wine, and spoils always goes to us! He's promised us lordship and dominion over the many cities we conquer and will grant us whatever we want! Come forth and live!"

The Coalition murmured to each other and many looked to Salt. The sailor spat, his face masked by rage. Before he could shout anything, there was movement from nearby. Two Star-Children broke ranks and ran past Salt, running through the rice stalks. It was Scarecrow and Mole-Face.

"Wonderful!" Portious giggled. "Wise you are, the two of you! First of many, I hope?"

When they'd reached a safe distance, the two stopped and turned around. "Altin!" one called out. Finn's throat tightened. "Altin, come with us!"

Altin took a few steps forward, stepping near to Salt. The sailor held a deep sense of betrayal. The man had given his all to his Star-Children. He looked heart-broken. Finn could see the Coalition leader's arm slowly moving toward his blade. Altin's face was red and blotched, his long yellow hair pulled back. He was hesitating in place.

"Don't stop, fool! Hurry!" Scarecrow called out. "You'll die if you stay! What have they done for you? Nothing! You know it's a lost cause!"

Altin moved and Salt went for his blade. Finn sprinted. No, even now he couldn't—couldn't let Altin leave them! Altin dropped to his knees, yanking out his crossbow. Salt's blade swiped over Altin's head, missing him. An arrow launched out. It flew true and straight, crossing the expanse and hitting Scarecrow through the neck. Everyone stopped, frozen. Altin stood, then hovered above the water, bracer activated, putting another bolt to his weapon. Mole-Face was already running away, the water he churned red from his friend's corpse. The second bolt whined out, missing the traitorous target.

"No!" Altin shouted, now lowering back down as Mole-Face ran into the cult's ranks. "It's not a lost cause! It—it can't be!"

Finn was stunned. He'd been sure Altin was leaving them… giving up… Even Salt was bug-eyed. The Coalition leader, for the first time, was at a loss for words. Finn kept moving forward, sloshing through the water in a daze. He reached Altin's side. Altin scowled at him and turned away. "If you think that means anything—it doesn't."

But Altin was wrong and they both knew it. It did mean something. Finn smiled, not even caring that within the hour he might be dead. "You're the biggest idiot I've ever met Altin." Altin spun, anger in his face.

"Fools!" Mole-Face shouted, his body hidden behind the slaves.

Salt breathed in and cleared his throat. "Leave those of ye that are wise, stay those of ye that are fools! For if I won't budge, a fool I be!" The coalition leader trotted back and forth on his horse in front of them, a blush to his face and a wild look to his eyes. He stared at Finn and Finn gave him a nod. The Coalition leader pursed his lips. "For I shall be a fool and a fool I shall be, marching through Lenova, sword in hand, defending those that can't fight! A fool shall I be on the day I die by the weapon of my foe! A fool shall I remain, from now until the end of all time, having challenged unstoppable enemies, unbreakable armies, even fate itself! And when Mal'Bal is at his highest…" He stopped dead center in front of his Coalition, his curved sword upraised. Finn's heart hammered like a caged animal, fire ran through his veins, ice through his marrow. It was time to save Lenova.

"When Mal'Bal is at his highest… he will be defeated by the greatest fools of all."

Shivers ran through the crowd and arm-hairs stood on end. Weapons were gripped tight. Portious was running back into his army, shouting commands. Salt nodded in approval, turned, and readied his horse. "Now, come ye fools: let our swords drink. They're thirsty."

Finn joined the Coalition in a roar so fierce, it pierced the soul. All around the rice-field bracers activated, lights shinning out in magical splendor—every color of the rainbow. *Stars in the day.*

Metal suits embraced their hosts, wrapping around limbs, conforming to strange designs, showing-off their potential. Alien powers came forth, ready for battle. A man's eyes glowed purple and he hovered, behind him, a strange symbol etched in the air materialized floating swords. Another man grew spines on every joint and a woman's skin became translucent, showing strange blue lights flickering and floating where her internals once were. A younger woman turned into some form of fanged four-legged creature with bat wings and multiple tails. The powers went on and on, each as unique as the other.

They charged as a whole, uniform and electrified by the heat of battle. Goblin and Leeya brushed shoulders with Finn, their weapons out and at the ready. Salt and the twins raced out front and Petreamus pulled back, readying a medical station. A Star-Child stayed with him, dipping his head into the water and whistling, fish and frogs floated to the surface, hypnotized and ready for sacrifice.

Portious VoidGrasper drew a large mace and roared. The cult's army moved forward, rushing to meet them. The golems shook the earth with their steps, water misting the air around them. The slaves shrieked in terror, wielding their blades with tremor. One of the Cult's Star-Children, a young man, sang out-loud and the slaves stopped struggling, instead growing quiet and obedient.

> *Go now my pretties,*
> *die for me pretties.*
> *Swing your weapons for me.*
> *Still your fear,*
> *and feel my fever,*

SUNRIDER

my pretties you shall be.

The rice field churned as great masses came for each other. Water rushed into their noses, forced its way down their mouths, and weighed their clothes. Finn was slowed, but his many weeks of conditioning kept him far ahead of most of the Coalition. At the forefront of the cult were the Star-Children, golems, and the poor slaves who were being dragged by the neck.

The first to meet in the middle were all eight evil Star-Children, Mole-Face, Salt, and the twins. Salt smashed his horse into one of the Star-Children and jumped off, twirling twice in mid-air, throwing his net over another, and coming down on a third with his sword. The Star-Child Salt had engaged was already collapsing to the water, blood spewing from his throat. Salt was then onto Portious, who fought with the ferocity of twenty men. The evil Star-Child was incredibly skilled and a seasoned fighter, able to block and counter blows that would leave others dead.

Finn was taken back: Salt had been playing with them in the pit. The way he fought, his technique—it was the polar opposite of how he'd engaged Finn. Here he was a wrathful titan. A storm of spinning metal and jabbing edges. Leeya had been right: there were warriors in Lenova beyond compare. The twins were no second-hand fighters either. One bent down and head-butted a Star-Child in the chest while his brother ran up the other's back, spun upside-down and beheaded an unprepared man. With Salt, the three pushed back the remaining seven Star-Children.

An explosive shout cracked the air and Salt was thrown twenty meters away by the sound, bouncing and skipping over the water, his limbs flapping like loose rags. Another, whose suit let out a beam of light from a glass facemask over a metal helmet blinded the twins. They staggered back, covering their faces with their arms, eyes squeezed shut in pain. A third had his suit open a cavity in his stomach, where dozens of poisonous-looking snakes poured out into the water, swimming for the twins. Some were large and thick, black and viscous, others were thin and short, a dull brown. The seven Star-Children surrounded the overwhelmed brothers and readied their weapons. But then Leeya and Altin were there, swooping in with skill and grace. Leeya tackled one, opening room for the twins to navigate and fight. Altin shot bolt after bolt at the snakes, killing as many as he could. Mole-Face jumped forward, his cheeks blotched as he opened his bag and whistled. Finn didn't see what came out of the belt-tied sack and Altin cried out as red lines slashed his skin. He ducked, wove, and dodged—but it was pointless—his blood rained over the water.

Before Finn and Goblin could join in, the ground shook, throwing them down. Looming over them, the weapon-covered golem let out the ear-splitting sound of metal grating on metal. It was the battle-cry of an abomination. Behind it, a stone golem drew close as well. "I have this one!" Goblin roared, throwing himself without regard at the monstrous metal behemoth. The weapon golem twisted in a circle, flailing at the smaller target that danced around it. Goblin drew it back and away, leading it into the depths of the battlefield. They were swallowed by the chaos as in the background a large green explosion blew upward, sending water and bodies in every direction. Finn was left to fight the stone golem in one-on-one battle.

The creature brought down both fists, each wider than a man. Finn tightened his leg muscles and dove forward, knowing his only hope to not get crushed was to be *within* the golem's grasp. But near its legs were the many slaves tied by metal chains. Eerily silent—controlled by one of the Star-Children—they swung their weapons at him. Finn did everything he could to block and dodge, shouting for them to stop. Using his spear, he kept them at bay. A dagger scraped his chest-plate and a sword glanced off his arm. Both stung and the later made him gasp. He spun to block the attackers behind him. The golem stomped, lifting half the slaves as it brought its body back, then down. Finn dove away, hearing the snap of necks. A chained man was crushed by the stone foot, yet the others stayed silent.

Pulling out his sword, Finn ducked a club's blow and swung, catching a chain between golem and blade. The metal snapped with a ring and one of the slaves dropped free. The restraint hissed like a dying animal. The slave gasped and shook his head, his persona changing as he fell into the water. Breaking the chain freed the slave from the Star-Child's command. Finn shouted the revelation at the top of his lungs and many in the Coalition cheered in acknowledgement, meeting the other golems and their trapped slaves.

Finn spun and danced, picturing Leeya beside him, guiding his moves. A stone hand came down and he ducked at the last second. While low, his chin to the water, he swung his sword out again, catching another chain against the arm as it passed by. A second slave was freed.

"Go!" he shouted to them. "Run while you can!"

But the two freed slaves gripped their weapons and rushed to Finn's side, defending him.

"For Kazma!" one shouted.

"For Vestés!" spoke the other.

Finn was overwhelmed by their bravery. In turn, he fought with greater ferocity, freeing a third slave. As the golem reared back and a broken chain slashed out, Finn grabbed it and was suddenly lifted out of the water. He lost his sword but held onto his spear, flying high into the air with a shout, fear and adrenaline rushing through his veins. At the peak of his accession, he came down on the creature's featureless boulder face. He landed there for a brief moment before it shook wildly, throwing him off. Still holding to the chain, he swung sideways in a loop around the creature, wrapping around its body. After a full swing, he arched toward its gem heart.

"Lenova!" he roared, bringing his spear forward.

The aim was true and his weapon smashed into the gem, splitting in two. The spear snapped as the golem exploded, showering the landscape with rubble. Its head flew out, spinning with a resounding groan. The oblong projectile sped through the air as if trying to escape its destroyed body and struck a wooden golem in the chest. It tipped with a crash, both its oak arms broken into splinters. Finn fell belly-first into the water, splashing straight to the bottom. He was miraculously unharmed and shot up, spluttering. The remaining living slaves blinked in confusion, brandished their weapons, and gave out weak cries of joy. Stuck in place—their chains caught beneath the golem's rubble—they banded together, back-to-back.

Finn found his sword sticking straight out of the water and pulled it up in time to block a scythe from a charging cult member. Without hesitation, he spun into the man and lacerated him across the belly. A second stroke finished the job. Adrenaline coursed through Finn and his lungs heaved, bringing in the smell of blood and marsh plants.

"SunRider!" someone shouted out.

Finn spared a glance, watching Goblin climb the chest of the weapon golem and tear free a broadsword. Cuts covered every centemeter of his body, yet he moved as if he was climbing a soft tree. The creature threw itself forward, belly-flopping and rolling away, killing men and women from both sides.

"Goblin!" Finn shrieked, running to the moving golem.

A sound rang out so loud, Finn thought his head would explode. He was moving at incredible speed: rolling, bouncing, and bowling through people. The noise propelled him forward across the field of battle and his neck nearly snapped against a shield. Smashing against it, he came to a stop, coughing out blood and water. He lay there stunned, half-submerged. Forms moved about him as blurs, coming together and apart like dancing shadows. Water heaved to his chest and was sucked away. Lightning rang out and twenty cult members dropped dead. A bandit flew through the air like a ragdoll, disappearing from sight over the edge of the battle, his broken body bent in half. Another bandit hacked the arm off a dead Star-Child and sliced the bracer free. He put it on and dropped to the ground, receiving the visions all Star-Children get when first donning the devices. Before he could recuperate, he was already dead, one of the other thieves holding him under and drowning him. *That* thief didn't even have the chance to cut the bracer off his companion before he too was killed—this time by a member of the Coalition.

Finn stood, wobbling in place. He picked up the shield—heavy enough to stagger him— and turned, looking for a weapon. Another golem exploded and a rock hit the shield, throwing Finn once more. His thigh burned and water found its way down his nose. Heaving and spluttering, he pushed himself up on one leg, reaching down and retrieving a scythe—the weapon that'd torn his flesh. He hobbled forward and ducked as an arrow hissed above him. Nearby, a large group of freed slaves turned on their captors.

Finn shook his head to clear it. Ahead, one of the evil Star-Children was running in his direction, not seeing him. The man was in a blind panic and his fancy clothes billowed about him, tangling his limbs. He opened his mouth and a visible beam of sound ruptured out, launching men and women to the side. The man turned too late to see Finn in front of him. Finn didn't waste the opportunity but hacked out. The scythe rolled across the man's jugular and no more sound ever escaped his lips again.

Finn continued to stagger forward, looking for Leeya and Goblin. Where were they? Were they alright? Around his body the water was warm and a deep maroon. What seemed like hundreds of lifeless bodies floated belly-down across the field, pushing at the reeds. The battle was dying down. Nearly a score of golems and but a few handfuls of cult members remained—it seemed as if the Coalition was gaining the upper hand.

Ahead, Finn spotted the central battle: Altin was fist-fighting Mole-Face; the two throwing furious uncontrolled punches. Mole-Face's bag had been slashed and sand poured out. *So that'd been his invisible weapon.* The twins fought four evil Star-Children at once, barely holding their own in the onslaught of combined powers. A bruised Salt and a tired Leeya were working together to push Portious back. The man blocked a blow from Leeya with his mace and launched a hand out toward Salt. The Coalition leader grasped at his throat, clawing for air that was no longer there. Leeya rushed forward and Portious broke her spear with a swing of his heavy weapon.

"Stop!" Finn shrieked to the Star-Children. "Stop or you shall all die!"

Portious hesitated, looking to Finn. His eyes were wide and skin taunt. He lowered his hand and Salt fell, gasping. Surprised, Finn licked his lips, trying to figure out what to say.

a place of death

40

—Circa 5,616 E.E. (Economic Era-The 17th Era): Piscus of Pittance follows Finn SunRider's instructions and finds Nozgull's vast wealth in the heart of a nameless forest. It takes him nearly a month of morbid work to clean the treasures and cart them to his village by night. Through the help of Miriam, whose honest loyalty to Finn binds her to the secret, both her and Piscus hide all the gems in her family silo, which has sat empty for nigh a century. Nozgull's bracer is hidden within the wax of a massive candle, which Miriam keeps unlit above the headboard of her bed. They await patiently for Finn's instructions on what to do next with the wealth.

—

"Halt!" Portious shouted.

Finn checked to see if his bracer had stopped the battle. Had it activated? No, it was still silent. Portious stepped back, gasping in exhaustion. The cult members, thieves, murderers, and remaining evil Star-Children paused, seeing their leader lower his weapon. The only fights to continue were those with the golems, which raged in the background. The greatest chaos came from the weapon golem, who spun in place, shredding anyone foolish enough to draw near. A man screamed, his limbs missing. Others—dead—stuck to the creature; impaled victims. It stomped its battle-axe feet in an attempt to kill the one individual that dared attack it: Goblin. The boy looked to be covered in more blood than skin, yet rushed forward, tore free a spear from one of the golem's legs, and threw it toward its heart. He did so again and again. The weapons bounced off a wire-mesh cage surrounding the gem and the golem continued its rampage. It rolled forward in a ball and when it stood back up, water, mud, plants, and people exploded skyward. Goblin was smacked sideways, crying out. Members of the Coalition ran forward to aid the gypsy boy in his struggle.

"It's over, Portious." Finn called out, narrowing his eyes at the nobleman. He scrambled for the proper words to say. Half of him wanted to attack the man and the other half wanted to turn and run to Goblin's side. "Your army's falling apart. Call it off and no more lives will be lost from either side."

Finn looked to Salt for guidance. Bruises dotted the man's face and his bottom lip was split open. The sailor had a crooked smile on his face. "It's true." he agreed. "Seems Mal'Bal underestimated our might. End it or we'll obliterate ye."

Portious' eyes moved back and forth between them. Leeya approached from the side with caution, flanking him. He backed away, his weapon pointing to each of them in turn. Sweat dripped from his face and his lavish clothes sloshed in the red water. "Name your terms." he hissed. The other evil Star-Children and Mole-Face drew behind their leader. They also held their weapons out, half of them severely wounded and dazed. The twins joined Salt's side, silent as the day Finn had met them.

"Term one," Salt spoke, "ye assist us in disassembling these golems. They obviously don't listen to yer direct command but to Mal'Bal alone. They must die. Term two: ye will free the slaves. Term three: ye will allow our healer to surgically remove yer bracers. He'll fix whatever injury that might cost. This will ensure ye cannot attack us any longer."

A mixture of emotions ran through Portious. His Half-suit, covering his arms beneath a thick lavender robe just like Antina, seemed to vibrate. His face grew furious, terrified, then relieved, before once more becoming furious. "I'll help you with these golems—I have no love for them anyways—and I'll release the prisoners. But I won't have me, nor the other Ventri subject their bracers to you! Never!"

Salt's face grew stone-like. "This is yer only offer. Don't let yer pride kill ye."

Portious attacked without warning, moving in a blur. He smashed one of the twins to the side with his mace and pointed his free arm to Salt. Salt gasped as air left his lungs. The Coalition leader collapsed to the water, clawing at his face. His chest contracted abnormally, as if imploding. Veins stuck out of his skin and blood-droplets seeped out. Portious was taking all the air from Salt's body. "Never!" the man was shrieking. "The bracer makes me a God! Me! A ruler of men! I bow to no one! Not even Mal'Bal, you hear me?"

The other evil Star-Children—the Ventri— jumped into the fight and the battle resumed.

Finn tackled the lantern-headed Star-Child and pushed him to the water, his weight landing on the man's chest. The man threw out wild punches and Finn ignored the pain, jabbing his fingers beneath the helmet. Water rushed in and the man panicked, gargling on the liquid. Finn was thrown back, but the man was no longer paying attention to him. Instead, he stood and floundered, deactivating his bracer. The helmet came apart as metal plates, contracting and sliding to his wrist. The water fell out, no longer drowning him. Finn rushed the man and landed a solid punch. The Ventri staggered and fell back down.

Punishment, Justice, and Leeya worked to push back the remaining Star-Children. Apart from the twins—who couldn't deactivate their bracers—and Portious, no one was using their powers. They were all too tired to continue with the devices. It became a battle of fists and weapons. Sparks flew as metal clashed on metal. Screams once more rang out loud enough to shake the rice-field as the remaining army of cult members reengaged with the Coalition.

The weapon golem roared past, taking Goblin on a ride as the poor boy hung-on for dear life. A second golem smashed into one of the twins, who hit it with his white blade. The other twin was suddenly there, slashing at the same spot. The golem fell apart, immediately dead.

Finn limped toward Salt, his scythe at the ready to defend the man. Portious noticed him and swung his mace. Instead of blocking it, Finn ducked and counter-attacked. Portious though, incredibly skilled as a fighter, immediately switched tactics. He caught the mace with his other hand, blocked Finn's strike, and pointed his free hand toward him. The mace he then swung at Salt.

Finn felt as if he'd been bowled over by a vat-worm. He could no longer breathe at all. In fact, it was as if his insides were being sucked through his mouth and skin. The pressure sliced through him and tightened every one of his muscles. In a final spasm, he lifted his scythe far enough to avert the mace's blow from smashing into the side of Salt's face. The scythe flew off into the distance and the mace slipped from Portious' hand. Finn's fingers were bent the wrong way and his arm was electrified. His hand was broken.

Portious howled and tackled Finn. Finn fell into the water backward, unable to defend himself. His body was a stiff wood board, clenched in unimaginable pain. With one hand, Portious sucked all the air from him while with the other he punched Finn in the nose, shattering it. Finn couldn't even scream as there was nothing in his body to make noise. Water swamped over him as Portious held him under. The nobleman's eyes bugged out red in desperation and rage. His straight teeth were clenched and spittle flew from his lips.

Then the man was gone and the power no longer assaulted Finn. He floated up, gasping and groaning as tears escaped his eyes. His lungs inflated at agonizing speed. Finn choked on the blood pouring from his nose and rolled over, belly-down. His good hand pushed up and he adjusted into a sitting position. His body was too weak to stand, so he waved about, eyes filming over.

Portious was stumbling back, shrieking at the top of his lungs, blood rushing down his face. A section of his scalp was gone, exposing skull-bone. He tripped and fell into the water, his robes swirling over him. Above them, Altin flew by, a bloody dagger in his hand. Portious clawed back up, gasping. "RETREAT!" he bellowed.

The remaining Ventri turned in place and ran, Portious joining in a zig-zag drunken line. The cult members, thieves, and murderers scattered in every direction, screaming in terror at the turn of events. The only battle that remained was of the golems, who were now being surrounded by groups of Coalition members. Quickly they were one by one demolished, overwhelmed by the Star-Children. Gem hearts cracked. Wood and stone flew like rain.

"Don't let them escape!" Salt gasped out, also sitting in the water, only a few paces away from Finn. The man looked half-unconscious, rice-stalks around his body.

Leeya, along with Altin, Antina, and Cion gave chase after the five Ventri and Mole-Face. Ribbons of blood rose out of the water like living paint and solidified into a path beneath the Ventri's feet. They ran at greater speed, no longer hindered by the sloshing environment. One of the Ventri, a small bald man, had activated his bracer once again, using his ability to make a way for their escape. Antina shot a controlled bolt of lightning through the water but the Ventri, protected above the current, weren't hit. The move brought the warrior woman down and she shook in exhaustion. Cion and Leeya tried to climb up the blood path but the Ventri turned off his power behind him. The blood returned to liquid form, no longer a platform. Only Altin continued, but he too stopped after a while, his shoulders sagging in exhaustion. His suit retracted and he dropped. With visible pain, he got up and trudged to them, his long hair dripping water. The Ventri were soon specks in the distance, running to the North where they knew their master continued his march, with-or-without them.

A cheer rang out behind Finn and he turned in his head, vision losing all color and going misty. Dizziness fought to swallow him as he watched Goblin topple the weapon golem. The gypsy boy was tearing at the creature's chest with the ferocity of a wild animal. He exposed the gem heart and brought down a broadsword, smashing it again and again until with a final crunch, the golem sagged, no longer humanoid in shape, but a large bundle of wire-wrapped weapons—inanimate and dead. The battle was over. The Coalition had won.

Finn tried to stand but fell back into the water, landing in Salt's lap. The sailor smiled at him, the veins on his body still pronounced and sticking out. Finn was sure he looked the same.

"We did it." Finn mumbled, his vision fading. Salt's eyelids were fluttering as well, consciousness leaving the man. The leader of the Coalition was staring off into the depths of the horizon, perhaps thinking of the sea, wishing for his old life, yet stuck with a destiny he did not want. Finn realized that like he had once been, Salt was now: a slave to a fate he did not want.

"The war has just started, Finn-for-Finn's-sake." Salt croaked.

"We have a way to go before we get to Mal'Bal."

RAFAEL HOHMANN

a quest given

41

—Circa 5,600 E.E. (Economic Era-The 17th Era): Finn SunRider, StreamCrosser and holder of many other worthy titles, is born in unknown circumstances and to unknown parents. —

Although having won, the aftermath of the battle was terrible. Many floated belly-down, dead in the water, marking the terrain red. The still bodies of lifeless Coalition members and slaves were separated from those of the cult. Tears were shed for friends lost and vows of revenge were shouted. The numbers were counted while Petreamus did everything he could to heal the Coalition survivors. Soon, apart from the three horses, no animals could be found alive in a five-kilometer radius. Nineteen of the Coalition had been killed.

Many chased after the escaping cult members. For the ones caught, there was no mercy. Of the cult army, only the few Ventri lived. There were over two-thousand dead in all.

Once healed, instead of continuing their pursuit of Mal'Bal, Salt declared they were to travel West to the city of Nthum, where dry land, food, and warm beds could bring them rest. It was also a means to escort the remaining former slaves to safety. They left behind a large mass-grave made of golem stones where they buried their brothers-at-arms. The bodies of the enemy were left out to rot, too numerous to deal with. The sky turned black with vulture-snakes and crows as they cawed and fought among themselves for flesh. In turn, Petreamus had more animals he could use for healing. The land had turned into a place of death.

Although only taking two days, the journey was difficult for the battle-weary men and women. Salt took the horses and gave them to the slaves. Finn and Altin didn't mind. The Coalition was commanded to keep their pace slow: the slaves weren't as strong as the Star-Children and wouldn't be able to keep up otherwise. Salt was quiet for most of the march but at one point he sang out, his voice a sweet tenor. It brought fire to their steps and got them the rest of the way to dry land.

By my deathbed there stands Death with the rags of a travelin' man,
he speaks softly "Don't ye cry, life's doors close, but do not slam.
"Go calmly to yer voyage beyond Lenova's blue-tinged edge
"There laughter hugs yer bosom, warmth eternal, that I pledge."
Death's comfort was a songbird who landed on my sill,
it flew into the sunlight to the next life with a thrill.
Death tapped my hand in waiting, saying "I am busy, we

must go.

"I cannot accept denial; I cannot accept yer no.

"Tell the ones ye leave behind to not cry nor shed a tear,

"For ye go to golden meadows, unmolested by pain or fear.

"Say goodbye to mother, father, say goodbye to yer old friend.

"For 'tis not 'til forever, one day we'll all ascend."

Near Finn, Cion sobbed. In his hand he held the bracer of someone he'd known—one who'd been with him for a long time. "T'was beautiful, it was—that song." Finn agreed, tears in his own eyes, thinking of all those who'd died in the Crust and in Kazma. His hands clenched and unclenched in sadness until Leeya wrapped her fingers through his, her face as emotionless as ever. To the side, Altin stepped away, sullen and with eyes downtrodden.

They arrived in Nthum and separated ways with the former captives. The city was a hub of medicine and orchards, a welcome for the broken slaves. Mal'Bal had missed Nthum only by a few kilometers. The city was well-hidden within their own groves, the entire outer edge surrounded by a variety of trees and thorn-bushes. Only those who knew their way or were guided could navigate inside. The former slaves ran out into the streets, shouting praise and sharing stories of the brave Coalition. After that, the populace of Nthum welcomed them with open arms.

On his first day, Finn rented out a room for himself, Goblin, and Leeya. He offered for Altin to join them, but the boy denied, having found a separate place to rest. Finn took those few days to spend with his friends, reminiscing on the past and wondering over the future. They spoke of everything: the wonders of Lenova, their dreams, what Finn's power might be, but not of Mal'Bal. They didn't allow themselves to talk of dark subjects.

They'd all survived incredible odds, beaten terrible enemies, and seen horrible events—yet each time Goblin prepared a home-cooked meal, Leeya taught them a new sword move, or Finn attempted a joke to see if Leeya would laugh, they grew a thicker skin, mentally preparing themselves for whatever else would come. Finn knew as long as he had his friends around him, he'd be able to do anything.

When nights came, he would fiddle with his SolarStone wristband, mind wandering back to Tuliah's prophecy and her nectar. The words rang through his head in concentric circles, confusing him. The prophecy sounded as if it should be simplistic yet was far from it. If there was one thing Finn knew, it was one day—maybe far in the future or possibly soon—he'd face Mal'Bal again, regardless if the prophecy held even a grain of truth to it. The prophecy told him Lenova would be threatened with destruction, and that had certainly been correct.

When Salt knocked on their door, Finn had a feeling he was about to be given an opportunity to continue his dream. Goblin answered and both Salt and Altin stepped inside. Together, they dragged a closed chest into the middle of the room. Finn startled. Salt's bracer was no longer on his wrist but activated. It'd formed into a simple metal cover over his right index finger, sticking out over the tip like a long thin stick. It closely resembled a quill.

"Sit, my friends." Salt asked. Finn, Goblin, Leeya, and Altin obeyed. Salt drew a key from a chain around his neck and unlocked the trunk. Inside were many thin brown books. Salt clicked his tongue and pulled them out, carefully stacking them in piles. "Hmm, seems I'll have to buy more journals in case we recruit more for the cause." He spoke as if talking to himself. "Granted I have no idea if I'll be able to write more names."

Each journal contained an inked name on the cover, all written in the same jittery, looping scrawl. *Antina, Petreamus, Justice...* It went on. At the bottom of the chest, beneath all the brown thin volumes were five thicker red tomes. On them Finn spotted five names: Salt, Goblin, Leeya, Altin, and Finn. The two thickest belonged to Finn and Altin.

Finn was perplexed. What was he seeing? Apart from Goblin, his friends looked at a loss for words. Finn remembered Goblin had been told what Salt's power was.

"As an old sea-dog, I have two treasure chests." Salt began. "One of bracers, and one of books. Neither contain normal items: they are not regular bracers; these are not yer regular reading material." The Coalition leader yawned. The man had hardly slept since arriving in Nthum, but instead had kept busy sending out spies to watch Mal'Bal's progression.

"I bought all these books on impulse after activating my bracer for the first time. What a strange activation that was. While others go on a mad fighting spree, trying to kill those around them, I went on a mad shopping spree. Does that reflect my personality? Damn, I hope not." He chuckled. "No idea what I was doing—the bracer had control. I sat in the dark of a tavern and grabbed each book one by one, writing names with this here quill-finger." He wiggled his suited finger; the strangest thing Finn had ever seen in his life.

"All the names I wrote were unknowns to me except my own. Strangely enough, five of the books I bought were red. No idea why. Still don't know. Perhaps the people whose names are written on them have some higher calling to attend to—I'm not sure." He tapped the quilled finger on one of the books. "We still know nothing of these bracers or their twitchy-tempered, furiously-frustrating mystery.

"I spent all night writing names and in some of the books, I wrote on the pages as well. The words made no sense to me at the time but are now growing clear in my head. Ye wondered why I was so trusting of ye Finn; when yer group first came to Jakitta I knew ye were to be a great man. My bracer had foretold it."

Finn's mouth dropped as Salt spoke, his mind trying to understand the man's power.

"Don't mistake what I can do." Salt warned. "I can't see the future. The journals are a means of communication with the select people whose names have been written. Watch."

He grabbed Leeya's red book, opened it to a random page and put his quill-finger to the surface. On it, he wrote in red ink *Salt is the most handsome man in Lenova*. Leeya startled and stared at her bracer. On it, a faint carving of the words appeared, then faded. In Leeya's book, the words disappeared as well, the ink no more. "My bracer grew warm." Leeya told them.

Salt nodded. "I've only used the technique with Petreamus and the twins. No one else knows. It's limited—I can only communicate with Star-Children whose names have been written."

"What about Goblin? You have a book with his name." Finn asked.

Salt winked. "Yer a spry one ye are. I wondered if Goblin counted as a Star-Child. Had to test it, me being a scholar and all. 'Tis why the boy knows of my ability." The sailor grabbed Goblin's red book and wrote in it. *Salt's a charming fellow with a perfect body*. Goblin stared at the scar on his wrist where he'd attempted to don a bracer. Words were fading from his skin.

"It-doesn't-hurt." he shrugged. "But-I'm-glad-they-don't-stay. Imagine-me-with-love-poems-written-to-this-vat-pig."

"Ye know ye'd love it." Salt spoke, a fake look of hurt crossing his face.

"Was there anything written in my journal?" Finn asked, remembering back in Jakitta when Salt had let slip about a book. Back then, he had no idea what Salt had been talking about and had forgotten the conversation. Salt grew quiet and retrieved Finn's book. He opened it to the first page and handed it over. Finn read the words multiple times.

Men become Gods, and Gods become dust. Rise SunRider, Rise!

Salt closed the book and took it back. "From that, I knew ye wouldn't need much from me in the way of guidance. Yer path seems to be laid out Finn. There are grand events in store."

Finn swallowed. "Why are you showing us this?"

Salt put all of the books back into the chest. He took his key out and locked it back up. The man beckoned them to stand and he grabbed them each by the shoulders in turn. "The Coalition will continue forward, preparing cities for Mal'Bal's sieges, gathering wild Star-Children, and fighting the Lich. But ye are not to come with us."

"What?" they exclaimed.

"There's a quest I can only entrust to those most loyal to Lenova. I have a feeling that they be ye four. We must find a way to stop Mal'Bal. The man cannot be killed in conventional ways—his power's too vast. So that's why I am sending ye all to Lyria, the floating island-capital of Lenova to meet with the king. There ye will find my brother Darius, Captain of the Paladins." Finn blanched. He wasn't the only one. Salt raised a hand. "I know, the family history is crazy, it is. Save the questions for another day. He's agreed to help ye convince the king to join us in battle against the cult's mighty forces. We need the king on our side. We can't afford a three-way war. But that's not all.

"Altin, ye hail from Lyria. There's a library there: The Library of Lenova, full of books and magical relics. Lead yer friends there. With so much information stored in one place, I would hope ye will find what kind of gem this is," Salt pointed to Goblin's chest and pulled out another shard—one taken from the weapon golem. "and if there's a weakness to them. With information like that, we can greatly increase our ability to defeat Mal'Bal's dreaded creations."

Salt stepped back from them and gave a large proud smile. Finn had been correct: he was about to embark on a quest; one which would help fulfil his dream.

"Go forth my friends! Ye mange-ridden, wobble-necked, rump-dancers! The wonders of Lenova await ye! When we meet again, it'll be upon the great battlefield, where we shall hold Mal'Bal's corpse in the air and smell the freedom of a new dawn! Perhaps when that day comes, we'll finally solve the mystery of these sky-fallen bracers!"

Wahala staggered behind the Lich-Lord, her exhausted body trembling. She was alone now. None of Salastine's people had come forward after his death. No one showed her any support. There were no whispers of *Queen* or *Lady Silver-Heart.* Sweat coated her striped skin and she swayed. The Golden Puppet pushed past her and she fell to her knees. Mal'Bal halted, standing on the peak of a grassy hill. Behind them, the vast cult army slowed, tired and worn. But it was alright, there were many farms to their right and left, full of fresh food and farmers who'd become their slaves. Ahead were many cities and kingdoms to conquer. Behind them lay the ashes of those they'd defeated. Thousands of golems shuffled about: Mal'Bal had made a goal to create as many as possible every day. Wahala pitied the men and women that were tasked with harvesting materials for Mal'Bal to build his creations.

Wahala knew there was something Mal'Bal wasn't telling them. He had a greater plan. A larger vision. He'd seen all possible futures and yes, he wasn't right in the head anymore, but he *knew.* And he was unstoppable. Far ahead, merely a dot on the horizon many kilometers away, the edge of another city could be seen. The campaign would continue. Mal'Bal looked to Wahala and grinned, his eyes tiny pinpricks.

He pointed to the distance. "Anti-life." he spoke.

His voice was chilling and promised a great annihilation to Lenova.

THE END

If you liked, or loved this story, please leave a review of the book on www.amazon.com and come talk to me by visiting my website www.rafaelhohmann.com

You can also request to join my mailing list via my website for additional content on the SunRider Saga and updates on upcoming projects!

SUNRIDER

RAFAEL HOHMANN

THE NECROMANTIC LANGUAGE

Meî — our
Muî — their
Gasta — melt
Za — *to*
Zah — (after a name) honorary term/holy
Shavazol — nothing
Shavazolum — nothingness
Dë — we
Culathas — transcend
Gav-da — the black
Deoth — rot
Baj — death
Uah — kiss
Mudah — marrow
Vindisca — heart
Bith — blood
Vetis-fin — liquefy
Ginda — solidify
Duna — swallow
Vel — her
Meyoh — spear
Bek — bite
Mull — down
Spita — shatter
Püd — stop
Thyd — slash
Rambushik — calves
Yuzah — push
Jujik — choke
Rumbin — break
Plohnz — hands
Ventri — power-thirsty

For my readers:

There's a great satisfaction and a slight sadness to be at this point, seeing this chapter of the story finished. Although it's as if we're temporarily departing from friends just made, feel giddy for what's to come. (Perhaps some answers to the mystery of the bracers?) Finn, Leeya, Altin, and Goblin's adventures are just beginning in the vast and strange continent of Lenova. Stay tuned for what will come next for them and help support them through continuing your journey at their side! But enough of me and them, this is really about you, the reader! A deep thank-you for reading the story is in order. So reader, for taking the time out of your busy life to trek through the fantastical lands of Lenova, *thank-you.* I hope you have enjoyed yourself and are thirsty for more!

Please feel free to leave a review on Amazon and recommend this story to your friends. Stop by and visit my website. Shoot me an email! As Salt would say: *Until we see each other again, farewell ye mange-riddled, wobble-necked, rump-dancers!* (I'm kidding, Salt would never insult any of you!)

About the author:

After all the vat-worms have slid underground and the dust of battle has settled, echoing the footsteps of departing heroes, Rafael Hohmann tiptoes out from behind the rock he was cowardly hiding behind to write out the events that he witnessed. As the author of the SunRider Saga, he hopes to one day be even half as cool as Salt, as tough as Leeya, and as ridiculous as the merchant Quinta. For now, all he can do is write, write, write and hope someone, somewhere out there is willing to read what he puts on parchment.

To learn more about the author, please visit his website at:

http://rafaelhohmann.com/

More works by the author:

In the Land of Hershel: A short story from the World of SunRider

55704598R00278

Made in the USA
San Bernardino,
CA